Praise for the InCryptid novels

"The only thing more fun than an October Daye book is an InCryptid book. Swift narrative, charm, great world-building . . . all the McGuire trademarks." —Charlaine Harris, #1 *New York Times*-bestselling author

"Seanan McGuire's *Discount Armageddon* is an urban fantasy triple threat—smart and sexy and funny. The Aeslin mice alone are worth the price of the book, so consider a cast of truly original characters, a plot where weird never overwhelms logic, and some serious kickass world-building as a bonus." —Tanya Huff, bestselling author of the Blood series

"McGuire's InCryptid series is one of the most reliably imaginative and well-told sci-fi series to be found, and she brings all her considerable talents to bear on *[Tricks for Free]*. . . . McGuire's heroine is a brave, resourceful and sarcastic delight, and her intrepid comrades are just the kind of supportive and snarky sidekicks she needs."
—*RT Book Reviews* (top pick)

"A joyous romp that juggles action, magic, and romance to great effect."
—*Publishers Weekly*

"*That Ain't Witchcraft* tells the kind of story that all series should be so lucky to have: one with world-bending ramifications that still feels so deeply personal that you don't question if this could have been someone else's book to narrate. McGuire has honed her craft over a decade-plus of writing, and if you call yourself a sci-fi or fantasy fan, yet haven't picked her work up, you're doing yourself a disservice." —Culturess

"*Discount Armageddon* is a quick-witted, sharp-edged look at what makes a monster monstrous, and at how closely our urban fantasy protagonists walk—or dance—that line. The pacing never lets up, and when the end comes, you're left wanting more. I can't wait for the next book!"
—C. E. Murphy, author of *Raven Calls*

"Seanan McGuire is one of my favorite urban fantasy authors and her InCryptid series is part of that reason. *Imaginary Numbers* is a stunning installment and one that every urban fantasy reader is sure to relish."
—Fresh Fiction

SPELUNKING THROUGH HELL

A Visitor's Guide to the Underworld

An InCryptid Novel

SEANAN McGUIRE

DAW BOOKS, INC.

DONALD A. WOLLHEIM, FOUNDER

1745 Broadway, New York, NY 10019

ELIZABETH R. WOLLHEIM

SHEILA E. GILBERT

PUBLISHERS

www.dawbooks.com

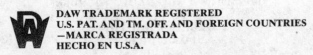

For Kory. Buckley owes you a lot more than
we ever could have realized.

And for Tyvar, for being a true source of joy in a dark time.

Price Family Tree

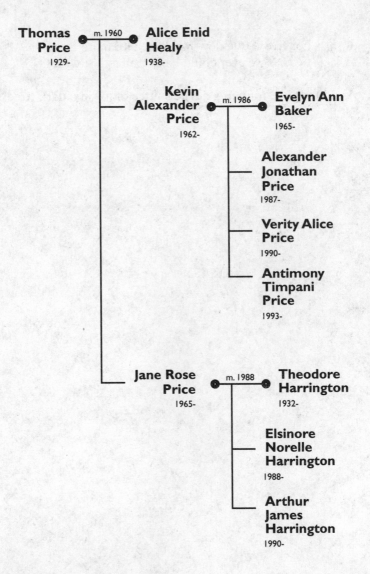

Thomas Price
1929-

m. 1960

Alice Enid Healy
1938-

Kevin Alexander Price
1962-

m. 1986

Evelyn Ann Baker
1965-

Alexander Jonathan Price
1987-

Verity Alice Price
1990-

Antimony Timpani Price
1993-

Jane Rose Price
1965-

m. 1988

Theodore Harrington
1932-

Elsinore Norelle Harrington
1988-

Arthur James Harrington
1990-

Baker Family Tree

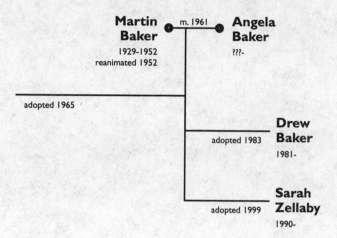

Martin Baker — m. 1961 — Angela Baker
1929-1952
reanimated 1952
???-

adopted 1965

adopted 1983 — Drew Baker
1981-

adopted 1999 — Sarah Zellaby
1990-

Love, noun:

1. An intense feeling of deep affection; may be romantic, filial, or platonic.

Passion, noun:

1. A strong or barely controllable emotion.

2. Enthusiasm, interest, desire.

3. See also "obsession."

Prologue

"Never could handle working on the trapeze, me. The one thing I never learned how to do was let go. I guess it's just not something I'm built to do."

—Frances Brown

The old Parrish place, Buckley Township, Michigan

Fifty-six years ago

THE OLD PARRISH PLACE—SO called because the man who'd built it, Theodore Parrish, had committed the unforgivable but extremely memorable crime of killing his entire family with an ax as a sacrifice to a horrible swamp god who thankfully seemed to have existed only in his imagination—was never entirely quiet. No matter the hour of the night or day, the pipes rattled, the foundation creaked, and the windows shook in their panes, rattled by the wind whether or not the wind was truly there.

Alice Price-Healy had grown accustomed to the sounds of the house around her, and while she often missed the less intrusive creaking and rattle of the house where she'd grown up, a childhood spent with a colony of pantheistic mice living in her bedroom walls had left her a deep sleeper, if only in self-defense. She was dead to the world, one arm thrown up over her head, the hard arch of her stomach pointed to the ceiling. At this stage of pregnancy, sleeping in any other position was a fairy tale, and the suggestion was likely to result in something being thrown.

She was snoring. She'd done that during her first pregnancy as well and had denied it until Thomas got the mice to back him up. (The mice were rather more enthusiastic about the phenomenon than he was, declaring jubilantly that the Noisy Priestess had finally mastered the art of living up to her name even in her slumber.) After a shouting match during which she declared that if her snoring bothered him so much, he could damn well figure out how he was going to carry their next child, or else she was going to start taking that pill the ladies at the library kept talking about, he had decided sleeping in the living room was a better choice.

But oh, some nights it was hard to leave her, even when she was so loud that he couldn't possibly sleep in the same room. After five years of marriage, he still couldn't fully believe they'd made it here. And even after everything it had cost them, everything it had cost *him* in specific, he didn't have a single regret. She was lovely in the moonlight slanting through the window, casting shadows on her skin. She was lovely in the daylight, too, although considerably more likely to be covered in blood. With the baby expected sometime in the next month, he had finally managed to convince her to stay out of the woods. He'd been worried for a time that he was going to miss the birth of his second child when she went into labor while halfway up a tree in the middle of a forest that carried a distinct dislike toward him.

It was funny, in its own ironic way. He lived in the sight of an eco-system that actively and impossibly didn't want him anywhere near it, trapped inside the house that had been intended as his punishment for daring to question the Covenant, and he couldn't imagine a world where he'd have been happier. Even trying to imagine a world where he was still capable of leaving the house didn't work, because it re-quired a world where he'd chosen not to bargain with the crossroads for Alice's life.

She was his happy ending, if a man like him was allowed to ask for one. She was his reward for turning his back on everything he'd been raised to be and choosing a better path for himself: Alice, and their children. Kevin would be three soon. He was talking more every day, constantly discovering the world around him, and now that he'd mostly learned not to play too roughly with the mice or tailypo, he was an endless source of joy for their small family. His excitement over his new baby brother or sister was big enough to fill the whole house. Sometimes Thomas thought he might be even louder than the mice.

As if anything could be.

Alice made a snorting noise in her sleep, and for a moment, it looked like she might be waking up. Thomas reached over and smoothed her hair back from her face, and she stilled, slipping into deeper slumber. Yes. This was definitely one of the nights where he slept elsewhere. During the summer, his tendency to radiate heat like a broken furnace did neither of them any favors: her, because she would get too warm and wake up; him, because it meant he would be sharing a bed with his angry, extremely pregnant wife. Retrieving his glasses from the bedside table, Thomas swung his feet around to the floor and rose, heading for the door.

(Later, when Alice was climbing the walls in furious, impotent panic, she would demand the mice tell her exactly how the evening had gone, over and over again, until she had a perfect vision of events. The one thing they could never tell her clearly enough to satisfy her was whether she had managed to wake at all, or whether she had simply slept through the moment when her husband walked away from her, possibly forever.)

As for Thomas, he didn't pause on his way out of the room, not to kiss her temple or even to look back at her. He simply left, unaware that this night was anything other than exactly like the night before.

Like so many of the other important people who had left Alice alone, Thomas Price never looked back.

Thomas eased the door carefully shut behind himself, trying not to wake Alice. She needed her sleep. If she woke, he would have been happy to make her toast and tea, or whatever else she wanted that they had on hand, but it would be better if she could sleep until morning.

Handling an increasingly rambunctious young boy who seemed to have inherited her fondness for the forest had been hard for her even before her pregnancy started to show, and—of course—he couldn't help in any meaningful way. Everything outside the house might as well not exist for him and hadn't for almost nine years.

Not since his bargain with the crossroads, which he had made with full understanding of the costs and possible consequences, and one he would gladly have made again if it had been required. What he'd gained had been more than worth everything he'd lost.

And if he needed to remind himself of that from time to time, when Kevin was having a tantrum or Alice was in a mood, well, it was a small price to pay to remain happy within what world he had remaining. He made his way down the hall toward the stairs, pausing to look into Kevin's room and reassure himself the boy was fine.

The mice were sometimes a little overenthusiastic about reciting the catechisms of Daniel, Alice's older brother, who they referred to as the God of Early Arrivals and Earlier Departures. Thomas had been forced to sit down and have a long talk with the head priests, explaining how much they were upsetting Alice, before they would stop. But the damage had been done, and it was rare to make it through a night without at least one of them looking in on their sleeping son, half-afraid he would have been snatched out of his bed.

Not that most things potentially inclined toward snatching could get through the layers of protection Thomas had thrown over the house: wards and enchantments and thick walls of elemental energy. Even perfectly mundane home invaders would have trouble muscling their way inside. Every time Alice woke up crying out of concern for the brother she'd never known, he would research and add another protective screen, trying to keep his family as safe as he could.

It was something he could still do for them, even though he wouldn't be able to drive Alice to the hospital, or take Kevin to school, or attend any of his milestone events as he grew older. No field trips or science fairs or graduations or weddings for Thomas Price. No, those things were for other men, men who hadn't sold their souls to save their wives.

A jet of something that tasted too much like bitterness tried to force its way up his throat, and he forced it down again. He knew full well that the crossroads had only allowed him this much because they were sure, in their terrible, inhuman way, that he'd be suffering every day for the rest of his life. The happiness he'd been able to snatch was all the sweeter for being stolen, and he was going to keep stealing it every day for as long as he was able.

The stairs creaked as he descended, one more quiet message from a house that never stopped talking, and he stretched, beginning to fully waken. A cup of tea and then back to sleep on the living room couch, which was comfortable enough and would let the tailypo curl up with him. They didn't like to sleep with Alice; she smelled too often of blood and gunpowder, and it unsettled them, but he had come to enjoy their company as a man might enjoy the company of a beloved dog, and it would be good to wake in their tangled, furry midst—

Then he stepped into the living room, and the gentle wakefulness he'd been stumbling toward evaporated in an instant, replaced by something cold and clear and altogether cruel.

Mary Dunlavy was waiting for him.

As always, their semi-resident ghost looked like a teenage girl with a pleasant face, the sort of girl who could be found in any American school or diner, except for her long white hair. She was even dressed in what he was sure was the latest fashion, a gray pleated skirt and a yellow button-down cardigan with a pressed Peter Pan collar. She looked at him solemnly, with nothing but sorrow in her eyes, which were the exact color of the sky above Penton Hall on a frozen winter morning. He shivered and forced himself to keep walking.

Finding Mary in the house was nothing unusual. She sat for Kevin when Alice needed a break, and she would be responsible for the new baby at least some of the time. She was the family babysitter. She had been since she died.

She was also the local representative for the crossroads, and the person who had helped Thomas broker his deal with them. Everything he had, he owed to her.

And if she was waiting for him in the living room in the middle of the night, it was because she was finally coming to collect.

"Please," he said, and when she gave a minute shake of her head, he sighed. "At least, not here?"

"You don't have a lot of options, Tommy," she said. "I was able to convince them to let me wait until you came down instead of snatching you out of the bed, but that was all they were willing to give, and they only gave it because there was too much of a chance Alice would have been able to force her way through after you if they'd taken you upstairs."

If not for Mary, Thomas might have protested that Alice would never do that, would never risk leaving Kevin alone. But he knew his wife, and he knew how much faith she placed in Mary's ability to protect the children, and he could understand how Mary had been able to spin it into letting him wait. Into giving him just a few more precious hours.

He hadn't kissed her before he left. He should have kissed her. He knew she would ask the mice, and they would tell her the truth: they would tell her he'd walked away without even kissing her on the forehead, and that would be the last she knew of him before he left her a widow with two children to raise alone.

They'd be able to unlock the Price family vaults if they needed money, but they'd have to go to England if they wanted to do that, and Alice's sensible fear of the Covenant would close that avenue before it ever had the chance to open. He was leaving her with nothing.

"Please," he repeated. Then, with a bit more certainty, he added, "At least the kitchen? You can take me in the middle of a cup of tea. It will hurt her when she finds it in the morning."

He knew it was true, and still he hated himself for saying it *because* it was true, because it had to be true to convince the crossroads. And the last thing he wanted to do was hurt his wife.

Mary sighed. "You're right, of course," she said. She cocked her head to the side, listening to something he couldn't hear. "They'll allow a cup of tea, although you won't finish it."

"Excellent. Thank you." He bowed stiffly in her direction, overly formal for a man in a nightshirt and shorts, and walked toward the kitchen, pausing to grab his wallet from the bookshelf next to the door. Mary didn't stop him. Her instructions hadn't said anything about preventing the man from picking things up along the way. Once again, he didn't look back.

The ghost of Mary Dunlavy followed him. Water ran, and a few minutes later, the tea kettle whistled. A few minutes after that, there was a sound like a sheet of tin foil being ripped, and everything was silent. For the first time in years, the old Parrish place sat completely quiet and serene.

It was the silence that woke her, rather than the absence of another body in the bed. Alice opened her eyes, blinking blearily up at the darkened ceiling. "Thomas?"

There was no reply from the empty room. Not even the mice seemed to be stirring, which was odd but not alarming. Alice rolled onto her side and levered herself into a sitting position, grunting with the effort. Pregnancy was rewarding in its own way, but it was also so *stupid*. She had never felt this alienated from her own body, not even when she'd been recovering from the damage done by the Bidi-taurabo-haza that almost killed her. Standing up shouldn't have been so hard.

"Thomas?" she called again, louder. She didn't want to wake Kevin, but she had the distinct, itching feeling that something was wrong, and you didn't survive in Buckley as long as she had by ignoring feelings like that.

Resting one hand on the slope of her stomach, she left the room and made her way down the hall, only pausing to peek into her son's room and reassure herself that he was still there. Kevin was on his back, one hand loosely gripping the taxidermied jackalope that was currently his best friend in the world. She smiled and eased the door shut again, continuing on.

For the second time in one night, a Price descended the stairs and found Mary Dunlavy waiting. Mary's clothes had changed, replaced by the simple cotton dress she had most often worn when babysitting for Alice herself.

Alice froze, hand clenching on her belly until her nails dug into her skin. "Where is he?" she asked.

"Alice, you know this isn't my fault. You know what he did, and you know why I'm here. I'm so sorry, sweetheart, I would have delayed it longer if I'd been allowed, but he—"

"Where *is* he?"

"Not here."

Silence fell, heavy as a thunderstorm, nearly smothering. Alice broke into a run, straight through the spectral babysitter and into the kitchen. She didn't slow down, not even as the chill of Mary's disrupted form wrapped around her limbs.

Mary was proud of her for that, and a little bit proud of herself. She'd helped raise a child Frances Healy would have been proud of and had managed to balance her duties to the crossroads and her duty to the family long enough to see that girl grown and starting a family of her own. Part of this was hers.

Mary disappeared, reappearing in the kitchen behind Alice, who was staring at what looked like a rip in the air, a jagged hole through which glimpses of a long, blue-tinted tunnel could be seen. She looked like she was gearing herself up to jump.

"Alice, you can't," said Mary. Alice's head whipped around, blue reflections dancing in her eyes. "You can't. Think of the baby. Think of both the babies."

"You'll be here," said Alice. "You can take care of the babies."

"I can't go into town. Everyone knows I died years ago. Is there enough food in the house to get us through to when Laura comes?" Mary kept her tone soothing, not pointing out the obvious issue with her staying to take care of the babies: if Alice jumped, the baby she was still carrying would jump with her. "And what happens if the crossroads call me while I'm alone with the children? You know they'd love the chance to take out the whole family."

"You can't just expect me to stand here and do *nothing*!" shouted Alice.

The rip was closing. It had been more than twice this size when Thomas was yanked through; if Mary could keep Alice talking, she wouldn't have the chance to follow him. All she had to do was keep her talking. All she had to do was distract her.

"I expect you to allow your husband, a grown man who made his own choices, to pay his debts before my employers decide the sins of the father can fall to the son," said Mary. "You *know* he's been waiting for this. You know you can't go after him. You have a responsibility to that baby in your belly. You *know* that."

Alice made a sound, and it was the worst sound Mary had ever heard. It was tight and choked and brokenhearted and crushed, all at the same time, and all she wanted to do was go to the girl she'd loved for longer than she'd been alive and take her into her arms and hold her, and tell her things were going to be all right. All she wanted to do was fix this.

All she *could* do was stand exactly where she was as she watched the rip seal itself, until there was nothing hanging in the air at all, and the normal sounds of the house in the night returned, and Alice put her hands over her face and wailed like her heart was broken.

That was fitting enough, since Mary supposed it was.

Thomas Price—husband, father, sorcerer, debtor to the crossroads, former member of the Covenant of St. George—was gone.

One

"I only ever made one choice that wasn't for the sake of my family, and I'll pay for it until the day I die. Doesn't mean it was the wrong choice. Just means that sometimes the right thing can hurt like hell."

—Enid Healy

The Red Angel, a bar of somewhat disreputable character just outside Buckley Township, Michigan

Now . . . and Then

NORMAL PEOPLE AREN'T SUPPOSED to rip holes in the membrane that separates dimensions. That petty pleasure is reserved for sorcerers and umbramancers and the various forms of cryptid who have managed to evolve a more symbiotic relationship with the stuff. For a human like me, it's a violation of the laws that supposedly govern the natural world, and it comes with a price.

I fell through the doorway I had opened on Helos—Helos sucks, don't go there if you have any choice in the matter, it's *never* a good vacation destination, no matter what your travel agent says—severely injured and hoping for nothing more than a quick, easy crossing. Instead, I found myself hanging by one hand from a very familiar tree branch.

I grimaced. I remembered this. Of course, I remembered this; what was the point of tormenting me with intensely vivid flashbacks from my own life if I didn't *remember* them? This was the summer of 1950, about four years before Thomas Price arrived in Buckley. I was twelve years old. I had returned home from summering with the Campbell Family Carnival less than a week before, and my father was already making me regret coming back. So I had done what I always did when

home felt too confining for me to live with. I had fled to the Galway
Woods. Like my family, they loved me. Unlike my family, they didn't
want me to be someone else. They liked me exactly the way I was.

Unfortunately, loving me didn't mean they wouldn't hurt me. I had
startled a peryton nesting in the higher branches of one of my favorite
climbing trees, and it had lashed out with its hooves, knocking me from
my perch and leaving me dangling.

As soon as I let go, I was going to break my right leg. I'd spend the
next six hours alone in the Galway Woods, trying not to cry so the
sound of a wounded animal wouldn't attract any predators too big for
me to deal with, trying not to move so I wouldn't pass out from the
pain. I'd be half-delirious by the time my grandmother found me and
carried me home. Like I said, flashbacks. But being here before didn't
mean I could do anything differently, and no matter how tightly I tried
to hang on, I was going to fall.

My fingers were already slipping. I bit my lip, tensing in anticipation of the pain to come, and let go.

How long the flashbacks last is shaped by how thick the membrane
I've pushed through was. The wall between Helos and Earth is pretty
thin, which meant I wouldn't be here long. It was still long enough to
feel the impact with the ground, and the sickening snap of my tibia
breaking.

I blacked out briefly, and then I was crashing through a window.
Great. Welcome back to the present day.

The location hadn't changed much. I was still in the Galway Woods,
or close enough for zoning laws: the Red Angel is technically outside
the tree line, but only barely. Cynthia was behind the bar pulling a
drink for a river hag with algae in her hair when I smashed into the
bar and rolled across the floor, a tangle of cut skin, broken glass, and
bruises. I couldn't see myself, but I know my body well enough to be
pretty confident in saying that I didn't look good. If anything, I probably looked like somebody's grandmother's meatloaf right before it
went into the oven.

A few drinkers flinched at the sound of breaking glass, their attention flicking more to the damage to their favorite—and in many cases,
only available—watering hole than to the woman now lying on the
floor, but once they'd confirmed nothing else was coming through the
window, no assailants or human police or anything else that might
bring down the mood, they turned their attention to me.

I was pretty sure Cynthia was shouting my name and rushing toward me, but my head was ringing like a bronze church bell, ears filled

with distorted static, and I couldn't hear a goddamn thing. I also couldn't move. I wasn't in the flashback anymore, but my right leg still felt broken, and judging by the shooting pains in my calf, it was some kind of spiral fracture, one that had split the skin in multiple places. That meant I was probably also bleeding even more than I'd realized. Dammit.

Cynthia had reached me, seeming to move in jumps, like a bad stop-motion animation. That wasn't a good sign. Her voice was starting to become audible, intermittently, mostly drowned out by the ringing.

"—pened to—can you—bleed—okay?"

"Sure, Cyn," I said, as cheerfully as I could manage through waves of pain and shrieking sound. Consciousness seemed like too much to ask of me in that moment, and so I closed my eyes and let myself pass out, slipping into the soft, welcoming dark.

I woke up on something soft. Not a bed. There's a distinct feeling to a bed, a sort of flattened-out smoothness that's at least semi universal. This was lumpier, formed of multiple layers piled up on top of one another. I opened my eyes, looking up at a ceiling choked with dusty cobwebs, and pushed myself upright, confirming the nature of the surface beneath me in the process.

Furs and sheets of birch bark, all piled up in a heap about as high as my waist, occupied fully half the room. Looking around, I guessed we were probably in one of the storerooms at the Red Angel. The place seems to have a virtually unlimited number of them, most un-used. Either Cynthia's mom was wildly optimistic about how many humans would want to drink at a cryptid bar when she built the place, or the nonhuman population of Michigan used to be a hell of a lot bigger.

I was honestly willing to bet on a combination of the two. Even when humanity isn't actively hunting down and killing the competition, we have a nasty tendency to push them out and eliminate them through attrition, if nothing else. We're kind of assholes that way.

And I, an asshole, had done enough woolgathering for one . . . day? Evening? Afternoon? There were no windows, and massive blood loss always throws off my sense of time. I groaned and flopped back down in the furs. I could have lost *days*. I didn't have days to lose.

My name is Alice Enid Price-Healy, and despite what my family will try to tell you, I am not a widow.

Sixty-five years ago, my husband, who wasn't my husband at the time, just the man I was ridiculously in love with, sold his future to the crossroads in order to save my life after I'd been attacked by a rare kind of venomous serpent called a Bidi-taurabo-haza. Their venom is always fatal, and their victims literally rot alive before sloughing off of their own skeletons. There wasn't time to come up with a miracle cure for something that no one's been able to defeat in centuries, and so he did the only thing he could, and traded himself to keep me from dying.

Four years after that, we were married, and we got almost five years together, time to create two beautiful children and pass our genes to a whole new generation of cryptozoologists who've done an astonishing job of carrying on my family's mission to protect the cryptids of the world. Our time ended when the crossroads came to collect, pulling Thomas through a rip in the fabric of the world as we knew it, leaving me alone with our babies and what few allies I had managed to make and maintain as the only daughter of a man who'd done his level best to burn every bridge his parents ever built.

The worst part is that I don't regret a single one of the choices that brought us to that point. Thomas paid too much to save me, but the crossroads wouldn't accept anything less. I'm just self-centered enough to think the world is a better place with me in it, and that if someone was willing to pay to keep me, they had the right to do so. Marrying him was probably the second smartest thing I ever did, after convincing my grandfather to teach me how to shoot, and I love my kids, even if my own daughter can barely look at me. We had good times together. We were happy.

The memory of those five years has carried me through the last fifty, because I've been looking for him almost since the night he disappeared. Mary had been able to convince me not to follow him through the rip while I was pregnant, but that state had only lasted for another month, and once the baby was outside me and breathing on her own—breathing and screaming, which was Jane's favorite pastime for the weeks we spent together—I'd handed our children off to my best friend, Laura, my sister in all but blood, and I'd run.

I'd run for every door I could think of that might take me to the world where he was lost and looking for me. I'd run for sorcerers and rumors of sorcerers, for routewitches in their tatty campers and for trainspotters in their boxcars, and I'd come uncomfortably close to my own crossroads bargain, only to be pulled back from the edge again and again by the ghost of my babysitter, Mary Dunlavy, who knew her employers wouldn't treat me as kindly as they'd treated Thomas.

And then I'd found my answer. The stupid snake cults hadn't been so stupid after all. They—

The sound of a door opening snapped me out of my woolgathering, and Cynthia came into the room, carrying a plastic tray that looked like it had been stolen from the Buckley High School cafeteria while I was still a student there. She smiled thinly at the sight of me.

"I wondered if you were going to wake up any time soon, or whether this was the time I got the dubious pleasure of calling your family and asking them to come collect your corpse from my stockroom," she said, walking over to me and putting the tray down.

We were alone, and she wasn't taking any measures to hide how intensely inhuman she really was. She had a fairly ordinary face, pale and lovely, with sharp Nordic features that would have made her a hit in any singles bar in the country, if not for the long cow's tail that extended from the base of her spine and swished idly near her ankles, and the fact that she had virtually no internal organs. Her back looked like it had been scooped out, revealing an empty, flesh-lined shell where most of her body should have been, and it was a sign of how comfortable she was with me that she was wearing a low-backed top that allowed that cavity to air out.

Her hair was a shockingly vibrant shade of red, and that should, I suppose, have been a hint of what her species eats, but it still took a surprisingly long time for us to convince her to trust us enough to answer some basic questions about huldrafolk biology. They're plants, essentially, specifically an extremely sophisticated and advanced form of pitcher plant, and like most meat-eating plants, they absorb their prey. Anything Cynthia can stuff into the cavity of her back, she can consume. Blood for the bloodthirsty usually works out in the end.

"How long was I out?" I asked. My leg didn't hurt; it hadn't since I'd woken up. I glanced down. And there was no break. The skin was perfectly smooth and unblemished. That either meant I'd been unconscious for six months, or I'd been awake enough at some point to activate one of my tattoos. Please, please, let it be the latter.

"About six hours," she said. I sagged in relief. Cynthia either didn't notice or didn't care. She continued, "After you broke my window— and don't think you're not paying for that—you bled all over the damn floor and passed out cold. What the fuck *happened*, Alice? You're not usually that easy to get the drop on."

"You know I got confirmation that Thomas isn't dead?"

Cynthia nodded, a wary look in her eyes. She's known me since I was way too young to be drinking in her place; she's been running the

Angel long enough that she knew my grandparents and still talked about them fondly when she got a few drinks in her. Wariness made sense. I've known for a long time that most of the people I love think I'm crazy, chasing a dead man across dimensions like it might actually change things, and I don't hold it against them. Maybe I *am* a little crazy.

You don't spend more than fifty years doing the same thing even when it doesn't work if you're not at least a little crazy. And given the alternative, which is a world where the crossroads killed my husband and I ruined my relationship with my children for nothing, I don't mind being slightly off my rocker. It's the best option I have left.

"Well, I know he's out there, but I don't know where he *is*, and the universe is pretty big, even if I'm just talking about the parts of it I can get to. I'm sure there are layers of reality I can't access." The ones occupied by the dead, for example, are pretty solidly closed off to the living. I've been trying to find a way into the twilight that Mary and Rose sometimes refer to for more than thirty years, and I've come to the conclusion that the only way it's possible is to die—something I have no interest in doing.

"Okay," said Cynthia, in a "get the fuck on with it" tone.

"This means revisiting a lot of dimensions I've tried before without any luck and using them to springboard into less friendly realities. And some of those people know me at this point. I was passing through a world where my rep is . . . let's call it 'colorful,' and I got jumped by a gang of assholes who wanted to prove themselves by taking out a pan-dimensional bounty hunter."

So yeah, that's what I do with myself, and it's part of the reason my own daughter can't stand me. I was raised to prize conservation above everything else, to believe it was my duty to pay back the debts my family had incurred through generations of service to the Covenant of St. George by helping nonhuman intelligence thrive in a world that was all too often set against it, and then as soon as shit got hard, I picked up my mama's six-guns and started killing things for money.

That's a massive simplification, but when you're talking about fifty years of dead ends and fruitless decisions, fifty years of lonely nights and too much alcohol, a little simplification is essential, or we'd be here all day and I'd never get anything done. Earth is mostly exempt from my extracurricular activities, since it's the one place I know Thomas *isn't*, but everywhere else . . .

It's not endangerment or oppression when the person you're bringing to justice is not only a criminal but a member of the dominant species, and worlds where the humans won—where people whose greatest superpowers are "endurance" and "breeding like rabbits" even managed to survive long enough to build a civilization—are punishingly rare. So yeah, I mostly hunt what we'd think of as cryptids, because off Earth, cryptids are what you get. Or aliens, I guess.

The nomenclature has never been entirely clear, to me or to anyone else. Finding common language was hard enough on me and Thomas, and he was a British immigrant while I was the granddaughter of same. We could still never agree on what we were supposed to call a damn cookie.

Cynthia looked disapproving, as she always did when I mentioned my current profession. At least her judgment was less "how can you hunt and sometimes kill intelligent creatures" and more "how can you waste that much meat." I like people with simple priorities.

"And what, they got the jump on you? Sloppy work, Healy. That's not how you impress the people."

"There were fifteen of them," I protested. When she looked amused, I shrugged and added, "There's about five left at this point. They were good. I'm still better. The only thing they had on their side was scale. Fuckers were seven feet tall."

Cynthia looked grudgingly impressed. "How's your leg already better?" she asked. "It was busted all to shit when you came through the window, and you had enough glass in your skin to qualify as a kaleidoscope."

"Nice one," I said. "I'm stealing that."

Grabbing the bottom of my shirt, I hiked it up to just below the band of my bra. Cynthia made a sour face.

"Put those *away*," she snapped. "I'm not a human-fucking pervert and I don't need to see that."

"Tits are staying in the bra, I promise," I said, and spread my fingers over the bare patch of skin at the base of my rib cage. "This was a very nice tattoo of a comfrey plant with its roots wrapped around a bone. Specifically for fractures. I must have woken up enough to activate it at some point."

"And then passed out again?"

"Yeah," I said vaguely. I'd lost a lot of blood, and my body had probably cannibalized something I was going to miss later in order to replace it. Which explained why I felt like I could mug Cynthia for the contents of that tray. "Healing is hungry work, whether or not you're awake while it's going on. What did you bring me?"

"Nothing that exciting, so don't get too excited." Cynthia pushed the tray closer, so I could see what was on it. A bowl of clear, yellowish soup with spots of fat floating on the surface, recognizable and somehow appealing despite that; two slices of buttered toast; a neatly peeled boiled egg. Hangover food, the lot of it. I raised an eyebrow.

"I didn't have time to start drinking before I passed out," I said mildly.

"Yeah, and I'll fire up the barbecue now that you're awake, but I wasn't going to waste perfectly good chicken on my usual clientele. They never appreciate it."

That wasn't entirely true; Cynthia's patrons who ate cooked food generally appreciated her barbeque. They just weren't the majority. I could still understand why she hadn't gone to the trouble. I pulled the tray toward me, trying not to drool like a starving wolf.

"Chicken would be great," I said, proud of how level my voice stayed as I picked up the first slice of toast.

Cynthia, who's seen me bounce back from some pretty extreme injuries and has a slightly better idea of what it costs than most people, watched with sympathy and sorrow in her face. "You're going to stop soon, right, Alice?" she asked, voice gentle. "You're almost done?"

"I know he's out there," I said. "All I have to do now is find him."

She didn't say another word as she turned and left the room.

I ate my toast and garlicy chicken broth and egg in silence.

Let's get one thing straight right here: I am not a sorcerer. Neither am I a witch, or a medium, or anything other preternatural thing that it's possible for humans to be. Most of them require a trace of magical talent or power, neither of which I possess. The only thing remotely special about me is a lot of training, and a bit of the Healy family luck, which is sometimes good and sometimes bad, but is never, ever boring. My mother had it, too—from what I've been able to put together, she's the one who brought it to the family—and she still died alone, unwitnessed, in the forest that loved her almost as much as it loves me. Luck alone isn't enough to save you. It never has been.

But the other thing I have is a remarkably high tolerance for pain, thanks to both genetics and a childhood spent running around the woods firmly convinced of my own careless immortality. I've been falling out of trees, breaking bones, and trying to shake off blood loss almost since I was old enough to walk, and when you learn to treat all injuries as a mild inconvenience, you can handle almost anything.

I also have—had—*have* a husband who figured out how to combine traditional tattooing techniques with his own sorcery to embed charms and protections in his own flesh, and I still have access to tattoo artists from another dimension, who have been able to expand and build upon Thomas' work. Anything magic can do, we can put into a tattoo. It costs, of course, and it hurts like hell, but it also *works*, and it means that a girl like me, who has the innate magical talent of a rock, can recover from a life-threatening injury in hours if I have tattoos containing the right spells and the mental acuity to activate them.

With my lunch done, I slid off the bed of birch bark and furs, relieved when my legs didn't buckle. I still felt weak as a tailypo kit; I needed to eat something much more substantial before I'd have the strength to leave the Angel and resupply. I took a deep breath and wobbled out of the room, into the narrow hall that would lead me to the Angel proper.

The window had already been repaired, and all the broken glass swept away. There were no bloodstains on the floor, but that was easily explained; all Cynthia needed to do was take her shoes off and walk where I'd bled, and her hungry, hungry skin would pull every drop out of the weathered wood flooring. It's convenient to have a vampire vegetable running the local watering hole, at least from the perspective of the cleanup crew.

Only a few seats were occupied, mostly by people who looked at me warily when I appeared. One young gorgon actually squeaked, his hand tightening on his beer bottle and his snakes writhing wildly around his face, all of them staring in my direction. I felt a little bad about that. My parents and my children dedicated their lives to repairing our family's tattered reputation among the cryptid community, and me?

I'm the monster under the bed, even for the literal monsters under the bed. I'm the thing they ask their parents to check for in the closet before they go to sleep.

I slid onto an open seat at the bar, trying not to let on how much effort that little walk had taken, and looked around for Cynthia. She was nowhere to be seen. I frowned, resting my weight on my elbows. Normally, this would be when I called for one of the family ghosts. But I wasn't in the mood to chat with Mary, and Rose is a bit more than I was really feeling up for. I didn't even have any grenades, having spent or lost them all in my last encounter.

Grudgingly, I added a return to that nasty little shithole dimension to my list of things to do. Nobody gets the drop on me and lives to keep bragging about it. My pride alone makes that unacceptable, and they had like half my gear. I needed it back if I wanted to go any further off the beaten path.

The list just kept getting longer. Eat enough to feel like I could handle a dimensional crossing. Go home to resupply and check the house. Check in with my employer. Get back to looking for my husband. For someone most people consider an unstable loner, I sure do wind up with a lot of obligations, and I don't like any of them.

A door opened and closed, accompanied by the smell of barbecued chicken. I raised my head. Cynthia was walking toward me with another tray, this one piled with red-sauced poultry and a bowl of baked beans. She set it in front of me and stepped back, holding up her hands in protective surrender. I smiled at her.

"It's always nice to see a woman who knows what she needs to do to keep her fingers," I said, pulling the tray closer before grabbing a drumstick in each hand. "Thanks, Cyn. You're a lifesaver."

"Yeah, Healy, I know. Now eat up and get out. You're scaring the customers."

She wasn't wrong about that. No one in the room looked like they were breathing, and most of them needed to.

So I ate up, and I got out.

Two

"Until Thomas came along, I wasn't sure that girl was
ever going to fall in love with anything the way she fell in
love with the forest. Or that anything was ever going to
love her back the way that forest did."

—Mary Dunlavy

*Leaving the Red Angel, to the relief of basically everyone inside,
even as they try not to show it*

CYNTHIA WALKED ME TO the door after I finished demolishing my
second lunch and wiping my hands meticulously with a towel. I
wasn't going to risk washing my hands in the Angel. There might still
be blood under my nails, along with all the barbecue sauce, and while
I didn't mind making the occasional donation to Cynthia herself, she
had some customers who might be willing to take the sink apart to get
a bit of me for themselves. Not cool, and not something I wanted to
encourage.

"Try to stay gone for a little while this time, huh?" she said, the
warmth of her tone belying her words. "Or come back with Tommy.
That asshole still has a twenty-dollar bar bill to settle, and that's in
1950s money. He needs to pay me back with interest before he's welcome to drink here again."

"You don't mean that."

"No, I don't." Her smile faded, replaced by an expression of deep
concern. Of all the living people in the world, Cynthia's the one who's
known me the longest. Huldrafolk live a long, long time. She knew my
mother. That's not something many folks can say anymore. Not even
Rose.

"Alice . . ." she said, and I braced myself, because I knew I wasn't
going to like whatever she said next. Cynthia only remembered I had

a name when she wanted to use it like a cudgel to keep me from doing something she'd decided would be stupid. Which, in her defense, my great ideas frequently were. "How sure about this are you? That's he's out there for you to find? What, exactly, did Mary say?"

"Mary didn't say anything," I said. "We're not exactly on friendly speaking terms most of the time. Antimony told me when she and her friends were here. After she defeated the crossroads."

"That was almost three years ago," said Cynthia.

Dammit. Sometimes moving in more distant dimensions means breaking my tether to Earth time, but it always sucks to hear that I've been out of contact with my family for more than a few months. "Doesn't change the intel."

"All right. What, exactly, did Antimony say?" asked Cynthia, dog with a bone, not letting the subject go.

I sighed. "She said the crossroads sometimes took people and put them somewhere far away, someplace where they couldn't get home. It didn't kill them. That's what I've been banking on this whole time, that when it took them away, it didn't kill them."

"It's been a long time, and whatever it is you've been doing to stay young longer than humans are supposed to, he hasn't had access to that."

"No, he hasn't." I was glad. I'd rather be married to a man fifty years older than I am than see him go through what I've willingly done to myself for his sake, what he never would have asked or expected me to do. It's always easier to set yourself on fire than to allow someone else to burn for you.

But there's a reason I've never discussed my methods with anyone. I try not to think about them except when it's time to submit to another treatment. Sarah—my adopted granddaughter, the telepath— has brushed up against the edges a few times, and she's never been willing to ask me to explain. She's a cuckoo, but I love her anyway, for letting me keep that secret from my family. They would never understand.

"He was already older than you. And time doesn't always run the same way between dimensions."

"All true. Are you going to get to a point any time soon, or are we just going to stand here with your tail out, waiting for a tourist to come along and take a picture?"

"What are you going to do if he's already dead from the things humans just die from, and not from anything the crossroads did?" She looked at me gravely. "Are you really sure you want to know?"

"Honestly, that's all I've ever wanted. This whole time. Do I want him back? Yeah, but I'm not even sure he'll have me. I'm not the sweet little wife he left behind anymore."

Cynthia snorted with the effort of holding back her laughter. "Alice, if you think you were ever a 'sweet little wife,' I should drag you back inside and make you sleep off the concussion you're clearly suffering from."

"Sleep doesn't cure a concussion," I objected.

"Whatever. You are only and entirely what you were designed to be by nature, nurture, and the forest, which I can see you stealing glances at. Go run wild in the trees for a while and then get back to your fool's errand. But remember that no one's promising you a happy ending."

"I wouldn't dream of asking for one. Thanks, Cyn."

"Don't mention it."

I blew her a kiss and ran for the tree line. The trees couldn't move, couldn't reach out to meet me, but it still felt like they were welcoming me home. The same way it always did, and always had, and always would, for as long as we were both alive.

On paper, there's nothing special about the woods around Buckley Township. They're a fairly standard Michigan forest type, various hardwoods with a spattering of aspens and hickories. Thanks to the proximity of the lake, the ground trends swampy in places, but never commits all the way into becoming wetland; our swamp is more mud putting on airs than anything really literal.

It's relatively geographically isolated, which is part of why my family settled there in the first place; my grandfather used to say the township was built in the hand of the forest, and he wasn't wrong. And thanks to three generations of Healys working to protect and preserve the land in all its diverse glories, the woods around Buckley have a higher population of the various North American cryptids that used to be endemic to all similar ecosystems than just about anywhere else. These days, most places, you could camp for a week and never see a single tailypo or hear a single fricken call. Not in Buckley, though.

In Buckley, we've managed to keep it all, and the woods are grateful. Or at least that's how they've always felt to me. When huldrafolk like Cynthia reach the end of their lives, they either turn to stone or trees, groves of white aspen with interconnected roots. Cynthia's mother, who was the one to actually build the Red Angel, had become trees before I was born, and she grew nearby. Cynthia still spent time with her, still talked to her and kept her up to date on the world, and while most trees aren't related to the huldra, if Cynthia's mother could be a thinking organism and a grove of trees at the same time, who was to say the same wasn't true of the wood?

It loved me like I loved it. I knew that. I had always known it. And as I stepped into the shadows below their branches, my feet following a path I had worn through the brush over the course of decades, I smiled. I only ever felt at peace in the trees. I kept the house where Thomas and I spent our time together for the sake of those trees. It had some pretty bad memories to balance the pretty good ones. It also had close proximity to my trees.

My mother died in the forest. So did my grandmother. It knew them both to the end of their lives, and part of them lingers there still, even if their ghosts have long since gone to wherever it is that ghosts go when they don't have reason to hang around. Much like Cynthia going to visit her mother, going to the woods is a way to visit mine.

Frickens chirped in the branches above me, so comfortable with my familiar presence that they didn't stop their constant communications with each other. The tiny, feathered frogs used to be everywhere in the world, and now most of them are extinct, lost forever, because humans were careless. Well, I won't let them be careless with my forest. I've never managed to save anything else I loved without hurting it in the process, but I can protect the woods.

They never liked Thomas, not the way they've always liked me. He used to mutter about it when I'd come home from hunting with blood in my hair and a peryton in the back of the truck, how if he'd been able to come with me, he would have been tripped up by every tree root and stuck his foot in every hole until I was forced to help him back to the safety of civilization. Not that he was a poor woodsman, or that he was wrong about the woods around Buckley: he could handle himself in almost any environment that wasn't actively out to get him.

The only times I could remember the trees being kind to him, he'd been trying to help me after I got in over my head with one problem or another. Bears, both alive and reanimated by body-stealing slime molds, were not nearly as affectionate toward me as the trees. Neither were dire boars, or any of the other predatory dangers that sometimes had to be confronted to prevent them from eating the locals. Part of keeping humans from being careless involves keeping the local wild-life from giving them a reason. On those occasions, the woods had been more than willing to let Thomas in and help him find me before I could suffer something he couldn't help me survive.

According to my grandmother, and to Mary, the woods were the same way with my mother. They loved her. They couldn't save her, though—whatever happened, it had happened too quickly for something as slow and deliberate as the trees—and she had lain in state among them until morning, when her body was found. To be honest, I was surprised they'd been willing to let her go. But the memory of my mother was enough to teach me the one lesson she never learned: just because something loves you, that doesn't mean you can stop being careful when you're alone with it. The best-trained dog can bite. The most devoted forest can hide a striking snake.

The most loving husband can go when the crossroads call without looking back or kissing you goodbye.

You have to stay careful if you want to stay alive. That's not even up for negotiation.

I emerged from the woods feeling better than I had when I stepped into them, and relaxed at the hideous, familiar, beloved shape of the old Parrish place, the house that started as a punishment and became a palace because it was where we'd been happy. At this point, I'd lived there longer than I'd lived anywhere else. The house loomed over the field around it, teetering and shabby and painted an unpleasant gray-green, like rotting flesh. It didn't matter how often I hired people to repaint it; the color always faded to swamp muck within a season, like the house remembered what had been done there.

I loped across the field, whistling as I drew close to the house and warning the tailypo that it was me. A chittering greeted me from the porch as I reached the steps, and by the time I got to the top, all five members of the current resident troop were clustered on the porch swing, tails draped possessively across one another, creepy little hands folded at quiet attention in front of them. Nothing looks attentive like a tailypo that thinks you might have food.

"Well, hello, darlings," I said. "Sorry, no treats today. I'm just passing through."

They're about as smart as any other breed of lemur, but they knew the word "no" well enough to give me disappointed looks before they chittered and vanished into the brush around the house. I smiled as I watched them go. The tailypo is virtually extinct everywhere in North America except for the woods around Buckley, and I get to feel at least partially responsible for that. I took care of them when I was a teenager, and I managed to trick Thomas into doing the same, and the old Parrish place has served as a sanctuary for generations of the long-tailed little monsters. Given food and shelter and a safe place to raise their kits, the population has stayed pretty stable, and the woods have stayed a little weirder than they'd be otherwise.

They definitely keep the local kids from poking around the place looking for spare keys. I leaned up onto my toes and felt the top of the porch swing, running my fingertips along the high rail that was meant to be a support for hanging flowers until I found the little hook where the door key was kept and took it down. Thomas didn't hide any keys while he was here. Thomas also didn't spend the bulk of his time wandering around parallel dimensions looking for me; I think I can be forgiven for loosening the outer ring of security a little.

The living room was cool and smelled slightly musty, as it almost always did these days. Only being used by a human occasionally, while being occupied by relatively clean wild animals almost full time, will do that for a place. Tailypo are even more notorious for their denning hygiene than racoons, sometimes traveling as much as a mile to urinate and marking their territory with scent glands that are almost undetectable by humans. They make for pleasant roommates, even more so since the development of the oral rabies vaccine in the 1980s. We haven't had an outbreak near Buckley in over forty years. No Stephen King novels for us.

Just a few monster movies, and those are more than enough.

I walked across the living room to the stairs, shedding clothes as I went. The ones I'd been wearing were torn and bloodstained, and while that might feed into the aesthetic I'd been crafting for the last fifty years, it wasn't comfortable against the skin. I like cloth that bends when I do, doesn't snap and crackle and shove flakes of my own dried bodily fluids into every crevasse it can find. Besides, one of the best parts of a stop off in my home dimension is being able to take a hot shower.

The water at the old Parrish place has never been turned off. Neither has the electricity. The bills are paid on a regular basis, and Kevin comes out every two or three years to replace the water heater, whether or not it's needed. Between that and Mary making sure the pipes don't freeze, the place stays pretty functional.

I left a trail from the front door to the master bathroom like the teenager I'd been the first time I stepped into this house, only pausing to grab a towel before I turned on the water and stepped under the stinging spray. I had no cuts or bruises left for it to aggravate, but my skin still knew it had been abraded recently, and the body remembers injury, even after it's been erased. I may not have any scars, but I know where every single one of them should be.

The first time I saw myself in a mirror after this journey began, I didn't know who I was looking at. I don't think I can ever be said to have been innocent, not really; I'm the daughter of people who dedicated their lives to saving monsters, raised as much by the dead as by the living, gun in my hand before I could do long division. My future was set from the day I was born. But I used to at least be able to act the part.

Now, though . . . Thomas was heavily tattooed because the tattoos helped him to keep and amplify his magic, and because he liked the way they looked, enjoyed the aesthetic of carrying a record with him everywhere he went, something the Covenant couldn't overwrite or take away. I got the idea from him. With no magic of my own and no way to guarantee anything I carried with me would survive the trip, I had to embed any charms I needed access to into my own flesh. It had been a quick enough process when all this started. A few protection and passage runes etched into my arm, a healing charm or two down the outside of my thigh. Now . . .

Every inch of skin below the neck on my right side was covered with a dense, ever-changing tapestry of images, drawn and redrawn after every use. Only a few stayed consistent between trips, the ones I'd learned I would always need, no matter what situation I was throwing myself into this time. I filled my hand with shower gel and began scrubbing it across myself, removing the sticky remains of a fight my body only half-remembered.

There was so much I couldn't wash away. Best to handle what pieces I still could.

Rinsing away red-tinted suds, I turned off the water and stepped out of the shower, toweling myself roughly dry. The urge to linger here, in the place that still felt like home, was as strong as it had ever been, coupled with the need to run and keep running, to never stop or slow until I found the man I was looking for and brought him back where he belonged.

The questions Cynthia asked me were nothing new, and nothing I hadn't asked myself a hundred times. What was I going to do if I found a ninety-year-old man who barely remembered the wife he'd only known for a fragment of his life or, worse, a grave? Some featureless patch of earth with a tombstone and a pretty widow weeping over it like she had a right to swoop in and replace me just because I was a dozen dimensions away and not there when he needed me?

The answer was always easy, and always the same. I yanked open the top drawer of the dresser, pulling out clean clothes and dressing as quickly as I could. I would *know*. I've never been happy not knowing things, and getting the answer, even if it hurt, would be better than not having it. So if I found him and he wasn't mine anymore, for whatever reason, I'd be able to come home and finally figure out who I was and how I fit into the family I had left, how I could live with a son who treated me like a dangerous animal and a daughter who hated me.

Laura used to tell me, after she'd had a few too many glasses of sherry, that we learn how to love from our parents. They teach us what a healthy—or unhealthy—relationship looks like, and I guess she was right, because I love the same way my father did, and his way of loving nearly killed us both. He never got over losing my mom. She died, and he turned into a hard, brittle man who was ready to fight the world to keep me safe, even if he killed me in the process.

Maybe that's what I learned from Thomas, or maybe the crossroads did me a favor when they made sure I wouldn't know if he was alive or dead. I'd been able to shove my children at my best friend and beg her to keep them safe until I was finished finding their father and could come home. If the search had lasted for their entire childhoods, well, at least I'd stayed away, and not tried to mold them into people who would never have anything to lose, the way my father had with me. And maybe that was unfair to him, but I didn't think so. Jonathan Healy had been a broken man who raised a breakable woman, and the only good thing I ever did for my family was let them go, whether or not they could see it that way.

If Thomas was dead, or had already let go of me, I could stop holding on. But until I knew for sure, as long as there was something that tasted like hope hanging in the air, I had to keep going. I stepped into my shorts and opened the bottom drawer, beginning to pull out boxes of ammunition and knives. Always knives.

Guns are great. Guns let you kill people before they get close enough to do the same to you, unless they also have guns, and then guns just make the fight shorter. Knives, though; knives don't jam or run out of ammunition. Six bullets to each of my mother's revolvers. Twelve chances to make the kill before I get gunned down in some backwater dimension where my body will never be found. Infinite cuts in a knife, if you treat it well and respect the weaknesses of the metal. I like knives.

I like guns better, but I like knives more than I like many other things. A life like mine doesn't encourage a lot of affections.

By the time I finished gearing myself up, it was a wonder I didn't rattle when I walked. That's sometimes the only thing I miss about having long hair; poisoned hairpins really are a miracle that more people should pray for. Still, the loss of a handle people could easily use to grab me was worth the small reduction in my personal armory, and I felt prepared for just about anything as I walked back down the stairs.

A few things of mine had been lost in the attack. I wanted them back. Time to go and get them.

Dimensional keys are often surprisingly generic. You can't tie them specifically to places you've never been before, so you lock them onto attributes and assumed directions. Not that "north" or "west" or "deeper" or whatever actually matter on a cosmic level. The human mind always starts from "here," and anywhere else you want to be is in relation to that point. So the keys I use are tied to one of two things: a relative direction, or a place I've been before. You can also tie them to an idea—if there's a world near you with a great beach, focusing on "a beach would be nice" can potentially pull you toward it. That only works if your available options include one that fits the bill, and since every crossing drops you in the dimensional point closest to where you started at the moment of transition, there could be a world just *filled* with gorgeous beaches, but none of them are close enough to make the list, and so you wind up in the extraplanar equivalent of Coney Island, broken bottles and tourists everywhere, not tropical vistas and silence.

Oh, and just to make things even more confusing, every dimension contains dozens of worlds. Start with the wrong assumed direction in mind, and the crossing you thought would put you in New Jersey could leave you on Olympus Mons, on Mars. No Jersey hot dogs there. No air either. Good luck!

I try not to navigate by ideas when I can help it. My primary idea is always either home or Thomas, depending on which way I'm headed, and that can throw things off no matter what I'm trying to do if neither one is directly in range.

The workbench in the basement was exactly as I'd left it the last time I'd been here: clean and organized, maybe the only thing in the house the tailypo never put their tiny hands on. Magic again, and again, not mine; Laura was an umbramancer before she disappeared, and for all I know, she still is one. Her magic was mostly about warding and seeing possible futures, and she'd set up a complicated ward over my workspace that apparently worked by shuffling through every possible future on a constant basis, always choosing the one where the spiders spun their webs someplace else and the dust fell in a different direction. Seemed like the sort of thing that could have been used to keep a house cleaner than I'd ever managed, but I didn't mind. It was nice to know that everything was as pristine as I'd left it.

I sat down and placed my right arm on the bench, turned so the back of my hand was resting on the wood. Then I picked up a bottle of ink, and a needle.

I am not a sorcerer. I'm not a tattoo artist, either. But anyone can learn freehand tattooing, and as long as I use ink that's been prepared for the purpose, I can amend what I already have, even if I can't create something new. I grimaced, looking at the runes running in a line from wrist to elbow. Too many blank spaces. I had two transits left before I'd need to sit down in a proper chair and get myself redone. I started off with fifteen—the maximum number I could carry without overloading myself. There's an upper limit to how much magic can be embedded in my flesh at any one time. We were already brushing up against it.

Two transits would be enough to get me to the dimension where I'd lost my pack and then back to base for a refresh and renew before I went deeper in. I took a breath, dipped my needle in the ink, and got to work.

Three

"Seeing the future has never done anything good, for anybody, and if I knew who had first linked seeing the dead and seeing what's possible in the same chain of talents, I'd beat them bloody."

—Juniper Campbell

The basement of the old Parrish place, preparing to leave Buckley Township

THE TATTOO ON MY arm was red and angry. I pressed my fingers against it and bowed my head, eyes closed. All my tattoos require intent to activate, although how much intent is on a case-by-case basis. If I accidentally blow a healing tattoo on a stubbed toe, well, sucks to be me. If I accidentally trigger a dimensional crossing when I didn't mean to, that's more of a problem.

The air around me got hot, then cold, then very, very still, like it had forgotten the way movement was supposed to work. It got difficult to breathe. This was all normal. I'd added the hooks to the basic rune that should tell it to take me back to the dimension I'd left the most recently, regardless of direction or distance. It was a risky move.

Dimensions aren't organized in a neat stack, like the layers of a lasagna, or even in beehive hexes, although some of the more scientifically-inclined travelers I've met have tried to use that model to explain cosmology, like something this big and complicated and messy would ever be that straightforward when it didn't have to be. Near as I can tell, reality is less like lasagna and more like a body. Sure, it has layers and divisions and strata and necessary membranes to keep your liver from winding up in your stomach or something, but it's alive. Pieces move. I was essentially aiming for a single blood cell that had been moving since the moment I activated my emergency out and fled, and since I didn't know where I was going, I had to trust the magic not to miss.

That meant I had to trust my own crappy handwriting, and the enchantments on a pot of ink that had been sitting unattended in the basement for months. If I'd gotten any piece of the process wrong, this moment could be the end of me.

That didn't make it special. The pressure in my chest got worse, and I opened my eyes to find myself standing in the Buckley Township Children's Library, surrounded by bookshelves packed with brightly colored volumes. The piping voices of children pretending to be quiet drifted through the air. I tensed.

Whatever mechanism triggers these flashbacks when I cross a dimensional membrane, it rarely lets me see Thomas. It never lets me see my children. It never takes me *home*. Instead, it seems to take me to whatever will upset me the most—and it never takes me to the same place twice. I remembered this day. I always remembered them.

I had time to take a deep breath before familiar footsteps came thundering down the hall connecting us to the main library. I spun toward it, following a script set sixty years before, an artificial smile plastered on my face.

"Daddy," I said warmly. "How nice to see you. Did you need something from the children's section?"

"Alice Enid Healy," he snapped, grabbing my arm and yanking me toward him. The action pressed against a bruise I had almost forgotten in the intervening years, and I hissed through my teeth, trying to pull away.

That only made him pull me closer, the same way it always had.

"You were in the woods again last night," he said, voice a sepulcher rumble, like he was laying down a proclamation of my own damnation. "You *know* how I feel about you sneaking out and risking your life."

"The Galway needs me," I protested. "It's not sneaking out. It's— it's going *home*."

He released me so abruptly that I stumbled backward, bumping my hip against a low bookshelf. He stayed exactly where he was, and I knew that he had framed this entire confrontation so that anyone watching us would see a superior scolding an employee, within the reasonable limits of their position.

I hated him. He was my father, and I loved him, and I hated him.

"Our house isn't home?" he asked, tone just on the edge of mocking. "Your grandparents would be so ashamed to hear that from you."

I squeezed my eyes shut before anyone in the library could see me cry and felt the air around me shift as the transition between dimensions finally concluded itself. Opening my eyes, I fell into a defensive crouch. It would look ridiculous if I'd appeared on a calm street corner or in the middle of a children's birthday party—both things that have happened more than once—but it might save my life if I'd dropped onto a battlefield.

I was standing on a low, rocky bluff surrounded by sheer hillsides. Scrubby thornbushes grew on every flat surface, almost dense enough to count as bracken. My charms may not give me much leeway in the steering department, but they're pretty good about not materializing me inside things, and that's good enough. They took some time to refine to that degree, and there were several times early in, where I'd returned to base early with something embedded in my calf or shoulder. I would have died if I'd ever caught a piece of the local landscape in the throat. Good thing I didn't.

Naga likes to say that luck is on my side and coincidence loves me. I can't really argue with that, even as I get the shit kicked out of me on a regular basis. I crouched lower, taking stock of my surroundings.

It was night, the sky bright above me with the swirls of what I would have called the aurora borealis if I'd been on Earth, bands of color dancing through the air and reducing the stars to bit players in their own nightly performance. Three moons capped off the image. There was no visible light pollution. It wasn't because we were too far from the city; it was because Helos was more focused on magic than technology and had never centralized their society in urban spaces the way we did back home.

That, and the dominant species was made up of viciously aggressive seven-foot–tall assholes with anger management issues who didn't like to live in large groups. It made them cranky, and when you're already talking about people who have twenty-eight words for "wound" but only two for "friend," you don't want to deal with them when they get cranky. They mostly formed small settlements a decent remove from one another and waged small, violent wars against their neighbors, complete with the occasional bout of recreational arson.

Nice folks. Unfortunately for me, Helos was an artery, for lack of a better way to describe it: from here, I could go off in half a dozen directions, some of which were inaccessible from Earth. I'd been here often enough to start developing a reputation, which was where the original problem had started.

But they didn't get to break my leg and keep my pack. It just wasn't allowed.

Moving closer to the bluff's edge, I looked down at the rocky land-scape. Nothing moved. This dimension didn't have many local preda-tors; the local sapients had long since wiped them all out, and there wasn't much bigger than a rat that could cause me any issues. I still stayed low as I began picking my way down the slope, taking it slow and easy. I didn't need to break another bone when I only had one crossing left on my arm; I could justify one detour for the sake of my stuff. Two would be pushing it.

The flickering light of a campfire burned about halfway down the slope. It was hard to tell from here how level the ground was around it, but I had to assume at least level enough that they wouldn't have to constantly be chasing embers as they rolled down the hill. The laws of combustion and gravity aren't consistent across dimensions, but they worked in this one about the way they did back at home, and no one enjoys an uncontrolled brush fire. Shapes around the light told me my former assailants were relaxing in their evening, probably smugly con-fident that nothing was going to give them any trouble.

That's me. I'm nothing. And I was going to give them all the trouble they could carry.

Reputation aside, I generally don't kill people without good reason—and yes, being paid to do it can constitute good reason, al-though I don't pull a single trigger without confirming what I've been hired to do. I'm a bounty hunter, not an assassin, even if some lan-guages use the same word for both, and some people can't see the difference. I don't kidnap people; I bring them to justice. I also help people get home after they've been yanked into dimensions that aren't their own. All the charms that let me cross dimensions are designed to carry at least two, and most of them allow for three, since for a long time I was traveling with a pair of Aeslin mice from my clergy.

It was my granddaughter Antimony, the one who told me I was right and Thomas was potentially alive somewhere, who called me on the fact that if I was traveling with two mice and hoping to bring my husband home, my charms should have been set to four. I've been losing hope for a long time. Fifty years is longer than any human should spend on this kind of fruitless quest, and even if I'm physically in about as perfect shape as it's possible for a person to be, I'm tired. I want to go home.

It's just that home is rarely a place. It's a combination of conditions. For me, home requires the Buckley woods, and the mice in the attic, and the tailypo in the trees outside the window, and Thomas by my side. I've been lost since the night he left me, and until I can be sure that he's gone for good, I can't start building something new. It's just not possible.

The size of the locals meant it was easier for me to crouch and pick my slow way through the darkness toward them. I didn't even have to take particular care to stay under cover. There was virtually nothing my size left in this dimension except for their own children, and that meant if they saw me at all, they wouldn't register me as a threat. There was enough cover, thanks to the darkness, the unpredictable flickering motion of the sky, and the brush, for me to descend without much chance of being seen as long as I was careful.

And I was very careful indeed. According to the mice, my mother never learned to be careful, and I guess that's the one thing I can say I definitely do better than she did. I crept downward one easy step at a time, placing my feet with exquisite slowness to avoid kicking loose pebbles, and hoped I wouldn't step on anything that made too much noise for them to brush off.

The trick to sneaking up on people isn't total silence. It's making sure the noise you can't avoid making fits into your environment. I crept closer and closer, not stopping when something rustled, but stepping carefully to the side, so that anyone looking toward the sound would be looking at where I'd been and not where I was.

When I was almost there, I unholstered my revolvers and balanced them lightly in my hands. The residents of Helos were big and fast and proportionately strong. They could break me in half if they got hold of me, which meant my preference for blunt force trauma couldn't come to the party. But they weren't resistant to bullets. That was the sole saving grace of a world that was otherwise pretty unpleasant. No good food, no good conversation, no local culture bigger than the equivalent of a few assholes yelling at each other across a puddle of blood, just an easy conduit to some useful pathways, and people who died when you shot them.

People I would have been perfectly happy to leave alone if they hadn't insisted on jumping me first. Killing folks for fun isn't my gig, no matter how inconvenient they may be. I know my rep says otherwise, but believe me, if I'd been in this game to bathe the multiverse in blood, things would have gotten a lot stickier a long, long time ago.

Revolver in each hand, I stepped up to the edge of the firelight and smiled my sweetest smile, the one that used to convince my father I was a sheltered darling who would never so much as dream of crossing any of the arbitrary lines he'd drawn around what I was and was not allowed to expect from the world. The two locals with a direct line of sight on me quailed, leaning back in silent shock.

"Howdy, boys," I said. "I believe you've got a few things that belong to me. Now, if you want to give them back, we can settle this without any more bloodshed. If you'd prefer to argue about possession being nine tenths of the law, like assholes always seem to want to do, we can get violent."

The man who'd been their leader when they jumped me before stood up, and kept on standing until his full, substantial height had unspooled from the ground. He turned to face me, smirking, already so sure how this whole scene was going to play out.

"You shouldn't have come back here, little thing," he said, voice rough and irregular as the ground around us. "Little things ought to stay broken the first time it happens, to show they're paying proper attention. Now I'm going to have to break you again."

I sighed and shot him in the knee. Very few bipedal things can stay standing with a bullet in their knee. It's just physics. He yelled and went down hard, and his companions began to rise, reaching for their own weapons as I sighed.

"Guess we're doing this," I said. "Come on, boys. I need to get home before morning, so let's make it quick."

The locals, as I've mentioned, stand about seven feet tall on average and don't care for the company of strangers, or their own kind, or much of anybody else. It seems to be a biological thing; get more than about a dozen of them in one place and they'll just start eating each other. I don't think most humans realize how lucky we are to have evolved from primates, who tend to be social and get along with each other. There's a lot of talk about how humans are inherently aggressive and will always devolve into conflict, but at the end of the day, we're the cosmic equivalent of puppies. We trip over our own feet and try to make friends with everything we meet.

These folks didn't evolve from primates. These folks didn't evolve from *mammals*. Seven feet tall, yeah, with pebbled black-and-orange skin and yellow eyes, like giant Gila monsters. They even have the hooked claws and stubby tails, although those were more decorative than dangerous. When they scratched, it was like being hit by somebody who'd had a really intensive manicure, not like being slashed with multiple biological knives. I was pretty sure they'd held onto them solely because with that skin, fingernails alone wouldn't have been enough for them to scratch anything that itched.

But that was ascribing intent to evolution again, which is one of my worst habits, and something I should probably work on. With their leader on the ground, clutching his knee, the other two he'd been sitting with were on their feet, one holding a nasty-looking machete, the other a length of chain.

Because oh, right, that's the other thing I should probably mention. Without any real population centers, they don't really produce much for themselves; it's hard to run a manufacturing plant, or even a smithy, when everyone keeps killing everyone else. So the locals mostly equip themselves by mugging helpless passers-through. Turns out there's a lot more cross-dimensional traffic than I would ever have guessed back when I thought Earth was actually important, and not the dimensional equivalent of that one neighborhood where all the weirdoes wind up living.

I mean, Earth *is* important, because *everywhere* is important. No-where matters as much as your hometown. That's another thing we get from our primate roots. We prioritize the familiar, we know what's "home," and we defend it as much as we possibly can. We form a circle around family, and we take care of it.

But in the greater cosmic sense of things, Earth is no more important than anyplace else, including this shitty little pass-through reality, with its giant asshole scavenger lizards who figured out that sometimes when people walked through their yard, they could knock those people down and take their shit. Which was how I'd been hired to swing through here in the first place. They'd mugged some tourists who took the wrong route between destinations, and the tourists in question wanted their shit back.

Which was currently less important to me than getting *my* shit back, but which I'd be perfectly happy to pick up also if I had the chance. It's always good to keep the customers happy. The one with the chain muttered something in the local language, beginning to spin it in a menacing fashion, so I did the only thing that made any sense.

I shot him in the throat.

De-escalation makes sense when you're just getting started. Maybe there's a chance you can work things out, so everybody gets away. Maybe this isn't one of those days where you add another bloodstain to your soul. Maybe. But there had been fifteen of these fuckers when they jumped me, and they'd been down to five when I whisked myself away, blood in my eyes and radiant pain all through my bones. Now they seemed to be down to three, which either meant the others had been wounded too badly to be worth taking care of, or they had been waiting for me to come back.

None of them looked surprised enough, within their limited reptilian range, for the former to have been true, which was annoying. I'm happier when I don't have to worry about people coming up behind me. But the one with the machete was looking at his fallen companions, the one still writhing and clutching at his knee, the other motionless in the dirt. Not everything is allergic to bullets. For most things that are, a throat shot will settle things with gratifying speed.

"Do we *really* have to do this?" I demanded. Machete guy looked past me, face relaxing marginally, and I ducked just in time for something that looked like a morning star with delusions of grandeur to whisk over my head. Dammit. Our other players were coming to the party.

At least if they were all here, I could be relatively sure my stuff was nearby. I took advantage of my bent position to put two more bullets in leader guy, before running straight toward machete guy like I thought that was somehow a good idea. He only looked surprised for an instant before he squared his stance and raised his weapon, clearly expecting me to run myself straight into it. What a charmer.

Instead, I whipped around and flung myself toward their fire, leaping over it and skidding to a stop on the other side. I was supposed to be injured. Even if they didn't have a detailed understanding of human biology, they knew enough to know I shouldn't be this spry, and they weren't expecting me to dodge. Machete guy snarled as he pivoted to advance toward me.

Issue with the machete as a primary melee weapon: it's not very aerodynamic. He was still holding onto it, clearly intending to do some hacking. I holstered one gun and produced a hand's-worth of throwing knives and tossed them his way, hard enough to break through his layer of natural scaled armor. Only one actually hit an eye. His scream was more like a bellow. The other two knives went wild. I'd have to retrieve those later.

Two more shots and my first gun was exhausted, but he was on the ground, not moving, and I only had two more partners for this little dance. I shoved the gun into its holster, trading it for its twin as I whipped around. The opponent with the morning star was coming up on me fast, almost back in range for another shot, and he'd been joined by a companion, who was holding something that looked a lot like a javelin. Oh, that was going to hurt if it hit me.

Neither was a great option for letting them get just one shot in. I jumped back over the fire and snatched the machete from the dead one's hand, digging it into the embers and using it to fling them at the one with the morning star. He howled and reeled backward, clawing at his face. I took advantage of his distraction to shoot his friend, twice. Four bullets left, no javelins in the air. Not bad.

Morning star guy finished clawing the embers out of his eyes and began advancing toward me. I lowered the machete and tried to feign cowering. It wasn't easy, not with a fire between us and him moving at a speed commensurate with his size. Still, he seemed to buy it, making a noise like laughter as he advanced.

Issues with fighting a nonsocial species: any primate who'd just seen their friends mowed down the way these ones had been would have at least paused, if not elected for a full-on retreat. Not this guy. He kept coming, apparently happy to charge straight through the fire to keep bothering me. No worries. I shoved my gun back into its holster and bolted, trying to circle around behind him.

He snarled and spun, clearly anticipating the move, and whipped his morning star around over his head. If he could get enough momentum on that thing, he could just let go and trust gravity to do the rest. Nice guy.

I waited until I was close enough to have a clear shot, then flung the machete as hard as I could at his stomach.

Like I said, machetes aren't very aerodynamic, but even a brick can fly short distances if thrown with enough force. Morning star guy made a startled noise that sounded a lot like "urk" and staggered backward, looking slowly down at the two feet of steel now protruding from his gut. He dropped the morning star, narrowly missing his own foot, and reached down with shaking hands to grasp the handle.

"Don't!" I said sharply. He glanced up at me. I sighed. "I know you speak some English. If you pull that out, it's going to take your internal organs with it. You'll bleed out."

He looked disbelieving. I was the one who'd put the machete there, and *now* I wanted to worry about whether or not he ripped out his own intestines? It was all very confusing, and he was losing a decent amount of blood. I sighed again, more heavily this time.

"Yeah, all your friends are dead. Maybe you're not, if you tell me how to find my stuff and I help you get that thing out without doing any major damage."

He snorted and pointed toward the hills to the west. There, not far away, was the mouth of a low cave. Then, making eye contact the whole time, he reached down and yanked the machete out of his own stomach.

He was dead before he hit the ground. "Great," I said, as I walked forward and took the machete away from his corpse. "And I'm sure your well-timed suicide has nothing to do with the caves being home to something that's going to try to eat my ass, right?"

Being dead, he didn't reply. I considered the virtues of kicking him a few times, just for the comfort of it, and decided that harassing the dead wasn't worth my time. Not when I had other things to do. Sighing one last time, I turned to face the cave.

Time to get this over with.

Four

"No one ever really dies. We live on in the memories of
our children, and it's down to us to make sure that we're
remembered kindly."

—Alexander Healy

Heading into a dark, unfamiliar cave in a dark, only semi-familiar dimension, because that's a great plan

I PAUSED OUTSIDE THE cave to dig bullets out of my pocket—not the
best bullet storage location, but when you don't have a pack and
need to move while you can still get it back, you make do with what's
available—and reload my revolvers. Whatever was waiting inside here
would be susceptible to bullets if it was somehow immune to stabbing.
Weird damage immunities like "fire" and "blood loss" only really
crop up in that fantasy game my grandkids like, the one where they
pretend to be elf warriors who seduce dragons or whatever.

Here's a tip: do not attempt to seduce a dragon. They don't have the
right pheromones, and they think humans are gross. Which, to be fair,
we kind of are. Lots of fluids in a human.

I wanted to keep my fluids where they were, which was why going
into this cave without a light or a guide was probably not the best idea
I'd ever had. Still, it was so far from the worst that it was fantastic by
comparison, and so, after a moment to wish I still had any grenades,
I gripped my new machete and stepped inside.

The cave was dark, as expected, although not *as* dark as expected;
glowing fungus stuck to the walls, almost matching the colors of the
sky outside—greens and blues and soft whites. It wasn't proper lighting, more like Christmas lights strung around the edges of a room, but
it was enough that I could see the outlines of the things around me,
rocks jutting up from the cave floor, the walls themselves. The air

smelled stale and musty, like a basement that had been closed off for too long. I paused once I was a few steps inside, listening intently. Nothing moved.

Wasting charms is never a good idea, but I was going to have to be redone once I got home anyway, since I'd burned through all my gates, and that meant I didn't need to be as frugal as I normally would. I slipped the first two fingers of my free hand under the strap of my tank top and pressed the small star I knew was tattooed there. "Light, please."

None of my tattoos actually have a verbal component—they're all intent—but sometimes saying what I want out loud helps. I closed my eyes for a moment.

There are two kinds of light spell that can be embedded in ink. The little ones give you a nice, easy, long-lasting glow, but it's better if you give your eyes time to adjust. The big ones are more like a sudden nuclear flash. There is no letting your eyes adjust. They're either closed when you trigger the effect, or you're going to be walking into walls for a while. I can power both, but the second kind knock me on my ass for a couple of hours after the adrenaline wears off, and they're really a last resort kind of thing.

Naga frequently reminds me that both types of light spell pull electrolytes and sugars out of my system, which can lead to seizures, rapid heartbeat, and unconsciousness if I don't take steps to correct it and could presumably eventually kill me. That's not the goal most of the time, so I'm as careful as I can be while dealing with situations that sometimes require me to write checks my body doesn't understand how to cash. Once I found my pack, I could take a few packets of the powder that's supposed to put things back to normal. It was just a matter of finding the pack.

When I opened my eyes, my entire body was glowing a soft white, like one of those weird glow sticks that are so popular with the kids. The cave, thus revealed, was a pretty standard representative of its kind, although the ground was smoother than it would have been naturally; someone or something had been moving through here for a long time, long enough to wear a path into the ground. The only real question was whether it had been the charming gentlemen who'd welcomed me to this dimension, or whether it was some sort of local monster my last friend had been hoping to feed me to.

Well, nothing like a little caving to liven up an already too-lively night. I started walking deeper inside, machete at the ready, watching for any sign of movement.

About twenty yards from the entrance, I had it, as something that looked like a hellbender if a hellbender were the size of a portable toilet stomped out of the shadows and opened its mouth in silent threat display. Its teeth were tiny nubs in its gummy jaws; it looked like it was built to eat larger bugs than any I'd seen on this world, which didn't make me optimistic about the depths of the cave. I was usually in and out, exterior only, when I had to pass through here. While I knew there were no big predators left in the open, there could be giant bugs in the depths of the earth. Why the hell not? Everybody seems to love a giant bug.

Almost as much as they love giant snakes. The universe is full of giant snakes. Earth got off easy, since most of our snakes are too small to swallow people, but not everywhere has been that lucky. And some snakes are very nice people, not interested in eating anyone they can carry on a conversation with.

I have yet to meet a giant bug, except for maybe the Madhura, who I would classify as "a very nice person." Sarah and Angela don't count. They're biologically cuckoos, but they're culturally human in all the ways that matter.

And that's probably a shitty way to talk about assimilation, but since their actual species is made up entirely of assholes who mostly want to kill or absorb everyone they meet, I can't feel too bad about it. I don't like bugs. Never have, never will.

The salamander continued to show me the dark, faintly glowing inside of its mouth, cautioning me not to come any closer. Since it didn't look like it was sitting on a trove of ill-gotten goods, I nodded politely and kept walking. It wasn't a big enough threat, even in the dark, to explain the smirk on the last jerk's face just before he spilled his own guts out on the ground; I couldn't lower my guard.

The cave grew closer and darker around me as I made my way deeper, and when something moved in the shadows, I understood why the dying man had thought it was a good idea to send me in here. The creature that abruptly loomed out at me was easily three times the size of the salamander and armored like a clawed tank. The closest earth equivalent I could come up with was a burrowing crayfish, albeit one the size of a bull elephant. Each of its claws was the length of my leg.

With that kind of natural armor, this was the fabled "immune to both bullets *and* stabbing" variety of fucker. It charged forward, claws waving, and made a horrifying bubbling noise deep in the cavernous gape of its throat. At least it didn't have a lot in the way of teeth. I leapt aside, taking refuge in the one advantage of being the smaller combatant in the unexpected fight: I was substantially faster and more agile. That was a good thing.

There weren't many good things in this situation as I could see them. I didn't have any grenades. Even if I had, setting off grenades underground is never an awesome way to stay alive, and so I tend to avoid it when I can. Until I found my things, I didn't have access to anything bigger than what I was carrying, and luring this fucker into the open didn't seem like it was the world's best idea as far as survival goes. For all that my tattoos can be used to hold effects of various sizes, none of them are as impressive as summoning fire out of nothing or freezing enemies in their tracks. That would be a whole extra set of upgrades, and I don't think my system could sustain them.

So I was pretty much screwed. Well, shit. It lunged again, and I jumped again, grabbing a rocky outcropping and trying to plan my next move. It waved its claws in a threatening fashion. I paused.

For all that it was enormous and covered in irregular protruding spikes, it really did look like a crawdad. Its armor was segmented, with clear divisions between the plates. If I could get myself above it, I might be able to do something. I started eyeing the various rocks with a more assessing eye, trying to figure out how I could get close enough to the ceiling to grab for some of the dangling formations that hung suspended there. I've never been able to remember which ones are the stalactites and which are the stalagmites, but I know that both are formed slowly, one drop of lime-rich water at a time, and back on Earth, damaging them can get you into serious trouble.

This wasn't Earth, and as I began my series of carefully timed leaps, I was grateful for that fact. Every landing was a jarring thud and a frantic scramble to get a handhold without dropping my new machete, which was going to be absolutely key to surviving today's stupid Healy trick. The crawdad continued pursuing me, waving its claws and gurgling unpleasantly. I wanted to avoid being caught at any cost, since one solid snap of those claws could have me down a limb, or possibly down an entire torso. I *like* my torso. It's where I keep my lungs.

After eight leaps and two near-misses, I was above the crawdad, which reared and waved its claws at me. I shot it in the eye. It roared and dropped back down level with the ground, no longer quite as invested in trying to threaten the biting thing on the ceiling. It wasn't going anywhere, just not trying to climb after me, and under the circumstances, I'd take it.

I watched carefully as it circled, and when it passed directly beneath me for the third time, I dropped onto its back, machete held in front of me with the point facing downward.

One of the things people tend to forget when they're listing off my admittedly eclectic list of skills: I started out with a slingshot and a row of glass bottles, and if you missed the target too many times, that was it, you were down for the day. I'm not the *best* shot in the world, but most of the time, when I'm aiming for something, I'll hit it. And that goes for knives, too.

I hit the crawdad's back with a bone-rattling thud, the blade of my machete going right between the plates of armor covering its head and its torso. At the same time, spiky bits of shell went into the flesh of my thighs and calves. The crawdad bellowed. I screamed, shoving the machete farther down. Creature like this, it had to have some kind of ganglia connecting its front end to its back end, even though it wouldn't have a spinal cord, since it didn't have a spine. If I could sever that . . .

Twisting the machete got me another bellow, and the crawdad's thrashing got less severe. The spikes jammed into my legs didn't get less sharp, and the pain was incredible, but I stayed where I was. Hurting myself and losing however much blood I was going to lose when I pulled myself free wouldn't do me any good if I then had to try and fight this thing again while already injured. No, I had to finish this now. I twisted the machete again. There was no bellow this time, only a pained, burbling exhalation, and the crawdad stopped moving.

Great. It was either dead or dying, and either way, it wasn't going to be trying to scissor me in half. That was good enough for me. I pulled a knife from inside my shirt and bent forward, following the gently glowing curve of my thigh to where it pressed against the crawdad's shell. The spikes had been faintly hooked, which made sense; they were both natural armor and a method of gathering food. If something attacked the crawdad and left pieces of itself behind, the crawdad could pick those pieces off later and eat them. Disgusting, but effective.

Pulling the spikes out would have caused further damage and blood loss, and some of them were too close to my femoral artery for me to feel comfortable messing with them in the field. Better to just leave them where they were for right now. Bending close, I was able to slice them off, one by one, as close to the skin as possible. After about five minutes of exceptionally painful personal surgery, I was able to dismount from the crawdad without leaving any major parts of myself behind. Under the circumstances, I was willing to call that a win.

I did pause to scowl at the shell of the thing before I yanked my machete free. "Thanks for playing," I said to the corpse, almost chipperly, and turned to head deeper in.

I was limping now, thanks to the spikes embedded in my legs. They were effectively plugging the holes they had made, and only a little blood leaked from each wound. There were enough of them that it was still a problem, and I was starting to feel woozy by the time the tunnel bent and I found myself confronted with Aladdin's cave of wonders.

This gang had been jumping tourists for a while, and this was apparently their favorite place to stow their ill-gotten gains. My pack was near the front of the pile, and nothing appeared to menace or attack me as I stepped forward and reclaimed it, settling it back on my shoulder with a feeling of the utmost relief. This bag was never supposed to be parted from me, much less stolen and stowed in another dimension.

The bags I'd been sent to retrieve were nearby. I grabbed those as well, taking a moment to scan the remainder of the pile before I activated my passage home.

Some of these things had clearly been here for a long, long time. Guess there wasn't much of a local market for these items, since they couldn't be used as weapons, smoked, or drunk. I paused at the sight of a large leather map roll next to a stack of old books held together by a leather book strap that looked a lot like the ones I'd used when I was in college. They weren't local make. Meaning they'd been swiped from a trans-dimensional tourist, and they might contain something relevant. After a momentary inner debate about whether it was stealing when those things had enough grime on them to have been down here for years, I grabbed them both, hooking the map roll over my shoulder and tucking the books under my arm before pressing the first two fingers of my right hand against my last remaining doorway tattoo.

"All right," I said, as I closed my eyes. "Let's get the hell out of here."

The world blurred. The world shifted. The sound of carnival rides whirling and singing their electronic songs to themselves suddenly rose in my ears, accompanied by the sugared-oil scent of funnel cake. I opened my eyes on the midway of the Campbell Family Carnival, Laura in front of me, both of us somewhere in her teens, her thrusting a corndog in my direction. She had a smile on her familiar, beloved face, which dimmed a bit as she looked at me.

"You're not my Alice right now, are you?" she asked.

This was another moment I remembered, and that question put

everything else into context. We'd been seventeen, me hopelessly in love with Thomas Price—and utterly convinced that it was hopeless. He was engaged to a woman from the Covenant, and I was just the useless local teenager who'd gone and nearly gotten herself cored out from the inside by a predatory alkabyiftiris slime. He was never going to love me the way I loved him.

When this had actually happened, I had been utterly baffled by Laura's statement, which had come entirely out of nowhere, and made no sense at all. Now, looking back across a gulf of decades, it made all the sense in the world: Laura was an umbramancer. They may be the least well-understood of the naturally occurring types of human magic user. They can see the future. They can talk to ghosts, even the kind who don't normally have the strength to make themselves manifest in the material world. They mostly work in wards and protections, out of self-defense; Laura had been fending off unwanted spirits since we were just kids.

And apparently, they could also tell when their best friends were possessed, however briefly, by their selves from the future.

"What?" I asked, in the voice of my innocent teenage self, the girl who had been completely baffled by this moment, the girl who had no reason to think anything was happening.

"Don't worry about it," said Laura, and handed me the corndog. "Whatever's bad enough to make you do something like this, it's probably bad enough that you really need a corndog."

"Um, okay," I said, and took a bite.

We walked along the midway, Laura shooting little worried glances at me that I appreciated now, in what was for her the future, but had baffled me utterly when this had been our shared present. Context changes everything.

The corndog was hot, savory, and far less confusing. We walked, and I ate, and the carousel music played, and overall, it was a much more pleasant flashback than most of them tended to be.

"Come on," she said, beckoning me toward a tent. "Darkness will help the transition."

We stepped inside, and everything went black, as the temperature rose by at least six degrees, the air growing suddenly humid and ripe with the smell of snake. I opened my eyes, which had still been closed in the present if not the past, on the dim, familiar confines of my bedroom in the dimension where I currently spent . . . not the majority of my time, but the majority of the time when not actively in transit from one world to another. This was my home base, as much as I had one, and the place I returned to, always. If I only had one crossing charm left, it brought me here, not back to Buckley.

Much as Buckley was and would always be the true home and haven of my heart, this had to be my final stop, if only because this was where Naga and my tattoo artists were. Without them, my journey would be over. I dropped everything I was carrying onto the floor next to the bed, including my pack, and staggered out into the hall. Every step sent another wave of pain through me as the spikes in my legs shifted and tore, but I kept walking. It wasn't like they could do any permanent damage.

The hall outside my room was long and gently curved, and entirely undecorated, without even pictures on the walls or a rug on the floor. It used to be jarring, when I first started spending time here, the way they left all communal spaces as bare as possible. Now, it seemed only natural, and human-decorated residences, like my own, were almost unbearably cluttered. Only the fact that I hadn't redecorated since Thomas disappeared kept me from getting rid of half the things in the house. But he might object, and I wanted him to be comfortable when I brought him home, assuming I got the chance.

Walking was slower than normal, the spikes working their way deeper and deeper into my flesh and slowing me down still further, but I forced myself to keep going. The smell of snake grew stronger. My room was about as far as it was possible to get from Naga's office without being in another building altogether. He found the smell of live mammal as disconcerting as I found the smell of live snake, and we both had to make allowances. Still, I was grateful. He'd been under no obligation to help me when I'd first come sobbing to his side, and he could easily have turned me away.

Instead, he'd offered to do whatever he could to get me back to Thomas, arranged for my first set of tracking charms, and sent me on my way. Without him, even getting off Earth would have been the next best thing to impossible, given my lack of personal magic. Because he was willing to lend me his resources, I'd traveled farther, seen more, than any other human I knew. Maybe than any other human, ever. We're not a species that encourages a lot of cross-dimensional exploration, and it's not easy for us.

I tried to focus on my gratitude as I limped down the hall, and not on the fact that I didn't know how close we were to his dinner time. Naga has a long-standing policy, as befits a Professor of Extra-Dimensional Studies at the University of K'larth, of not eating anything or anyone to who he has been formally introduced. I accomplished that introduction myself when I was six years old and had been snatched by a group of snake cultists intent on sacrificing me to him as part of a ritual bid to seize control of what they mistakenly believed to be a snake god—it's always snake gods with snake cultists, and somehow they believe that he who has the biggest snake will get to rule the world, not just have to clean up after the biggest snake.

I'm sure Freud would have a few things to say about that, if he weren't a dead hack who would probably also be happy to say that my fondness for knives stemmed from a bad case of penis envy. I do not have a bad case of penis envy. I have a bad case of wanting to own more knives, and those are not the same thing.

Anyway, Naga and I have known each other a long time, and he wasn't going to eat me, but that didn't make it polite to tempt him. I stopped when I reached the door to his chambers, which was large and round to admit his not insubstantial bulk, and knocked as I leaned up against the hallway wall, trying not to whimper. The spines had worked themselves so deep by this point that I wasn't sure I could have removed them on my own if I'd tried, and I wasn't trying. If it had been unsafe before, it was potentially fatal now.

When there was no answer, I knocked again, harder. If Naga wasn't here, he was probably in his office, and if he was in his office, I was in trouble. There was no way I could walk that far in my current condition, and now that I'd stopped moving, I wasn't actually sure I could start again. Even getting back to my room felt like an impossibility. I bit my lip to stop myself from whimpering and slumped against the wall, closing my eyes.

I don't know how long I stood there like that before there was a slithering sound behind me. I didn't bother trying to turn. Either it was Naga, or it wasn't. If it wasn't, maybe it was one of his grad students who thought of me as an annoying pet and might try to eat me. That would be a lousy way to end my multi-decade quest, done in by a giant crawdad and a hungry scholar, but I was exhausted and injured and basically *done*.

"Alice," said Naga, sounding horrified. "What have you done to yourself this time?"

Arms wrapped around my waist, lifting me easily, and I found myself tucked into a bridal carry against the smooth, scaled chest of my patron and benefactor. I managed to open my eyes and smile weakly up at him.

Naga looked sternly back. He was well-equipped for looking stern, at least by human standards, what with his total lack of hair, yellow, slit-pupiled eyes, and finely scaled skin. The scales grew larger as they moved down his body; by the time they reached his waist, they were as large and hard as the scales on any snake his size, and since that size was fairly substantial, we were talking about a *lot* of scales, many of them larger than my palm.

"Got myself jumped on that retrieval gig," I said, and winced as he turned to slither down the hall. I knew he was heading for the infirmary. That, at least, was normal.

"And that explains why you're leaking on me how?"

"Had to go back to . . . Earth to patch myself up after the initial fight . . . hurt worse then, if you can believe it." I mustered a weak smile. From the look on his face, he didn't believe it at all. Oh, well. It was the truth, and the truth was always worth trying. "Got back to business with one crossing left, had to finish with what I had on hand." I closed my eyes again. "Did it. Got what I'd been sent to get. Got my own stuff back, too."

"Got a nasty case of what looks like some form of septic shock, too," said Naga. "You've used all your crossings?"

I managed a minute nod. He sighed.

"It's soon, but I think it's time for another session," he said. "You've used so many of your tattoos it looks like you've been shedding, and this damage . . . I don't know if the thing that left those needles in your body was poisonous to humans, but I wouldn't be surprised. Are you ready?"

No. I was never ready. That didn't mean it wasn't necessary, or that I didn't understand the reasons; I'd been going through this process for fifty years, and any good reasons I might have had to put it off had long since fallen by the wayside. I sighed.

"As long as it gets them out, I don't care."

"It gets everything out," he said, and slithered on.

I didn't open my eyes once during the trip. I didn't need to. This was a familiar journey, one that I'd made in both better and worse shape than I was in now. Naga carried me down the hall to one of the courtyards that dotted his estate, then turned to head into a narrower hall, one he wouldn't be able to fit down for too many more years. Lamia like Naga keep growing throughout their lives, which can span almost a thousand years when all is said and done, and they get steadily larger the whole time. He'd been twenty feet long when we first met, and I'd been a child. Now, I was an adult holding herself frozen in time, and he was almost fifty feet from the top of his head to the tip of his tail.

Hopefully, I wasn't going to need him to take care of me by the time he was too big for this estate and had to move to one of the larger ones. I've never been sure how lamia society handles that transition, and I wasn't overly interested in finding out firsthand. I huddled in his arms, a feeling of rotten wrongness radiating out from the puncture wounds on my legs, and tried not to shiver. He was probably right about the poison. If he wasn't, it could still be a slow allergic reaction or just a response to the filth that had been on those spikes when they went into me. They were there now, and probably killing me. The mechanism didn't make that much of a difference.

He ducked as he carried me through a door, and I heard other people for the first time. He said something in the rough sibilants of his own language, and they responded in kind. Most of the medical staff had never taken the time to learn English, which their mouths could handle, while mine couldn't handle their language. I'd tried. It just sounded like so much hissing to my ears. According to Naga, I couldn't even hear the upper registers of his language.

At least my tattoo artists spoke English. I could tell them what I needed to stay safe and do my best work, and they could help me choose the right designs. They were good about steering me away from things that might take too much out of me, pulling too much power and depleting my reserves to the point where a little electrolyte replacement powder wouldn't help.

"Can you stand?" asked Naga.

I consulted silently with my body and sighed. "I don't think so," I said.

"I'll have to undress you if you can't stand."

"That doesn't make my legs hurt any less," I said. "No, I can't stand."

"All right." He sucked air through his teeth, a sharp, tight sound. "Alice, the injuries on your upper legs are severe enough that I'm not sure I can remove your shorts in one piece."

"Nothing special about them," I said. Waves of exhaustion were starting to wash over me, alternating with the waves of pain. The recovery I'd managed at the Red Angel was long gone at this point, and I was done. "Cut 'em off."

"Good girl."

He slithered forward, setting me down on the hard metal surface of an operating table, and a moment later, I heard the snick of scissors being opened. A few quick cuts and I was naked, still too tired to move or cover myself. Not that I needed to. Lamia aren't attracted to mammals, and unlike many of the humanoid reptiles on Earth, they never developed mammalian mimicry. No breasts for these serpents. No hair, either. And while I'd met quite a few of them by this point, I had yet to encounter a single one who saw a naked human as anything other than a novelty, or, on a few unpleasant occasions, as something easier to eat.

One of the medics hissed above me. I tensed. A hand brushed my shoulder, accompanied by a hissed interrogative, which Naga answered before sighing, and saying, in English, "They want to know how many dimensions you touched. I told them you began with fifteen crossings, but they need to position the blades appropriately."

"Right . . ." It was getting hard to think. I took a few deep breaths, trying to buy myself time, before I said, "Here to Ithaca, Ithaca to Xxyres, Xxyres to a series of sub-dimensions whose names I don't know . . ." On and on the list went, ending with, "Helos to Earth, Earth back to Helos, Helos to here. How many is that? I can't count."

"Thirteen," he said, with some satisfaction. "You touched thirteen dimensions, including this one and your own."

"Not . . . quite . . . a record, then." Each word felt like an effort, and when the last of them was out, I sighed and relaxed into the table. Tension wouldn't do me any good anyway, and I knew it. I'd been here before.

"No, but close enough." He reached down and smoothed my hair away from my forehead. "How deep shall they go?"

"Shallow," I said. "Don't want to get . . . any younger."

I was already functionally, physically in my early twenties, and it had been a fight to get that much ground back, after the time they'd gone too deep and left me effectively seventeen again, still growing, still a little gangly. Naga had scolded them roundly after that incident, reminding them I couldn't do my job *or* hunt for my husband if my hands were too small to hold my gun, but it had meant several seasons of slower work, never going too far from either Earth or Empusa, for fear that I'd get hurt enough to need another session.

Naga chuckled. "And here when your snake cults call on us, eternal youth is one of the most common requests," he said.

"Not . . . worth it," I replied.

"No, I suppose it's not." He stroked my forehead again. "Here's where I leave you. Try to keep the screaming to a minimum this time?"

"No . . . promises."

He laughed outright as he slithered away, heading back to the door. I heard it open, then close, and then I was surrounded by the medics, their hands lifting me away from the metal table and the remains of my clothes. Fingers dug into one of the larger wounds, grasping the end of a spike and yanking it out.

I did not keep the screaming to a minimum. Removing that spike hurt just as much as I'd been afraid it would, ripping through tissue with the fierce precision of something that had not evolved to be *nice*. If the medics had an issue with it, they could damn well cope.

Judging by their aggravated hissing, they didn't like the noise. That was fine. As long as they didn't go too deep, it wasn't like there was much they could do to me that they weren't already going to do. And they didn't drop me, which was the only thing I'd been particularly worried about.

Still hissing to each other, they lowered me into a warm liquid and let me go. Whatever this stuff was, it was thicker than water, and I floated easily, at no danger of slipping under, even as I remained completely limp. The longer I could keep myself from tensing up, the less this was going to hurt.

Not that anything could actually *keep* it from hurting—pain was inevitable in this process—but hurting *less* was something to hope for, no matter what the surrounding circumstances. One of them moved away, scales scraping on the floor, and I heard the rattle of metal. They were almost ready to begin.

"Please," I said, voice small. "Please, I can just take some antibiotics. You don't have to do this. Please . . ."

This was one of those moments when I was glad none of them had ever learned English. My begging wouldn't stop them, and I trusted Naga. He wouldn't do this to me if it wasn't necessary. I would never have made it this far without him. This was just what had to happen, because I'd been careless enough to get jumped, to get hurt and use my only healing charm before getting hurt even worse. This was my fault, really.

This was always my fault.

Then the first blade was pressed into the skin just above my collarbone, biting into the flesh with very little pressure, and I found exactly how much screaming I had left inside me. As it turned out, I had a *lot* of screaming.

I always did.

Five

"There is no price too great to pay to ensure the safety of the ones we love. To question that is to question your love for them."

—Jonathan Healy

In the infirmary of Naga's estate, being skinned alive, again, by people who are very, very good at their jobs

EVENTUALLY, OF COURSE, the screaming stopped. There's only so much pain the mind can process before it starts shutting things down, and while the liquid I hung suspended in was designed to keep me from slipping into shock and dying from the sheer intensity of it all, it was impossible for them to deaden my nerves enough to keep the removal of my skin from being the worst thing I had ever experienced. It didn't matter how many times they put me through it, either. Every single time was the worst time. Cut shallow, cut deep, that didn't matter once the knives were tracing along my body, as intimate as a lover's hands, touching me in ways I had never allowed anyone to touch me, not since Thomas disappeared. And he had *never* touched me like this, not even when he'd needed to patch me up.

They flensed me one inch at a time, and I was awake and aware for the entire process, unable to lose consciousness thanks to the drugs in the nutrient bath around me, unable to even find that much peace. Bit by bit, they cut me away, leaving my face, as always, for last, so that my eyes could stay shut until they ran their knives along the inside of my cheeks to sever skin from muscle and peeled it away, taking my eyelids in the process.

They appeared above me, three smaller members of Naga's species looking dispassionately down at me, all covered in blood to their elbows. One of them was holding a pale, boneless thing I knew I would recognize if I looked for too long, and so I didn't look. My exposed nerves were on fire.

Another of the medics produced a small ivory jar, and only the fact that I had screamed myself raw stopped me from demanding it right now. She opened the jar and sprinkled its contents, a pale ocher powder, into the liquid around me, and finally, mercifully, I lost consciousness. The pain went with it and was the greatest kindness I had ever experienced.

.It always was. Every single time.

I woke up naked, dry, and stretched out on that same metal table I had been placed on when Naga first brought me here. Nothing hurt. I lifted my right arm and held it up so I could see, and was greeted by the sight of smooth, unmarked skin. No tattoos, no scars, not even a single freckle. I'd asked Naga once, why they couldn't give me pain-killers; why they had to knock me out when they finished skinning me, and not before. He'd replied that it had something to do with the skin itself. If they wanted the procedure to function correctly, my nerve endings had to be active during the removal, and reasonably quiescent while my skin was regrown.

It didn't exactly make sense to me, but it had been working thus far, and it was keeping me moving, which was the important part. Maybe it would have been better if I could have understood what was being done to me. Probably not. I'd still have to go through the process, which cut away all the damage I'd done to myself since the last time I'd been skinned, doing it in a way that went all the way down to my bones—hence why I kept getting de-aged every time I went through it. It cut away distance and time in one fell swoop, leaving me purified.

Best of all, once it was over, nothing hurt. No old aches, no unexplained sore spots. I got a clean slate every single time. And maybe that made up for the fact that it was literally torture and was slowly driving me out of my mind. I didn't really know, and I absolutely didn't have another option.

I sat up on the table, swinging my legs around so my feet were pointed at the floor, and stood. Naga and his people trusted me; all the surgical equipment was still here, and if I'd finally snapped, I could easily have outfitted myself for a fight. Instead, I ignored the trays of shining knives and scalpels, shivering a little as I remembered what those same instruments had felt like slicing through my skin, and crossed the room to where a robe was hanging on the hook next to the door, waiting for me.

Naga was always thoughtful like that. It had taken a few years for him to figure out where the soft, squishy aspects of my mammalian biology came into play, and then he had started arranging things for my comfort as much as possible. Robes in any room where I might be expected to be naked, for whatever reason. Fruit in the kitchen, along with pre-killed meat of indeterminate origin that I could cook, rather than needing to slaughter my own lunches. Pillows for me to sit on. Little things, designed to make me feel like I was a valued member of his household, and not just the equivalent of a tailypo moving in and making myself at home.

(And if some of those "little things" were horribly reminiscent of the ways Thomas had adapted his home to the tailypo before I moved in, the sort of kindnesses you showed a pet, not a guest, there were worse fates in this world than being someone's beloved pet. At least Naga took care of me. It was nice to have someone who was willing to do that, even if the methods they chose weren't precisely the kind a human would have used.)

The robe, which was made of some relatively smooth flannel, was nevertheless soft enough to be momentarily distracting when I put it on. I paused, taking a deep breath as I processed the sensation and pushed it to the back of my mind. This was a natural side effect of what I'd just done to myself. My new skin was an adult's skin in terms of toughness and appearance, but it was also brand new, and everything it experienced was a surprise.

Which just made what had to happen next all the more unpleasant. I sighed and pushed the door open.

The hallway was empty. It always was. No one was ever there when I woke up; they hadn't been since the first time, when I'd opened my eyes to find Naga looming over me, stroking my hair and hissing soft words under his breath, like some sort of impossible serpentine fairy godmother. (The storybook kind, not the kind we set traps for.) I'd blinked up at him, still half-drunk on endorphins, the ghosts of pain still echoing in my nervous system.

"I'm sorry," he'd said to me. "I wish there were some other way. But this will help."

And it had helped, then and every other time. It had kept me going long past the point where I should have been broken by the things I'd been through, the things I'd experienced, and if it hurt, maybe that was a good thing, too, because it kept me from getting careless. A painless rejuvenation would just have encouraged me to take more risks than I had to, to do things like that stunt with the crawdad on a more regular basis. This way . . .

We only did it when I'd been injured enough to make it necessary. Sometimes I could run through more than thirty crossing charms before it was necessary to skin me. And sure, it was necessary often enough that it had probably happened a hundred times by now, if not more, but it could have been so much worse.

Holding my robe shut, I walked down the hall toward the door at the end. I could hear buzzing and rattling from behind it. The tattoo parlor wasn't always active before I went in for a session, but it was always active after, and I assumed it was because Naga called the artists and asked them to be ready for me. There were four of them present when I stepped into the room: two members of Naga's species, one vaguely feline humanoid with close-cropped fur and a small, jutting muzzle, and a Johrlac.

I offered all four a polite nod as I closed the door and shrugged out of my robe, hanging it on the hook next to the door, placement identical to the one in the surgical suite. I'd tried asking them, a few times, whether I was their only client. Surely this whole system couldn't exist solely to benefit me. It had all come together too quickly for that. None of them had ever answered.

The lamia artists changed every decade or so as they grew too large to use the equipment and were replaced by their own apprentices. The feline was new, having shown up within the last seven years, replacing a very sweet sylph who had been willing to sneak me sips of water between sessions. I'd liked him. It would have been nice to try and chat with him again, now that he no longer worked for Naga and might be willing to talk to me with more candor. Not that I thought Naga was lying to me. It was just . . . hard.

I've never had the easiest time making friends. I was the school weirdo in Buckley, the librarian's daughter who always had blood in her hair and mud on her clothes, who cared more about bullets and books than boys. Then I married the town foreigner, a recluse who hadn't left his house in years, and became part of the landscape.

Marrying a man who literally couldn't go outside hadn't done much for my social life. Oh, we'd been happy, but I hadn't exactly built myself what you'd call a wide social network. My whole family was dead, apart from Thomas; and somehow, only Mary had decided to stick around after her body went into the ground. And then there'd been the babies, and I'd loved the babies, but they weren't exactly *conversationalists.* Outside of Laura's occasional visits and my own work at the library, I'd been almost as isolated as Thomas was.

And I'd never minded. I want to be absolutely clear about that. I was never a social butterfly, and so it doesn't bother me as much as it probably should. My choices and my nature made me a relatively isolated person, and I do okay with that. The friendships I do have are scattered across half a dozen dimensions—Bon, back on Earth, Naga, here in his own estate, Helen in Ithaca—and none of them travel with me as easily as I wish they could.

Still, it would have been nice to have someone to talk to while all this was going on. Someone apart from Lybie, who watched my approach with cool blue eyes, as serene as any Johrlac born of Johrlar.

Not many of them choose to leave their home dimension and still carry that name. For Johrlac, the risk of drifting too far from the communal dreams of their hive mind is too great, and mostly we see their exiles, the ones who carry the name "cuckoo" and aren't allowed to return home, no matter what.

The chair had been adjusted to fit my measurements so precisely that it barely felt like I was sitting down—more like I was floating. As always, we'd do my front first, and then, after kitty-cat wiped away the bruises and swelling, we'd flip me over and do my back.

"May I enter?" asked Lybie, voice level and measured, as Johrlac almost always were. They don't do big emotions when they're around other people. They don't think we deserve them.

"You may," I said, only somewhat grudgingly.

She leaned forward to rest her fingertips on my temples. Any skin contact would work—proximity to the brain doesn't matter—but since I had thus far refused to allow any tattoos above the neck, my head was a safe place for her to anchor herself. The soft hum of active telepathy became an overlay on my thoughts, all the more noticeable because it was foreign. Foreign things shouldn't be inside my head.

"May I suppress?" asked Lybie.

This was a familiar script, and one I had learned to follow. "Please," I said.

What little pressure I could feel from the chair went away, taking every other sensation with it. It felt as if my entire body had been dipped into Novocaine, as if it belonged to someone else; I was inexplicably able to operate it. I tilted my head back, focusing on the feline.

"Standard array, two more bone sets, any extra healing you can cram in without killing me, same number of transits," I said.

"Keep the transit power at the same level?" he asked, always the professional.

I used to find the artists cold. There was always someone who could speak my language, always a telepath to make sure the pain wouldn't interfere with the procedure, and the two artists of Naga's own breed, who viewed me as a renewable canvas, a palimpsest girl somehow wiped completely clean over and over again for them to practice their art upon.

And they *had* improved over the course of our time together, even as they grew too big for the room and their equipment and were replaced by their apprentices. In the beginning, almost everything I'd had tattooed on me had been brute force, the magical equivalent of using a crowbar to open a motel window. Some things probably got broken in those early rampages through the dimensional walls, and they learned more and more about what they could pack onto my skin, and what I needed to have in my pocket, as it were, if I wanted this to be a trip that I came back from.

Currently, my dimensional punches were set to carry up to three people, designed when I'd been traveling with my mice, before I'd passed them off to Antimony for safekeeping. That had been a reduction from four, and it had taken my number of jumps from ten to fifteen. But I couldn't just add more dimensional crossing charms without exceeding the amount of magic we knew my body could handle. I still hesitated before I asked, "Would reducing the number of people I can carry with me from three to two let me have more jumps?"

The feline turned to the artists and hissed a long series of sibilants, which the artists answered in kind. He nodded before returning his attention to me, and replying, "Not in any meaningful way. If you'd allow them to reduce the number to one, we could double your number of potential transits."

"No," I said immediately. Reducing the number from four to three had been an admission that I was starting to lose hope, starting to believe that Thomas wasn't out there to find. Now I knew he might be, now I had hope again, and dropping the number of people I could take with me would be the same as giving up on him completely. I might as well get out of this chair and go back to Earth if I was going to do that. "Tell them to keep the power levels the same."

"If you're sure . . ."

"I'm positive." I closed my eyes. "You can start whenever you're ready."

There was no pain when they set to work, only a distant feeling of vibration, like being on a moving train. I'd been running hard for a long time, and being knocked out after being skinned alive isn't the same thing as sleeping. Gradually, I slipped under, until even the vibration was gone, and I was alone with my dreams.

They might not be the kindest dreams I'd ever had, but they were mine, and I welcomed them, even as I remained distantly aware that Lybie could see them all. My brain's private movie was playing for an audience of two, and while I could probably have pushed her out if I'd woken myself up and made a genuine effort, that would have been enough to bring back the pain. I didn't want more pain today.

According to Mary, pain leaves marks on the nervous system, and enough pain, over enough time, can scar. She said it was a miracle the pain hadn't scarred my mind beyond functionality already, after everything she knew I'd put myself through—and everything she didn't know but had come to suspect from the times when I wasn't careful enough: the times she'd seen me flinch away from the light glinting off a knife or refuse to pick up a scalpel. She knew that there was damage she couldn't see, damage that I wasn't ready to tell her about.

I'm not *stupid*. Yes, my family thinks I'm delusional, thinks I've left my sanity behind somewhere in one of the uncounted dimensions I've gone running through over the last fifty years, one more trinket tossed aside because it didn't fit in my pocket anymore. That doesn't mean they're right, and it doesn't mean I've lost what sense my mama gave me. I know enough to know that if I told my babysitter that the reason I've stayed young and functional for all these years is because I'm letting my childhood friend skin me alive on a regular basis, she'd nod and listen and say all the right things to make me think she was going to keep my secrets, and then she'd run straight to Kevin and tell him what had been going on.

It's hard enough to keep my family from calling an emergency meeting and trying to nail my feet to the floor of my home dimension without giving them more ammunition to use against me, and Naga was helping me get back to Thomas. He'd been helping me all along. And soon enough, he'd be done helping me, and I'd be going home.

One way or another, I'd be going home.

My dreams devolved into shape and color. There was a mountain made entirely of ice cream, and if I didn't eat the whole thing, something terrible was going to happen. I approached it with a spoon the size of a snow shovel in my hand and hoped, perhaps irrationally, that it would be enough to let me tackle the problem at hand—

The mountain shattered and fell away as hands coaxed me out of the chair and over to the waiting table, where it was even easier to sleep, stretched on my stomach with my face pressed into the pillow, Lybie sitting beside me with her hand now on the back of my head, keeping me numbed and serene. It was virtually impossible for me to stay awake while all this was going on, even when I hadn't let myself get beaten to death's doorstep before the rejuvenation process. Between the sedatives that finished out the flensing and the soothing presence of a telepath I'd voluntarily allowed into my mind, consciousness was something meant for other people.

The mountain came back, and I went to the mountain, and nothing mattered except the soothing numbness that had become the entire world. Everything else fell quietly away and was forgotten.

Once again, I woke up someplace else. I was wearing my robe and had been moved to a low couch at the side of the room, installed for my use after the third session that had ended with someone needing to wake me up so I could walk back to my bed. Naga hadn't been able to fit in my room since long before it had officially become "mine." If he'd been married, it would have been set aside for the youngest of their children, it was so small by their standards. It was more than large enough for me.

I blinked at the ceiling for several long seconds before sitting up and pushing the right sleeve of my robe toward my shoulder. Fresh new tattoos greeted me, bright as anything, including a marching line of fifteen runes that would allow me to accomplish the necessary dimensional crossings. I squinted at them. They looked, and felt, exactly like the last batch, and when I checked, there were no matching runes on my left arm. I sighed, relieved. The artists didn't usually ignore what I asked for, but there had been a few incidents, and being effectively drugged insensate for the whole process meant that there was no reasonable way for me to object.

Lybie had prevented me from feeling the pain while it was happening, and the oil the artists had rubbed into my skin when the procedure was over—and whenever necessary while it was still going on—had repaired all the damage. My tattoos were effectively as healed as they would have been after almost a month's recovery, and I was ready to get back on the road.

I asked Naga, in the beginning, how I was supposed to pay for all this. He shook his head and said that among his people, there could be no debts between friends. And maybe it was, again, because I was his tailypo, but I believed him.

It wasn't like I really had a choice.

The hall was empty when I stepped out of the studio and started the walk back to my room. I didn't pass anyone along the way, and honestly, I was grateful for that. I wasn't really in the mood for conversation. I wasn't in any pain—one of the nice things about the way all this was handled, if any process that begins with being literally skinned alive can be referred to in any way as "nice"—but I wasn't feeling up for people. Most of the people on Naga's estate were other lamia, and while they were perfectly nice, the majority of them didn't speak English, and just looked at me like I had somehow slipped my leash and needed to be brought to heel as quickly as possible. No, better to just move quickly, get my stuff, and get moving.

Naga wouldn't mind me leaving without saying goodbye. He never did. This was just a waystation for me, always had been, and always would be, at least until I brought Thomas home and didn't need it anymore. I kept my head down as I walked, moving fast, and didn't relax until I saw the door to my room.

That was when I remembered. I *couldn't* leave, not until I gave Naga the bags I'd been sent to retrieve. I didn't pay for the services he provided me, but when he showed up with a job—which was almost always, essentially, "go to this world in this dimension over here, get something, and bring it back," with a decent side order of recreational murder—I did it, no questions asked. I owed him, whether he wanted to acknowledge it or not. Retrieving a person and retrieving an object meant essentially the same thing, and they were part of why the artists had already known how to amp up a gateway tattoo to carry more than one person.

I paused, frowning. I did enough retrieval that they should never even have asked if I was okay reducing my gateway tattoos to a single-person carrying capacity. That was a little odd, and I didn't entirely like it.

Oh, well. I could worry about that later, *after* I had given Naga the bags and gotten back on the metaphorical road. I can't stay still too long, or I get twitchy. I'm always twitchier after a procedure. I opened the door and stepped into my room, this time pausing to turn on the light.

After Thomas had had a few drinks and let the last of his guard down, he used to tell me about his days at Penton Hall, back when he'd been a ward of the Covenant. His parents had died before he was old enough to remember them, victims of the Covenant's endless, unnecessary war against the cryptids of the world. He grew up in a plain white room that was essentially part of a barracks, and nothing he did could ever have made it seem more like a place where people actually belonged. It was part of how he'd been able to adjust to the old Parrish place so quickly. Sure, the house had been actively hostile, but at least it had been *his*.

My room at Naga's made me think I understood him a little better. No matter how much of a mess I made or how much stuff I packed into the reasonably small space, it never looked like anyone *lived* here. There was a bed, flat and round and designed for a very young lamia, but sufficient to my needs. There were two dressers, both constructed from hard red wood that smelled faintly of turmeric, sized for human use and probably built by some of the same people as assisted the artists; there was a wardrobe that matched the dressers. There was nothing else. Nothing on the walls, which was my own fault. Naga wouldn't have stopped me from hanging pictures, or maps, or charts, and sometimes I'd been tempted.

But it felt like there were very few steps between truly starting to make this space my own and starting to think of it, not Buckley, as home. And once I stopped thinking of Buckley, of *Earth*, as the place where I actually belonged, something would be over. Something I might not ever be able to get back.

My bag was where I'd dropped it, along with the map roll and pile of books. Might as well look at those now, see what I'd stolen, and figure out whether they were anything Naga might want to keep.

The map roll was so old it didn't have a zipper. The top was capped with a hard leather "lid" that creaked and stuck as I wiggled it off. I immediately tipped the case upside down over my bed, figuring that if anything nasty had managed to creep its way in there, it would spill out along with whatever else was inside. Nothing came. I turned it back toward me and peered into the dark interior. Something was mashed up against the side, and bit by bit, I wiggled it out, until I was holding a sheet of vellum approximately three feet long.

Someone had been mapping for quite some time before they'd ended up on Helos and lost their possessions. Their possessions and, given the surrounding debris, very likely their life. Oh, well. Dead people could still have opinions, and if this map had been haunted by someone who didn't want to give it up, they would have told me so by now. Picking up a couple of knives to serve as weights, I began unrolling the map on my bed, placing a knife on each corner to keep it flat.

When I was done, I was looking at something very much like a star chart, except that the things it showed weren't stars. It was the unfinished point that told me what I was looking at. Our long-lost cartographer, whoever they had been, whatever had happened to them, had been on their way to Helos to chart the dimensions branching off from there.

Using that as my starting point, I was able to trace back to familiar lines and pathways, finding worlds I knew in the web of interconnected lines. Some of them were connected in ways I hadn't seen before, new shortcuts and directions that might be useful in the future. And then I reached Empusa in the chart and had to pause.

Because every dimension is a blood cell or a hex in a hive or a grain of rice in a sack or whatever metaphor you need to let you picture something that literally cannot be pictured by the human mind, there are always a lot of directions you can go. It's not like being a person standing on a flat plane, where you can walk almost any way that isn't barricaded, but you can't go up without a jetpack or down without a shovel. It's more like being a deep-sea diver. You can go in any direction, three hundred and sixty degrees all-immersive, and because you've presumably got a tank of oxygen strapped to your back, you don't really need to worry about drowning.

But if you don't have a guide, you pretty much have to go by what you're told. You have to follow directions from your dive instructor, basically, the people who've been there before and know where the giant eels that like to eat novice divers are lurking. Naga's dimension, Empusa, was one that had been familiar to me for most of my life, and since he'd been summoned by a Buckley snake cult, it had been relatively easy to get there after Thomas disappeared, requiring just a little blood sacrifice and a little help from a routewitch who'd started out her life as part of a snake cult.

I say, "relatively easy," which means it wasn't impossible, the way it should have been for someone as magically inert as I was. I didn't have to give up my firstborn child, my name, or any body parts, and I got a one-way ticket out of Earth and into the domain of the only person I knew who might actually be able to help me.

And Naga had been willing—almost eager, even—to help. He'd started recruiting tattoo artists who knew how to seal sorcery into skin almost immediately, and I'd been on my way within a month, passage charms etched into my arm and no real destination in mind beyond "wherever Thomas is." I'd been trusting the Healy luck to make me trip over the right rock and fall down the right rabbit hole, like my namesake, coming out in Wonderland.

It hadn't worked. Again and again, it hadn't worked, and again and again, I'd returned to Naga, until the first time I returned with a septic gut wound that was driving my fever through the roof and my blood pressure through the floor at the same time, leaving me barely able to stand unsupported, and he'd taken me to the treatment room while I was still lucid enough to consent.

I'd sworn it would be the only time, and Naga had agreed, and kept researching possible directions for me to go, but had always told me not to go in one general direction from Empusa, or one general idea of a direction. "There's nothing that way that's capable of supporting life," had been his final word on the subject. "I feel a great deal of responsibility toward you, after the service your mother did me. I'm not going to let you wander off into a blasted hellscape and die from lack of biochemical reactivity in your cells. Stick with the directions we know are safe."

But that didn't match this map.

According to the map, there was a whole cluster of verified dimensions and worlds off in that direction, and if I was reading the symbols correctly, the nearest of them was environmentally very close to this one. That probably meant it was full of giant snakes, and where giant snakes can survive, so can I, as long as I can avoid the giant snakes before they eat me. All the destinations were labeled, and they all had the tiny runic marks that I had learned in order to amend my tattoos.

Naga didn't know. Clearly, Naga didn't know. It was an easier explanation than Naga lying to me over and over again for fifty years. I rerolled the map and tucked it back into its case, glancing at the pile of books. They looked like they had come from the same place. Maybe they had more information about the mapped dimensions I didn't recognize. I sat down on the edge of the bed and unbuckled the strap, opening the first book.

It was written in a language I didn't recognize, much less understand. Of course. Naga was a professor of extra-dimensional studies, and I briefly thought of bringing it to him for translation, then rejected the idea. If there was any chance he *had* been keeping this from me for some reason . . .

No. I couldn't think like that, but I couldn't show him the book, either. And I couldn't explain what I was about to do in any way that would make sense, but I didn't use my translation charm on about half my trips. I'd be fine without it. Pressing two fingers against the hydrangea tattooed high on my bicep, I concentrated, and felt a wave of dizziness as the tattoo flared and disappeared, used up by the intent to use it.

When I glanced back at the book, it was written in English, the handwriting neat and precise. It was a cartographer's diary, of sorts.

2nd Glorn, fifth year of the reign of our Lady of Pleasures.
We have found another of the bottle worlds, which must be avoided by those who wish to survive navigation of the great weave. It opens from . . .

And there the entry went into a list of worlds and dimensions, six in all, before concluding with:

. . . which opens from Cornale, in the upmost when Cornale has been approached from the correct direction, and with the proper intent. It is a small and a terrible place, and better left forgotten. What enters it does not emerge again, and it is my belief that we have found a place of prisonment. That it contains life is unquestionable. That this life is beyond all access by those who wish to see their homes again is equally unquestionable.
We will return home via Helos, to document the branches which open from this world. We have heard that it is well-connected to its portion of the weave, and we might use it to discover yet more wonders. Perhaps this will prove true, and we will return home heroes.

I closed the book, slowly, and stared off into nothing. Eight jumps—nine if I included Ithaca, which I would have to do to access Cornale, that being the only name on the list I recognized, apart from Helos, where their journey had ended—would leave me too far out to get back. If I entered this "bottle world" they referred to, I'd be down ten, leaving me with five. And five wasn't even enough to make it back to Ithaca. I should tell Naga about this. We couldn't pack a single additional crossing charm onto my skin without risking some sort of permanent damage to my nervous system, but maybe he had something external I could take with me, some sort of charm or pendant I could carry.

And maybe I could ask him why he'd told me there was nothing past Ithaca worth even looking into, when clearly the dimensions in that direction could sustain life, and life that was compatible enough with humanity to draw maps and keep diaries to document their travels.

Yes. Talking to Naga was the right thing to do, despite the small, nagging voice at the back of my mind telling me not to do this. He was my friend. He would tell me how to proceed. He would help me.

He'd been helping me for fifty years.

Six

"Alice doesn't trust fast, but once she decides it's safe to trust at all, she trusts absolutely. I love that girl, but it's going to get her killed one of these days, and I don't know what I'm going to do when that happens."

—Laura Campbell

About to enter the office of Naga, Professor of Extra-Dimensional Studies at the University of K'larth

NAGA'S DOOR WAS SLIGHTLY ajar, as it always was during his office hours. I paused outside, listening for the hisses that would have meant he was consulting with a student. I might have free run of the estate when I was there, but that didn't mean I was allowed to just go busting in on him while he was at work.

Only silence greeted me. I took a deep breath and pushed the door open, holding the first of the three books under my arm and carrying the bags I'd been sent to recover in my opposite hand. "Hey, Naga," I said, by way of greeting. "I was just about to get back on the move, and thought I'd drop these off with you first."

He was behind his desk, the great bulk of his body coiled beneath him and his humanoid upper body held at attention. I've never been able to understand how he could make that look so effortless, and I would absolutely love to get my hands on some X-rays or a skeletal model of a member of his species, because I want to *know*. He had a parchment in his hand, and he put it down as he turned to look at me, lightly scaled lips tilting upward in a smile.

"Alice," he said. "I wasn't sure you'd come to see me before you left."

"I know, I know, but I'm not in as big of a hurry this time as I was last time." I put the bags down next to the door, where they wouldn't block his path if he tried to slither out. "I don't know if everything's there. I didn't want to go digging around in a client's stuff. But the packs are still tied, and the raiders didn't seem to be looting the things they stole very thoroughly before they tossed them in the pile. They got my pack, too, and they didn't even steal the TNT."

"You shouldn't run around with explosives in your bag the way you do," he said, somewhat chidingly. "One day that's going to go very poorly for you, and if it happens far enough away from here, I'll never know what cliffside I need to go and scrape you off of."

"Yeah, but when that happens, at least it won't be my problem anymore." I smiled at him, trying to look as charming as I possibly could. Naga sighed. He's never been easy for me to charm.

"You want something," he said.

"We redid my tattoos," I said. "I have to keep the power on my gateways the same in order to bring Thomas home, but I think I might want to go a little farther afield this time. Is there anything portable I can take with me, to make sure I won't get stranded someplace where I don't have any allies?" And why had I never thought to ask that before?

The question was almost surprising enough to make me lose my train of thought. I blinked, waiting for Naga's reply.

Naga looked dubious. "Why would you need to go farther afield?" he asked. "I know there are directions off of Tartarus that you haven't finished exploring, and there are still bounties around Helos to be cleared."

I blinked again before frowning. "You do remember the point of all this isn't collecting bounties, it's getting back to my husband, right? That's all I'm trying to do. Everything else is just consequences of something that was going to happen anyway."

"Of course, forgive me," he said smoothly. "Still, the question remains, if slightly modified: why the sudden rush to go farther than you have before? Fifteen jumps should allow you to go as far from here as seven layers of reality, and you've yet to make it more than six without serious injury. What kind of friend would I be if I sent you into the void knowing that you might break yourself when too far from home to return?"

"But this *isn't* my home. It's my home base. That's not the same thing. Once I find Thomas, we're going back to Buckley, and we're going back to our house, and we're going to be happy." I was going to find a way to fit myself into the space that used to fit me perfectly, even if I had to slice something off to do it. I couldn't keep doing this forever. I needed to *rest*.

"I know, Alice," said Naga. "I've never forgotten why you started all of this, or why you allow me to help you. No one wants you to find Thomas more than I do. He always seemed like a very nice man when I knew him."

"He wasn't," I said. "He isn't, I mean. A very nice man. He's a very practical man, and a very generous man when he cares about someone, and a very earnest man, but he's never been a very nice man. The Covenant doesn't encourage niceness in the people they train." Thomas had never liked Naga. He was willing to accept that the lamia was a family friend, and had known me since I was a child, but something about him had rubbed Thomas the wrong way, and there had never been time to really figure out why.

There hadn't been time for so many things. We deserved time, and I was tired of wasting it. It was time to bring him home.

"So please forgive me for saying this, but I don't care about the bounties around Helos. I didn't commit to them. The only job I was committed to was bringing back these bags, and look, I did it. Hurt myself pretty bad in the process. We need to update the threat description for Helos. The entry says there's nothing dangerous left apart from the locals, and unfortunately, that's just not true."

"I wondered how you had managed to fill yourself with chitinous spikes," admitted Naga. "My question remains. Why the sudden press to go farther afield from Empusa? I thought you had charted all the main roads from here."

He was a professor. Professors like research and documentation. Holding this in mind, I dropped the book onto his desk. "I don't recognize the language it's written in, but it's not encoded," I said. "A simple translation charm should do it."

Almost reverently, Naga opened the cover. "Where did you find this?" he breathed.

I was struck with the sudden firm conviction that I couldn't possibly tell him about the other two books, or the map, if I wanted to have time to study them. His entire posture had turned possessive, and he was all but curling his arm around the book as he pulled it gently, gingerly closer to his body. Telling him that finders keepers meant it belonged to me wasn't going to do me a scrap of good, I could tell that much already.

"It was in the junk pile the raiders on Helos had been assembling," I said. "I saw it when I was retrieving the bags."

"This is one of the lost journals of Aikanis," he said, in a reverent tone. "He was one of the great dimensional cartographers. We have a library named after him. He vanished on his last charting expedition. His remains—and his research—have never been found. The scribes of Ithaca use a unique ink for their notation. It can't be faked. You found what no one else has been able to."

"Well, I don't think he made it any farther than Helos," I said. Crabs can break down a body in near-record time; they don't eat the bones, but they take them away. Those books had been in the pile long enough to accumulate a layer of dust my grandmother would have grounded me over, and this researcher had been gone long enough to have a library named after him, so I was willing to bet that any forensic evidence was long, long gone.

"You read this?" Naga raised his head and looked at me, tone wary and surprisingly envious. I was the first person to have touched a work applicable to his field, and now I got to see what professional jealousy looked like on his face. It wasn't pretty.

"I skimmed it," I said. "Why did you tell me there was nothing past Ithaca?"

He looked surprised. "What do you mean?"

"The first page," I said. "He says there are dimensions and habitable worlds past Ithaca, and if he could survive on Helos, I can survive wherever he went. I want to follow his trail. I want to see what he found."

"He was a satyr," said Naga. "His environmental needs were similar to a human's. If he survived past Ithaca . . . yes, you could survive there, too. But your body cannot carry any more crossings than it already holds."

"Hence why I'm here, asking you if you can give me something external," I said, trying to sound patient. Everything about this was making me uncomfortable, stillness most of all. I had a direction now. I could *go.*

"We decided on tattooing to match your husband's example, and because you would be unlikely to lose them without losing parts of your body too large to survive," he said. "Possessions can be lost. External things can be torn away. You would be taking a dear risk if you chose to carry something that was not embedded in your skin."

"Not until I'm more than seven jumps out, I wouldn't," I said. "If I can get that far without using my own charms, I can get back."

Naga looked dubious, but put the book down on his desk, fingers lingering on the cover, before slithering over to one of the shelves. "If you lose these, we'll lose you," he cautioned. "I can't send someone to retrieve you."

"I know." For all that he was a professor of extra-dimensional studies, Naga didn't travel much himself. Neither did many of the people who thronged around him, the other professors, the employees, the younger students. The University of K'larth attracted scholars from dozens of dimensions, but apart from coming to class and popping home to see their families, most of them found my predisposition for wide-ranging as strange as my own family did. No one had ever been able to tell me precisely why that was the case, or maybe I just hadn't pressed them for an answer.

It's funny, really. For some species, dimensional travel was as easy as doing a bit of math or casting a spell or closing their eyes and concentrating. For others, it was virtually impossible. I couldn't do things the Johrlac way—their math was miles beyond me—and without magic to fuel my crossings, I can't travel using any of the natural mechanisms of those species, but it seemed like we should have been able to find a method to make this easier. To go all *Star Trek*, but with dimensions instead of outer space.

Naga's species had found the keys to dimensional travel, probably aided by the fact that snakes have very little friction and can slide through dimensional membranes with distressing ease, and then decided that while it should be studied as much as possible, it shouldn't be *done* when it could be avoided. I didn't understand it. I didn't understand much about their culture. Most of my time with them had been spent here in the estate, passing through.

Naga reached into a deep vase and pulled out two . . . I suppose the best English term for them would be "charm bracelets," although each of them was large enough for me to wear as a necklace. They jingled faintly as he slithered back to me and held them out. "Here."

I took the necklaces from his hand, trying to handle them as carefully as I could. They had to be at least stable enough to deal with ordinary movement, or he wouldn't have let me touch them, and anything that couldn't take at least as much jostling as a grenade wasn't going to do me much good.

Each of them had five little glass beads on it, and each bead contained a swirling silver liquid. I glanced up. "One crossing each?"

"Break the bead and open one door," said Naga. "You can go ten out before you have to start using your own charms, if you're careful, and don't get yourself so badly hurt that you can't go any farther. Please try not to die out there."

"I'll do my best." I slipped the necklaces on over my head, and fought the urge to ask him why, if we had crossings in such an easy, portable form that he could have ten of them in his office just waiting to be used, I needed to have them etched into my skin. The answer wouldn't have mattered. The crossing tattoos took up so little real estate, body-wise, compared to everything else, and everything else was there because it needed to be. He'd been anticipating my future needs, not trying to keep me away from a resource.

"Each one will use up as much of your bodily reserves as a crossing etched into your skin, so be careful."

"I'll pack extra electrolyte powder," I said. "Thank you."

"Of course, Alice. All I've ever wanted to do is help you in your quest."

I smiled at him, touched the necklaces now hanging against my chest, taking some reassurance in the weight of them, and turned to leave the room.

Naga apparently hadn't realized that for me to have read the books at all, I would have needed to activate a translation charm, or that it would still be in effect, because before I could move out of hearing, he hissed, in his own language,

"Curse the endless curiosity of monkeys."

I couldn't stop and tell him I understood, not without starting something I didn't have time for and that wouldn't make any difference right now anyway. I left the room, pausing in the hallway for a moment to blink, then took a deep breath and continued on. I needed to get my things.

It was time to go.

My pack—which was important enough to me that I would have gone back to Helos to get it even if I hadn't been in the middle of a job—contained mostly weapons, ammunition, and spare clothing. I filled the remaining space with electrolyte powder, more bullets, and the other two books before untying my robe and dropping it to the floor, turning to the dresser that held more clothing than weapons.

I was never the most fashionable girl in Buckley, and spending most of my time around people who have no idea what's attractive for a human hasn't helped with that. Pretty much all my drawers were filled with the same things, simple, practical clothing that I could move in without getting snagged on something, cut to accommodate as many knives as I could cram under a shirt. So I didn't have to think about what I was going to wear, just pull it on and fasten the buttons, and then I was ready to go.

Strapping on my weapons took longer. Mama's revolvers went back to my belt, as always, and from there, it was a game of hide and seek with everything else. The last thing I put on was my boots, sturdy enough to run over crusted lava if I moved fast and the convection didn't kill me, sufficiently broken in that if I had to wear them for the next three days, the worst thing I'd have to worry about would be the smell. All told, it took me less than ten minutes to get ready.

I spent the whole time watching the door, waiting for Naga to realize that I must have translated the text somehow. I didn't know why his last words had left me with such a bad feeling, but it sat in my stomach like a stone, too heavy to carry for long, making everything else seem uncertain and sour. He didn't show up. No one did.

Sighing, I slung my pack over my shoulders and hooked the map case over one arm. The same bad feeling that told me I needed to be concerned about how Naga was going to react to having spoken candidly in my presence was telling me not to leave it behind, and I trust my feelings, especially when I don't understand them. They haven't steered me wrong yet.

Time to see if these beads worked as advertised. I took a deep breath, reached up, and snapped one off the necklace where it dangled, dropping it to the floor and grinding it under my heel. A wave of dizziness washed over me even as I closed my eyes and focused on Ithaca, a world that was familiar enough by this point that I didn't even need to think of a direction, just the destination. Everything shifted around me.

Abruptly, I could smell the sea. Opening my eyes, I beheld Ithaca. No flashback. No moment of total disconnection from my own life. I lifted the necklace and stared at it, reeling. I could have been traveling this way the *whole time*?

Oh, Naga and I were going to have *words* when I got back.

I already touched on this a little, but it's important to be as clear as I can, so: there are dimensions, and there are worlds. If every dimension is a body, then every world is an organ—or again, more accurately, a cell. When you enter a dimension, the direction of your approach will determine which world you wind up on—and that's why intent matters. Every dimension I've visited has been as large and complex and complicated and confusing as the one I'm from, full of worlds with their own natural laws, climate, civilization or lack thereof, and inhabitants. But to go back to the blood metaphor—I know, I know, too many metaphors, like I said, I'm trying to explain the unexplainable—in order for me to cross into a new dimension, I have to have *something* in common with it. So while there are dimensions that would kill me instantly, I don't have access to them, no matter how close they are to my starting point or destination. I can go to worlds that don't want to support human life, and that's part of why I listen when people say a direction isn't safe.

A dimension whose physical laws don't allow for my existence wouldn't let me in in the first place, and that's the difference.

Naga says he assumes less than twenty percent of reality is accessible to any traveler, and honestly, that sounds more than generous to me. There's a lot of places where humans can't survive.

But what this really means is that everyplace I go has at least a few commonalities with the world where I grew up. Gravity, oxygen, consistent laws of physics. It's nice. It makes a real difference, where comfort is concerned. Ithaca is only two steps removed from Earth, since Empusa is directly connected, and I found myself standing in a loose circle of old stones that were probably once part of some sort of foundation. Grass grew between them, green and sweet-smelling, with just a hint of spice.

So far, I hadn't found anything on Ithaca that I was allergic to in pollen form, which was nice. Some of the food, yeah, which isn't always something I have time to discover about a new world, since I tend to be in and out in short order. I was suddenly grateful that Ithaca was my best starting point. According to Naga, Aikanis had been a satyr. Maybe Helen knew something about him.

I tromped out of the circle and started down the hillside, moving toward a rustic brick-and-wood house in the middle of what looked like an entirely untended field. Appearances can be deceiving. I'd never been much more than a mile from my standard arrival spot, and while I knew all of Ithaca wasn't a bucolic coastal paradise, that was mostly what I'd experienced. The locals were incredibly good at making things look natural and unattended while simultaneously cultivating them to within an inch of their lives.

It made walking down the hill surprisingly fraught, since I knew nothing here would be regarded as a "weed" by the people whose house I was approaching; it was all incredibly intentional. Helen's wife once cried for three days because I'd stepped on a wildflower she'd been trying to cultivate for years, and only stopped when Helen was able to successfully harvest seeds from the flowers I *hadn't* squashed.

Phoebe still didn't fully trust me. I couldn't blame her, since by satyr standards I was clumsy and unobservant. Anyone who stepped on a flower was suspect to her.

At least Helen liked me. I kept descending the hill, fully visible in the afternoon light, and by the time the ground leveled out beneath my feet, the front door was banging open and Helen herself was making her appearance.

She was a reasonably tall woman with the sturdy build of someone who farmed for a living and enjoyed the fruits of her own labor a great deal, belly contained by a flowered apron and arms thick as planks. If not for the fact that from the waist down, she had the body of the largest goat I'd ever seen, she would have seemed perfectly normal.

Well, that, and the horns. "Alice!" she called jubilantly. "I didn't expect to see you so soon."

"Just passing through, I'm afraid, but I wanted to ask you about something, if you have a little time for me."

"For you, my friend? Anything. Come into the kitchen. Phoebe's been baking, and there's fresh bread and butter if you have a hunger to you."

"That would be lovely, thank you." I've learned not to eat before going to Ithaca. For them, refusing food is a greater insult than physical assault. My grandmother had been similar, if less codified; she didn't offer people who turned her down second chances.

One of the theories I've been vaguely poking about dimensional travel is that not only are the worlds closest to us almost always ones where we can survive, they're the source of many of the cryptid species we know. The ones that seem just a little out of alignment with the local biology, that don't make any sense from an evolutionary standpoint? Yeah, there's a reason for that. Ithaca, the parts of it I'd seen anyway, seemed vaguely Grecian in nature, and could easily explain all those old stories about the utopian fields of Mount Olympus. Not that I'd encountered any gods here. Mostly just satyrs, who were charming, friendly people, and the occasional centaur, who were . . . less friendly, to put things *extremely* charitably.

It wasn't hard to believe that a group of satyrs might have been exploring the dimensions near their own at some point, found their way to Earth, and been stranded there. It was sadly not hard to believe that they wouldn't have lasted long after that. Despite a skill with horticulture that felt like it verged on the supernatural, the only real inhuman talents any of them had demonstrated were the ability to walk up almost sheer cliff faces, and the power of eating virtually anything without having an allergic reaction. High levels of goatiness, in short.

Humans are not unique in the universe for violence. I've met plenty of people since I started traveling who believe that shooting first and asking questions later is absolutely the way to go and will make everything better when all is said and done. But humans *are* pretty unique in our narrow definition of what it means to be a person. Almost every other inhabited world I've been to has had multiple kinds of intelligent people living in accord, if not actually in harmony, while back on Earth, humanity's response to realizing we were not alone had been to build bigger guns and try to fix what we saw as a problem.

So drop some people whose main attribute is looking like livestock and really, really wanting to run their farms and be left mostly alone in ancient Greece, and you've basically created a recipe for mildly cannibalistic goat stew. Helen smiled at me as she turned to go back into the house, clearly holding no grudges over the fact that my ancestors had probably eaten some of her distant relations. That was all in the past. Here and now, it was time for bread.

The kitchen was bright and airy, like something out of a storybook about witches who lived in the woods and dried all their herbs by hanging them in bundles around the edges of the room. The air smelled of rosemary and lavender. Another satyr was at the table, rolling out a sheet of focaccia bread. She glanced at me warily, flicking long white hair out of her eyes with a tiny jerk of her head.

"Alice," she acknowledged.

"Phoebe," I replied.

She grunted and went back to kneading her bread as Helen bustled into the room and past me to the icebox, which looked as old-fashioned and antiquated as anything that we'd had when I was growing up, but opened to reveal a sleek white interior, brightly lit by low-impact LED bulbs and frosty with internal cold.

"I have lemonade," she said. "Fresh this morning, made from lemons out of our own grove. We didn't expect to see you today."

"We'd have been elsewhere if we had," muttered Phoebe. It took me a moment to realize her words sounded slightly odd because they were; she was speaking the local language, which was shaped something like ancient Greek if it had managed to stay the dominant form of communication for an additional two thousand years, and something not at all like that. Centaur had different phonemes than humans or satyrs, and they'd influenced the linguistic development as much as anyone else had.

The translation charm was still working, then. That was good, since it meant I'd be able to go over the books I was carrying *with* Helen, and not ask her to translate for me. "I didn't know I was coming until about an hour ago," I said, and shrugged off both my pack and the map roll. "Lemonade would be lovely, Helen, thank you."

"So you've just been seen to?" she asked, as she pulled a pitcher out of the icebox and closed the door.

The satyrs were always very noncommittal when discussing the process by which Naga had my tattoos redrawn. I wasn't clear on how many of the details they knew, and had never really wanted to explain, not least because my mice were never allowed in the procedure room. Something about the smell of rodents distracting my surgeons. They said farewell to me when I went with Naga and didn't see me again until I was clean and tattooed and equipped with a full measure of skin.

If the mice had ever known exactly what I was putting myself through to keep on going, it would have been the same as telling Mary. They would have informed the rest of my clergy, and the clergy would have told the family—whether they intended to or not, the first time they decided to celebrate the Festival of Flensing or something like that, Kevin and Jane would have figured it out—and then I would have been dealing with a whole new set of problems. So telling the satyrs had always been out, because speaking those words aloud would have meant speaking them in front of the mice.

"Yes," I said, and held out a hand as she poured me a tumbler of lemonade. It was sweet and tart and had a faint herbal taste to it that I couldn't quite identify. "Is that mint?"

"Meadowsweet."

"Ah. It's nice." I took a longer drink before saying, "I'm just heading out again. Found a new direction in a diary by some old dimensional explorer, a man named Aikanis. Naga said he was a satyr. I thought you might know something about him."

Phoebe turned and stared at me, hands still full of dough. "Aikanis?" she asked. Then, more loudly, "Did you find him?"

"I found some of his books," I said, and bent to retrieve the map roll from the floor. "And this map. I think they go together. I didn't check to make sure."

Comparing the handwriting could confirm it, but also might not prove anything; many explorers travel with cartographers, rather than drawing their own maps. I certainly don't draw my own maps. Couldn't work a protractor if you paid me. So maybe Aikanis had just been charting someone else's expedition.

I paused before uncapping the roll. "Is there a table where I can spread this out?" I asked, looking to Helen, who stared at me like she'd just seen a ghost. Ghosts didn't seem to be as common on Ithaca as they were on Earth. I'd never been sure why. Maybe Ithacans just died with less in the way of unfinished business.

"This way," said Helen, and gestured for me to follow her as she turned to go deeper into the house. "The dining room."

I grabbed my pack—maybe they'd want to see the books—and followed.

She led me to a room dominated by a massive oak table, which was covered by a tatted lace runner my grandmother would have admired endlessly. She pushed it aside and motioned for me to spread out the map, so I uncapped the map roll and did precisely that, producing knives from inside my shirt and laying them out on the corners.

Phoebe, who had come up behind me, gasped and pushed her way between me and the map, her hands pressed to her mouth. She muttered something, words too muffled by her palms for me to make them out, before reaching down and tracing one of the pathways with her finger, not quite making contact with the paper.

She lowered her other hand and turned her head to look at me. Her pupils were rectangular, like a goat's, but her tears were perfectly understandable. "We never knew what happened to him," she said. "He just . . . he didn't come home."

I blinked. "This map is very old, and there's a whole library at the university named after him," I said. "How long ago *did* he disappear?"

"Satyrs are very focused on the family," said Helen quietly. "Aikanis the mapmaker is known enough even now that his name has been taken to retirement, and his family has never known what became of him."

As my family would never know what had become of me if I insisted on going as far out as I was currently intending to and didn't make it back. That wasn't a thought worth dwelling on. "I'm sorry," I said. "I didn't realize either of you would be relatives of his, or I would have been more circumspect in my questioning."

"He was my októfather," said Phoebe, the word untranslatable but still twisting itself inside my head to "eight-father."

"That's a lot more efficient than the way we'd say it back home," I said. "We'd just repeat the word 'great' eight times, probably while counting on our fingers."

Both of them stared at me.

"And you don't care about that," I said. "Right. Okay. So you're a descendant of his. And he didn't come back from his last expedition. I have two books that were with the map. There were three originally, but Naga took one."

Helen's face hardened. "He knows the Ithacan government has declared all artifacts not specifically deeded to other dimensions to be cultural treasures and requested their immediate return."

Meaning I wasn't walking away from here with the map. That was fine. I have a good memory, and I could take notes. "Maybe he's planning to return it."

"Or maybe he was counting on the fact that you wouldn't know about the law and didn't realize you would think to tell us." Helen shook her head, then paused. "If you didn't know Aikanis and Phoebe were related, why *did* you come here and tell us? I know you've never used Ithaca for a jumping-off point."

"Not often, no," I said, and bent to pull the two books out of my pack. "The book Naga took included a list of jumps leading to what Aikanis called a 'bottle world,' whatever that means, and to get there, I need to get to Cornale to reach the bottle."

"Which means you need to start from here unless you want to go the long way 'round, and I'm guessing you're already going pretty far," said Helen. I blinked at her, and she gestured toward the necklaces that dangled against my chest. "It's nice to see you fueling something without burning yourself up to do it."

"These still throw me off balance, but yeah, I have to go farther than I've ever gone before. I thought there was nothing past Cornale that I could survive."

Helen and Phoebe exchanged a look, expressions turning concerned before they looked back to me.

"Alice . . . we told you that wasn't so," said Phoebe carefully. "The last time you were here. Don't you remember?"

"No, and I think I would," I said.

They exchanged another glance.

"Alice . . ." said Helen.

"No, Naga told me there was nothing past Cornale, and you've never told me any differently," I said.

"And you just *believed* him? Without seeing the charts or asking for any evidence?"

I bristled at her tone. "Of course I did. He's helping me. I wouldn't be here if he weren't. I'd have died decades ago if he hadn't taken me in and provided me with ways to survive. So when he said that none of the worlds past Cornale were capable of supporting human life, I believed him."

"Maybe he didn't understand," said Helen, catching the discomfort in my voice. "Phoebe, did you want to see those books?"

"They belong to my family," said Phoebe, watching me warily. "They should all be returned."

"And I'm happy to return them, although I'd like it if you can tell me anything I need to know about the path I'm planning to take, or 'bottle worlds' in general. I've never encountered that term before."

"Most of us would like to know how Aikanis was able to detect them," said Phoebe. "We have records that imply he entered some, and even left again, which is meant to be impossible."

"Bottle worlds are what remains of dimensions like any other after they have died and lost their souls," said Helen. "Nothing beats at the heart of them, nothing keeps them cleaved unto the great weave. When something stumbles into one of those, it remains there, until it is digested."

I frowned deeply. "I understood every word of that, but not the way you put them all together," I said. "Can you please try and make it make sense for a silly little librarian from a backwater world that doesn't even know other dimensions exist yet? Please?"

"Every living world possesses a pneuma of its own," said Phoebe. "A living spirit, as it were, that allows the world to sustain smaller life than itself."

"People are ecosystems, so I guess it makes sense that ecosystems would be people," I said slowly. "All of us are more bacteria by volume than we are the people we think we are. We're basically swamps that decided to go for a walk one day and haven't figured out yet that it's a ridiculous thing for a swamp to do."

"The pneuma—the soul of a world—is formed by the presence of so much life that it becomes another life through proximity to itself," said Phoebe. "If enough pneuma is gathered together, it will give rise to another life, even greater and more glorious than the pieces that comprise it."

"I'm with you so far," I said. "This swamp is following."

"This dimensional oversoul makes sure everything below it remains healthy and whole. When people move between worlds, that's what clings to them."

"The dimensional oversoul is the membrane?" I asked slowly, trying to make sure I was still understanding her.

"Not entirely, but the two are connected. The membrane is a physical thing, like air or water are physical things. The dimensional oversoul is the living energy of that membrane."

"Huh."

Dimensions are surrounded by an intangible membrane that, well, sticks to people whenever they pass through, for lack of a better metaphor. It's part of why snake cults gain so much traction; it's easier to summon your god when your god is essentially a tube. Very low friction. It's also why dimensional crossing is such an effort for someone built like me. Lots of friction. So much friction. I am an irregular shape being magically dragged through the fascia that's intended to keep one dimension from bleeding into the next.

The membranes around individual worlds are so thin by comparison that they barely register, so if these bottle dimensions didn't have any membrane left, there would be nothing to block my entry.

Helen put a hand on my arm.

"No, although I can guess what you're thinking, and it's not as clever as it seems," she said. "The dimensional oversoul is the source and sustenance of the membrane. It animates it and provides its strength. It's like an eggshell. It protects the entire egg. If you take away an eggshell, there's an internal membrane—the pneuma and membranes of the individual worlds—that will hold for a while, but that dimension's membrane will be dead. It won't renew itself or grow any longer. Gradually, it's going to get damaged. It's going to tear. And when that happens, you're going to lose the whole egg."

I blinked at her. "I'm not sure I follow."

"When you remove the membrane from a dimension, all the pneuma inside it will die," said Phoebe.

"Okay, so the pneuma is the same as the soul, and the membrane—or that internal membrane you were talking about, like the yolk sac of the egg—would be sort of like the body?"

She nodded.

Oh. An extinction event for the souls of literal worlds seemed like a bad thing to me. I frowned down at the map. "So a bottle world is really a . . . a dead dimension?"

"A dimension where something happened to kill the oversoul, and left the lesser pneuma defenseless, yes," said Phoebe. "Most of them collapse, like stars sometimes do. They warp inward and devour themselves, and there's nothing left to show that they ever existed. But a few will curdle instead. They twist into something new, and they're lonely, and they're hungry. Worlds in the places where dimensions used to be, eating until their own ends."

"Meaning . . ."

"Meaning that anything they catch never gets out." She turned to the map, all but glaring at the point that had been flagged as a bottle world. "They devour whatever they encounter. But you found these materials elsewhere. Aikanis found an exit."

"Maybe he wrote it out in one of these." I pulled the books out of my pack and offered them to her. She virtually snatched them out of my hands. "If you find it, please let me know."

"Alice, you're not planning to do something stupid, are you?" asked Helen.

"Bottle worlds swallow people," I said. "No witch or sorcerer I have been able to find in dozens of different realities has been able to tell me where my husband is. Wherever the crossroads put him, it's outside the reach of normal magic. And don't get that soft-eyed face that means you're about to try and make me accept some hard truths, because I know two things I didn't know last time we talked about this."

"Those being?" asked Helen.

"He's not dead," I said. "But the crossroads are."

Phoebe gasped, turning to stare at me. "You would speak so lightly of the end of your world?"

"What?" I frowned at her. "That's not what I said."

"But it is," said Helen. "Your world has a pneuma akatharton—an unclean spirit. That's why we cut off trade with you. It came through the membrane and devoured your world's native pneuma."

I blinked. "What?"

"The thing you call the crossroads is your world's pneuma," said Helen, words slow and deliberate, like she was trying to make a child understand. "It wasn't always, but it killed the original pneuma and took it over. It came from somewhere outside your dimension, and it darkened your world's spirit, such that we stopped traveling there. It's not the only case of parasitism I've heard of, but it's the only one I've seen for myself. I'm so sorry, Alice. Your world is doomed if it's not already dead."

"My granddaughter said it was something called the 'anima mundi' that told her my husband was alive when the crossroads sent him away," I said. "I always heard that translated as 'world soul,' so it sounds like what you call the pneuma is what she called the anima mundi. Does that sound about right to you?"

Phoebe and Helen exchanged a glance before Helen looked back to me and said, "It does, but it's not possible. The invader killed your world's pneuma. It can't be telling anyone anything."

"And I can't get wrapped up in whether the world is doomed when I'm trying to find my husband," I said. "For right now, let's just accept that everything was normal the last time I went home, and I have a job to do. We'll worry about the fate of the world later. Bottle worlds. Nothing gets out, but things can go in. Things like a sorcerer chucked across dimensional walls by an unclean spirit, maybe?"

"Maybe," said Helen reluctantly. "But, Alice, you have to understand that if you go into a bottle world, you'll never come back. You'll be trapped in a dead place, one that's falling apart all around you, and you won't be able to escape it."

"Aikanis did," I said. "He seems to have written everything else down, so I expect the answer to how he got out is either in one of those two books Phoebe has, or in the one that Naga took. I have to go, Helen. You'd go if it were Phoebe. You know you would. If Thomas is there, if he's still alive and waiting for me to find him, I can't make him wait because I'm finally stopping to worry about my own neck. My neck doesn't matter. My neck made a lot of choices, and none of them said 'hey, it would be fun to survive a long, long time.' Will you read the books? If Aikanis had a method for exiting the bottle dimensions, you can come and get me as soon as you figure out what it is."

"Why are you so determined to do this?"

I shrugged. "Because I've been hunting for my husband for fifty years without a single lead, and then I find out the crossroads are gone, I've potentially been right all along and he's out here for me to find, but also somehow outside the scrying range of literally any magic user or dimensional mathematician I've met, Naga hasn't been telling me about the dimensions off of Cornale, and I just *happen* to trip over a map pointing to a dimension people can get trapped in? Don't you see why I have to go?"

"Don't you see how likely this is to be a trap?" countered Helen. "Everything you've just said is true, but that doesn't make this an invitation, it makes it a lure. You could be getting set up."

"By whom, though? I know that ink can't be faked."

"Someone could have planted the books for you to find, knowing you'd be unable to resist the lure of answers." Helen looked almost sympathetic. "You have your share of enemies."

I thought of how close I'd come to dying on Helos, with those spines in my legs and the sepsis spreading through my bloodstream. "I do, and it's possible," I allowed. "But I don't think so. Healy family luck has always had a tendency to trend toward coincidence. Things either go really, really right or really, really wrong where we're involved. And I don't think the anima mundi would have rewarded my granddaughter for killing the crossroads by telling her something she could use to send me to my death."

Phoebe and Helen both stared at me. I blinked at them. "What?" I asked once the silence had stretched on for long enough to become uncomfortable.

"Your granddaughter killed a *world soul*?" asked Phoebe. "I'm sorry, but—no."

"She says she did, and I believe her when she tells me things," I said. "She's a sorcerer. Takes after Thomas. That's one of the reasons it's important I bring him home *now*. She's doing pretty well for herself, but she needs training if she's going to stop setting things on fire when she doesn't mean to."

Phoebe put the books down on the table and put her hands over her face, making a despairing noise. Helen put her arm around her wife's shoulders, still watching me with concern. "If your granddaughter told the truth, then she has accomplished something neither of us has ever heard of," she said. "I'll test the crossing point to your Earth, and see if it remains intact, and if so, I'll look to the other side to check the health of Earth's pneuma. If it confirms your story—and that's a very large *if*, Alice, this is impossible—then maybe you're right and your luck is arranging the universe the way you want it to. But, Alice, if you're wrong, if there's no way to get out in these books, or if Naga tries to claim he doesn't have the one you say he has, we could lose you forever."

I paused. "I've been to Helos a hundred times," I said finally. "A hundred times, Helen, on bounties, on pass-throughs, just to get back to Earth if I've been wandering. I've fought the people I fought today on dozens of occasions, and I've never seen their hoard before. I could have passed through a hundred more times without seeing those books, if I hadn't gotten lucky. I have to believe it's the same coincidence that's been keeping me alive all this time, and that if it had been trying to destroy me, it would have been a lot more upfront about it. A few inches to the right when I fought the big fucker guarding the treasure and I would have bled out in the cave. A few feet to the left and I might not have seen the books at all. I have to go."

Helen sighed deeply. "Alice Healy, when you die, they'll retire your name for generations," she said. "The line between bravery and

stubbornness is even thinner than the line between love and foolishness, and you cross them both so often it makes me ache. But you've
brought some of the treasures of Phoebe's family back to us, and we
will help you. I'll talk to your . . ." She paused, nose wrinkling like
she'd smelled something bad, and finally said, "Patron. I'll ask him for
the book. If he refuses me, I'll remind him of the treaty between his
university and Ithaca, and the number of items we could demand re-
patriated to us if we wanted to state them in breach. And if we find a
means of pulling someone from a bottle, we will come and rescue you.
We cannot stop your foolishness. We may be able to save you from its
costs."

"Thank you," I said, and hugged her. She smelled of healthy goat,
that warm farmyard scent that mostly reminded me of childhood pet-
ting zoos and summers with the carnival. I let her go and stepped back
before Phoebe could glare at me.

Phoebe glared at me anyway. "Is there anything else we can do for
you?" she asked. Apparently, the brief period of grace brought on by
my returning something her family had lost was over now. "A sandwich, maybe?"

My stomach growled. I smiled at her as endearingly as I knew how.
"A sandwich would be great, thanks," I said.

Phoebe threw her hands up in the air and stormed back toward the
kitchen, hooves clacking sharp against the floor. Helen and I exchanged a wry glance.

"She's never going to like me, is she?" I asked.

"Not likely," she replied.

"Ah, well," I said. "Let's go eat, and then I'm gonna go do something seriously stupid."

"A normal day for you, then."

I laughed and let her lead me to the kitchen. I was feeling better
already.

Seven

"I love my wife, but every time she repeats something her father told her, I want to travel back in time and slap the man. It would be worth it, even if it meant she grew up to be someone else. The Grandfather Paradox be damned."

—Thomas Price

Leaving Ithaca for a series of unfamiliar dimensions, culminating in Cornale, which has never been a pleasant place to visit

I'D BEEN TO CORNALE twice before, once with Naga, when he was still going with me on my earliest jaunts, testing the limits of what my body could carry, and once on my own, by mistake, after pushing my crossing charms to the absolute limit of what they were capable of. Neither visit had been particularly pleasant.

In fact, it was the climate on Cornale, coming as it did after a series of increasingly less pleasant dimensions, that had gone a long way toward convincing me Naga was being utterly sincere when he told me there was nothing more in that direction that could sustain human life. I still wasn't sure he'd been lying. A bottle world was, by the definition Helen and Phoebe had given me, already basically dead, and definitely not a place you wanted to wind up by mistake.

Naga could have had absolutely no idea that the bottle world would be the next place I needed to look for Thomas. He could have been acting in good faith.

And if I kept on telling myself that, I would eventually start to believe it, and everything would go back to fitting together neatly, the way I needed it to.

I stepped into the stone circle that would let me transition to the first dimension on the list of jumps, a place Helen called Mul, where it was apparently monsoon season. My sandwich—which had been closer to a gyro, packed with onions, tomatoes, mild, soft cheese, tzatziki, and ground poultry of some kind, lightly spiced and as delicious as it was unfamiliar—had come with a side order of both stuffed grape leaves and grudging advice about how to handle the chain I was about to embark on. Don't try to talk to the locals on Mul; they were aware of the dimensional space between the warp and weft of their local weave, but they didn't appreciate the people who sometimes came through. They wouldn't bother me if I didn't bother them, but if I made myself their problem, they would absolutely answer in kind. My last route from Cornale had been longer and less efficient. This was the straightest shot I could make to the bottle world, where Phoebe still said I shouldn't go.

And despite that, she had hung a waterproofed woolen cloak around my shoulders before I left the house and thanked me in a low voice for bringing her októfather's final journey home, even if her októfather himself was lost to them forever. The cloak was warm and heavy enough to feel reassuringly solid against my back, protecting me from bad weather yet to come, even if it was slightly too warm here in the Ithacan sunshine.

Phoebe and Helen both stood at the bottom of the path to the circle, watching me go. Phoebe would return home to her baking and reading after this, while Helen would head onward to request a meeting with Naga. It's good to have friends.

Transit circles aren't necessary for movement between worlds—if they were, it would be even harder to accomplish—but they ease the process somewhat when they're built at the location of a weak spot in the membrane, making it easier to find and push through. That was what Phoebe called "a space between the warp and the weft," which an interestingly textile metaphor. If I thought of it that way, I started to picture the barriers between dimensions as a pie crust, and the weak spots as the openings in the latticework on top.

Standing smack in the middle of the circle, I pulled another bead off my necklace and ground it under my heel, closing my eyes. Again, a wave of dizziness washed over me, followed by a sheet of stinging rain so cold that it made my skin feel like it was trying to become two sizes smaller as soon as it lashed against me. I opened my eyes on the present, no flashback gnawing at me. A girl could get used to this, if not to the weather.

I was standing on a boardwalk, oil-treated wood beneath my feet, a raging sea all around me, and the distant lights of a village on the shore. At least the local dislike of travelers didn't extend to routing the boardwalk around the weak spot and dropping us into the water. Given how hard the waves were roiling, I would have been swept away in an instant, and it would have been a pretty lousy way to end a fifty-year journey.

According to Phoebe, if I wanted to hit the next world on the chain—a place called Hríðarbylur, which I would have had no concept of how to pronounce if she hadn't said it aloud first—I would need to walk about twenty yards from my starting point, face west, and concentrate on the idea of snow. Going straight from a world of endless rain to one where the key to finding the right place was thinking about snow didn't seem like a great idea to me, but it was the route I had, and at least my cloak was keeping me semi-dry. Maybe I wouldn't freeze if I moved fast enough.

There was no need to linger, and it felt increasingly like doing so would result in being swept off the boardwalk by an errant wave. I walked as instructed, turned, and pressed my fingers to the inside of my arm under the cloak as I closed my eyes and concentrated. I hated to use one of my tattoos so soon, especially given how much harder that transition would be, but if I dropped a bead on this boardwalk, I was never going to be able to find it in the storm.

The feeling of wetness immediately went away. That was good. What replaced it was bad. The worst flashbacks are the ones that come with immediate sensory memories. Like, say, the acid burn of Apraxis nymphs gestating inside my flesh, getting ready to chew their way out into the open air and add me to their collection of copied, captive minds. Their telepathy isn't like the Johrlacs, or like anything else we've come across; it's a unique, terrible thing.

The waves of pain were as intense and immediate as they had been the first time, enough to make me lose track of the fact that this wasn't really happening; this had already happened. Maybe it was better that way. Maybe I could be happy if I stopped trying to live in the present when I was in the past, even though I was living in the past when I was in the present.

I never said I was psychologically healthy, okay?

I was lying on my stomach on a hard wooden table, and the air against my back was cool verging on cold, almost soothing on the spaces that weren't on fire from the developing nymphs. A hand touched my shoulder, pushing me down.

"I'm sorry, Alice," said Thomas' voice, familiar and tight with fear. "This is going to hurt."

"I know," I said, closing my eyes. When this had actually happened,

I hadn't been focused on looking at him, more interested in getting through the removal of the nymphs from my flesh without throwing up or passing out. Keeping my eyes open—fighting the flashback to keep them open—wouldn't change what had happened.

It never did.

"Take a deep breath."

I did, and held it as he began digging the first nymph out of my shoulder, fighting to yank it free, and the pain, the pain, the *pain*—

Again, that feeling of dizzying blur and transition, and the air got warmer. Warmer? That didn't match up with picturing snow. I opened my eyes, suddenly afraid I'd ended up in the wrong place, and looked around me at what seemed like a cozy hunting lodge. There was even a fire burning in the fireplace, although there weren't any people in sight. A piece of paper rested on the nearby table, held down with a rock. Curious, I walked over and picked it up.

Either my translation charm was still working—impressive, after more than three hours—or the note was written in English. Either way, it read, "Welcome, traveler! The fire needs no feeding. Cheese and bread have been left in the box by the door. If you choose to linger, we will see you when the sun rises. If not, we are sorry to have missed you, and glad to have supplied you with a moment of peace on your journey."

I put the note back down, smiling to myself. Sometimes people are pretty decent. Not that I was going to eat anything they'd left for me. Sometimes people are really good at pretending to be pretty decent when they're actually predatory assholes trying to set up nice little caches of meat on the bone to help them get through the winter. There was a door. I walked over and pulled it open, revealing a frozen, snow-swirled landscape that explained Phoebe's instructions, and made me even more grateful for the fire. I closed the door.

Well, I couldn't eat their food, but I wasn't hungry yet after lunch with Phoebe and Helen, and while my key for the next world involved thinking about jungles, I didn't really want to rush on before my hair was dry. I walked over to the fireplace and sat down on the edge, leaning as close to the flames as I could without actually setting myself on fire.

Dating and eventually marrying an elemental sorcerer whose magic liked to express itself in flames was a great way to get way too casual about the risk of immolation. I had to jerk upright several times to keep my hair from going up and was once again glad I'd been keeping it short.

Once I was sure I was dry enough, I stood, walked forward, and closed my eyes again, pulling a bead from my necklace. This had been a nice waystation, and maybe it was as innocent as it seemed to be, but it was time for me to move along.

That bottle world wasn't getting any less dead.

The next five worlds passed in much the same way, brief glimpses of one tiny slice of what they had to offer, what was accessible when traveling along this particular route. If I'd been approaching from another starting point, I would have passed through other dimensions along the way, which was how I knew Cornale in the first place; it had been part of a chain I'd run along to bring back a bounty, and taken from that direction, it had only been five jumps away from Empusa. But taken from that direction, there had been no bottle world. Reality is like a kaleidoscope. The angle you view things at makes a huge difference.

My last step dropped me into Cornale, but a whole different part of the world. Rather than the wide, open scrubland of my last visit, I was standing in an alley that looked like it could have been lifted from a period drama about Victorian England, tall brick walls rising around me and cobblestones under my feet. I couldn't tell whether the placement of my arrival was due to the alley being built to accommodate travelers, or whether the beads I'd been using to cross had shunted me out of sight of the locals. It didn't entirely matter.

I paused to shrug off my pack and pull out two packs of my electrolyte powder, ripping them open and dumping them into my mouth. They tasted like vaguely fruit-flavored dust, sucking the moisture from my tongue. There was technically nothing to chew, but I chewed anyway, trying to work up enough spit to let me swallow. Food is easy to carry between worlds. Liquid is more difficult. It's heavier, for one thing, and sometimes the different physical rules from dimension to dimension will make it start boiling, or freeze, or otherwise render it undrinkable.

I don't know why that doesn't happen to the water inside a person's body. There's a lot about dimensional travel that I don't know. Given how long I've been doing it basically full time, that seemed odd to me, like there were questions I should have been asking all along but somehow hadn't been. Thinking about it made my head hurt a little, and so I stopped. It wasn't going to help me right now one way or another, and it's better not to get distracted in potentially hostile territory.

The powder had absorbed enough spit to be a thick paste. I swallowed it, waiting until my head stopped spinning before I shrugged my pack back on and stepped cautiously out of the alleyway, looking around.

According to Phoebe and what she'd found in Aikanis' notes, the bottle world's opening would be approximately a league away in a westward direction. If his definition of league matched mine, that would be about three miles. Hopefully, there'd be something to tell me when I was getting close. Normal weak spots can sometimes show themselves in their environment—if you know how to look for them. Maybe they're places without any obvious water source and really lush flowers. (Of course, those could also be underground springs or body dumps, it's hard to say without a shovel). Or maybe they're narrow strips where the bugs are a different color, or a little too big, or behaving oddly. It usually manifests in plants and insects if it's going to impact anything living. It's never something that's super obvious. You have to learn how to look.

I've been learning for fifty years. Weak spots are easier places to cross, and when you're chasing a whisper across worlds, you start looking for easy whenever you can. They can also, as in this case, signal an access point for a world that's not widely accessible from anywhere else.

There were people on the street. Most were substantially more respectably dressed than I was, or at least they were wearing substantially more clothing, which I assumed meant the same thing; it was difficult to say without more context. At least none of them pointed at me, threw up, or fainted. That was nice.

Most worlds that are close enough to Earth to support human life as we understand it will have some sort of biped somewhere in their local food chain, regardless of what dimension it's in. The bipeds don't always win out—see also Empusa, where Naga and the other lamia ran the show without any native bipeds to offer conflict or competition—but we happen, at some point in the evolutionary chain.

That's nothing to get all smug about. Those are just the easy-to-access worlds, the ones where we can live. There are worlds that belong to creatures we wouldn't even be able to recognize as forms of life, entire dimensions so packed with snakes that they've basically given up on having anything in them *except* snakes, places where the things that have managed to catch on and thrive would make Earth's Cambrian period look measured and reasonable. The limitations of the human form keep us, mostly, from tripping and falling into worlds where the air would dissolve our bones, and it means that when we do run into the locals, they may consider us a little weird looking, but no more so than we'd think about a perfectly ordinary cryptid.

If the architecture made me think of Victorian London, the clothing was more akin to Meiji-era Japan, long, loose garments that looked something like kimonos on people of all ages and sizes. Almost everyone I could see was taller than me, thin in a way that could have been either genetics or fashion, with skin in varying shades of blue, green, and even pale purple. Their hair was a similar range of colors, plus red and black. All of them seemed to keep it long, and about half the people on the street had jeweled pins holding it in place. They weren't staring and so I didn't stare either, just turned in a slow circle as I tried to get my bearings.

Thus far, my trip had been environmentally annoying and occasionally exhausting, but had involved surprisingly little violence. I was starting to wonder how many of the fights I'd been in had been consequences of Naga sending me after criminals, and not a matter of the universe being an inherently hostile place.

Had he actually *asked* me before sending me on the first set of bounties? Or had he just added, after giving me a map to a potential lead on Thomas, that if I were to capture a few runaway criminals, I'd be able to make some money and put myself into a better position to keep searching? I wasn't actually sure anymore. It had been such a long time, and there had been so much suffering between then and now. I remembered everything before this all began vividly and with absolute clarity. Much of the last fifty years was a lot fuzzier.

Maybe that was bad. Maybe when I finished this expedition, regardless of how it ended, it was time for me to go home and talk to someone. Or maybe I needed to stay focused and not let myself get distracted by worrying about things that wouldn't change anything.

Naga had been helping me get back to my husband. If he'd decided to make himself a little profit in the process, I couldn't exactly blame him; not when he'd been feeding, housing, and caring for me for all this time. I'd never have been able to make it this far without him.

Some of the people on the street were starting to nudge each other and turn to look at me. More details about their physicality became obvious in that motion. What I'd initially taken for some kind of iridescent shawl worn by people of all ages and quality of clothing was actually the thin membrane of a pair of wings that sprouted from the shoulder blades and then folded down to approximately waist level before stretching upward and over the arms, meeting at the middle of the chest in two hooked claws that formed a shape almost like a brooch. Given the way ideas sometimes cross-pollinate across realities, maybe that was where humanity had gotten the concept, although fastening a thing with another thing seemed straightforward enough that we could have reached that conclusion on our own.

The direction I needed to go followed the line of the street, which was convenient. I started to walk, not rushing enough to attract more attention than my alien nature was already going to, but quickly enough to make it clear that I was going somewhere. I wasn't just a weird alien thing walking around their city for fun. Maybe that would be enough to let me avoid any awkward encounters with the locals.

Maybe not. When I reached the corner, three people dropped out of the sky, folding their wings as they landed. Their descent allowed me to glimpse bare, clawed feet and long, fringed tails that I would have assumed belonged to amphibians if not for the rest of the package they presented. All three were armed, holding long spears with shafts of polished metal.

Well, crap. So much for doing this quietly.

"Greetings, traveler," said the one on the end, one of the ones with jeweled pins in their hair. They bowed shallowly toward me, keeping their spear rigidly upright. That was nice. I can be calm about implicit threats. I'm not as good at ignoring explicit ones. "It's been some time since we've seen someone come through that gate. It had almost been forgotten. What brings you to our fair city?"

"I'm just passing through," I said, pleased that the locals either spoke English for some ridiculous—but not impossible—reason or had translation devices, magical or technological, that let us communicate. It didn't matter in the end how it was happening. It only mattered that it was. "Is there a problem?"

"Oh, no," continued the speaker. "We're simply delighted to receive a visitor."

The hair on the back of my neck stood up. I glanced over my shoulder. Three more people with spears had appeared there, watching me with studied carelessness. That's the trouble with people who can fly. They don't always approach from directions you can anticipate.

"In fact, we would be honored beyond reason if you would agree to come with us and meet the jaghirdar. They are always eager to meet new people and hear their impressions of our fair land."

"I'm sort of in a hurry," I said. "I'm sorry if that seems rude to you, but I really *am* just passing through."

If I remembered correctly, a jaghirdar was sort of like a prince crossed with a mayor. Someone who'd been born in charge and held near-absolute power over the land under their control, but wasn't considered royalty, due to whatever justification the locals had come up with. Maybe they were ruled by an emperor or despot who didn't like the idea of competing royals, or maybe they had reached the "no more kings" stage before they reached the "maybe feudalism isn't such a good idea after all" stage. I'd need a lot more time and a lot of information about the local social structure to understand, and quite honestly, I didn't want to take the time.

"I apologize," said the speaker, with another shallow bow. "That was not intended to sound like a request. All visitors are required to see the jaghirdar before they can be allowed passage through our territories. You will come with us now."

There was no please. I still made one last stab at getting out of this. "You said you would be honored if I agreed," I protested.

"Yes, and we would have been," said the speaker. "Sadly, that happy future has not come to pass, for any of us. You do us no honor, and we grant you no grace. Now we will take you to see our jaghirdar, and you will not fight, for it would go poorly for you."

I could see six of them, and none had any visible weapons apart from their spears. A spear is a useful thing. It's also a simple thing, and it's easy enough to take a spear away from someone who you feel has forfeited spear privileges. I could take six of them. I've taken on worse and won.

And what then? There were six of them here *now*, all summoned without any visible or audible alarm, and they could fly. I had to travel the better part of three miles before I could get out of here, or my entire trip would have been for nothing. Naga wasn't necessarily going to give me another free batch of beads to get myself farther afield than my tattoos could carry me. I frowned, mouth set into a hard line.

I can be impulsive. I have a tendency to shoot first and ask questions later. But I've also survived for a long, long time in a universe that seems to actively want me dead, and I know when the odds are so against me that fighting isn't the answer.

"Sure," I said. "Let's do this. Take me to your leader."

They walked me through the streets in formation, three in front and three behind, and none of them talked to me, not once I'd agreed to go with them. I wasn't formally their prisoner, but there really wasn't any other term for what I was at this point. They hadn't taken my weapons, but I wasn't sure how much of what I had on me they would actually recognize as weapons. Worlds with stable societies without guns outnumber the ones with guns at least ten to one. Maybe they thought I just had weird taste in jewelry.

And maybe it didn't matter, as we approached a low, imposing building that seemed to have been constructed on a different scale than all the buildings around it, roof held up by vast columns, topped with a series of slanted, irregular surfaces that broke with the general aesthetic of the rest. Then I blinked and saw the utility of it.

No one could land on that roof. Attackers coming from the air would have to go down to the ground before they could pose any sort of a challenge. And the low construction would also be a tactical advantage, reducing the amount of space they'd have to defend in case of a situation like that one. They would be prepared for a siege.

On Earth or Ithaca, I would have called this a courthouse, maybe a museum if I was feeling generous. Here, it was a palace. It was a fortress.

It was a prison.

My captors led me up the broad staircase and inside, into an echoing antechamber decorated with richly embroidered tapestries of animals I didn't recognize, surrounded by the wide shapes of things I assumed were the local equivalent of flowers. Given all of creation to spread out and get weird, biology does some shit. But for a world to evolve bipedal life, again, it has to follow certain understandable rules. This one had clearly embraced symmetry to a degree that made sense to my Earth-born eyes and kept this whole thing from being too jarring.

There was no furniture anywhere inside the frankly massive room, no adornment apart from the tapestries. Our footsteps sounded like thunder in the cavernous space, and I glanced up, catching a glimpse of a domed ceiling with a skylight at the center, presumably to allow people to come and go from above.

Huh. So they were well fortified, but they still left some avenues open. That could mean that they were too cocky to worry about attackers. It could also mean they were anticipating the need for a swift escape.

Either way, I didn't have a great feeling about this jaghirdar I was about to meet. My captors stopped abruptly in the middle of the room, and I did the same. The three in front turned to face me.

"Welcome, honored guest," said the one who had done all the

speaking since this whole thing kicked off. "If you would wait here, we will collect the jaghirdar for you."

Definitely not on the level of a prince, then, unless there was something in his throne room—or office, as the case might be—that they really didn't want a stranger to see. Still, I shrugged and said, "No skin off my nose," taking a small, petty comfort in their expressions of bewilderment at what must have been an unfamiliar idiom.

The three who had led the way turned, the speaker frowning, and walked the rest of the way across the room. There was no visible door. As I watched, they spread their wings, which were impossibly gauzy things that looked like they should never have been able to sustain the weight of their bodies, lifted off the floor, and soared through the center of the closest tapestry, vanishing into what I had assumed was an image of some sort of complicated plant.

Okay, third option: I was waiting here because I couldn't use the doors that they used to get around the place. That was a new one on me. I turned to my three remaining escorts, trying not to look too impressed. It wasn't that hard. I'd seen more elaborate architecture on a dozen different worlds, even if most of it had been built with a healthy respect for gravity.

"Any of you people understand me?" I asked. There was no flicker of comprehension in their eyes, which were, universally, matched to their skins, just a few shades darker. I nodded. "Didn't think so. Cool."

Since only one of them had spoken during our whole trip, I'd been assuming that was the one with the translator, and the rest of them were here to stab me if I tried to do something foolish, like run away from the flying weirdoes with the giant toothpicks. I folded my arms, resisting the urge to start studying my nails. When dealing with a completely unknown society, it's best to avoid as many potentially misinterpreted gestures as possible, just to be sure you don't accidentally insult them so profoundly that they decide the only solution is dumping you in a vat of the local acid equivalent. Instead, I turned to look at the spot where the other three had disappeared, waiting for their return.

Thankfully, I didn't have to wait long. One by one, they emerged from the center of the tapestry, trailed by four new figures with spears, then two unarmed people in longer, more elaborate robes, and finally a smaller figure in the most elaborate robe of all. The last figure was wearing a heavy crown made of what looked like gold mingled with bone, and if they'd been human, I would have put them at most at ten years old.

Having no idea of the local lifespan, I couldn't guess at actual age, any more than I could guess at gender, but I'd have been willing to bet actual money that however old they were, it wasn't adult. Their jaghirdar was a child. Maybe that explained how careful they were all being. When you've already changed who's in charge recently enough to wind up with a kid running the show, you don't want to risk anything else going wrong.

All ten of them landed a short distance away and walked toward where we were waiting, with two groups of three forming lines to either side of the jaghirdar, while the last guard and the two unarmed adults fell into place behind them. They bowed to me. I bowed back, as much out of reflex as intent, and then winced. If they took that as some sort of insult, I could have just made things worse for myself.

To my relief, their expression didn't change as they straightened and approached, clasping their hands right around where the navel would have been on a human their size. "Greetings, traveler," they said, the same translator the other speaker had used turning their voice into a bright, clear adolescent tenor. "You are welcome here."

"That's cool," I said, glancing to my guards. "I was sort of on my way somewhere, though, so I'd appreciate it if you'd say it was cool for me to leave."

"My adviser tells me you came from the direction of Atl," said the jaghirdar. "We haven't seen anyone from that way in many years."

I couldn't think of a polite way to tell them there were reasons for that. Cornale was a backwater dimension, no real exports, no real appeal to criminals, and they had no big incentives for the tourist trade, such as it was. They'd been fortunate enough to avoid colonization attempts thus far, mostly because the worlds directly to either side were also fairly unpleasant—the landing point I'd used on Atl had been a swamp the size of North America, humid and sticky and rich with mosquitoes and other nasty swamp dwellers. The approach I'd taken the last time I'd been to Cornale had been similar, but substitute "desert filled with cacti that flung their thorns of their own volition when you got within six feet" for the swamp. Yes, both were probably part of bigger, richer ecosystems, but if those were where the overlap occurred, it was no surprise they didn't get a lot of guests.

"Our tables have been poorer for the absence."

Or maybe they liked to eat their company.

The jaghirdar smiled at me, and for the first time, I realized how sharp and serrated the teeth on the locals were. "It was kind of you to come."

I uncrossed my arms, dropping my hands to the revolvers at my hips. None of the onlookers seemed to think this was strange. Guess they really didn't know what a gun was. Cool by me. We'd traveled about two miles to reach the meeting house, and while I'd need to course-correct a little bit, at least it hadn't been in the opposite direction of what I needed to do. I could still make it out of here.

"Yeah, I'm not here for dinner," I said. "I'm heading somewhere."

"There aren't many places to go from here."

Maybe these people could help me before I had to kill them all. "I'm looking for the entrance to a dead world," I said.

The jaghirdar's face hardened, and in that instant, we were no longer friends. "The parasite?" they asked. "You seek the parasite?"

"If that's what you call it, then sure, that's what I'm after."

"It drains the life from our lands," they snarled. "We were a thriving world once, part of the trade network out of Ithaca. We bought and sold with a dozen worlds, we filled our tables with the fruits of the field and the profits of the pasture, and we did more than just survive. We prospered. Then our neighbors dabbled in things that were better left alone. The blight came, poisoning our world."

That was something I hadn't heard before. I blinked and raised my eyebrows, hoping my silence would be a prompt to continue. Fortunately for me, some things are almost universal, and the lack of recent visitors meant the jaghirdar, young as they appeared, was already primed to let their frustrations out.

"The parasite refuses to be cut loose, and its taint infects our membrane, making us less and less appealing to travelers. It fuels nothing. It powers nothing. It only devours. We are gangrenous flesh, and one day, when someone finds a way to sever the infection, we may be banished with it for the crime of our location. Is that fair? Is that justice?"

"No," I said. "But neither is eating me because I'm passing through. Look, I don't know much about how this system works." I was starting to figure out just how ignorant I really was. Even after fifty years of running rampant through the dimensions, I didn't know how to contextualize half the things they were saying. That didn't feel right.

I could tell you more about how sorcery works after knowing Thomas for a year—not even dating him yet, just *knowing* him—than I could tell you about dimensional travel and interactions after fifty years of switching wildly between them. And sure, I've been sort of focused on finding Thomas and bringing him home, but that's long enough that I would have expected Naga to sit me down for a remedial class at some point, if only so I wouldn't embarrass him running around out there telling people I was getting his help and having no idea what was going on.

It didn't make sense.

"Clearly not," said the jaghirdar. "We haven't much here. Our larders are bare. It is an honor to grace my table."

So much for the vague hope that I was wrong, and these were perfectly nice people who weren't going to try to strip the flesh from my bones and devour me whole. "Yeah, well, I'm not big on honors. I was always a solidly average student."

"Not all honors can be refused."

"And not all honors are worth receiving." These people were starting to get on my nerves. They were making me ask too many questions about how this whole thing worked, and they were threatening me without coming out and saying it, like honest people would have done. Not that I've ever met an honest cannibal, using the term to mean "someone who eats other intelligent beings" rather than "someone who eats their own kind." I used to be a librarian; I can be pedantic with the best of them.

I drew my revolvers in one smooth motion, holding them out in front of me. Even after calling in reinforcements, there were fewer of them than I had bullets in my guns, and when you're talking about people who can fly, the trick is to shoot before they can get into the air.

None of them reacted. I started to feel a little bad. They really had no idea what was about to happen here.

And that couldn't be my problem, not when they were planning to make me their special dinner guest. "We have two choices at this point," I said. "You can let me leave peacefully, and not try to stop me again as I make my way to the exit, or you can decide that this is going to get ugly. I can do ugly. I can do ugly real, real well."

The jaghirdar actually looked amused. I began to feel bad. They were just a kid, and they were hungry enough to be considering eating random strangers. And here I was, planning to kill them without even learning their name. Maybe I was the monster people had started to say that I was.

And maybe the crossroads had set up their prison on the other side of a dimension full of people who were way too interested in travelers as part of the effort to keep people like me away. Maybe this was proof that I was on the right track. You can spend a long, long time in maybe. You can put down roots there.

But everything that matters happens a hell of a lot faster.

"Funny," said the jaghirdar. "We have our own skill at ugliness."

They smiled then, and this time their smile grew and grew, well past what I would have guessed to be the reasonable outline of their mouth, extending almost from ear to ear, and every inch of that smile was alive and bright with teeth. The threat in that expression was unmistakable, even before the seven spear carriers swung their weapons down to point at me.

I shot the first five of them before they had a chance to do anything more. They fell heavily, bodies hitting the ground with a soft, heavy sound like sacks of wet cement. I turned. The other two spear carriers were already in the air, positioning themselves above me, while the jaghirdar and the two unarmed adults were still staring in shock.

"That enough of a dinner for you?" I demanded. "Because if we're done now, I'd really like to be going."

"You *killed* them," said the jaghirdar, sounding stunned. "They were just standing there, doing their jobs and serving me as they were sworn to do, and you *killed* them."

"They had weapons," I snapped. "They pointed those weapons at me. Anyone who's ever met me knows that's a shooting offense. Now unless you want me to kill more of your loyal lackies, you'll call them the hell off and let me leave."

"You have made enemies here on this day," said the jaghirdar. "You will never walk untroubled in my lands!"

"Let me leave now and I won't give a shit," I replied. "I don't want to linger here, I don't want to be a thorn in your side, I don't want to shoot anyone else. I just want to leave."

"Then go."

I didn't turn. Turning your back on enemies is a clever way not to have any more enemies, because corpses aren't big on rivalries. Instead, I backed toward the door we'd entered through, watching as the other two spear carriers landed and all of them moved toward the bodies, beginning to pull them into carrying holds. They'd eat well tonight.

No one stopped me from getting to the door. No one was waiting on the stairs, and when I descended them, looking around and up as rapidly as I could, no one appeared to threaten or interfere. This had been a painful interlude. It was done now.

Time to get back to business.

Finally turning around, I holstered one revolver and kept the other in my hand as I began to run.

Eight

"Never knew my folks, and I turned out okay. It's the love that matters, not whether or not you're related to the people giving it to you. It's always the love."
—Frances Brown

Running through Cornale, which is just as unpleasant as anticipated, heading for something that's probably even worse, because that's a great *idea*

I MADE IT TO the edge of the city—about a half mile, if I was judging the distance right—before anyone sounded an alarm. A great bell rang from the center of the city, and the sky was suddenly alight with winged bodies, so many that for a moment they seemed to blot out the sun. I had time to hope that what I'd just heard was all of them being summoned for dinner, and then they began to wheel overhead, clearly pursuing me.

Great. This was just what my day needed, and not an intrusion by an uncaring universe. I ran full tilt down the narrow road leading to the door in the gate, shouting, "Come the fuck on!" at the sky full of bodies. Some of them had spears. More of them carried no visible weapons. It didn't matter. They had numbers on their side, and I didn't know the terrain like they did.

The gate in the wall was swinging shut even as I approached, which was ridiculous. These people could fly. Unless they shared this world with a ground-dwelling species that liked to come over without being invited—which might well be the case—there was no reason for them to bother with gates, *or* with walls. I pulled one of the ancient grenades that my grandkids are always giving me shit for carrying off of my belt, glad that I had thought to keep gearing up even as I was in transit. Never assume you're going to be safe unless you control the perimeter completely, and even then, it's probably best to check for traps.

I waited to yank the pin until I was almost at the wall, then chucked the grenade as hard as I could for the closing gate, wheeling around and running back the way I'd come. My sudden change of direction confused the people wheeling overhead. Some of them tried to change directions to match me and slammed into their neighbors, raining down from the sky in a tangle of wings and limbs. Good for them. I hoped hitting the ground would hurt.

And maybe they'd be grateful for the fall once their lower altitude kept them from being caught in the blast.

I ducked into another narrow alley and crouched down, putting my hands over my ears. A great, concussive boom came right on the heels of the gesture as the wall learned why it didn't want to make friends with grenades. I waited until the screaming and the sound of falling debris mostly died down, then stood and strolled out of the alley, holding another grenade overhead.

"I can do that again," I shouted. Even if not everyone would be able to understand me, they would understand the implied threat of the grenade in my hand. Winged bodies littered the ground. Others, who had been helping them, froze and stared. It was nice to not be running for a moment. It would be even nicer if I didn't have to start back up. "If you stop chasing me, I won't."

I turned to jab the grenade at the nearest people, who shrank back. The ones with spears either dropped them or pointed them ostentatiously away from me, which was fine. I didn't need them defenseless, especially not when I'd just blown a huge hole in their wall. I needed them to leave me alone.

"I'm out," I said, and continued toward the hole I'd made. "Maybe you should learn about explosives."

Even if I'd just triggered a new evolution in local warfare, it wasn't going to happen soon enough to stop me at this point. I picked my way through the rubble, turning to look back at the stunned, staring locals once I was safely on the other side.

"My name's Alice," I called. "And I am out of here."

Then I continued on my way.

This time, they didn't pursue.

The land outside the city was the barren, blasted scrub I had been expecting from my last visit, but this time I looked at it with new eyes, noting the places that could have been gullies or could have been dry riverbeds, the high-water marks on rocks that had no water anywhere nearby, the fallen, dried-out tree trunks too large to have been supported by this ecosystem.

No wonder the people were hungry enough to be willing to eat strangers. Their land was dying.

I kept walking, trying to follow the directions I'd been given, reorienting myself as I adjusted for the trip through the city pulling me off course. Eventually, I was sure I'd gone at least three miles—possibly closer to four—and I sat down on a large rock (after giving it a few solid kicks to be sure it wasn't secretly a large turtle that would bite my ass off) and put my hands over my face, taking a moment to just breathe.

I'd come all this way. Not just this trip, which had allowed me to foolishly get my hopes up, but over the last fifty years. I'd given up so much. I'd killed so many people who wouldn't have needed to die if I'd just stayed on Earth like I was supposed to, never crossing their paths in the first place, and for what? To miss my opening because some hungry assholes pulled me off the path?

I needed my own white rabbit to follow, or I wasn't even going to find the rabbit hole, much less have the chance to go tumbling down it into whatever wonderland was waiting on the other side. I needed to breathe. I needed a moment. That was all. Just a moment, to sit and seethe and feel sorry for myself, freed from the pressure of moving forward.

So I pressed my hands over my eyes and slumped, and listened to the wind rattling the scrub, and the trickle of water in the distance, and—

Hold on. I uncovered my eyes and sat up straighter, focusing on the sound of running water. I'd seen nothing to indicate that there was any running water left in this wasteland. I followed the sound, pausing to close my eyes occasionally and reassure myself that I really was hearing what I thought I was hearing. The sound got louder. I smelled water, petrichor, dust becoming mud, and I opened my eyes, looking down at a narrow creek running where it shouldn't have been able to run.

It emerged from a crevasse in the rock and flowed lightly downhill, which made sense, wetting the ground around it. Small insects filled the air, the first signs of real life I'd seen out here, and even as I watched, a tiny brown lizard-like creature streaked out from between two rocks and snatched one of them out of the air. This place was still trying to survive. Despite everything the people in the city had said, despite the condition of this scrubland, the world was still *trying*. I couldn't help but be grudgingly impressed, even as I followed the creek, trying to see how far it went.

Something was calling the water up from the rocks. Given everything else around me, I didn't think it was likely to be natural hydroponics, an assumption that I felt briefly smug about when I realized the water was flowing, however briefly, along an uphill slope. I kept following it, moving deeper into the rocks, listening carefully for signs that I might be disturbing the sparse local wildlife. There wasn't much left out here. What there was probably wouldn't be of the friendly variety.

The creek finished its uphill run and began to flow downhill again, toward a small pond that had formed at the bottom of a shallow depression. It was a spot of green in a gray-brown landscape, ringed with tall waterweeds. Even one of the blasted old trees was still growing here, branches putting out leaves and small, pale-yellow fruits that looked something like wrinkled apples. Larger insects flitted among the branches, and tiny winged lizards whose scales shone the same colors as the skins of the locals.

This had probably been a beautiful place, once, before whatever had happened to kill the soul of the neighboring dimension and infect the world next door, trapping them all in the spreading haze of its decay. How many worlds could be sickened by one dead one refusing to release its hold on the membrane between dimensions? The world next to Cornale had clearly been rotting for some time. How long had it taken for things to get this bad? Would Cornale get better once the dead world was cut away and the wound was allowed to heal, or was it too late? Was this world's anima mundi also doomed to keep getting sicker and eventually die?

And I was oversimplifying again. What was on the other side of the gate I was about to open wasn't a dead *world*, it was a dead *dimension*. Everything an entire reality had had the potential to be, gone, reduced to the slow decay and constriction of decomposition. If this world's pneuma died, it wouldn't kill the dimensional oversoul of this reality. There could be countless life-bearing worlds in this dimension, a whole cosmos of people who would start dying as Cornale's rot sickened their worlds' pneuma.

No wonder the jaghirdar had mentioned the possibility of Cornale's membrane being separated from the ones around it, isolating this world so the infection couldn't spread. And if I wanted to get Thomas back before that happened, I needed to move. I walked to the pond's edge, studying the water long enough to reassure myself that there were no large predators present, then stepped up onto a large, flat rock and pulled a bead from my necklace.

It was almost denuded. If I was in the wrong spot, I would only have so many tries before it was stop trying or don't make it back to Ithaca, much less home.

"Healy family luck," I said, looking at the bead in my palm. "Sometimes it's good and sometimes it's bad, but it's never, ever boring."

No matter how this went, it wasn't going to be boring. If I could be sure of nothing else, I could at least be sure of that. I dropped the bead to the rock, put my foot on top of it, and closed my eyes.

I had no direction to aim for, no details about the bottle world except that it was dead and things that went in couldn't get back out. But I also had the soothing conviction that I was on the right path, and so I held to that in lieu of anything else that might have served me as a guide. If I went this way, I would find my husband. I would find my answers. He might be alive, and he might be dead, but either way, I'd *know*, and once I knew, I could finally put down the burden I'd been carrying for so long and go home to the family who loved me, hated me, and mourned me, all at the same time. This was the door that would let me have my life back, and all I had to do was force it open.

The air grew thick and heavy, with the reeling, unsettling feeling that normally came from a dimensional crossing, but nothing happened. The heavy feeling lifted, and I opened my eyes on the same landscape, now feeling a little dizzy. I scowled. Of course it couldn't be that easy.

Another bead, another stomp, another long pause while I thought as hard as I could about where I wanted to go, and another failure. My head was starting to spin, and my heart was beating way too fast, which is a potential sign of low blood sugar that I wanted to avoid if I possibly could.

Fine. I was going to have to force my way through this. I let go of the necklace and pressed two fingers against the highest remaining gate tattoo on my arm. It would take more out of me, but it might let me push harder, and there was *something* there. I could tell that much, even if I couldn't tell exactly what it was. There was *something* on the other side of my shove, some pressure resisting me coming through. I could manage one more push, probably, before I'd need to eat something and get my blood sugar back toward normal.

That could wait. I looked around, reassuring myself that this was the most likely place. It felt almost like I was slamming myself up against a door that had been intentionally locked to keep people like me from coming through. Well, that made sense, I guess. Any locals who knew how to manage dimensional math would have wanted the door to the all-consuming gangrenous death dimension closed before it ate everyone in sight, and if dead places were easy to reach, the rot would probably spread even faster than it already did.

The water was collecting here. The world was slightly out of sync with what it had become here. This was the soft spot if anyplace was.

I pressed my fingers harder against my arm, closed my eyes, and *shoved*.

This time, the membrane let me through. It didn't feel like any membrane I'd ever experienced before. Transition via tattoo was usually a blur, a twist, and some scene from my past that I didn't want to experience, thanks. Transition via the beads left out the home movie but was otherwise identical. On the rare occasions when I've had to move through a membrane thick enough to provide resistance, it's been a longer flashback and a sensation something like pushing through a soap bubble and something like pushing through a spiderweb—solid enough that you notice it, so ephemeral that most of the noticing happens when you're already through to the other side, free to focus on wondering whether you need a shower.

This was like pushing through a moldy shower curtain that had been slashed into ribbons for use in a haunted house, or through a literal fleshy membrane. I kept shoving, trying to force it to yield, and it snapped, so abruptly that I could almost feel it.

The air, which had already been dry and arid, suddenly turned abrasive, all moisture gone. I opened my eyes.

The wasteland was gone, replaced by a different, even less welcoming expanse of barren ground. There was a group of low buildings about two hundred yards away: weathered, sun-bleached sandstone with no visible windows. Something about the shape of the compound was familiar, like I had seen this before, only in a better setting. The sky was the color of dirty dishwater, less cloudy than clogged with the ghosts of countless dust storms, but when I blinked, I could almost see the same building under a different sky, pale violet and beautiful.

I must have run into this style of architecture on some other world. Maybe the original residents had time to get out before everything fell apart. I didn't have time to dwell on the thought, because when I tried to take a step forward and get my bearings, my head spun and I dropped to my knees.

My body and I aren't always friends, but we've been together a long time, and I've had years to chart the effects of magical overexertion on a system that isn't built for it. My blood sugar was in the toilet. My heart was beating too fast, and my head was still spinning, leaving me dizzy and disoriented. Thoughts were difficult to pull together, resisting my attempts to assemble them into a coherent shape. I knew I needed to get into my pack, needed to swallow some electrolyte powder and probably some glucose gel, but the steps involved in taking it off and working the zipper seemed like a set of insurmountable tasks.

I closed my eyes. If I just let myself rest for a moment, I'd be fine. I'd bounce back the way I always had before, and I'd be ready to pick myself up and keep on going. This was no big deal. I'd done worse, and I'd survived.

My last conscious thought was: *This is a really stupid way to die.*

And then the ceaseless hammering of my heart drove me down into the dark.

Nine

"Sometimes you have to let go. Sometimes it's the only
way. I learned that lesson, and it hurt like hell. Not sure
how I failed so hard in teaching it to my son."

—Enid Healy

Not sure, but not dead either, and that's a good start

I WOKE UP. THAT was nice. I hadn't entirely been expecting that when I
passed out, and yeah, it would have been a stupid way to die, but also
a fitting one. I was already a ghost story in half a dozen dimensions, so
disappearing in the middle of nowhere without a trace would just have
guaranteed I'd stay a story forever. Behave or Alice Price-Healy will get
you. Behave, be a good kid, or she'll be in your closet when you go to
bed tonight.

But my family would never have known the truth, and my clergy
would have waited for me forever, holding out hope that one day they
were going to come into the kitchen and find me baking cookies, wearing a borrowed apron, and trying not to have opinions about the contents of the fridge. No, it was better for me to be alive.

Alive, but still weak and a little shaky, like I'd gone to bed after
running a marathon without taking the time to hydrate first. I
stretched, checking that all my parts were still there, and froze as I
realized what *wasn't* there.

If I wasn't naked, I was wearing something so light I could barely
register it without opening my eyes, and I definitely wasn't armed.
None of my weapons felt like they were where they were supposed to
be. That was enough of a surprise that I rolled onto my side, pleased
when I realized that nothing was being used to restrain me, and opened
my eyes on a plain, unornamented white stone wall. It looked like it
had been assembled from individual bricks and then painted, rather

than being a single piece of something, but it was spotlessly clean, and must have been maintained on a regular basis.

The light was warm and diffuse and didn't hurt my head, so I risked pushing myself upright and answered two questions at the same time.

First, I could sit up without vomiting or passing out; someone had managed to get some sugar into me while I was under, although they hadn't used an IV, since there wasn't anything attached to me. Good. I don't like needles much when I'm awake to agree to them. I like them even less when people are jabbing them into me without asking first, even if it's to save my life.

Second, I *was* dressed, although the filmy, diaphanous robe I was wearing was barely worthy of being considered clothing. It wasn't transparent despite its weight, which was pleasant, but it felt like wearing a dress made of gauze, or flower petals, or something equally unsuitable.

Whoever had redressed me had also taken my underclothes, and the fabric I'd wrapped around my wrists to stabilize them. I was more naked even with a robe than I normally was any time short of stepping out of the shower or moving between rejuvenation treatment and the tattoo station. I didn't like this. Big surprise there. I was, at least, reasonably sure the fabric was thick enough to let me hide a few knives if I could get my hands on them. I've had years upon years of practice to determine exactly how much clothing I need where in order to go armed enough to feel comfortable. One of my granddaughters does something similar with fringe and sequins when she puts on her ballroom costumes—it's all about knowing both your body and your wardrobe. Nothing hurt. The people who'd stripped me had done it without injuring me.

That was good. It wasn't going to stop me from injuring *them*, but no one ever said I was into proportionate response. And either I'd somehow forced my way into the wrong dimension, or I'd just confirmed that the bottle world I'd been looking for had people in it. Either way, I was still alive, and all I had to do from here was get my stuff back and get the hell out of here.

"You're awake!" The voice was light, easy, and incredibly bright, like the speaker was on the verge of bursting into a happy ballad about how nice it was when the company woke up. I turned. A woman had entered through a small door I hadn't turned to notice before; it was round at the top, like a Hobbit hole, and had no sharp edges.

The woman herself had plenty of them, thanks to the fact that she had what looked like thorns growing out of her shoulders, upper arms, and the sides of her neck. Her throat, chest, and face were free of thorns, and her skin was a pale, rosy pink. I couldn't have explained exactly what about her face wasn't quite human; she was one of those species who would have been called cryptids back at home, close enough to pass through humanity's world, not quite close enough to blend in.

She was wearing a short dress with a toga-style neckline, made of the same diaphanous fabric as my robe, and beaming at me brilliantly, all sunshine and sparkles. "They don't always wake up as fast as you— you were lucky to break through where you did, and Sally heard the wards when you arrived, so you weren't alone out there for *too* long. But it's all right now. You're safe here. Oh, and our Autarch is going to be pleased to see you. You look like you're probably the same species he is. You even have the same kind of skin."

I blinked, very slowly. "All right . . . let's start with the easy ones. Where am I?"

"The Palace of the Autarch," she said. "All newcomers come here first—and have since he claimed and warded it to provide us with safety. I mean, if that's not precise enough for you, you're in the women's quarters."

"The women's quarters?" That sounded suspiciously like a polite way of saying "harem," and I didn't like it. Then again, I hadn't liked anything since I woke up, so why should this be any different? Liking things was no longer a part of my job.

"Yes. All who come through the great barrier are taken under the Autarch's protection upon arrival, to keep them safe." Her smile got somehow even brighter. "He's a very good man. You'll like him. And oh, he'll like *you*. I don't think I've seen any females of his kind except for Sally, and she's of a different phylum. I didn't even think their females had the markings."

"Uh." I do not like passing through thick dimensional walls. I like losing consciousness even less than that. I like waking up without my weapons so much less than that that it's almost comic. And more than all of those things, I do not like being confused by pink, thorny women who tell me I've been dumped in a stranger's harem like it's a good thing. "Do you have a name?"

"Oh, yes! Rubina is my name. It's a pleasure to meet you . . ."

"Alice," I said. "Are we speaking English?"

"No, we're speaking whatever language brings you the most comfort. The Autarch was concerned, as so many of us come from dissimilar worlds, that we would be unable to find commonality. He arranged for translation runes to be painted in all the rooms, to be sure we'd be able to speak with one another freely."

She was still smiling. Either this Autarch of hers was a great guy and would be totally willing to let me out of this supposedly protective custody as soon as I met him and explained exactly what I was doing here and who I was looking for, or he was a monster operating a girl collection and she was too afraid to say anything bad about him.

"Okay," I said. "Cool. Can you do me a favor?"

"Of course! Anything to make you comfortable here."

"Okay, then, is it possible for you to take me to get my stuff back, please? A lot of the things I was carrying when I arrived have sentimental value." And the ones that didn't could be used to hurt people. Which might be necessary if the Autarch wasn't miraculously awesome.

People who call themselves "Autarchs" and start collecting people who need their inexplicably benevolent "protection" are very rarely awesome, in my experience. Whoever this guy was, he was probably already a dead man walking. He just didn't know who was going to pull the trigger. I was happy to volunteer.

"Of course," repeated Rubina. Either she was naturally good-natured, or I needed to be careful about what I put in my mouth while I was here. Drugs in the water would be pretty solidly on-brand for an "Autarch." I was really starting to dislike this guy, and I hadn't even met him yet.

She walked over to the Hobbit-hole door, still smiling. It opened easily when she pressed the latch, and I relaxed slightly. So they weren't locking me in here.

"Belongings of new arrivals are temporarily kept in the storage rooms for safekeeping," she said. "Come with me."

I didn't have to be invited twice. She walked out of the room into a winding hall, and I followed her, relieved when no wards activated to keep me locked in. All this could still be a trick—send your friendliest, most unassuming representative to work on the paranoid stranger while you get her to drop her guard—but I was starting to suspect that it might not be.

"You know," I said carefully. "This isn't what I was expecting."

"No?" The walls out here were something smooth, plaster or clay or drywall, and had been painted as white as the walls in the room where I woke up. There was something industrial about it, like the color had been chosen because it was easy to repaint, and not for any aesthetic reasons.

She led me down the hall to a large, circular doorway leading to what I would have called a community room at a library: it was built on a scale that fit the entry, large enough to hold a small 4-H assembly. Pillars supported the ceiling at regular intervals, necessary due to the lack of load-bearing internal walls, and people were scattered around the space. Most of them were women, dressed in the same diaphanous fabric as Rubina and myself, although the cuts ranged from something that looked like pajama loungewear, with long sleeves and actual pants, all the way to dresses much shorter than Rubina's, or my robe.

The only men stood to either side of the arch we'd just entered through, or to the sides of the matching arches on each wall, four in all. The men, all of whom were bipeds of roughly human conformation and proportions, wore brown leather, lace-up vests and tight trousers, and held an impressive assortment of polearms.

I like polearms. They're not the most practical weapons under most circumstances—you need too much room if you're going to use them effectively, and while they're great for keeping people at a distance, if you're dealing with someone who mostly works with firearms, they'll quickly cease to be your friends, as the jaghirdar and their lackies had learned to their dismay. None of the guards—because that's what they were, harem guards, whatever fancy description they liked to use locally—were carrying the sort of spears I'd seen in the last dimension. That was good. I wouldn't have wanted to deal with more of the same.

But they *were* carrying spears, or at least some of them were. The rest—and there were seven in all—had an assortment of blade designs that made them look like a medieval recreation troupe with very poor historical accuracy. Fauchards and bardiche and billhooks don't belong in the same armory, much less the same guard. I downgraded my weakly forming assessment of the local security a few steps for sloppy equipment reconciliation. Not that it would matter. Any of those things could stab me, whether or not they should be used together.

But none of the men were making any threatening moves with their weapons, and Rubina smiled at several of them as we entered.

Once I took my eyes off the polearms, I found the assortment of visible species in the room much more distracting. No two of the women looked like they'd come from the same starting dimension. While they were all vertebrate bipeds, that was about where the similarities ended. Some were covered in fur. Others had scales, or wings, or extra arms. One of them looked like she would be nine feet tall if she stood up, instead of lounging on a pile of beanbags on the floor.

Any Autarch who could maintain this kind of wide-spectrum buffet of women and still want more wasn't going to be a nice man.

Rubina led me straight across the room, waving and smiling at the women we passed, all of whom looked at us with curiosity, though they didn't stop her or speak to me directly, even as they assessed me with their eyes. Checking out the competition if I was making my guess correctly. Wouldn't they be surprised when they found out that I was nothing of the sort?

The entryway opposite the one we'd come through was equally large, while the entries to either end were smaller, limiting the shapes and sizes of the people who'd be able to use them. Some of the women in this room wouldn't have been able to walk upright through those doors

Rubina stopped at the far entryway, knocking lightly on the wall. "Sally? New arrival is awake, and she wants her things back."

"Yeah, well, some of 'her things' are weapons of mass destruction, so I'm not necessarily in a rush to return them," answered a voice. Like Rubina, the speaker's words came through in English. Unlike Rubina, she had an accent I recognized, solid Mainer. She didn't talk like a lobsterman, but she had the inland accent, an inhale on her "yeah," soft "r"s, and vowels that didn't subscribe to any other region I knew, not even quite Boston.

Not the accent I would have expected to hear in a place like this, but it wasn't the strangest thing that had happened to me today, so I was willing to roll with it.

"Sorry," I said. "But they're mine and I didn't consent to having them taken, so I want them back."

"You were practically in a coma when we found you and brought you into the compound for medical attention. I would think you'd be a little grateful," said the speaker, who emerged from the dimness on the other side of the opening to lean against the archway and look at me flatly. "Not every day you pass out in a freezing field and wake up in a nice bed."

Rubina seemed to have no sharp edges, despite the thorns growing out of her neck and shoulders, a woman designed for softness, like a rose from a safely walled garden. This woman was nothing *but* sharp edges, every inch of her. She was dressed in the same basic uniform as the guards, in contrast to all the women I'd seen so far. Interesting, that, given how much she looked like a human being. Her hair was long and black, and her skin was a tawny beige. If I'd been asked to peg her to an Earth ethnicity for some reason—something it was hard not to do, given how much she sounded like home—I would have guessed Asian-American, probably Korean-American.

"I thought you'd be out for a lot longer," she said, casually pushing away from the doorway and moving closer. I tensed. She stopped, holding up her hands. "Whoa, no, not planning to hurt you. Just wanted to ask how you're doing, see if maybe there's anything you need. You were down pretty hard when we found you. I'm guessing you're diabetic? And from Earth, to boot. I found the glucose paste in your bag and put it on your gums when you wouldn't wake up. I figure that had to have helped."

"Not diabetic," I said, more curtly than I meant to. It had been a long, hard, weird trip, and a chatty Earth girl dressed to audition for the new *Mad Max* wasn't what I'd been looking for. "Not a sorcerer either. So."

"So you sucked all the sugar out of your own body to fuel the crossing? Nice. Innovative. And really, really stupid." Her voice turned hard. "Shouldn't the big-ass 'Keep Out' signs have been some sort of a warning that maybe this wasn't the best stop on your vacation tour of the dimensions?"

"Excuse me?" I asked, eyebrows climbing toward my hairline. "Listen up, young lady. This isn't a vacation tour. I'm on a mission, and I needed to be here, so I came in. I could have killed myself getting past those 'Keep Out' signs you mentioned. Did you set those?"

"Nope," she said, with what seemed to be far more relish than the word warranted. She spoke like someone who'd been spoiling for a fight all day and was happy to accept it from the woman who'd just shown up if that was what she had available. "Boss did that. He wanted people to stop falling out of the sky like assholes we'd have to patch up and feed and rehabilitate. He'll like you, though. He likes the human ones." She looked me deliberately up and down. "Blonde's just a bonus."

"What the hell are you talking about?"

"Didn't whoever told you to try in our direction tell you? This is a roach motel. You can check in, but you can't check out." Her shrug was deliberately broad. It was like she was actively trying to get under my skin. Which maybe she was. Again, she stood like someone who wanted to have a fight.

Maybe she was head wife or something, and me looking human made me the competition. I didn't actually care.

"Yes, I knew that part," I said carefully. She might be antagonistic. That didn't mean I had to be. "I came here on purpose after I found a cartographer's record indicating that this was a bottle world. He got in *and* he got out. Some friends of mine back in Ithaca are going over his papers to see if they can figure out how he did it and extract me."

For a moment, what looked like hope flared in her dark eyes. She tamped it down and scowled at me. "So you really are on a vacation tour of the dimensions," she said. "Ithaca's a long way from here."

"Earth's even farther," I said, somewhat cautiously.

To my relief, there was recognition in her nod. "Yeah, it is. Can't imagine there's anything this far out to be worth making the trip for. Especially not when you're probably stuck here with the rest of us."

"Let me worry about that," I said. "Can I get my things?"

"Can you tell me why you're armed like you plan to start a war against whatever gets in your way? Some of these grenades are older than my grandfather."

"Like I said, it's a long way from Earth, and I did the whole trip on foot and by myself," I said. "And like I said, I'm not a sorcerer. I can't just fling a fireball at somebody if they decide I shouldn't be allowed to keep going."

"Most people aren't sorcerers, and yet most people don't go around with half an armory on their back," she said, and looked me up and down again, apparently coming to a decision. "I'm sorry, I really am, but I can't. Not until you've seen the Autarch. If he says you can have your things, you can have your things. Boss calls the shots, the rest of us just count the bullets."

"Nice effort to fit the metaphor to the person you're talking to, even if it fell a little flat in the execution," I said. I turned to Rubina, who had been watching us with confusion and concern. "All right, since you came to get me, when do I see this Autarch of yours?"

"Please, as if you didn't come here specifically to try and play the lost Anastasia?" said Sally, snapping my attention back around to her.

"I'm sorry, what?" I asked.

"You look human," she said. "You say you started from Earth, but you don't have an accent I recognize, and you mention traveling through other dimensions like that's something someone from Earth would know as anything other than science fiction. Which they wouldn't, by the way. Whoever prepped you forgot to mention that Earth is still isolated enough that we mostly don't know other dimensions even exist, much less how to move between them."

"But you're from Maine, and you know those things," I said.

"Yeah, because I attracted the attention of the crossroads and got slingshot across creation to wind up here," she countered. "I'm stuck.

You came here voluntarily. Forgive me if I'm suspicious. And then just look at you."

I raised my eyebrows again. "Look at me?"

"Whoever prepped you missed the mark by a couple of decades, Princess." Sally gave me another up and down look, not even bothering to hide the way her lip curled. "Too young to be the wife *or* the daughter, assuming either of them survived, and the wife, which I assume is the goal, didn't have any tattoos. You're not good enough. You're not going to pull it off."

I stared at her, a hard, cold feeling starting to gather in the pit of my stomach. It had begun with her casual mention of the crossroads throwing her here, which was exactly what I'd been hoping for but somehow sounded upsetting coming from someone else's mouth. If the crossroads had been putting their victims here, then I might be in the right place.

In the palace of an Autarch who grabbed every woman who entered his territory. "I don't need to be good enough for anything," I said, tightly. "I'm moving between worlds because I'm trying to find my husband. He disappeared, and I'm looking for him so I can take him home. I'm not here to steal anything that belongs to you, or to mess around with whatever system you've got going here." I waved my hands vaguely, indicating the whole room. "I don't *care*. Maybe that makes me a bad person and I should be worrying about how to set you all free from whatever messed-up form of communal bondage you've gone and fallen into, but I've been doing this for a long fucking time, and I've had plenty of opportunities to learn that sometimes you don't want to mess around with the way the locals do things."

Sally pursed her lips. "Rubina, go tell the guards that we're going to need an escort," she said. "I'd like to chat with the new girl in private for a minute."

"Oh, I'm sure that won't be—"

"*Now*, Rubina."

"Yes, Sally." The thorn-skinned woman turned and hurried away toward the nearest set of guards, leaving me alone with Sally, who gave me a slow, measuring look.

"If you have a way to leave, you should leave, now," she said. "I know what you're trying to do, and they didn't prep you as well as they probably think they did. Something got lost in translation."

"I don't know what you're talking about."

"Don't you?"

She was fast, I'd have to give her that: she grabbed the front of my robe and yanked me toward her, stepping backward through the archway as she did. The room on the other side was smaller than the main room, about the size of my bedroom back in Buckley. Shelves lined the walls, piled with a wide assortment of bags and boxes. She let me go once I was safely in the room, waving a hand at the wall across from the entry.

"See?" she snapped. "He'll *know*, you fucking imposter. He'll know."

I said nothing. I just stared, silent. Because there on the wall, looking back at us, was me.

Not literally me. A painting. I even remembered the picture it had been painted from. The year between Kevin and Jane, the library had decided that we would treat staff photo day as an occasion and asked us all to come to work dressed for a formal portrait. I'd worn a pink dress and my grandmother's pearls, and I'd done my hair in pretty curls, the way my mother always wore it in the posters.

Thomas had liked that picture so much he'd carried a copy in his wallet. His wallet, which had disappeared the same night he did. Guess I knew where it had gone now. Guess I didn't have to wonder anymore.

"They should have modeled you off of the historical records, not whatever messed-up assumptions they've made about how the family would change," said Sally, not appearing to notice the sudden tension in my stance, or the way my breathing had gone fast and shallow. "They didn't do you any favors. They didn't—"

She was so confident about being in the right that she didn't even block as I brought my knee up and slammed it into her stomach, grabbing her hair at the same time and jerking her head downward, so that her forehead connected with the hard surface of my lower thigh. When I let her go, she staggered backward, off balance.

"Shut the fuck up," I snarled, and punched her twice in the face. She was unprepared for the sudden additional assault, and clearly too dazed to hit me back fast enough. I took the opportunity to strike her under the ear with my forearm. She went down without a sound, landing in a heap on the floor. That was no guarantee that she'd *stay* down. People are frequently sturdier than they seem.

I heard voices just outside. I didn't have time to tie her up or to really properly loot the place. None of my things were immediately visible. Fuck. I'd have to find a way to come back for them later. Sally might be armed, but—if so—it wasn't obvious. I decided my best bets were still speed and the element of surprise and left her where she was as I stepped back into the main room.

Rubina had returned with one of the guards, an anxious-looking green-skinned man with the facial features indicative of the dominant species on Cornale, gauzy wings wrapped around his shoulders and a fauchard in one hand.

"Where is Sally?" he asked.

"Indisposed," I replied. "Can I see your polearm, please?"

"No," he said. "We don't arm strangers."

"Kinda think you do, though," I said, and punched him in the throat. Not the most subtle introduction, but absolutely an effective one—again, especially when the person being punched doesn't see it coming. I've never been much of a brawler, she says, while assaulting people left and right. I prefer my fighting to happen on the other end of a bullet or a blade. Thomas used to despair of teaching me to throw a punch without telegraphing it.

But I've improved enough over the years to stay alive, and I can still hit with sufficient force to get my point across when I feel the need. People who aren't expecting to be punched in the throat don't care about your form, they care about their tracheas. Tracheas are crunchy when you hit them hard enough. The guard staggered backward, gasping, and I snatched the fauchard out of his hands, bringing it up to shoulder level and holding it like a barrier between us as I kicked him between the legs.

That maneuver works better when I'm not barefoot, but again, the element of surprise was on my side. Dainty, sweet little harem girls aren't supposed to start whaling on the people assigned to protect them, and maybe I shouldn't have been doing it. Maybe I should have stayed polite and demure and let him lead me to the Autarch like an offering, but right now, all I felt like "offering" to their Autarch was fifty years-worth of extreme disapproval. I've always found disapproval easier to express through violence.

Rubina recoiled, visibly shocked by my actions, as the guard stumbled into the wall and sank slowly down to floor level, pulling his knees toward his chest. I didn't know whether his genitals were in the same place a human's would have been, but whatever I'd hit seemed to have been an effective target. I whacked him in the side of the head with the butt-end of my new fauchard, before spinning to point it toward the rest of the room, turning in a slow arc to make sure every single person there saw that I was armed.

"All of you stay where you are, and I won't have to knock any more of you down," I said. They blinked at me, some more slowly than others, and didn't move. Guess this Autarch wasn't as good at inspiring loyalty in his people—or his "wives"—as he probably assumed he was. Well, that worked for me.

Sally probably wasn't going to be as passive when she stumbled out after me in a minute or two, and from the musculature I'd felt when I hit her, she wasn't as soft as this guard had been, either. I'd won only because I'd surprised her. Yeah, I had a weapon now, but here's the thing about most weapons: you shouldn't use them unless you're willing to kill the person you're using them against. Sally was complicit in this system. She was also trapped here and may not have had any choice in the matter. As long as she stayed out of my way, I didn't really want to hurt her. What I had done to her could be pretty disorienting, so hopefully she'd stay down long enough for me to get out of here.

"I'm going to be leaving now," I said, loudly and clearly. "None of you are going to stop me. You won't like how things play out if you try."

They continued to watch me, saying nothing. I leaned over and grabbed Rubina by the arm, careful to grip below the point where the thorns stopped.

She whimpered, and I immediately felt terrible. I'm not normally in the business of terrifying people who can't defend themselves. It's not kind. That didn't stop me from pulling her toward me like a hostage, and hissing, voice low, "Which way to the Autarch?"

"You don't have to do this!" she said, voice rapidly approaching a wail. "We were going to take you to see him!"

"Yeah, well, I prefer to take myself," I said. "Just get me pointed in the right direction."

Not surprising me in the least, she pointed to the leftmost archway, one of the ones too small to be used by some of the women. The guards on that door were holding a boar spear and a voulge. Whoever was in charge of their armory needed to get a little consistency into the program.

I wanted that voulge. A fauchard is nice, although it's not much of a stabbing weapon, but it's not as nice as a voulge, which has a longer cutting edge and a better spike at the bottom, making it ideal for hooking things that don't want to be hooked.

"Thank you," I said. "You did nothing wrong." Then I let her go, giving her a little push away from me to make it clear that I wasn't going to grab her again, and walked toward the door she'd indicated, giving my fauchard a spin as I walked, like I was completely unconcerned about what was going to happen next.

I paused when I reached the door, getting a little closer than was probably wise, close enough that either of them could have tried to hit me if they'd had the presence of mind to do it. Also close enough that they would have been fighting against their own weapons in the process. Never let it be said that we aren't limited by our tools.

"Hi," I said to the one with the voulge, holding out my fauchard. "Wanna trade?"

He looked utterly nonplussed, taking a step backward. "I am loyal!" he snapped.

"Never said you weren't. I have a weapon, you have a weapon, I'm not asking you to *give* me your weapon, I'm asking you to do an equal exchange, at the end of which, you'll still have a weapon, and so will I." The other guard, with the boar spear, brought it down to level with my gut.

Boar spears are a bitch if they break the skin. They're designed to disembowel more than anything else, and I don't approve of them. I spun my fauchard in my hands again, pointing the butt end of it at that guard, and whacked his fingers before he realized what I was about to do.

The sound of his weapon clattering to the floor was beautiful. I put a foot on it to stop him picking it up again and drove the butt of the fauchard into his stomach, eliciting a loud "oof" as he staggered away from me. They were all going down so easily, I was starting to feel bad about it. These people didn't seem like very good guards. Only Sally had presented any real challenge, and one kid from Maine was never going to be enough to protect this many people.

If they could have shaken off their passivity and swarmed me, it would have been over in minutes. I wasn't willing to really hurt them, and sometimes there's not a way to win a fight without really hurting people. I whacked my current playmate again, this time on the head, and pointed the blade at the one still holding the voulge.

"Trade, or I take it away," I snapped.

He held his weapon out toward me, cringing.

"Thank you," I said brightly as I plucked it from his hand, replacing it with the fauchard. The weight on the voulge was much more balanced to my liking. I gave it a spin and smiled at him, bright as anything. "I really appreciate it. Now, you want to get out of my way?"

He stepped to the side, staring at me like I was all his nightmares come to life and rolled up into one perky blonde package. I smiled at him and stepped through the archway, into another long, featureless white hall.

I'd made it about fifteen feet before someone sent up the alarm. Awesome.

Time to party.

Ten

"If there is anyone in this world or the next more stubborn than Alice Healy once she gets her teeth into something, I truly hope to never meet them."

—Mary Dunlavy

Running hell-bent for leather down an unfamiliar hallway, hoping I won't have to kill anyone

THE ALARM WAS A loud, shrill belling sound that seemed to pour out of the walls themselves, filling the air. It wasn't quite loud enough to disorient, but it definitely made it harder to focus on what I was doing. Footsteps filled the hall behind me, running after me, and a spear clattered to the ground some feet ahead of me, thrown by a guard who clearly hadn't stopped to consider that when you only have one weapon, throwing it at people isn't the best plan. I paused to duck down and grab it, whipping around to face the sounds of pursuit. All the guards who hadn't already been knocked down were running after me, accompanied by about half a dozen more who had apparently answered the call.

And all of them were carrying polearms from the same grab bag assortment of ways to stab people. When I found the Autarch, after I finished beating the everloving crap out of him—twice if my suspicions were correct—we were going to have a serious talk about diversity in armaments.

I threw the spear back at the one in the front. My aim was better than theirs. It hit them in the shoulder, embedding itself there and sending them rocking backward into the rank of guards behind them as they clutched at the wound. The blood that spurted forth was darker than I would have expected. Biology is fun sometimes. I turned my attention back to the hall ahead of me and kept running.

I had a head start and a lot of practice fleeing from angry mobs. I was also barefoot and dealing with the aftereffects of physically and magically exhausting myself breaking through the dimensional barrier. That meant we were probably on roughly equal footing.

The hall widened ahead of me, into another of those wide, round openings. I plunged through, into a tiled courtyard lined with unfamiliar vegetation, like something out of a home décor magazine. I kept running.

The guards, when they reached the opening, didn't. They stopped there, piling into one another, but didn't cross the boundary. That probably wasn't a good sign.

The branches around me weren't rustling. I slowed down, coming to a stop right around the center of the courtyard, and looked at my surroundings more closely. Most really predatory plants are attracted to motion. If they were going to strike, they would strike at me while I was moving. Still nothing rustled in the brush. Still nothing appeared to threaten me.

Then I smelled apples mixed with strawberries. It was a characteristic perfume, and one I hadn't been expecting to find here. Looking more closely at the trees, I saw the vines wrapped around them, green and edged in white, the thorny "teeth" of the bromeliads outlining them. I looked down at the ground. Thin white roots snaked across the tile. This whole place was a bromeliad feeding nest.

And here was I, barefoot in the middle of it. No wonder the guards had stopped. I'd step on a vine or a mature enough root any second now, if I hadn't already, and the soporific sap would get into my veins. After that, it was only a matter of time before I collapsed.

Or it should have been only a matter of time. You don't run around the disreputable parts of several dozen dimensions without finding a way to avoid roofies. I pressed my fingers against the ammonite tattooed over my hip, pressing hard to make up for the lack of skin contact. Like hell was I taking off my robe, thin as it was, with the guards looking on.

The tattoo warmed beneath my fingers as it dissolved, and a brief wave of dizziness told me that the price had been paid for temporary poison resistance. I began walking across the courtyard again, watching my step. The thorns might not be able to incapacitate me, but they would still sting like the dickens if I stepped on them directly.

What kind of person keeps a courtyard full of *swamp bromeliads* in a place easily accessible from his *harem*? Not a person who worries much about the women supposedly under his protection. I scowled as

I angled for the archway on the far side of the courtyard. I was liking this Autarch less and less, and that was pretty impressive, given where I'd started. I was honestly beginning to hope I was wrong. The man I was looking for would never have been this careless about the safety of others. Time changes everyone. I didn't want it to have changed him like this.

The archway on the other side was as open as the others had been. I stepped through into a narrower hall. The air was cooler here, probably in part due to the high windows on the walls, which allowed the wind to pass though. The air hadn't been stale in the other wing, but it had been still, something I hadn't really noticed at the time. There were doors along this hall. All of them were circular, matching the rest of the local architecture, but unlike the majority I'd seen in the wing where I woke up, they actually had *doors* in them, closing off the rooms on the other side.

I ignored them and kept going. The alarm was still ringing, but no additional guards had shown up to complicate my day. Either there *were* no additional guards, which didn't make a lot of sense, or they assumed they would only have to wait a few more minutes before I passed out from the bromeliad sap, becoming much easier to collect without further risk to life or limb.

Or maybe they just didn't like their Autarch all that much. It would make sense. People don't usually like the guy who takes all the women. Mostly because that guy is usually a jerk.

At the end of the hall was another, much larger circular arch, containing a pair of tall, closed doors. I gripped my voulge tightly and strode toward it. The end of my long journey might be on the other side. If that was the case, I didn't know what I was going to do next. I also didn't know whether it would end well, and I wasn't ready for that. And it was too late to turn back now.

It was too late by fifty years. I approached the door. I pushed the latch.

It swung open, and I stepped through.

The room on the other side was a throne room. There wasn't any other way to describe it: it was too big, too grandiose to be anything else, like something out of a Gothic castle as designed by architects from Hobbiton, who couldn't think in terms of things being impressive without them also being round. A single worn rug ran from the door all the way to the back of the room, a distance that felt as long as a football field but was probably more like a hundred and fifty feet in reality, where it reached the foot of an ornate wooden throne.

Unlike almost everything else in here, the throne had hard edges, and looked like it had been crafted according to more familiar-to-me rules of design. It was stained dark with some sort of resin, and the smell of apples and strawberries hung distantly in the air, telling me where at least some of the materials had originated. And I was focusing on the throne to avoid focusing on anything else.

Like how empty it was. This should have been the seat of the Autarch, but there were no guards here, no attendants . . . and no Autarch. I walked forward, the carpet muffling my footsteps and the room swallowing what sound managed to escape. Something about the rounded ceiling stopped echoes from growing the way they should have, rendering the room almost entirely silent. It was uncomfortably so.

I stopped when I reached the throne, reaching out to touch the cushion on the seat with careful fingers. It was still warm. Maybe the lack of guards had been a logistical one; I'd been running away from the wives, so they didn't need to be protected, and the guards who hadn't already been behind me had been busy getting the Autarch away from the madwoman with the polearm. It was good tactics, even if it meant I still hadn't had the fight I was absolutely spoiling for.

A door opened in the wall behind the throne itself, about a dozen feet farther back and small enough to blend in with the paneling around it. It didn't match the other doors I'd seen so far: instead, it was rectangular, swinging out like a part of the wall and vanishing when it swung closed again. A man stepped out into the room. I swung around to face him, voulge held at the ready. Maybe not the nicest "hello, honey" anyone has ever managed, but it was the one I had in me at the moment.

The man was human, or close enough to human to have passed even on a busy street back home, head bent slightly as he studied something in his hands. His hair was brown, still short enough to count as "short," but long enough to have become slightly disheveled, and barely starting to gray at the temples. He was wearing a white shirt, sleeves rolled up to his elbows, and brown slacks of the same kind I'd seen on Sally and the guards, and it was suddenly very, very difficult for me to breathe, because his forearms were a riot of colorful tattoos, and similar images were just barely visible above the collar of his shirt, working their way along the curve of his neck. I managed to raise the voulge so that it was no longer pointed directly at him. That was about all that I could do while otherwise frozen.

With the acoustics of the room swallowing the sound of my breathing, he made it several steps closer before he realized he wasn't alone. He stopped and lifted his head, blinking from behind the frames of unfamiliar glasses. That was almost a relief. If he'd been wearing the same pair after fifty years, I would have assumed this was a hallucination.

The glasses were the only thing about him that were unfamiliar. I knew that face, almost as well as I knew my own. He'd lost some weight since leaving Buckley, but I'd seen him worn thin and wrung out before; when I came back from college, after my one abortive attempt to leave the life I'd been born to behind, it had been to find him a prisoner in his own home, dependent on the charity of the local Women's Aid Society, hungry and unkempt and imprisoned by his own choices. He looked better now than he had then.

His jaw was still sharp, his cheekbones so pronounced that they looked as if they could be used to slice cheese, and his eyes were still very, very blue. Not Johrlac blue, but still startlingly bright for a human man. The tattoos I could see were familiar ones, all save for the cameo now tattooed in the hollow of his throat, higher than any of the others around it. Since unlike me, he did his own tattooing, the position of the image was impressive. I just couldn't imagine what magical benefit the profile of a human man was supposed to provide.

I couldn't imagine much in that moment. Even as he stared at me and I stared back, my thoughts were skipping like a scratched record, dancing around admitting who he was, even as I knew exactly who he was; I couldn't bring myself to think his name, despite the fact that his name had been the only one occupying my thoughts for so long that it had drowned out almost everything else, the loss of him transforming love into an obsession. I had become my own cautionary tale in the search for just one man, and now that I had found him, I couldn't even think his name.

He was holding one of my mother's revolvers in his long-fingered hands; he'd been studying it before I managed to catch his attention by being an unexpected person in his space. His hands tightened around the gun as he stared at me, and I stared back, and neither of us moved. I wasn't absolutely sure that I was even breathing. If his hands hadn't moved, I wouldn't have been sure he hadn't passed out without falling down. It's a neat trick, and one that I've seen people accomplish before, if not very often.

Finally, he took one hand off the gun, reached up, and adjusted his glasses, a gesture so familiar that it felt almost like he had punched me in the gut.

"You made it farther than I expected," he said, and his voice, like everything else, was the same, British accent so different from the one I'd grown up with. He and my grandparents were all former Covenant, but they'd been from the west, and he was originally from London. The difference was subtle if you weren't accustomed to hearing both voices on a regular basis, but growing up the way I had, it was as noticeable as the difference between Massachusetts and Maine. "How many of my people did you kill?"

"N-none," I managed. This wasn't the conversation I'd imagined us having on our reunion. That conversation had sometimes been a cliché out of a romance novel, all tears and inexplicable string quartets, and sometimes it had been a string of shouted recriminations, me blaming him for leaving me the way he did, him blaming me for getting hurt and causing him to make a crossroads bargain in the first place. It had never been a calm accusation of murder.

He raised his eyebrows, expression politely disbelieving.

"I knocked a few of them down, and when one of them threw a spear at me, I threw it back and hit him in the shoulder, but that's all," I said. "Considering I passed out in a barren wasteland and woke up stripped of my clothing and weapons in something that pretty much looked like a harem, I don't think that was an unreasonably violent reaction. I mean, *really*, Thomas—what else would you expect me to do?"

"Impressive," he said, then smiled in a way that didn't reach his eyes, looking oddly relieved. "You even sound like her." He kept smiling as he raised my mother's gun and aimed it levelly at my chest. His hand didn't shake at all. That was almost worse than him pointing a weapon at me. The fact that he did it, and he didn't flinch.

"I admit, when they described you to me, I had a moment's hesitation, even though I knew better. I know better. People change, you see, and while my wife may not have been magically gifted, she knew people who were. If she'd been fast and foolish and made unwise bargains, she could have held herself together long enough to reach me. I desperately want to believe that you might actually be real, and not another damned imposter—which is why I can't do it. So, as I'm done hesitating, I suppose now is when I ask you: who sent you here to kill me, and how long ago did you kill my wife?"

Silence fell over the room like a hammer, so heavy and all-consuming that even if the acoustics hadn't been so well-designed, I wouldn't have been able to hear anything beyond the frantic pounding of my heart. I swallowed, bile and bright, metallic adrenaline in my throat, and tried to keep on breathing. Thomas was *alive*. I was right, I'd *been* right all along, and he'd been out here for me to find . . . and he thought I was an imposter who had killed his wife to take her place. This wasn't the worst scenario I could have imagined. This wasn't a scenario I had ever imagined.

I stared at him, trying to figure out how I was supposed to react, and horrified confusion curdled in my chest, recovering the rage that had carried me here. I swung my voulge back into position, aiming it at him, like a polearm could ever win against a six-shooter, and snarled, "No one sent me here but *me*, and I wasn't planning to kill you—not if you turned out to be *you*, anyway. I just wanted to bring you home. And I'm not gonna lie. I'm not a big fan of this Autarch guy you've turned into."

"You are a poor imitation of the woman I lost," he said, voice imperious and cold. "Whoever trained you should have primed you better for success, not just thought I'd be turned by blonde hair and a pretty face. You don't even *look* like her."

"Are you fucking *serious*?" My temper has never been great at the best of times, and even if Thomas didn't believe I was who I appeared to be, he knew how to press my buttons. "I've been killing myself crossing dimensions looking for you, and now you point my mother's *gun* at me?! It's like you *want* me to kick your ass!"

I ran straight at him, gambling on the idea that he thought I was a paid assassin, someone who wouldn't be interested in risking their own life by putting word to action so quickly, and that that might be enough to throw off his aim. I can't dodge bullets. There's trained to stay alive and then there's superhuman, and I don't cross that line. But I know how Thomas tends to aim, and he always pulls a little to the right; not enough to miss what he's aiming for, but enough to result in imperfect bullseyes. I used to tease him about it, and he'd counter by pointing out that my lousy left hook was the reason I'll never be a boxer. Everyone has their weaknesses. Train with someone for long enough, and they'll turn familiar.

My instincts proved correct, and his shot missed me. Seeing him shoot my mother's gun just made me angrier, though. How could he think I wasn't me when he was holding my mother's gun? "You better have both of those," I snapped.

I was close enough at this point to throw my voulge. Unfortunately, my aim is very, very good, and I never learned how to miss to make myself seem more helpless. Competency can be a curse when it's not optional, and impaling my husband immediately after finding him didn't seem like a *great* plan, even if he *was* shooting at me. I can be pretty annoying sometimes.

His mouth thinned, lips forming a grim line, and I knew he wasn't going to miss a second time. Planting the end of the voulge against the floor, I jumped, using it as a pole vault.

My granddaughter, Verity, uses poles for dance and exercise equipment, and she's taught me a few tricks I would never have thought of on my own. Using them as a launching point is on the list. My feet hit him in the chest, knocking him back several feet. That was good. The blow didn't knock him down, which was less good, and it didn't cause him to lose his grip on the gun, which was worse. I wanted him unarmed if at all possible.

Raising my fists, I fell into a fighting pose, all too aware that as soon as he brought the gun back up, I'd be in real trouble. There would be no evasion at this range, and all teasing aside, he wasn't going to miss when I was in closing range. "Get your hands off my mother's revolver," I snarled, and went for a roundhouse kick.

"She wasn't *your* mother," he countered, blocking the blow with his arm, only to wince and take a step back. I kick hard.

"Frances Healy was so my mother." I paused for half a beat, considering. I knew closing with him would put me at a disadvantage, but as long as he still had the gun, getting close enough to disarm him was my best bet. I stopped, running the math in my head, and smiled. "Did you bother to reload my guns after you stole them from me?"

"I wasn't expecting I'd have to use them!"

His eyes narrowed as he pointed the gun at me and pulled the trigger again. At this range, he couldn't possibly miss.

The hammer clicked down on an empty chamber. If I hadn't been so understandably furious with him, the look of surprise on his face would have been a beautiful thing. As it was, I beamed and moved closer. "Hi," I said brightly. "I shot five people on my way to reaching you, you bastard."

Then I punched him in the face.

The blow snapped his head back. He stumbled, losing his grip on the gun. I glared at him as it clattered to the floor. It had taken harder hits while in my hands, but it was *mine*, not his, and he didn't just get to throw important things aside because he didn't think they mattered anymore.

Maybe I was projecting a little. I didn't care.

"That hurt," he said, and raised his hand, a ball of fire forming above his palm. It was weak and wavering, barely substantial enough to qualify for the name "fireball." He flung it at me anyway. I raised my arm to block it, taking the hit just below the wrist. It stung, but didn't really burn, and dissipated quickly enough that it might as well have been nothing.

"Magic not working right?" I taunted. "I hear that happens to men your age."

Not that he looked his age. He could have been here less than a week, to look at him. Only the women I'd met so far, and the painting of me on the wall, which was weathered and aged and had clearly been exposed to direct sunlight before it was moved to the back of a closet, told me that he'd been here any longer. Time can run differently between dimensions. It still didn't explain why he looked so much like I expected him to.

"Who sent you?" he demanded, and surged toward me, aiming a blow at my solar plexus. I blocked, but barely, and was rewarded by my arm going numb.

He was still wearing his wedding ring. That was enough of a surprise that my guard dropped for a moment, and his next punch caught me on the edge of the jaw, rocking me back and filling my mouth with the bright, sharp taste of blood. I spat it onto the floor.

It's bad to get distracted during a fight. That's how you lose. I spat more blood and glared at him.

"I came because I knew I'd find you one day," I snapped, and swung for his head. My right arm was still numb, so I used my left. Less effective, but still good enough.

Sometimes good enough is all you have.

He blocked the blow with too much ease, eyes going wide, and took a step back, conveniently leaving himself wide open on the left. If it wouldn't have been tactically stupid, I would have assumed he did it on purpose. Under the circumstances, I didn't particularly care. I swung again.

This time, he ducked easily out of range of my fist, and just stared at me. Voice spiking slightly, like he couldn't actually believe what he was saying, he asked, "Alice?"

"Oh, no," I said. "This isn't where you get me to drop my guard by pretending to finally know who I am. That isn't how this goes."

I rocked back to reposition myself, and launched another round-house kick, this time aiming for his midsection. To my confusion and surprise, he took the blow, not even flinching away from it, and went down hard, hitting the floor on his back.

I dropped down to straddle him, landing with one knee on either side of his hips, and pulled back my right fist, arm cocked to hit him hard enough to knock him out if my aim was right. He didn't even try to defend himself, just kept staring at me like I was an illusion, like this couldn't possibly be happening. Like none of this was happening. I didn't move.

He was staring at me, and so I just stared at him, and the two of us formed a frozen tableau marred by blood on the floor and trickling from the corner of my mouth, running from a split on the skin of his left cheek, and blotching both our knuckles. A bruise was forming around that cut on his cheek, burst capillaries darkening with damage. Still I stared, and still he stared, and it felt like neither of us was breathing.

Since my fist was still raised for a blow that felt like it was never going to land, I wasn't holding down his arms. Hands shaking, he raised them toward my face, like he was going to cup my cheeks. "*Alice*," he repeated, less disbelieving, more amazed.

I pulled back, stopping him from grabbing me the way he had been intending to. "As soon as you're losing, you believe me?"

"Alice," he said, for a third time, like repeating it was what made it true. Then, starting to laugh as he spoke, he said, "No assassin would know how you telegraph your swings to the left. I told you to work on that. You should have listened."

"Yeah, well, you should have learned to *aim*," I countered.

This time, when he reached for the sides of my face, I didn't pull away. And while his hands were warm—a sorcerer's hands are always warm—they didn't burn me. This wasn't some sort of a trick to get me to drop my guard. I did lower my fist, finally, and just stared down at the laughing man beneath me. He looked almost exactly the way that I remembered him, except for the tattoo I'd already noticed, the one that must have been almost impossible to complete without making a mistake, and he was watching me so closely that his gaze was almost a physical weight. There were tears in his eyes.

He made a sound somewhere between a laugh and a sob as he let go of my face in order to grab hold of my shoulders, sitting halfway up and wrapping himself around me as he pulled me into a hug so tight it bent my ribs and made everything about me ache.

After a moment of stunned surprise, I wrapped my arms around him in turn. This wasn't the reunion I'd imagined. It was apparently the one I had, and that was what honestly mattered. That I had it. That I'd been right all this time, and here he was for me to find, waiting for me, holding me like I was some kind of a terrible miracle, something he'd never even hoped to have.

Then he pulled back, returning one hand to the side of my face. I leaned into it, taking a deep, shaking breath that felt like the first real one I'd had in more than fifty years.

Eleven

"Nothing is lost forever. Sometimes we just pretend not to understand what it would cost to find it."

—Juniper Campbell

In a throne room the size of a cathedral, kneeling atop the man I've been hunting for the last fifty years, who just stopped trying to attack me

EYES STILL BRIGHT WITH tears, Thomas looked up at me. My eyes weren't exactly dry, either, although I'd been working toward his reunion, while he'd just been invited. It was understandable that he was looking a little poleaxed, considering the circumstances.

He began to pull his hand away. I grabbed his wrist before he could complete the motion, holding it in place, and he smiled, a little unsteadily.

"Always did know what you wanted," he said. "Didn't you?"

"Hi, Thomas," I said, still holding his hand against my face. "Miss me?"

"Oh, well, it's not like I'm any stranger to being locked up while you go gallivanting, so I suppose I shouldn't have, but I missed you when you went off to college, and I missed you when I went off to hell," he said, shoulders dropping slightly as he started to relax. He didn't try to pull his hand away from my face again. Instead, he reached up with his remaining hand and slid it around behind my neck, pulling me down toward him.

Adrenaline is fun. It tries its best to keep us alive during a fight, and then when the fight is over, it does all sorts of clever things. Sometimes it exhausts us, or makes us hungry, or makes absolutely everything seem funny, no matter how inappropriate laughter is. It can bring relief, or it can bring crushing depression. Or it can bring the urge to be close to another person, to ground yourself in the act of touching and being touched.

I've always fallen at least partially into the last camp, which has made the past fifty years even more fun. When getting into a big fight makes you want to be touched so badly it causes physical pain, and there's no one around who you want touching you, you spend a lot of time feeling like your skin doesn't fit quite right. As Thomas pulled me down to him, I had to swallow the urge to shout with relieved joy, and then he was kissing me, and there wasn't room for much of anything else in my head.

Fifty years apart, and he still remembered the way I liked to be kissed, and I still remembered how to kiss him back. I'd been a little worried about that. I finally let go of his hand in order to wind my fingers into his hair. I was still angry, but that only added fuel to the last fifty years of helpless, hopeless longing, and so for the moment, I just kissed him, and he kissed me back, and it was enough. Dear God, it was enough to pay for everything I'd lost and everything I'd given up and everything I'd left behind.

At first, I didn't even register the distant sound of shouting. It was happening somewhere else, and it wasn't my problem. The door slamming open, that *could* become my problem, as could the footsteps that ran across the floor behind us, moving fast enough that the acoustics of the room didn't have time to swallow them the way they'd been swallowing every other sound. They slowed as they got closer, and I should probably have been concerned about that, should probably have stopped kissing Thomas long enough to look, but honestly, I didn't give a fuck. Let them stab me in the back, let this be where I died; at least I'd go knowing I'd been right all along. I hadn't thrown my entire life away for nothing.

"Boss?" said Sally, Mainer accent impossible to mistake for anything else.

Thomas was underneath me, and the floor was underneath *him*. He couldn't exactly pull away. What he could do was stop kissing me.

I decided to hate Sally a little bit.

"I'm fine, Sally," he said, breath hot against my cheek. It was one more reminder that he was here and real and alive, not an illusion or a cruel trick. Some sorcerers can do a lot with illusions. I've yet to meet one who can make a mimic of a man believable enough to keep seeming real to a woman when she's straddling him and they're making out like a couple of horny teenagers behind the diner. There were too many physical tells and reactions for even the most elaborate spell to keep track of.

"But she *hit* me," protested Sally, sounding furious.

Thomas sighed.

I knew that sigh. It meant he needed to pay attention to a problem, and I needed to stop distracting him. I hated that sigh almost as much as I hated Sally. I pushed myself away from him, sitting up, but didn't get off of him as I turned to glare over my shoulder at Sally and the four guards who had come with her.

One of them was the guard I had originally taken the fauchard away from, presumably looking for a little redemption. I didn't spare him from my disapproving expression. Couldn't they see that we were too busy for them to come crashing in and breaking the mood?

Also, now that I was no longer actively making out with my husband, my split lip was starting to ache, and I didn't like it. Kissing was not going to resume until I'd had some time to patch myself up, and that was enough to make me even crankier.

It showed in my face, too, because the guards looked even more uncomfortable. Beneath me, Thomas pushed himself up onto his elbows—not the most dignified position for an Autarch—and sighed again as I turned my attention back to him. "I'm sure she did," he said. "Alice has always been prone to thinking with her fists when under pressure. I apologize for the lack of introductions. Sally Henderson, meet my wife, Alice Price."

"Alice Price-Healy," I corrected smoothly. He flashed me a quick, semi-startled look. "I'll explain later, sweetheart."

I didn't start habitually hyphenating my last name until sometime in the eighties, when it became a common enough practice in America that I realized it was an option, and I discovered that some doors that slammed shut on the name "Price" would crack open, just a little, for the name "Healy." I have pride. That didn't mean I could afford to leave any tool unused during my search.

"Quite," he said, and returned his attention to Sally. "As I was saying, this is my wife. I'm sure she was unsettled to wake up disarmed and surrounded by strangers." He shot another glance at me. "We still have a great many things to discuss, but now that we've established our bona fides, I'm sure she won't be assaulting any more members of the household."

"Only if they make me," I said. "Don't start none, won't be none."

"Even so." He looked past me to Sally. "Does this address your concerns?"

"Not in the least," Sally said. "Your wife's *dead*. You've always been very clear on that point. 'She was the love of my life, but walls have more common sense than she did, and it's been fifty years. Even if Mary was able to keep her from doing something stupid right away, she'll have found plenty of opportunities to be stupid between then and now. I'm a widower, and it would be cruelty to try to tell myself otherwise.'"

"It would seem I underestimated her resourcefulness," said Thomas.

"I'm a human cockroach," I said blithely, and turned again, to see Sally glaring daggers at me.

"Or she's a trick intended to get you to lower your guard," she said stiffly. "This . . . woman . . . looks young enough to have been in the grade below me at school. She's not your wife."

"Yes, and we're going to discuss her apparent age as soon as we get a moment to ourselves," said Thomas. "I promise you, she has passed every test I've set before her, even the accidental ones, and I am convinced of her identity."

"I'm sorry I hit you," I said. "I may have thought I had good reasons, but I could have tried to discuss things further before I resorted to violence." Given that she'd been trying to convince me I'd never be able to get Thomas to believe that I was myself, I wasn't sure there had been any other ending to our conversation, but I was trying to apologize, not make excuses.

Sally scowled at me. "You're making a mistake, sir," she said. "This is a trick, and you're going to regret it."

"If so, it's my mistake to regret," he said. "You may all go. Thank you for your concern. Please tell the others I would like to be undisturbed for the rest of the afternoon."

Sally looked like she wanted to argue. She didn't. Instead, she took a long step back before turning on her heel and storming away, the guards following after her. The one whose fauchard I'd stolen paused to recover the abandoned voulge from the floor, then scurried after his companions, and in another minute, Thomas and I were alone again.

"Alice . . ." he said, reaching up to grasp my hips and pull my attention back around to him. He looked up at me, expression filled with what looked like genuine regret. "You have to let me up now. I need to *see* you."

There was still a note of genuine awe in the way he said my name, and that alone kept me from arguing as I pushed myself away from him and rose, leaning to offer him a hand. He took it. and I pulled him to his feet.

He looked me up and down as we both stood, not bothering to disguise the motion in the least. With me wearing nothing but a thin robe, it wasn't like I had a lot he couldn't see. He paused when he reached my left calf, asking, "Alice . . . where's the scar from the Bidi-taurabo-haza?"

"Oh, I got rid of that ages ago," I said. The damage the Bidi-taurabo-haza's venom had done despite the intercession of the crossroads had been severe enough to leave my left calf dented in and make long skirts a requirement for my job at the library. Hard to look like a demure lady who never causes trouble when something has so visibly taken a bite out of you.

Thomas frowned, a crease forming between his eyebrows. "I need you to be completely honest with me now."

"I didn't come all this way to lie to you."

"Did you find a way to make a bargain with the crossroads so you could come after me? I won't be angry if you—no, that's a lie, and if you're not allowed to lie, neither am I. I will be *absolutely furious* if you made a bargain with the crossroads after promising me you wouldn't, after seeing what it cost up close. But I'll understand." He looked briefly regretful. "I would have made another bargain after they took me if it had been the only way of getting back to you. I would have done virtually anything. But they never answered when I called. They never even let Mary come to see me."

"She wasn't allowed to tell me you were still alive," I said, stepping forward and taking his hands. Even being able to do that was a small thrill, and my hands remembered the shape of his so well that it was like finally remembering what shape *I* was supposed to be.

Your partner shouldn't complete you. Everyone is an entire person all on their own, and you don't need someone else to make you whole. But sometimes you know what the world is supposed to be so absolutely that when it changes without your consent, the absence of the people you've chosen as your own can be a gaping wound. Holding onto Thomas' hands, standing close enough that I could see him breathing, made me feel like that wound might finally have a chance to heal.

That's good. Some injuries are too dire to carry for long unless you want them to go septic. This one had started killing me a long time ago. Allowing it to heal wasn't going to take the damage away, but it might stop it from getting any worse.

"So how—"

"The crossroads promised you they'd never let me make a deal, and they wanted me to suffer," I said. "I got downstairs while the rift was still open, and Mary wouldn't let me go through after you because it would have hurt the baby. They took you while I was pregnant, so they'd have a head start on hiding you someplace I couldn't reach on my own. If I hadn't been pregnant, I would have been right behind you."

"Then I'm so glad you were," he said as he freed one hand from mine in order to cup my cheek again. "No one should have been here the way it was when I first arrived. This is a dead world."

"It's a dead world in a dead dimension, technically," I said. "That's why it's so hard to get in."

"I'm afraid that's on me," he said. "The nature of this reality is more connected to the reason that no one can get *out*. No one can manage it. Not even a Johrlac without the processing power of their entire hive mind behind them. Anyone who crosses the boundary is trapped in a world with no exits." He glanced down, eyes going dark. "I tried. For so long, I tried. I beat myself bloody against the walls of this place, I did everything I knew how to do and some things I had to intuit on my own, and some things I probably shouldn't have, and nothing changed a thing. I was trapped. We all are." He looked alarmed. "You shouldn't be here. You won't be able to leave. The children—"

"Are in their fifties now, and aren't my biggest fans," I said. "The grandkids will miss me. I'm sorry not to meet the great-grandkids. But our kids never met our grandparents, and they turned out okay."

"They did?" he asked, voice aching with need.

I smiled, nodding. "They did. They both got to grow up and start families of their own. They keep colonies in their walls and put up with me bopping in and out whenever my travels take me back to Earth. The mice call Kevin the God of Decisions Made in Necessity, and they call Jane the Silent Priestess, and they're happy, and they're loved, and they lived."

"It was a girl?"

"Yeah. She was a girl." I smiled a little, wistfully. We'd both been hoping for a daughter, someone to keep Kevin company and give the mice a new priestess to focus their adulations on. The birth of a God was exciting. The birth of a Priestess was a week-long revel that had come close to breaking several windows and had almost been enough to break me out of my misery for a few moments. Not quite; I'd been sunk so deeply in despair at that point that if not for Laura and Mary practically holding me down, I would have been halfway to the crossroads before the baby was even dry.

Jane and I never bonded, not the way Kevin and I had. She was born into a world with two missing parents, even if I was physically there for the first several weeks while I waited for my traitor body to recover enough to let me run. Laura had placed her in my arms, and she'd looked up at me with those big, dark eyes, and I'd felt nothing but resentment for the fact that she'd been the thing that kept me in Buckley when I needed to be going after Thomas.

Was it right? No. Was it healthy? No. But we learn who to be by watching who our parents are, and for most of my life, my example had been my father, the man who never learned to love in a way that allowed for letting go. I couldn't let go of Thomas. Kevin already adored Mary almost as much, if not more, than he loved me—he'd be fine. Loving Jane would have destroyed us both, and so I didn't even try. I looked at that little girl and I saw a punishment, and I hated myself for doing it, yet I did it all the same.

"She was beautiful," I said. "She still is. She and Kevin live near each other in Portland, Oregon, with their families. The kids stayed together."

He smiled a little, grief in his eyes. "I'm glad to hear that. I'm sorry to hear they aren't your biggest fans."

It wasn't a question. It still felt like one. I shrugged, not meeting his eyes, and said, "They didn't really know me when they were little. They mostly grew up with Laura and the Campbells. Kevin was apparently one of the best midway barkers they've ever had. The show still tries to lure them back when it passes through the Pacific Northwest."

"Alice . . ." His fingers fell away from my face. "Why did our children grow up with your mother's carnival, and not with you? Where were you?"

"I think you know where I was."

"I knew you'd have gone looking for me before you showed up here, but Alice . . . *fifty years*?"

"The minute I was well enough to get out of bed after the baby was born," I said. "In case they were still moving you farther away from me, I had to catch up. I had to reach you as fast as I could. And look—

even with a start that early, they kept you away from me for fifty years. I wasn't fast enough."

"Oh, *Alice*," he sighed, and folded me into his arms, and held me. I didn't resist. I just leaned into him, letting him hold me up and hold me to him in the same moment, and I couldn't imagine a world where I would have wanted to pull away. If I could chase the man for fifty years, surely I could hold onto him for just as long?

Eventually, however, he took a step back, tugging me along with him. I blinked. "You're leaving?"

"*We're* going someplace where we can have slightly more privacy." He shook his head, wryly amused. "And more furniture."

"Privacy works for me," I said, although I really didn't care that much about the furniture part. I pulled my hand out of his and took a few steps away. He watched me go, looking hurt and oddly calculating at the same time, like he was measuring my gait in some way I couldn't quite put my finger on. It made me uncomfortable, which wasn't right—Thomas watching me walk should have been the sort of thing that made me want to swing my hips harder and make him laugh, not something that made me want to stand perfectly still until the watching stopped.

"I'm just getting Mama's gun," I said, and stooped to retrieve the revolver from the floor, quickly popping the cylinder and verifying for myself that there were no more bullets inside. Sure, it had failed when Thomas tried to shoot me, but the first rule of gun safety is that no gun is unloaded unless you verify it for yourself. The second rule of gun safety is that it still isn't unloaded, because invisible bullets can happen to the best of us.

Maybe invisible bullets aren't really a thing, but acting like they are prevents a lot of accidents.

I snapped the cylinder shut and turned back to Thomas, smiling. "All good," I said, then paused, slightly taken aback by the expression on his face. He was watching me with a look of such all-encompassing fondness that it was almost confusing. Nothing I'd done justified that face, at least not that I could see.

"I'm sorry," he said. "I should have realized you'd be worried about the gun."

"It was my mother's."

"I know. I have the other one, if you want to put them back together." He offered me his hand, almost hesitantly. "Will you come with me?"

"I crossed a universe to find you," I said, and slid my hand back into his. "I'll go anywhere you want me to."

The narrow wooden door Thomas led me through had clearly been designed to blend in with the panels around it, virtually disappearing until you got close enough to see the seams. There weren't even any hinges on this side of the door. I raised an eyebrow.

"The people who originally constructed this place were gone long before my arrival, and they had a tropism toward circles," he said. "Any door with sharp edges was built by people who came later and took over what they'd left behind."

"Is that your polite way of telling me that you finally learned how to hang a door?"

"I'm handy!" he protested. "I patch drywall like a champion."

"You put holes in drywall like a champion," I corrected. "I had to hang all the doors for the mice, and those were so small that you should have been able to manage them one-handed in the dark."

He smiled and pressed a kiss to my temple before undoing a latch on the front of the door. It swung open easily. "I missed you so much," he said, and stepped through, pulling me with him into a dim, narrow tunnel that smelled of wood resin and time. No dust, though, and no spiders; just a faint underlying scent of strawberries and apples, making me suspect he'd been treating the wood in some way with bromeliad oil.

Interesting. Maybe he'd finally found a decent use for the stuff. The door swung closed behind us, throwing the hall into darkness. Thomas kept walking, pulling me along. He didn't create a light to guide us to our destination, and that was a little strange—once he'd fully relaxed into the idea that it was safe for him to be a sorcerer around me, he'd become casual about showing his magic, casting near-constant little spells to make things easier on the both of us. After a lifetime of hiding, he'd finally been able to relax and be himself. It seemed odd that he wouldn't do it here.

The hall was only about ten feet long. At the end, Thomas opened another door, revealing a small, square room with the same whitewashed walls I'd seen throughout the rest of the building.

There was a small, round window high on one wall, allowing sunlight to trickle into the room. The window was open, but largely choked off by a tangle of bromeliad vines. One opportunistic bromeliad flower had actually poked halfway into the room, and I could see small insects like moths with too many wings stuck to the petals, already in the process of dissolving. The scent of its pollen hung ripe and heavy in the air.

"I'll get that," said Thomas, and pulled away from me, picking up a heavy wooden paddle and using it to nudge the flower gently back outside before closing the window behind it. The pollen that was already in the room lingered, but it already seemed lighter without the flower emitting more. I took the moment to look around.

The room was simply furnished, which made it all the more jarring, because the furnishings were the sort of thing that wouldn't have seemed out of place at home in Buckley. A low bed was shoved into one corner of the room, too small for more than two people to sleep comfortably, and for two only if they were content to be piled practically on top of one another. There was a dresser, four drawers and a cluttered top, one drawer partially open to reveal a tangled welter of clothing. A single bookshelf dominated the wall opposite the bed, mostly filled with rocks and oddly shaped pieces of wood, rather than actual books. The top shelf was entirely devoted to a tattoo kit that looked half as sophisticated as the one I had at home, which was already an antique.

Something small was stuck to the wall above the bed, too distant from the door for me to see it clearly, even at this short remove. The bed itself was unmade, covers tangled and tossed and entirely unprepared for company. My pack leaned against the foot of the bed, top open, and my other revolver was on the bed itself, gleaming in the light from the window.

I crossed to the bed and knelt to check that my bag was still closed and retrieve my second gun, feeling better once both of them were in my hands where they belonged. "Do I get my clothes and the rest of my gear back eventually?" I asked.

"All your weapons are with Sally, except for the revolvers," said Thomas. "I kept those, because I thought . . ." He trailed off, looking momentarily like he wasn't sure whether he should continue. Then he nodded, apparently coming to an agreement with himself, and continued, "I thought, based on the description she'd given of our newest arrival, that you were the latest in a long line of assassins. One clever enough to have disguised yourself as my wife, but not clever enough to have started from an accurate description of her. And since you weren't the real Alice, you must have been responsible for her death as I couldn't see any other way she would have allowed those guns to leave her hands. Forgive me for thinking you'd be so easily overcome. After this much time . . . it grows easy to confuse what I know for the truth with what I hoped to be true. I'm afraid I've forgotten many of your failings in the intervening years, and remembered only how much I missed you, and your absolute conviction that there was no possible threat too big for you to handle. I had a shamefully easy time picturing a younger, faster assassin getting the drop on you in order to complete their disguise."

"So you kept my guns because you thought they were the only real thing about me?"

"Not to put too fine a point on it . . . yes." He looked at me hopelessly. "It's still somewhat difficult to believe you are who you claim to be."

I glanced back at the wall, at the small item stuck there. It was the original photograph that the painting Sally showed me had been based on. Of course it was. It was faded and worn, with tattered edges, but still recognizable, and looking at it, I could so easily understand his concern. I looked nothing like that girl.

The anger washed out of me, replaced by an exhaustion I had been fighting back for decades, never quite allowing myself to feel it, for fear that it would slow me down. I sat heavily on the edge of the bed, setting my revolvers on the mattress to either side of me, and just looked at him.

Thomas. My Thomas, the man I had loved since the first day I saw him, long before it was appropriate for me to go falling in love with an adult man. The man I had spent what sometimes felt like my entire life trying to find. He was still looking at me like I was a miracle. He was just looking at me like I was a stranger at the same time, and the dissonance of that expression in his eyes was painful. The silence stretched out between us.

"So this is where you live," I said finally, choosing to smash the silence rather than allow it to fester.

"Yes," he said, walking toward me. "And this is where I sleep. Alone."

There were no signs that anyone else shared this room with him, but hearing him confirm it reminded my body what it had been doing before we were so rudely interrupted. My breath caught, and I met his eyes, not letting myself look away.

"I know you still have questions," I said. "So do I."

"My questions can wait." He picked up the revolvers, placing them gently on the floor beside the bed, his eyes never leaving mine. "Can yours?"

"I've waited this long," I said. I expected him to sit beside me, but instead he slid down to kneel on the floor in front of me; from that position, he was still tall enough to be able to reach out and rest his hands on my hips.

"So have I," he said, pulling me toward him.

I wrapped my legs around his waist and my arms around his neck. "So we can finish this discussion later?"

"You were always less prone to prevarication in the afterglow," he said, and kissed me.

Kissing Thomas was like visiting a place I knew well but hadn't visited in years, long enough that everything was familiar and strange at the same time, that I felt like a tourist again, when I would have expected to feel like I was coming home. He pressed closer, still kissing me, and I responded in kind; my split lip protested, but in the rush of endorphins flooding my body, it was nowhere near enough to make me stop. Honestly, the sting just lit me up more.

I shoved myself backward to the middle of the bed and pulled him down on top of me, fumbling with our clothes. My robe was easy enough to remove, a simple tug on the knot letting me shrug out of it, but his clothes were a bit more complicated, trousers tied at either hip and shirt requiring us to pull apart long enough for me to work it off over his head.

A bruise was already forming where I'd kicked him. I wanted to touch every inch of him, to relearn the taste and texture of him with my fingers and tongue. The smell of swamp bromeliads hung in the air, and only the absence of an Aeslin choir celebrating our reunion kept it from feeling like home.

Except that it did. Everything about it felt like home and simultaneously like a dream, but I had had this dream so many times and this was too vivid for that.

Too real. Everything was magnified, my mind struggling with the disconnect; even the overwhelming pleasure felt like too much. I tried closing my eyes, but that just took me deeper into the feeling of the dream, and opening them was like double vision, reality overlaid by memory. His hands on my body felt as new as if he were touching me for the first time, and yet everything he did was so familiar, so right, that soon what was the same and what was different stopped mattering as my mind and body finally came together, and I didn't know where I ended and he began.

By the time he rolled away from me, panting and staring at the ceiling, I was no longer a stranger in that once-familiar country; I was back where I belonged. We both were.

I laced my fingers through his and rested my head against his shoulder, luxuriating in the mere warmth of his presence. He was here. He was real. This was really happening. I'd been right all along. That, or this dimension was a honey trap of hitherto undiscovered quality, and I was going to while away the rest of my life in a happy illusion of fucking, eating food that wasn't really there, and feeling like I'd finally found what I'd been looking for all this time. Under the circumstances, I'd take it.

If my choice was a perfect lie or continuing to run long after my quest turned hopeless, I'd take the lie. Maybe that makes me weak, but I honestly don't care.

Thomas turned his head to kiss my temple, burying his face in my hair. "You still smell right. God help me, you smell like yourself."

I pulled away slightly, not far enough to make him think I was going anywhere—not far enough to make my own skin start longing for him again, which seemed like a genuine danger right now—and looked at him. "You sound like you weren't sure. Were you not sure?"

"Alice . . ." He sighed and smiled wryly at me. "The crossroads stole me from my home and family and threw me so far away that even the hope of homecoming faded. I know how much time has passed here. Sally's arrival . . ." His smile faded. "I won't say I had been *very* hopeful before she came, but Sally's arrival carried with it something terrible: a date. The year the crossroads took her, which was so far in the future of our lives together that it was unbearable. She was able to tell me precisely how many years I had been away from my family, and when she spoke, I knew that you were long gone. I love you too dearly to have any illusions about whether you'd ever have learnt how to be careful."

"Not a skill of mine," I admitted. Being careful isn't something we Healys have ever been particularly good at. Both my mother and my grandmother died alone in the woods after going out on what had probably seemed like perfectly normal hunting trips, too commonplace to need backup. I know better than most how easy it is for a moment of carelessness to cost you everything you have.

"So when Sally told me a woman had appeared, and told me about the weapons you'd been carrying, I knew you had to be an assassin. And then you came to me, and you fought like my Alice, and you spoke like my Alice, and when you got angry, you even glared at me like my Alice, and I wanted so badly to believe that you were the woman I had lost. I wanted it badly enough to lie to myself, if necessary, but not badly enough to betray her if I was wrong. And I knew I had to be wrong. I knew there was no way. But then I kissed you, and . . ."

He stopped, and I held my silence until it was obvious he was going to do the same. Finally, I asked, "So that's why you slept with me?"

The idea was like a knife to the gut—and that's something I've experienced more than often enough to have a solid sense of what it feels like, and to be a lot calmer about it than I probably ought to be. I took a deep breath, tamping down my initial reaction, which involved assaulting him, and wouldn't have been a polite way to say, "Thanks for not being dead after I spent five decades trying to find you." My second reaction was similar, if less violent, and by my third, I was able to pull away and sit up, gathering the blankets around me as I looked at him.

To his credit, he knew he'd fucked up; I could see it in his eyes. He sat up, widening the space between us, and let his hands rest between his knees, staring down at them. "You're not the first, you know," he said. "Only the most recent. I've had an 'Alice' show up here on a fairly regular basis since I arrived. Some of them were even human, people who'd made their own crossroads bargains and been convinced that killing one little villain would let them go back to their lives. Most weren't. Humans are rare, pan-dimensionally, but people who look like humans are common as rocks. The crossroads . . . I always wondered why they cared so much about me, when they didn't seem to care about anyone else they left here." He chuckled, mirthlessly. "They were afraid of exactly this. That you'd beat them somehow, and find me, and bring me home. You terrified a cosmic entity by being too damn stubborn to give up when it should have been the right thing to do. So they sent their assassins, and I thought . . ."

He sighed. "It's been a while since the last one. I thought it was finally over, and then you asked me why I had kept Fran's guns, and—I used to *repair* them for you, Alice. I *know* those guns. I knew they were yours. And them being here meant that either they were here with you, or you were gone. They were the proof that you were gone. By the time you put me on the floor, you were either the best imposter they had ever sent, and I was a widower, or you were the woman I'd been grieving for all this time. Either way, there wasn't anyone for me to betray."

He looked back at me and winced. "Say something. Please."

I took before I took another breath and asked the only question that still mattered: "And *now* do you believe me?"

"I believe you either *are* my wife, or such a good imitation that even she wouldn't blame me for being fooled," he said, looking briefly, deeply weary. "Or at least I hope she would forgive me, but I couldn't ... I just missed you so much. I tried, Alice. I tried so hard to get out of here and come home, but I couldn't. The walls are all but unbreakable. I couldn't find a way back to you, I couldn't find—"

"It's all right," I said. "You found a way to wait for me, and now I'm here, and we're going to find a way home together."

He looked at me, and his face fell, and with no more warning than that, he began to cry. I pulled myself closer and wrapped my arms around him, and just let him weep against my shoulder for as long as he needed to. If nothing else, I could do that much for him. I could be here.

Finally, after everything, I could be here.

Twelve

"My God, Enid, you beautiful fool. What have you done?
How am I supposed to keep on doing this without you?"
—Alexander Healy

Naked in a bed with a man everyone thinks is dead, but who is
most definitely and empirically alive, thank you very much

IT TOOK A SURPRISINGLY long time for Thomas to stop crying. Surprising mostly because my eyes stayed dry the whole while, watching him closely, but not shedding a single tear. When he finally wiped
his eyes, he looked at me somewhat bemusedly and asked, voice soft,
"Alice . . . why aren't you crying?"

"Oh. I mean, I guess because I don't have anything to cry about." I
pushed myself into a sitting position again, not bothering to pull the
covers around myself this time. It wasn't like I had anything he hadn't
seen anyway, even if much of it had been substantially more scarred
the last time he'd had the opportunity. "You were out here, separated
from your family and wondering if we were still alive for you to come
home to. Well, I was left on Earth with the kids, and no proof the
crossroads hadn't chucked you straight into the first event horizon
they had access to. So I had to convince myself. I had to spend so
much energy believing you were alive and out here for me to find that
it's been all that kept me moving for the last fifty years. I'm sure I'll
have a little breakdown later, when I realize I don't know what to do
with myself anymore, but right now, I'm mostly just relieved to finally
know for sure that I was right. Sally showing up here and knowing
what time it was at home may have made you lose hope, and I bet that
hurt. I bet that hurt a *lot*. Well, I never lost hope. I couldn't. If I had,
I would have fallen apart completely. So for me, this is all less

overwhelming and more . . . inevitable is I guess the term. It's inevitable. You were inevitable." I smiled at him. "We were inevitable."

"I see." He frowned. "Can we finish that conversation now, do you think?"

"Unless you want to go for round two," I offered. We had a lot of lost time to make up for.

He shook his head. "Perhaps later," he said. "I'm not as young as I used to be."

"All evidence to the contrary," I said, half-grumbling, half-appreciative. "But if it's answering questions time, can we start with how you've barely aged a day?" I paused. "Oh, I almost forgot." I pressed two fingers to one of the small stars tattooed along my hip bone, concentrating. The star flared and vanished, leaving a blank spot where it had been. My head spun, briefly, before my body equalized and recovered from the relatively small expenditure.

I pulled my hand away to find Thomas staring at me.

"Alice," he said. "what was that?"

"My tattoos are all single-use," I said. "They have to be, or I can't carry them. Anything larger would require me to have the magic to power them, and I don't."

"Not naturally, but you've been traveling between dimensions," he said. "The membrane that adheres to you should be enough to power . . . never mind." He shook his head, clearly abandoning the thought. "I know you can't have been doing your own ink, not if it's magically-imbued, and whatever your artist told you has to be what we go by. But Alice, what was the charm you just activated?"

"Contraception charm," I said. "I have five more. I don't think we want to be heading back to Earth with me pregnant, and I think we both have a concerted interest in repeating the activity that might risk it. I don't have an implant, and I don't travel with condoms."

Thomas blinked. "What 'implant?'"

"It's one of the options women have for contraception these days," I said. "If you have one, you won't get pregnant, even if you're sexually active."

"Ah," he said. "I'm sure catching me up on the ways the world has changed will be the work of several years."

"I'm looking forward to it."

"As am I. But Alice . . . why did you need contraception charms?"

"I'm a woman who's mostly been traveling alone through some dodgy places, filled with pretty dodgy people," I said. "It seemed like, well. Better safe than sorry if that makes sense. And it never happened." It seemed suddenly very important to be sure he understood that. "I was being cautious, for once, and I was always, always armed, and the sort of people who want that sort of thing were usually the sort of people who didn't want to be shot repeatedly."

"So why so many, if it was just a precaution?"

"Oh, because it turns out they don't just work to counter possible pregnancy," I said. "They also work on parasites and oviposited larvae."

He was silent for a long moment, but I could see his jaw working as he chewed over what he was going to say next, so I waited for him to catch up with his own thoughts. Finally, slowly, he said, "Alice, why do you know that?"

"A surprising number of the dimensions adjacent to Earth are overrun with Apraxis wasps," I said. "Seems like once they get in there, they tend to take over, and they see anyone who passes through as an opportunity to expand the hive mind."

"And did you learn this before or after you started requesting contraception tattoos?"

"It takes three days from implant to hatch. I made it to Empusa on time." I'd collapsed on Naga's doorstep with almost eight hours left before the infant Apraxis finished their gestation and emerged from my flesh, chewing their way out of me and swallowing my mind in the process. I'd been shaky and unsure of who I was for days after that, although there hadn't been any permanent damage that we'd ever been able to confirm. Naga had been so angry.

His anger was nothing to what I saw now, brewing in Thomas' eyes. "And you kept *going* in that direction?"

"It seemed promising," I said. "Contraception charms are small. They don't take up a lot of skin."

"That's not why I'm . . . Alice, didn't you ever stop to ask yourself whether it was *worth* it, if finding me meant you had to put yourself through that?"

"No," I said. "Never."

He was silent for a moment, and then said in a measured tone, "It's been long enough that I don't know whether I get to say I don't approve—I rather feel like I lost that privilege when the crossroads took me away from you and our children—but I don't like it. You are precious to me, Alice. You have always been precious to me, even when we've been far apart from one another. The idea of someone harming you makes me want to harm *them*. So how am I meant to react when the person doing the harm is you, to yourself?"

I didn't know how to answer that, other than with anger, and anger didn't feel like the right reaction, not yet. Still, a part of me wanted to rage. How dare he? After all this time, after I'd done all this work, how dare he judge me for how I'd done it? He was lucky I'd bothered to come for him at all, when he was the one who'd sold himself to the crossroads in the first place. I could have stayed in Buckley with my babies. I could have learned how to let go. Mary had been more than willing to help me do that if I'd wanted to. And instead, I'd chosen fifty years of running and bleeding and loneliness, for the sake of a man who wanted to *judge* me?

Even as the anger flared in my chest, I did my best to damp it down, reminding myself that he had made his bargain to save my life. If he hadn't done that, we wouldn't be here because I'd be dead. All my other choices had been my own. The only person who'd done any of this to me was me.

"I did what I had to do," I said. "I'd do it all over again if I knew this was where we'd wind up. And I'm not sure I approve of all *your* choices, either. To start with, what's with this whole Autarch deal? The last thing I expected to do was get here and find out that my husband has turned into some sort of dystopian warlord—and with a *harem*, no less!"

"A . . . harem? What are you talking about?"

"Don't all those women belong to you?"

"*God*, no." He looked horrified enough by the idea that I laughed. I couldn't help myself.

"Good," I said. "Because just so we're clear, I don't plan on sharing you with any other wives."

"I forgot how adorable you were when you let yourself give in to jealousy," he said, with the kind of smile that meant he was suppressing a laugh.

I glared at him. "I'm glad you're finding this amusing, but given that when I woke up—again, let me stress, basically *naked*—the first person I met told me I was in the women's quarters, and all newcomers were under the protection of the Autarch, perhaps you can see how I might have gotten the wrong impression."

"Yes, and I'm sorry about that," he said. "The situation is . . . somewhat complicated, and I owe you an explanation." He sat up, leaning back against the wall beside me with his shoulder touching mine, and reached out to intertwine my fingers with his, apparently feeling safe to do so. I didn't pull away. We had a lot of unpleasant conversations ahead of us, and we had to hold onto each other.

"When I first arrived here, I landed in the middle of a war," he said. "The crossroads threw anyone they'd made a bargain with and wanted to dispose of into this convenient killing jar, and some of those people . . . well, weren't very nice. They were killing each other. I arrived and realized I would have to put a stop to it if I wanted things to be stable enough to let me research a way out of here. So I took over."

He made it sound so simple. From the shadows in his eyes, it had been anything but. He looked like a man who'd seen things he could never unsee, done things he could never undo, and regretted that fact every day of his life.

"Some of the people making war on their neighbors were doing it for the control of resources," he continued, looking down at his hands, resting as they were between his knees. "Water is scarce here. Food was equally so before we began establishing the necessary safety to let us tend our fields. Both of those were things to be controlled."

"Guessing 'women' also made that list, huh?" I ventured.

Thomas nodded miserably. "Not only women—the strong enslaved the weak without much regard for gender—but yes. They were in hell. This is a hell world, and they were literally in hell. So when I took everything else as my own, I took the people as well. But it isn't quite how it appears."

I raised my eyebrows and said nothing, giving him the space to continue.

Thomas sighed. "I became Autarch by killing the previous Autarch, but he wasn't the only—how did you put it?—dystopian warlord this world had produced. There are still other factions here who are very much in that mold, and over the years I've found the most effective strategy is to let them believe that I'm cut from the same cloth, only stronger and more ruthless. If my people suspect a new arrival may have been sent to infiltrate our ranks, we don't let them see how things truly operate until we know if they can be trusted."

"So all that was just . . . what, a show for my benefit?"

"Much of it, yes. Do you really think all those women have nothing better to do than sit around all day pretending to be my concubines?"

"I'm sure some of them wouldn't mind," I muttered. "And I can see how Sally might be your type."

He raised an eyebrow. "My 'type'?"

"Human, stubborn, likes to get into fights?"

"If I have a type, it's only because of *you*," he retorted. "Sally was seventeen when she arrived in this dimension, and even were I not a married man, if you'll recall, I refused to see you in that manner until you were well into your twenties. What's more, Sally has no interest in the male of her species. She's quite content to serve as my lieutenant, and she has no illusions about our relationship."

He looked at his free hand, where his wedding ring caught the light. "I can't say others didn't offer, but I never took any of them up on it. It would have meant admitting that I had given up all hope of ever getting home. I couldn't do that. Not to you, and not to our children, and most of all, not to myself. Some days, the pretty lie of finding a way out of here was all that could keep me from giving in to despair."

I didn't say anything, just tightened my fingers around his. Thomas flashed me a quick, grateful look before looking away again, like this was all easier to say when he didn't have to face me as he said it.

"So you thought I was another of those crossroads assassins," I said, and shook my head. "But why were the crossroads trying to kill you? They already had you. I thought the point for them was to torture you as much as possible, and being trapped in hell seems worse than just being dead."

"You would think so. But 'the mind is its own place, and in itself can make a heaven of Hell, a Hell of heaven.'"

"Now you've lost me."

"I'm a sorcerer," he said. "A fully trained, adult sorcerer who understands what my own magic is capable of. This world doesn't have much magic remaining to it, but everyone the crossroads deposited here was ripped through multiple dimensional walls on their way to the final barrier, and they landed with a heavy harvest weighing them down. With their consent, I've been collecting it all this time, and using it to power various passive effects."

"Like the KEEP OUT signs Sally was talking about?"

"Yes, those are a major one. I can't actually *close* the border between us and the world we're still somehow connected to, but I can make it more difficult to penetrate. The translation spell that runs through the public areas is another. It slows language acquisition on the occasions when someone new does arrive, but also eases integration sufficiently that we have fewer conflicts and less panic. For the most part, my people cooperate to our common advantage, and we have no slavery, rape, or murder. I suspect the crossroads didn't care for my improvements to their terrarium."

"They wouldn't," I said. "So if the biggest standing spell is the barrier, what happens to the linguistics when you run out of magic taken from new arrivals?"

"We're working on learning to speak to each other outside the spell's border," he replied. "I don't have enough personal magic in this world to fuel that one on my own. The barrier will hold until it doesn't. You were the first person to arrive in some time."

I paused. "About three years?"

"Yes. How did you—"

"I think I might know why that is, but it's going to take a long time to explain and just distract us from the conversation we're trying very badly not to have, so if you could trust me on this? I don't think you need the barrier anymore." The crossroads wasn't going to be pitching anyone through the walls of the universe, and the locals on Cornale hadn't been the sort to go hunting for ways into the dead world they hated.

Thomas looked at me gravely for a long, long moment before he said, "I'll trust you, providing you will explain at some point. And I'll answer the question we're both avoiding first, but once I do, I'll expect the same reply from you."

"Of course."

"Very well, then. Using the magic I get from new arrivals to fuel the standing spells has freed up my own, limited as it is here, for more selfish uses." He let go of my hand to press two fingers to the tattoo on his throat. "This anchors a spell that keeps me from aging at the customary rate. It took me five years to design it and gather the necessary strength to power it, but once started, it continued running, and will until I make it stop."

"Why?"

He shrugged, looking briefly sheepish. "I still had hope, five years in, that I was clever enough to find a way out of this place, out of this predicament. If I could return to the wider reality, I could navigate my way home. I knew I needed to get back to you and the children before too much time had passed, and I know time can run at different rates in different dimensions. So I . . . stopped myself, for lack of a better phrasing."

He'd been afraid of the same thing I was: of adding too much time to the distance between us and not being able to find his way home. "That makes sense. Was that always something you could do?"

"It's something any sorcerer who's managed to grow past their element can do," he said. "Which brings us to the part I suspect I'm not going to like very much."

"I know what you want to ask," I said. "So go ahead. Ask."

He closed his eyes for a moment, taking a deep breath, before he opened them, looked at me, and said, "If I were a betting man, I'd lay odds that right now, physically, you're not of legal drinking age in the United States, unless it's been lowered to nineteen while I've been gone."

"Nope," I said. "It's still twenty-one." Thomas might be the only person who could look at me and accurately estimate the current age of my body. He'd been there the first time I passed through all these years, when I'd been moving at the normal rate, and not going in jumps and starts. "But I was never a big drinker, unless you count the cooking sherry."

"I've looked you over fairly thoroughly at this point, and none of the tattoos I've seen have been keyed to counteract aging. Nor would they be enough, as single-use charms, unless they were activated as soon as time had passed, and then you'd have no room left for anything else."

"That's not how we've been putting me back together."

"So what *have* you been doing?"

"Oh, it's easy," I said brightly, and began to explain the process, starting with the moment when they lowered me into the bath and continuing until I passed out. He only interrupted twice, the first time to ask if I was awake for the whole process, and the second time to ask how many sessions I'd been through. Neither of my answers seemed to make him very happy. After the second he got off the bed and started pacing around the room, still naked. It would have been funny, if he hadn't looked like he was getting ready to murder someone with his bare hands. I shrank back into the pillows.

"Thomas?" I asked, voice small. "Are you mad at me?"

"What? No. If anything, at myself. I should have anticipated that you'd continue to be yourself after I was gone and would orchestrate some means of coming after me. And I should absolutely, without question, have prepared you better to take care of yourself out there. This was all predictable. I should have seen it coming." He turned to look at me. "I am, of course, absolutely furious with your adoptive uncle, and will be seeing how much *he* enjoys being skinned alive while forced to remain conscious and aware of the entire process, although I'm afraid I lack the stomach or the malice to put him through the process once for every time he had it done to you. He'll die much more quickly than I believe is fair, or just, but at times we must accept our limitations." His eyes were hard. "As long as he dies screaming, I'll consider this debt paid."

I watched from the bed as he resumed his pacing, a frown on my own face "I don't understand why you're so angry," I said. "Naga has been helping me. If it weren't for him, I would never have been able to stay alive long enough to find you. I've been injured pretty badly a whole bunch of times now—badly as in 'verge of death' badly. And he's always gotten me back on my feet."

"Back on your feet, covered in carnival charms, and back to making him the richest man in his home dimension," Thomas snapped, before he paused and looked at my expression. Visibly calming himself, he walked back to the bed and sat on the very edge, twisting so he could watch me as he spoke. "He told you that you needed single-use charms because you weren't a sorcerer, correct?"

"Correct," I said warily.

"That's true under normal circumstances. If you're not magically gifted, you can't draw on the pneuma yourself. You can use portable charms and objects, like the darks that people make for bogeymen, regardless of any inborn capabilities. Tattoos are a riskier proposition. They're anchored to your flesh, and if you haven't the magic to power them, they'll consume you instead. I would never risk a non-practitioner with magical tattooing." His voice turned hard again at the end, and I had to fight the urge to shrink away.

This was *Thomas*. He was the man I'd married, the man I'd thrown away everything to make my way back to. More, he was naked. While I was naked, too, my mother's guns were at the foot of the bed in easy reach. If things went poorly, I'd bet on me before I'd bet on him.

"But those are normal circumstances," he continued. "In the case of someone like a routewitch, who can use distance itself to fuel their magic, tattooing is much safer."

"I'm not a routewitch," I protested.

"No, but you've been traveling between dimensions. Remember how they work? Every time someone passes between worlds, a trace of the pneuma from the membrane separating them adheres to the traveler's skin. It's why snake cults remain so popular."

"They don't have a lot of resistance, so they can pass through the membrane easily," I said.

"Precisely. Meaning that when a snake cult manages to summon one, they can harvest the membrane that has adhered to their new 'god' and use it to do great things. Pure pneuma is one of the most powerful magical tools there is. A dimensional traveler should be dripping with it. Especially one who's been pushing through membranes for fifty years." He paused, clearly expecting me to pick up on the thread of what he was saying.

I've never been a fan of picking up on threads. If you can't punch through something or blow it up, what's the point? I looked at him blankly for a long moment before shaking my head. "Okay."

He looked confused by my lack of curiosity, then shrugged and said, "You should be. And you're not."

"What?" I looked at my arm, like I would somehow be able to see the dimensional membrane that had never been visible before. "Not at all?"

"Oh, you have quite a bit adhering to you now, and I'll peel it away later, with your permission, to add to the standing effects. We'll be able to run the translation spell for longer than I thought. But, Alice, you don't have fifty years' worth. You could have been keying your tattoos to the pneuma you were harvesting just by moving between dimensions." He looked at me gravely. "You could have set up your own anti-aging tattoos."

I blinked slowly. It sounded like he was saying that it had never been necessary to flense me; like the energy generated by my travels would have been enough to do the same thing with substantially less trauma. But that couldn't be true. Naga had been helping me. Naga had been making sure I was put back together every time things went wrong, supplying me with maps and directions and bounties to collect while I'd been out there anyway, and . . .

"So every time they skinned me, it peeled off the pneuma?" I asked slowly, feeling out the words.

"Yes," said Thomas. "Every time. After fifty years, you should be carrying enough of a magical charge to power a continent. Or destroy one. Right now, you've got enough of it stuck to you to destroy a city, not crack a world in two."

"Naga . . . told me . . . he said there were no worlds capable of supporting human life in this direction," I said, still speaking slowly and deliberately. It felt like I was standing on the edge of a cliff that had started to crumble under my feet, throwing everything I thought I knew into disarray. "I tried to come this way more than forty years ago, and he said no. He said I'd never survive. He said there was nothing here to find."

My heart was beating too fast, and my chest was getting tight, making it more and more difficult for me to breathe. I stared at Thomas, but I wasn't really seeing him anymore. I was seeing the cracks in my relationship with Naga, the places where the things he'd told me and the things I'd been going through hadn't quite matched up, all the things that had never made sense.

The questions I should have asked—the questions Helen said I *had* asked but didn't remember asking. His personal Johrlac took my pain away every time they laid me down and covered my skin in new ink. What else had they been taking away? And for how long?

"He *lied* to me," I said wonderingly. Thomas reached over and pushed my hair back from my face.

"Yes, darling, I'm afraid he did," he said. Then, with more alarm: "Alice? Are you all right?"

It was getting harder to keep breathing. I dug my hands into the blankets, balling them into fists, and bent forward to stare at my own knees, shaking. I was distantly aware that I was having a panic attack but had no idea how to make it stop.

Thomas got off the bed. I grabbed for his hand, suddenly certain that if he left my sight, he'd be gone again, and I'd have to start looking for him from the beginning. Gently, he extricated himself and leaned over to kiss the top of my head. "I'll be right back," he said. "You have my word. I've made no further bargains, and even if I had, I have a snake to kill, meaning I can't go off to get abducted by cosmic forces of ultimate evil right now. Stay here, all right?"

I couldn't have moved if I'd wanted to. I managed to nod, barely, and dug my fingers into the covers again as he walked away, breathing faster and faster.

Naga had been lying to me. *Naga* had been *lying* to me. This could have been over *decades* ago. I could have gone home to my children while they were still *children*, I could have been a part of their lives, I could have saved my family, I could—

I could hear the click of the window being opened, and the snick of small shears. Then Thomas sat back down on the edge of the bed, and said, voice reasonable and very distant, "I want to give you something to calm you down. Do I have your permission?"

I still couldn't breathe. I couldn't even nod anymore. Everything was crashing down on top of me, walls eroded by relief and finally feeling like I could relax. How much damage had I done to myself in the process of running? How much of it could have been avoided?

"Oh, *Alice* . . ." Thomas put his arm around me, drawing me up against his body. "If I wasn't already convinced, this would convince me. I never wanted to see you fall apart like this again. But it's not something you can fake. Here. Please."

Carefully, he peeled the fingers of my right hand away from the snarl of blankets, lifting it in his own. I didn't try pull free, not even as he turned my palm upward and pressed the long, thorny stem of a swamp bromeliad into it, not quite hard enough for the thorns to break my skin. He gave me an expectant look and relaxed slightly as I curled my fingers closed around the stem, driving the thorns into my own flesh.

As always with swamp bromeliads, they were wickedly sharp, but so thin I barely felt them entering me as I slowly turned the flower toward my face and inhaled the smell of apples and strawberries. A wave of exhaustion swept over me, accompanied by a loosening in the bands around my chest, and I toppled gently over into the bed.

Thomas was still there, stroking my hair and watching me with open, obvious concern.

"Rest, love," he said. "Just . . . get some rest. I'll be here when you wake up."

You better be, I thought but couldn't quite say as my eyes drifted shut and I drifted off to sleep, soothed by the familiar, soporific scent of swamp bromeliads and sweat. It smelled like home. I inhaled deeply, and I was gone, slipping into the comfortable dark of peace.

Thirteen

"I only ever wanted to get her clear of the blast radius before the bomb went off. Was that so much for a father to ask?"

—Jonathan Healy

Still in the same bed, still naked, and somewhat tragically alone, because sometimes the world isn't fair

H E WASN'T.
There, I mean. I opened my eyes on an empty room, the light coming through the vine-clogged window much dimmer and more diffuse, the flower still in my hand, wilted from the lack of water, but otherwise fully intact. I hadn't rolled or thrashed in my sleep. I sat up slowly, groggy and still faintly sedated by the lingering effects of the sap. Swamp bromeliads are carnivorous plants, and they eat larger prey than most of their kind. They can do that primarily because their sap is one of the best sedatives I've ever encountered. It seems to work on everything with a circulatory system, and it has no real negative side effects. I probably shouldn't think about operating heavy machinery for an hour or two, but I hadn't been planning on doing that anyway.

"Thomas?" I knew I was speaking to no one but myself even before I opened my mouth. There's something in the quality of the air that tells you when you're alone. Uncurling my fingers from the half-crushed stem, I dropped the flower on the bed and stood, shaky and dizzy but functional . . . and grateful, honestly. If I'd woken up alone when I *wasn't* drugged, I would probably have lost my shit.

My guns and my bag were where I'd left them, and something new had appeared: my clothing, boots and all, was piled on the chair by the door, neatly folded and clean, with my weapons in a tidy stack off to one side. There was also a tray with a few covered dishes, and a pitcher and basin with a washcloth and towel beside it. It was hard not to take that as some sort of hint. I teetered over to it, too drugged to be offended, and gave myself a quick cold-water scrub-down.

The cold water was enough to clear some of the fog from my head, and the fact that I was alone suddenly seemed a lot more alarming. Food was the last thing on my mind, and my stomach was in a tight enough knot that I wasn't sure I could have eaten if I'd wanted to. I dropped the washcloth onto the tray and toweled myself briskly dry before turning to my clothes.

There's a security in properly fitted boots and support garments, a feeling of comfort in knowing that I could run if I had to. Maybe that feeling would fade once I made it home with Thomas by my side, and once I talked Thomas out of killing Naga, who might have been less honest with me than he could have been, but had still been helping me, keeping me alive long enough for me to get here.

I felt even better once I had my boots on and laced and my knives secreted around my body, their weight comforting against my skin. I finished by strapping my holster around my hips and pulling the chain that held my wedding ring and Mama's engagement ring out of a side pocket. I didn't always wear it, out of fear of losing them, but it should be safe enough here, at least for the moment. I fastened it behind my neck, shook out my hair, and wiped the last stinging remnants of bromeliad sap off on my shorts before turning for the door.

It wasn't locked. I was grateful for that. Waking up alone in a locked room might have been enough to convince me that everything from reaching the throne room of the Autarch on had been a dream, and I had just fallen into a nest of Johrlac or something similar. As it stood, I was unhappy to have woken up alone, but I wasn't doubting my memories.

Yet. That would come. The thing that didn't make sense to me was why, if Naga had been sending me the wrong way for such a long time on purpose, he had finally helped me go in the right direction. For him to have been intentionally misleading me, he would have needed to know where Thomas was all along, and if that was the case, then he'd been a fool to finally let me head in the right direction. It didn't add up.

But then, the crossroads hadn't been dead before I started this particular leg of my journey. And I hadn't told him they were gone. I'd been so focused on getting started that it just hadn't come up. Maybe their absence changed things somehow, made this all possible when it really wouldn't have been before. Maybe the situation was different.

And I'd had the map. The map, which changed everything I thought I knew about this end of the dimensional network, and which made it possible for me to make a solid case for heading in one direction over another. I was ascribing malice where there probably wasn't any. Naga was my friend, had been since I was a child. He might not always think like a human did, but that didn't mean he was going to *hurt* me.

Mammals and reptiles are different, that's all. I stepped into the short hallway, following it quickly to its end, and paused to listen; unfortunately, the door was too thick for me to tell if anyone was out there. Gingerly, I eased the door partially open and peeked into the room.

Sally was sitting on the short step in front of the throne, which was positioned so as to block my view of the occupant, if there was any. From the angle of her head and the fact that I could hear her talking now that the door was open, I was guessing that there was. I slipped through the door, easing it shut behind me, and walked forward, keeping my hands carefully visible.

I had made it about six feet before Sally noticed me and stiffened, rising. I held up my hands so she could see that they were empty, but I kept on coming.

"You," she said, tone utterly flat.

"Yeah," I said. "Do I need to apologize again? I didn't mean to be a bad guest and hit you."

"Yes, you did," she countered. "You hit me very intentionally. I was *there*."

"All right, yes, I hit you on purpose, but you took all my stuff, and then you called me names and said I wasn't believably myself, so you can probably understand why I was a little cranky at the time."

"I still don't think—"

"Sally." Thomas stood, coming into view. He was dressed again— pity, that—in essentially the same thing he'd been wearing before. I wondered whether he'd remembered to pack more weapons this time. I'd been too distracted by the novelty of undressing him after fifty years to really pause and count the knives, but he'd been carrying far fewer than I would have expected. "We've discussed this. I have verified her identity to my own satisfaction, and if that was sufficient for me, who knows her best, it can be sufficient for you as well."

"Yup, you said that the woman who looks almost exactly like your dead wife did when she was a college student is somehow *actually* your dead wife, who I would like to remind you would be an *octogenarian* at this point, if she weren't, you know, *super dead*, and then you smiled too much and walked around like a man who'd just gotten laid for the first time in fifty years, so you'll forgive me if I'm not really trusting your judgment right now." She flipped her hair, folded her arms, and tried to glare at us both at the same time.

I stopped where I was, lowering my hands. I didn't want to seem like a threat. I was absolutely a threat. No question of that. Instead of pressing the issue of why I'd hit her, and why I'd been justified to do so, I looked to Thomas and said, "I woke up and you were gone. Where did you go?"

"Matters arose which required my attention," said Thomas regretfully. "I would rather have been there. I'm sorry."

"Yeah, and while he may or may not be your long-lost husband, he's still the Autarch here, in case you hadn't noticed," said Sally. "There are hundreds of people who need him. I want to see you tell them you've come to steal him off to another dimension because you 'need him more.' I'd like to see you *try*."

"I don't think you want to get into that pissing contest with me," I said, voice gone low and tight. "No one wins if we start that. A lot of people lose a lot of blood, and we never figure out how to live with each other. And surprise, you're gonna have to figure out how to live with me. No matter what happens from here, you're going to be putting up with me for a while."

"Lot of assumptions in that," she said, almost casually.

I paused to consider how angry Thomas was likely to be if I broke his lieutenant. Sadly, "very" was the most likely outcome I could think of. People don't like to follow reunions with assault. "I know I am who I claim to be. Whether you believe that I've proven myself to my husband or not, I know I'm telling the truth, and that matters more than whatever you think of me. I also know, because I know the man I married—maybe not all the details of who he is right now, but the essential core of the man—that there's no way he's going to leave all the people he's promised to protect just because I show up and say that it's time to go home. So either we're all getting out of here together, or we're not getting out of here at all."

Judging from the look of profound relief that spread over Thomas' face, I had just identified and shortcut an awkward conversation that he hadn't been much looking forward to having with me, yet it only made sense. His loyalty was one of the best things about him. Not the first thing to catch my eye—I'd been a hormonal teenager in a small town, and he'd been the exciting stranger who moved into a house near my woods and made my father angry just by existing. Honestly, the rest had been a bonus to the fact that he made my father want to lock me in my room until I died.

We were both different people now than we had been before. I wasn't deluded enough to think that things were going to go back to the way they had always been, or that we could just go home and pick up where we'd left off. But just the fact that he'd still been wearing his wedding ring told me that he was still the patient, loyal man I'd married.

"What?" Sally blinked, glancing back at Thomas. "But you have kids. He told me—"

"Okay, wow, sexist much, assuming that he'd be willing to abandon the kids and I never would, just because I'm their mother? I genuinely think he'd have been a better parent if our situations had been reversed. More, it was fifty years ago. We don't have kids anymore; we have adults who happen to be related to us. We're on the verge of not having grandkids, either, since they're all grown up."

Thomas looked a little disappointed at that. I guess he'd been more excited about the opportunity to be a grandpa than I'd expected. Well, he'd be thrilled when I told him about Annie, and how much training she was going to need. We didn't have another adult sorcerer around, unless they'd managed to find one after I left, and I somehow doubted that.

Squaring my shoulders, I walked past Sally to stand next to Thomas, leaning over to kiss him on the cheek. "Next time, wake me up," I said.

He gave me a sidelong look, raising an eyebrow. "I expected you to be angrier about being drugged," he confessed.

"Normally I would be, but under the circumstances . . ." I shook my head. "You asked, and I consented. Bromeliad sap was the easiest way to calm me down, and I'm not going to blame you for taking care of me. Although I *am* going to ask why you've decided to start your gardening with swamp bromeliads. They seem like a dangerous begonia."

"They have medicinal applications," said Thomas. "We could all use a little help sleeping sometimes."

"How did you get them? Is this where they come from?" Not everything on Earth that science hasn't managed to nail down comes from another dimension, but a lot of the things that seem to have evolved according to a slightly different set of rules originated on the other side of the membrane. It makes for an interesting attempt to chart evolution across multiple worlds at the same time, and a nice headache for the traveling naturalist.

"No, they're native to our world," he said. "I was able to grab my wallet before Mary banished me here. I had some seeds in the billfold. Planting them gave me something to do in the early years, besides fighting, when we were still most focused on establishing and defending our territory. And then we realized how useful it was to have a natural sedative, for both medicinal and defensive reasons, and I encouraged more and more of them to grow. The smell always reminded me of you." His smile was small, brief, and painfully fond. "They're genuine Buckley bromeliads, if that makes you feel better about succumbing to them."

"Wait, wait," said Sally, with all apparent delight. "You mean you were *serious* about that? You literally knocked her out with a swamp bromeliad? She's been here less than a day and you're already sedating her. How do you think this is going to work?"

I took a deep breath and turned to fully face Sally. "I think we may have gotten off on the wrong foot for some reason," I said. "Let's try and start over, okay? Hi. My name is Alice Price-Healy, and I'm a cryptozoologist who's been looking for my missing husband since he was abducted by the cosmic incarnation of being a massive asshole roughly fifty years ago. We have two kids, both grown, six grandkids, and a colony of Aeslin mice and a troop of tailypo at home. I'm not here to take anything away from anyone, or to take anyone's place. I'm here because I want to take my own."

Sally blinked, several times, while Thomas made a small, half-muffled sound of surprise. I glanced at him. He was doing his best to hide a smile behind his hand. Well, whatever he found so funny was something we could deal with later.

"Hi," she said, hesitantly. I snapped my attention back to her. "I'm Sally Henderson, and before you say anything about my name, I was adopted, I don't speak Korean, I wish I did, but we didn't really have any good language classes in the town I'm from. I was abducted by the same cosmic incarnation of being a massive asshole about seven years ago, give or take a few months, after I tried to bargain for the freedom of my best friend. They said they could make sure he got the money for college, if I'd just agree to pay them something of equal or greater value, and when I agreed, they snatched me, and I wound up here. I was seventeen, and I had my whole life ahead of me, and now I'm living in an arid hellscape with a warlord who's turned out to be a pretty decent person, so you'll please forgive me if I'm a little wary of the weird teenager who fell out of the sky and assaulted me for trying to protect him."

I tilted my head, studying her. "Sally," I said.

"That's my name."

"Yeah. That best friend you mentioned. His name wouldn't happen to be James, would it?"

She moved with admirable speed. If she'd been a teenager from a small town when she landed here, Thomas must have been responsible for a remarkable amount of her training. Not all of it. Body language is like spoken language. People have dialects and accents, they use and repeat certain phrases, and they pass them along to the people they teach to "speak." There were elements of Thomas in Sally's stance, in the way she threaded herself though the needle of the open space between us, but they weren't all his. Some of it was natural talent, and some of it was a conversational style I didn't know, one which placed her directly in front of me in remarkably short order, her hand gripping the front of my shirt, her other hand pulled back like punching me in the face was the greatest idea she'd ever had.

"Where did you hear that name?" she demanded.

I remained perfectly still, watching her in mild silence. If I so much as breathed wrong, she was going to deck me, and then all hell was going to break loose. I can stand calmly while someone threatens me. I *will* react if I'm assaulted.

And that didn't even account for Thomas, who was staring at her like he'd never seen her before, like she was a stranger who had somehow managed to insert herself into his inner circle. He raised a hand, and I was relieved to see that he was holding some sort of throwing dart. Not relieved because he was threatening the woman who was threatening me—relieved because he was properly armed again. I'd been worried.

"It's okay, honey," I said to him, keeping my eyes on Sally. "She's not going to hurt me."

"Yes, I am," Sally snarled.

"That's what you think," I countered. "Right now, we're friends. As soon as you throw that punch, we're not friends anymore. I don't think that's what you want. I think you want answers, and if you hit me, I'm not going to be inclined to give them to you. Now how about you let go before someone does something you're going to regret?"

Slowly, Sally unhooked her fingers from the front of my shirt and let me go, stepping back. "Answer the question," she said. "Now, please."

"I'm here because my granddaughter said she'd spoken to the living spirit of our world, and she told me the crossroads weren't killing the people they abducted, just putting them somewhere they wouldn't be found," I said implacably. "She was traveling with a boy." Two boys, actually, but these people didn't want to hear about Sam, and if I got too far off the point, I was afraid Sally was going to *actually* take a swing at me. That would change the situation, and not in a good way.

"What boy?" she asked warily.

"Dark hair, blue eyes, impressive eyebrows," I said. "She said his name was James Smith, and he didn't like it when I called him Jimmy, and he was a sorcerer." I glanced at Thomas to measure his reaction. "Just like her."

He blinked. "She's a *sorcerer*?" he asked. "How in the world—"

"Uh, think you had something to do with that, sport, since you told me it was genetic. Took two generations and five grandkids, but they finally threw a sorcerer, and she sets things on fire just like you do, and she looks so much like you that sometimes it hurts to look at her, and I hope you get to meet her." I looked back to Sally. "Her friend James said the crossroads took his best friend, a girl named Sally, and because he never got what she bargained for on his behalf, they were able to use that as a loophole to reach the crossroads on their own ground and destroy them."

Sally made a choked sound, putting her hand over her mouth, tears gleaming in her eyes.

"Is he still looking for me?" she asked. "That stupid, stupid boy. I left him a *note* . . ."

"Oh, because leaving notes for the people who love us always works so well at getting them not to do stupid things." I shrugged. "Then again, Thomas didn't leave a note. So maybe it would have changed my mind. Maybe I'd be home and old and happy, and all my kids and grandkids would adore me, instead of being vaguely afraid of me and confused about how I keep not getting any older."

Saying that caused a brief bubble of panic to work its way up from the depths of my psyche, and I suppressed a shudder. This wasn't the time to fall apart again. Maybe that time was never going to arrive. Wouldn't that be nice? We could go home, and I just wouldn't let Naga hurt me anymore, and Thomas would ignore him, and I wouldn't have to deal with what he'd been doing to me all this time. It wouldn't be forgiven. It would just be . . . forgotten, swept aside in the face of so many better things to worry about.

"I wasn't afforded the opportunity to write anything down," he said, with the stiffness I had long since come to recognize as apology in his tone.

"I don't know if he's still looking for you," I said, eyes on Sally. If I looked at Thomas with the panic over Naga bubbling at the bottom of my mind, I would lose my cool, and everything would fall apart. Sally, though . . . Sally was essentially a stranger. Sally was safe. I could look at Sally.

"I don't know, because I wasn't really listening after the point where Annie said Thomas was really alive out there for me to find. I was losing faith. I hate to admit it, but I was, and I needed that moment to get me moving again, to get me looking properly, not just circling in dimensions I already knew, going through the motions and occasionally finding some new corner to explore. I was stuck. So Annie told me I didn't have to be, and I got going again, and now I'm here. But he's there, Sally. He got out of the town where you grew up, and he's with my granddaughter, which is about the best place he could possibly be, even if her boyfriend may not agree with that."

Sally snickered, eyes still overly bright. "Oh, James isn't going to be any threat to the boyfriend," she said. "Kids like us travel in packs for our own protection, especially when your school's too small to have a GSA."

"I don't know what any of that means, but good to know Annie won't be setting him on fire."

Thomas cleared his throat. The dart had vanished, back into wherever he'd been hiding it before, and I couldn't wait to get my hands on him and find out.

Later. "Does me knowing about your best friend who I couldn't possibly know about help you believe that I am who I say I am, or does it make it less believable? I just want to know how many asses I'm going to have to kick before you stop randomly assaulting me. A ballpark number would be great."

"If we're pausing for questions, I want to know what you meant when you said, 'Destroy them,'" said Thomas, tone measured. "Are you telling me the crossroads have been . . . how is that even possible?" I glanced at him. He was watching me, gaze sharply focused and understandably anxious.

"I don't have all the details because I was a little distracted and trying to get out of there; this was at the Red Angel, and Cynthia wouldn't have appreciated it if we'd stayed around forever. If I had my mice, they could tell you exactly what Annie said. I can just give you the gist."

"Please," said Thomas.

"She said that because the crossroads broke the rules they were supposed to operate by, she was able to ask Mary to take her for an arbitration?"

It turned into a question at the end, largely because I didn't know what an arbitration was in this context. Thomas, however, nodded, a look of satisfaction on his face. "Mary always did her best to be on our side," he said. "Even when she couldn't, she was sorry not to be. I'm not surprised our granddaughter asked her for an arbitration." He paused. "I am a little surprised Mary's still with the family. I would have thought you would ask her to leave after everything that happened."

"Mary is one of the first people I remember," I said. "I got in trouble in school because I was drawing pictures of a dead girl when they asked me to draw pictures of my family."

Sally blinked. "Dead girl?"

"Mary is our family babysitter," I explained. "She died about a year after I was born, and no one noticed, so she just kept on going about her life. My mama hired her to take care of me. And she liked our family well enough that she stuck around after we found out she was dead. We're the house she haunts."

"What my lovely wife," and Thomas stressed the last word just a little, as if reminding Sally of my place in all this, "isn't mentioning is that in addition to serving as the Healy family babysitter, Mary is a crossroads ghost."

Sally tensed immediately. "A crossroads ghost is bound to her family, and you still married the woman?"

I decided to let her anger slide, since she'd at least acknowledged me as his wife, instead of calling me an imposter again. I shrugged, spreading my hands. "Most of the time, Mary was just trying to keep me from licking the frickens. Unless we invoked the crossroads, she didn't bring them into things."

"My bargain was made under extreme pressure—but not because Mary convinced me it was the right thing to do," said Thomas. "She fought against me until it became clear that we were out of time. If we continued to fight, Alice would die, and the only thing that ghost cared about more than keeping her people away from her employers was the girl who had grown up in her care—and even then, she made a stab at convincing me that Alice would be better off a ghost like her than she would be with further ties to the crossroads, even by association." He turned his attention back to me. "I was worried you would have called for an exorcist after the crossroads called in my debts."

"Like I said, one of the first people I remember," I said. "It took me a long, long time to forgive her, even knowing the constraints she was under. But she helped as much as she could, and having her and the mice meant the kids grew up knowing about their family and where they came from, and that was important." I hadn't been able to raise my own children, but I'd been able to make sure they could take care of the mice and stay connected to their history, at least a little.

"I want to ask about these mice you keep mentioning, but I feel like we're already getting pretty far off the point," said Sally. "The crossroads were destroyed?"

"Annie said she went to the pocket dimension where the crossroads existed, and that it was somehow outside of time. She saw them come to Earth and displace the pneuma we were supposed to have. They were never meant to exist in our reality."

"A traveler," said Thomas thoughtfully. "That would explain how they knew about this place. If they had come from far away, they would have encountered dead realities that petrified instead of putrefying, turning into fossil reminders of what was lost rather than tainting and destroying everything around them."

"Or they created those places," I said. "We don't know that our world was the first the crossroads affected. They attacked our pneuma and took its place, until Annie bent time and fought them before that could happen. I don't really understand how that works—how could she have fought them before they displaced our pneuma when we've been suffering the consequences of that displacement for centuries? But they were all very firm on the idea that it had happened, and Annie's boyfriend talked about her killing the crossroads like it was something that definitely occurred."

"How long ago did this happen?" asked Thomas.

"They were driving home to Oregon, and James seemed like a comfortable but fairly new addition to a pre-existing group, so I'm going to say it all went down somewhere on the East Coast," I said.

"Maine," said Sally. "We're from Maine."

"All right. Maine to Michigan doesn't take more than a couple of days, and I ran into them at the Angel about four months ago as I experienced it, but I apparently hit some time mismatch between dimensions, so according to Cynthia, that was about three years ago," I said.

"That's when the new arrivals stopped," said Sally. "Before you showed up, we hadn't seen anyone in roughly three Earth years."

"Sally begged for an accurate cross-dimensional calendar when she arrived here, and it's become rather the standard," said Thomas.

"Without the crossroads banishing people, you stopped getting guests," I said.

"But most of the people here made their bargains on worlds other than Earth," said Sally. "How can choices made in our reality, fights fought on our world, impact theirs?"

"If my granddaughter had truly traveled through time, she would have created a paradox," said Thomas slowly. "Reality is malleable, but it refuses most great transformations as intrusions. So her actions could not unmake the choices we had made or undo the lives we had led. If we made bargains, they were still made, because they were part of our pasts, and we lived through them. The things we paid were still lost; the gifts we received were still given." He glanced at me, and he didn't need to say a word for me to understand the message in his eyes.

Out of all the things I'd been afraid of during my long search, Thomas falling out of love with me had never made the list. It was still nice to know that he wasn't sorry for what he'd done and didn't wish he could unmake the choices he had made. I was alive because he'd been willing to barter with the crossroads, despite knowing what it could cost us both, and our children and their children existed because of that choice. If not for the crossroads, our family wouldn't exist.

That was an uncomfortable reality to sit with. "If the pneuma of our world wasn't killed by the crossroads, just displaced, it could have gone looking for a new source of nourishment," I said. I didn't like to think of my own world turning predatory in that way, but we were all demonstrations of the fact that people will do almost anything to guarantee their own survival.

"And if . . . Annie . . . stopped our pneuma from being displaced, it would never have become the crossroads of whatever world it attacked, and that world's pneuma would never have done the same to the next world along the chain, and so on, and so on," said Thomas. "It's a paradox, and one that impacts us primarily because we were impacted by things that happened, but now didn't."

"That makes no sense," said Sally.

"Time travel never does," said Thomas. "In all my days, I only met one sorcerer who thought it was a worthwhile exercise, and he had gone quite mad due to isolation and alienation from humanity. We're all here because of what the crossroads did, and now they never did any of those things, thanks to my granddaughter being too untrained to understand that she was attempting the impossible."

"I'm pretty proud of her, too," I said. "She's a smart kid, always has been. We did okay."

"Yes," said Thomas. "I suppose we did."

"So what's the problem?" I turned back to Sally. "I woke up alone—why?"

"Your arrival did not go unnoticed by our enemies, and I'm afraid we'll have to make a show of force to prevent greater issues."

"Some of our neighbors don't like how the Autarch hogs all the hot babes," said Sally, and snorted with semi-private amusement, like this was some great and secret joke. "They were even more unhappy when the ladies stopped falling through the barrier. Sometimes they could get in ahead of our scouts."

There was so much about this place I didn't know or understand. "Is there still life in this world that didn't arrive via the crossroads?" I asked.

"Nothing very sophisticated: plants and some smaller creatures and the like," said Thomas. "This world has been dying since before my arrival. It's not capable of sustaining much life without magical aid. And without a healthy membrane and pneuma to protect it, it's not generating enough magic to provide the necessary aid. This is an . . . oasis, of sorts, a place of relative stability."

"Only because you made it one," said Sally. "We're not sure whether any of this world's original inhabitants have survived to be pains in our asses. The oldest people we've been able to find all had stories like ours, about falling through the barrier after their bargains went sour. It may be that the locals hide better, or that people don't tend to live that long here—"

"But we think we're an entire world, or at least an entire continent, of exiles," said Thomas. "I think that I, being British, may seem like an exemplar of an ethos that says, 'Well, you weren't using it right, so we took it,' but in this specific case, that doesn't seem to be the situation. When I arrived, this territory was being fought over by three different warlords, each of whom had originated in a different dimension, none of whom could communicate with the others. Granting them the ability to converse didn't solve anything. They're all long dead, of course, but their descendants still hold their territories as best they can, and all of them would like to reclaim the territory we've carved from the bodies of their own."

I nodded. "Gotcha. Anyone but Thomas here when all this was going down?"

Sally snorted. "Some of the guards come from really, really long-lived species, and they remember what it was like before Thomas became Autarch," she said. "But boss is the only one who decided to stop aging for funsies. The rest of us keep on getting older at a normal rate. Whatever you've been doing hasn't been an option."

"And it will no longer be an option for Alice, after this," said Thomas firmly. "That is finished, thank you."

I bristled a little at the imperious note in his tone—I've never liked being told what to do—but even if I could convince him not to punish Naga for helping me, he was right. "I don't need it anymore," I said. "I've only been going through rejuvenation to keep me capable of navigating worlds long enough to find my way back to you."

Sally looked interested. "Is this something ordinary people like me can do?"

"No," said Thomas and I together. I took a deep breath and repeated more gently, "No. It only worked for me because . . . because I have a very high tolerance for pain. I'm afraid it wouldn't work for just anyone. And we don't have any of the necessary equipment here. I'm aging just like you are right now."

"I'll keep my own charm in place until we're back to where we were when I left home," said Thomas. "But then I'll release that as well, and we can grow old together. My days as Autarch will end when I can no longer hold this territory, and I cede it to my heir."

"Your heir?" I knew Thomas hadn't been engaged in any activities that could result in him fathering any more children since getting to this dimension, but he could have adopted some. I wasn't sure how I felt about that. Mostly because he hadn't been able to be there for *our* children, and I'm just selfish enough not to want someone else to have had that time with him. What? I'm allowed to be flawed.

"Yes, my publicly acknowledged firstborn," he said. "Some of the people here are physically compatible, but their children, when children occur, are officially announced as mine. Ser is officially my heir, and I doubt his mother and I would have been compatible if I had been inclined to try, which I was not."

"Around here, you can found a dynasty if you hook up with someone you're capable of reproducing with and pass things on to your kids," Sally explained. "That means it's mostly only the assholes who have kids, because the rest of us are limited to one, maybe two members of our species. I'm the first human chick to touch down in decades, and even if the boss hadn't been pining for what we all thought was a dead woman, we would never have worked out. Scuttled a *lot* of hopes that the next Autarch would somehow look like this one, let me tell you." She sounded deeply amused by how wrong the people had been to be hopeful for some stability.

I nodded. "So these are the descendants of people who made bargains that got them banished, and did so in sufficient numbers that they could build a gene pool capable of sustaining multiple generations?"

"Bingo." She touched her nose.

"And these warlords are pissed?"

"Because of you," said Sally.

I blinked. "Come again?"

"Not directly," said Thomas. "As Sally mentioned, our neighbors have been attempting to beat us to new arrivals for some time now, and there had been a sufficient gap between the last and yourself that they've been growing anxious. They are rather worse at keeping their people alive than I am, as they will persist in making war on one another whenever the opportunity arises, and we simply defend ourselves."

"Lucky for us, assholes never learned to play nice with the other children, or to share," said Sally. "If they formed an alliance of all three, we'd be completely screwed. They could overrun us in no time. But they haven't all realized how many of our defenses are down, and they're still being careful."

"Those are the standing effects that you were powering with the bits of pneuma you peeled off the newcomers?" I asked, glancing to Thomas. He nodded. "Cool. I assume they were part of what was keeping you safe from these people up until now. Can you peel off the pneuma that's stuck to me and use it to get things back up and running?"

Thomas looked uncomfortable. "If you're sure you wouldn't take it as a violation of your trust, I suppose I could . . ."

"Will knives be involved?"

He looked horrified. "No!"

"Then it's fine. Honestly. Maybe we can get your security a little more up to snuff." I looked to Sally. "Any of these people marching on us right now?"

"The Haspers, to the west," she said. "They're a nasty bunch. Not that any of the neighbors are *nice*, but they and the O'Vera to the south are the worst of a bad lot. I think because neither of them are mammalian. They don't necessarily view things the same way we do. When they got their hands on new arrivals, they used them for dinner, not for breeding stock. Which may have been an improvement, considering our other neighbors, but I'm happier not knowing for sure."

"How long do we have until they get here?"

"A few hours. Maybe a day, at the most," she said.

"Then you must have a lot of preparations you need to make." I looked to Thomas. "I'm going back to your room so you can finish this without any more distractions. Come get me when you're ready."

And then I walked away, before he could protest. I needed some time to think.

Fourteen

"Yes. Yes, it was too much to ask. Raising your daughter to think that her only value is in sitting pretty and pristine on a shelf somewhere doesn't get you a functional person, it gets you a monster in waiting."

—Laura Campbell

Sitting on the same bed, no longer naked, and somewhat annoyingly alone, because sometimes being an adult means putting duty first

THE SMELL OF THE bromeliads was almost pleasant now that I understood where they had come from and why they been tended with such care. A lot of things are like that. They can seem off-putting or even bad until you get the proper context, and then they become vital and exactly as they're supposed to be. I left the window open.

There was still enough sap in my system that the pollen alone wasn't going to be enough to knock me out. I've never understood the mechanism by which swamp bromeliads do the things they do. I know some of the more insular cryptid communities use them in place of any more modern form of anesthesia, and it seems to work well enough. Thomas had probably saved a lot of lives by keeping those seeds in his wallet. And he probably kept that window closed and sealed whenever he had Autarch stuff to do.

I folded my hands under my head, on top of the pillow, and stared at the ceiling, allowing my mind to drift. It was probably for the best that I had this time alone: I needed it to sort through everything that had happened, and everything I'd learned. I'd always expected this moment, if it ever came, to feel like I was finished. Like I'd done everything I was supposed to do and could stop now. It was like as soon as

Thomas disappeared, I had thrown out my old, ever-vague life plan and replaced it with a simple list of bullet points: One: Find a way out of my home dimension. Well, I'd managed that, and then I'd done it over and over again—lather, rinse, repeat— until one day I'd looked around and realized the only real anchors I had left were a dead girl, a house that wasn't mine, a forest that loved me, and a colony of talking mice. My family was . . . well, they were people who were related to me, and I liked them, even loved them, but I didn't know them. They weren't enough to make me stay.

Two: Find Thomas. That was the one that had seemed impossible for a long time, and I'd been starting to lose hope when Annie found me at the Red Angel. It was a wild coincidence to base the rest of my life on, but being a Healy, I've learned to trust the wild coincidences. Grandpa used to say the family's luck didn't work that way before Dad brought Mom home from the carnival, but once he did . . . things just fell into place around her. Sometimes good things, like finding a dead babysitter who would stay with us forever. Sometimes bad things, like whatever eventually killed her. Always things that were just on the far edge of improbability.

I inherited my luck from my mother, and I passed it on to my kids, and it's kept us alive almost as many times as it's put us into extreme danger, and it was a big part of why I'd been able to keep looking for so long. Not just the last-minute saves and the pieces of evidence falling into my lap at the exact right moment, but the conviction that I wouldn't be doing as well as I was if he wasn't still out there for me to find. My luck wouldn't have allowed me to keep going at that point.

So now I'd managed both the first and second points on my three-point list. Only the third was left: Get home.

But I didn't know what that meant anymore.

I had always expected to find him and have him tell me we were going back to Buckley immediately. Would he even want that now? He had a life here, a community. Was I offering him anything he hadn't already grieved over and left behind? Sure, our family didn't have the mixed feelings about him that they did about me. How could they? He'd been missing longer than most of them had been alive. They'd be willing to welcome him with open arms, and Thomas . . . Thomas had always wanted a family.

I had one. I had my parents, and my grandparents, and Mary, and the Campbells, and all the weird aunts and uncles my parents collected before I was born, and even though my childhood had been marred by tragedies, I'd grown up never questioning whether I was loved. Family was like air. It was just *there*, until it wasn't, but you never questioned its existence.

Thomas didn't grow up the same way. He'd been an orphan from the time he was young enough for that to be a defining attribute, growing up in the communal dormitories of the Covenant's training center at Penton Hall. That upbringing was supposed to leave the young soldiers devoted to each other, a brother- and sisterhood of zealots, but Thomas had begun manifesting sorcery at an early age. Spending all your time trying to hide the fact that you were setting the sheets on fire when you slept led to a certain amount of isolation from your peers. He'd been an outsider, even within the Covenant, which should have been his home and heart and harbor.

And then he'd come to Buckley, and my father had hated him, and my grandparents had been wary of him, and I'd fallen in love with him practically from the moment we met, creating a weird tangle of relationships that had chafed at us all. But despite all that, we'd found our way to something that seemed stable. I think he was more excited to find out I was pregnant than I was. Which made a certain amount of sense—I was the one who was going to be grounded from hunting for weeks, if not months, and kept out of my beloved forest until I was no longer in danger of giving birth in a bromeliad patch—but was also an illustration of how much of his life he'd spent searching for a family he could count on.

So maybe he wasn't going to want to go back to Buckley. Maybe he'd want to stay here. Or maybe he'd want to go to Portland and settle someplace near the grandkids. I understand people do that all the time. But I didn't want to live in the Pacific Northwest. I wanted to live in the hand of my forest, letting the familiar shape of the world ease me into a future where I didn't have to keep running just to stay ahead of my own terror.

That was the problem. I'd never *thought* about any of this. I'd never thought beyond finding Thomas, confirming he still wanted to be with me, and maybe, on the days when my mind was really wandering, making it back to the house and letting him stand in his own living room, letting him see that I might have failed to keep our children safe, but I'd kept our home safe. I couldn't think beyond that point because there'd been no way of knowing how he would react. Would he reject me for letting our family fall apart in my desperate need to bring him home? Would he say I'd done the right thing and put his arms around me and tell me I'd done a good job, but I was allowed to rest now, I didn't have to keep running forever?

I was allowed to rest.

The ceiling wasn't doing anything interesting, so I closed my eyes and lay there quietly until I heard the door open. A lot had changed in fifty years, but Thomas still had the same basic stride: it's something that doesn't change much without an injury or other skeletal alteration. I didn't move.

"Alice?" he asked softly, after a few seconds of silence had passed. "Are you awake?"

"Strange place, alone, not currently drugged; of course, I am," I said. "Did you finish your meeting?"

"We did. You didn't have to leave, you know." The bed creaked as he sat down on the corner of the mattress, putting one hand on my calf. His palm was warm, as always. "You're welcome in any of my meetings."

"And I appreciate that, but your people are going to need some time before they feel the same way, and I don't want to undermine your authority more than I do by existing, so I figured it was best of me to opt out," I said. "Plus Sally doesn't seem to like me much just yet, and I want to give *her* as much time as possible." Both of which were true.

He laughed a little. "When did you get so reasonable?"

"Oh, I'm not," I said. "I'm extremely *un*reasonable about most things. But until we figure out how to get out of here, and get all your people out in the process, I figure I should at least pretend I'm not going to make your life harder."

"You don't approve."

"Oh, for—" I rolled onto my side and opened my eyes, propping myself up with one elbow. "You don't approve of me going and getting myself skinned alive so I could survive long enough to have this might-be-a-fight, still-finding-out with you, I don't approve of you deciding the only way you could save the people who got thrown into your backyard by the crossroads was by claiming as much territory as you could for England, God, and St. George. I think we both have some decent reasons to be a little annoyed right now. I'm still less annoyed than I am euphoric, and I can't quite believe I'm here, and you're here, and we're both here together."

"I'm having my own difficulty believing any of this is real," said Thomas, hand tightening on my calf. "It seems a little too convenient to be believable."

"What, that we both found ways to stop aging until we could get back to each other and go on with our lives?" I shrugged. "I always suspected it would be a possibility for you, if you thought of it in time, and as the years went by, I had to put more and more faith in the idea that you would have thought of it in time—that you'd want to come home as much as I wanted you to."

"I did," he said. "Of course I did."

"Honestly, it wouldn't have changed anything if you hadn't. I still would have kept going, because finding your grave would at least mean knowing you were at rest, and besides, once I knew you were dead, I'd be free to go home, strap twenty pounds of C-4 to my chest, and head for Penton Hall. Show the Covenant why they should have made sure we were dead before they declared our family line extinct."

Thomas blinked, slowly, like he was trying to process that. Finally, he asked, "You would have killed yourself if I had died before you?"

"No. Yes. Maybe." I flopped back down on to the bed. "I'm feeling sort of unmoored right now because this is all I've been trying to accomplish for fifty fucking years, and now it's done, it's over, I found you, good show, gold star Alice and here's your little red wagon. And now I have absolutely no idea what happens *next*."

The last word was more petulant than I intended it to be, the protest of someone much younger being told that it was time to eat their vegetables and go to bed. To my surprise and mild annoyance, Thomas began laughing.

I pushed myself onto my elbows again, glaring at him. "Hey. Wife, right here, reunited after way too damn long. Stop laughing at me if you want to get naked again any time soon."

"I'm sorry." He removed his glasses and wiped his eyes, still laughing. He had it mostly under control by the time he put his glasses back on and schooled his face into an expression of relative solemnity as he looked at me. "You have my sincere apologies. I wasn't attempting to make fun of you. I was simply reacting to the absurdity of the situation. Could you ever, in all your contemplations of the possible future, have placed us *here*? In this place, under these circumstances?"

"No," I admitted, easing up on the glare a little. "You still shouldn't be laughing at me."

"I know." He leaned over and kissed my forehead. "Expect a lot of inappropriate laughter over the next few days, I'd say. This is going to be an adjustment for both of us, and your demand for a little red wagon was so simply, essentially *Alice* that the size of it all briefly loomed up and overtook me. You'll forgive me, I hope, for being giddy and distracted?"

"As long as you're not giddy and distracted when you're supposed to be going to war." I finally sat up all the way, pulling my legs in so I could sit cross-legged on the bed. "What did you decide? And how does that work, anyway? Are you the only one in charge, or are you an Autarch with a democratically elected council of advisers?"

"I am the absolute authority on anything I decree myself the absolute authority on. My magic keeps this place safe and sustained; our greatest concern when the new arrivals stopped was how long I'd be able to do so without their regular deliveries of fresh pneuma to be harvested and redistributed among the effects."

"They do more than translate, I'm guessing."

He grimaced. "Quite. Without the spells I've been building into this place, agriculture is more difficult, as is water collection. Things we would never have had to worry about on Earth are major concerns here. And then there are the boundary alerts, the lines which keep our enemies from sneaking up on us, and the weather shields that prevent the worst of the local storms from slamming into us. In a few more years, we'll probably need more atmospheric shielding as well, or the oxygen will dissolve as the atmosphere itself continues to degrade."

I must have looked shocked. He shrugged, expression turning wry. "You knew this was a dead world. It's been rotting since long before I arrived here, and the speed of decay has only increased since the connection to the crossroads was broken. Soon enough, the few systems still working will collapse. You said I wouldn't be willing to leave here without freeing the people in my care. To be honest, I'm not sure I'll be willing to go without finding a way to get all the people in this world out of here."

I blinked slowly. Annie killing the crossroads might have opened the path that allowed me to get here in the first place, but it had also shut off the one channel this place had to any kind of fresh pneuma, any ability to recover itself from the damage that had been done to it. I should have realized it would be dying faster now. I leaned forward and put my own hand on Thomas' knee. He glanced at me.

"I won't let you hurt yourself to save people who've been trying to kill you," I said. "But I understand that it would hurt you to leave them behind if there's any way to get them out. Of course, we'll try to find a solution that frees them all. I have friends working on the issue of how we leave this place."

Thomas frowned. "Alice . . . this is a killing jar."

"I know. Jars can be broken." I shrugged. "I found a map that had this world marked on it, drawn by a dude who was apparently a pretty damn famous dimensional cartographer. Some friends of mine in

Ithaca are familiar enough with his work to decode his notes, and they're working on it now. They've been working on it since I left them with the map."

Thomas kept on frowning. "That's nice, but working on a thing isn't the same as actually accomplishing a thing."

"True enough, but the thing about this guy is that he'd *been* here." I said it with as much conviction as I possibly could. "He visited this dimension. Left notes about it and everything. And that means he knew how to get out of the jar. So if he wrote down the way he did it . . ."

"They may be able to recreate his work!" Thomas grabbed me by the shoulders and yanked me toward him, kissing me fiercely before letting go and jumping to his feet. "Alice Price, you're a bloody genius!"

"Not something people call me very often," I said, surprised. I wasn't used to being kissed at all anymore, and he'd never been that much of one for displays like that. I could have conquered worlds with the power of that kiss. It lingered on my lips. I turned to face him, slightly dazed. "As soon as I knew this might be where you were, I knew I couldn't go in after you unless I could get out. What if I'd been wrong?"

"What if you were only right once?"

"I found the map and the book together," I said. "Healy family luck."

"You've always put too much faith in a phenomenon we can neither replicate nor explain," he said, frowning briefly. "So you may have people coming to get you, and presumably they'll have prepared to possibly take us both, if they have faith in this luck of yours."

"They're Ithacan," I said. "Helen likes to say I'm blessed by Tyche. She thinks my luck is a literal gift from a goddess."

"Maybe she's right," he said. "It would be as believable an explanation as any other we've been able to devise. But all right. I'll put my faith in your friends, and that means we're not skimming the pneuma off of you until we absolutely have to."

I blinked. "Why not?"

"Among other things, if your particular brand of ridiculous fortune really *is* a gift from a goddess—which seems less absurd now than it would have before I got abducted by the spirit of a dead world that apparently never existed, thanks to the granddaughter I've never met—then it may or may not behave like ordinary luck, and even ordinary luck can be harvested by unethical sorcerers. We have to assume that it can be pulled away, however temporarily."

I frowned, nodding slowly. "And what would that do?"

"Harvesting someone's luck leaves them a blank slate, with only what they've managed to acquire from the universe around them. They'll gather more luck, attracting good or bad based on what's already there. An unethical sorcerer can sour someone's luck for the rest of their life. And luck tends to cling to the dimensional membrane."

"Remove one, remove both," I said carefully. "You think that's what's been going on with me?"

"I think it's very possible, and even if I had the equipment to do so, I wouldn't be skinning you alive to verify the theory," said Thomas. "But yes, I believe Naga has been harvesting your luck, intentionally or as a side effect of getting what he *really* wanted, for as long as this has been going on."

"I . . . see," I said.

Thomas nodded. "I'm glad. Now, if your ridiculous coincidences have continued since you started the rejuvenation process, and never turned sour on you, your luck is something you generate internally. I've always suspected that to be the case, given the way it seems to behave, but normal luck doesn't work that way. It accretes, like layers of calcium carbonate around a speck of sand forming a pearl. No one's luck consistently maintains the same form after it has been stripped away."

"My luck always gets a little funky for a while after a treatment, but it goes back to normal pretty quickly," I said, thinking of the way I stubbed my toes and stumbled more frequently in the wake of a treatment. I'd always chalked it up to being uneasy in my body while I adjusted to the changes, and not to having my luck literally peeled away. "So why does that stop you from peeling the pneuma off of me?"

"It's very likely to pull your luck off with it, and I would prefer for us not to go into battle immediately after taking away one of your natural defenses," he said. "Not to mention that unlike your luck, the pneuma we remove from you will *not* regenerate, and if the solution your friends have found for getting us out of here assume any measure of natural magic in this place, we'll need it."

"So we're saving me until necessary?"

"Precisely."

"Cool. Now I don't just have grenades, I get to *be* a grenade." I smiled at him brightly. "I've always liked to be the biggest danger in a room."

"Even so." He rose, leaving me cross-legged on the bed as he began pacing around the room. "The Haspers are already on the march and should be here well before nightfall. I'd give them perhaps six hours before they reach our outer barrier."

"Tell me about them," I said.

"About seven feet tall, on average, with black-and-orange skin and vicious claws," he said, and raised his arms like he was trying to mimic the outline of a bear. "Their skin is pebbled and hardened, and it serves them almost as armor."

I nodded slowly. "They're from a dimension called Helos. They're mostly scavengers, although they're not above attacking travelers. Earth-adjacent, you can get there from North America, and from there you can get to about a dozen dimensions that I know of, most of them capable of supporting human life."

Thomas blinked. "You recognize my description of the neighbors."

"Yeah, they're assholes. I'm not surprised that enough of them would have been making crossroads bargains to have a breeding population in the terrarium." Thomas had called this place that earlier, and it was an accurate description: this was a sealed, self-sustaining terrarium that was dying now that its owners weren't maintaining it the way they used to. My inner conservationist suddenly wished Annie hadn't killed the crossroads, so I could kick them in the metaphorical face a couple of times to make them understand that this wasn't how you treated your pets.

"I am a little surprised that there are so few humans," I continued. "Given how many of us seem to have made crossroads bargains, I would have expected a higher population density. How many of the neighbors are human, or descended from cryptids I'd know from home?"

"There are at least a couple within all three factions," he said. "The Murrays, to the north, are human-dominant. They have a large enough range to have a stable breeding population, and I think they resent my presence more than any of the others, since I share a world of origin with some of them and should thus presumably share their ideas about ethical behavior. They send assassins periodically, usually young women who've been raised to think of me as some sort of soul-swallowing demon from the depths of hell." He sounded deeply affronted by this, so deeply affronted that I had to laugh.

"I was raised essentially the same way, and we did okay," I said. "Any of those women here at the moment?"

"No, they don't tend to last long on the occasions when we're able to take them alive. Usually, they suicide as soon as their missions fail. The rest are convinced they'll be killed and eaten, not necessarily in that order, and we can keep them alive for a few weeks if we keep them away from weapons, but they won't eat our devil fruits or drink our devil water, and eventually we have to drop them at the border of Murray territory to save their lives."

I cocked my head to the side. "Do the Murrays let those women come back into the fold?"

"Yes . . . but if you're thinking what I can see you thinking, it's not happening."

"So how, exactly, were you planning to tell them all that it's time to leave this dimension, then?" I asked. "You said you wanted to try to get all the people in this world out, so we need to find a way to convince your neighbors that they can trust us, or we'll have to leave them behind when the extraction team gets here." I could handle him demanding we find a way to create a much larger rock to smash through this shitty dimensional window and get us all to safety. I couldn't deal with hanging back to abduct the unwilling.

"I'll send someone to tell them," he said. "They still fear me enough not to eat my messengers. But first, we need to fight off the people who are coming to attack us and figure out how exactly we're going to leave this place."

"I can help with the first part." I paused. "You are planning to let me fight, right?"

"As if I'd try to stop you." He raised an eyebrow. "I've never been able to do that, even when it was the best choice for everyone involved, and you've had fifty years to get even more stubborn. Even if I were foolish enough to attempt it, I doubt this is when I'd start succeeding."

"Really? Huh. I guess I'm not the only one being surprisingly reasonable today."

"Alice." He sat down next to me, leaning over to cup my cheek with one hand and look into my eyes. "If I had my way, I'd never let you out of my sight again. But yes, I remember who I married." He dropped his hand as he stood again. "Besides, we need every skilled fighter we can get."

"Why would you have to let me out of your sight?" I asked. "Aren't you going to be leading the charge like a proper warlord?"

"One benefit of magic having dwindled so dramatically in the last years—I'm not expected to go to the front line. It would diminish my mystique if I died like an ordinary man."

He managed to make that sound both disdainful and annoyed, when arrogant would have been so much easier, and I laughed, startled. He blinked at me.

"What? Is the thought of me dying so amusing?"

"No, 'cause you're not going to die. I forbid it," I said. "Just . . . you're still you. A little battered around the edges, I guess, and with some scars I'm going to need to learn, but still you. You have no idea how relieved I am."

"I think I may have some idea," he said, voice going dry. "And you . . . you haven't turned into someone I don't recognize either. I'm not sure how peaceful we'll be together after this, but it's not like we ever had a chance to figure ourselves out before, not without the crossroads hanging over us like an ax about to fall. We're going to learn it now . . ."

He leaned down again, this time with clear intent to kiss me. I met him halfway. When he pulled back, I smiled.

He blinked at me. "What?"

"Just missed your face," I said. "That's all."

This time I kissed him, and it went on for even longer before I regretfully drew myself away.

"Seriously, don't worry about me," I said. "I didn't make it this far or find you again just to lose you now. We're going to get out of here together."

"I'll hold you to that," said Thomas, and smiled. "Sally is explaining our plan to the guard now. We'll be shoring up our defenses at the appropriate points, calling all noncombatants to take shelter in the palace, and setting guards on the fields and the wells. Archers will be posted on the wall in case the O'Vera are foolish enough to attempt a frontal assault."

"Protecting what they'll see as your resources," I said. "What are the O'Vera, anyway?"

"Descendants of our nearest neighbors. They fly, and come in a dozen shades of jeweled green, and eat all flesh without consideration or compunction. I've seen them fall upon their own during battle. They seem to be always hungry."

"Okay, met them, too." Apparently, the way they handled things next door wasn't entirely due to the dead world damaging their pneuma. That was an unpleasant thing to realize. I'd been sort of hoping that if we could restore their world, they'd go back to being whatever they'd been before, and Cornale could stay on the list for safe transit. "They're assholes when they're at home, although I don't know if I can blame them. They run the world I used to get here."

"Meaning they have a rotting universe latched onto their own, poisoning it by inches."

"Yes. Not much to eat there if you take each other off the menu, and they don't seem too inclined to do that."

"Right." Thomas shook his head, eyes hard. "I don't want to know why you had to know that. I feel that the story of your life while we've been apart is going to drive me to drink."

"It drives me to drink on a fairly regular basis, and I was there," I said cheerfully, and rose. "So you're shoring up the defenses and setting guards. Anything else?"

"Sally will be taking a detachment of our men to meet the Haspers on the field. They're quick to act when they perceive weakness, but they will generally retreat with equal speed when met with proportionate force. She's repelled them before. Will you be able to work with her if I send you along?"

"That's more up to her than it is to me," I said. "But seeing as we both have a vested interest in keeping you alive, yes."

"Very well." He crossed to the door before turning back to face me. "I'll talk to her. But for the moment, will you come with me, please? There's something else I want you to see."

"You know I've been happy to go anywhere with you since I was sixteen," I said, and stood, stretching before I walked over to join him. Unhygienic as it might be, I hadn't bothered to remove my shoes before lying down on the bed, and since he hadn't said anything about it, I was assuming he didn't care about a little mud on the blankets. Which made sense, given that we'd both been bleeding when we made it to bed in the first place.

"Yes, and you know I've always been careful not to take advantage of that." He leaned over and kissed the crown of my head before opening the bedroom door and leading me out into the hall.

The throne room was empty when we reached it. Thomas took my hand, pulling me with him as he made for the far wall. I went willingly enough. Honestly, it was nice to be following someone I trusted for a change. That had been a rare enough occurrence over the past fifty years.

He pressed his hand against a seemingly unremarkable piece of masonry and murmured a phrase under his breath, too low for me to understand what he was saying. The air around him briefly flashed with the sharp pre-storm smell of ozone, and when he pulled his hand away, there was a door there. It hadn't appeared. It had always been there. I simply hadn't been able to see it before.

I gave him a sidelong look. "A little less shy about showing off the sorcery these days, are we?"

"When you're living as a wizard king, it seems a bit silly to pretend that you aren't one," he said, with a small, almost abashed bob of his head. "I'm sure it's been excellent for helping me get past some of my issues with the thought that others might see what I can do. I'm not as sure how I'll handle a return to Earth and the need to be more circumspect."

"Yeah, but you'll be circumspect with the tailypo and your family and access to chocolate, and that should make up for a lot."

He laughed and pushed the door open. "I apologize, but I may not be able to add you to the list of people who can access this space on their own. My magic has run low enough at this point that even modifying the protections on this space may be beyond me or may weaken the locks to the point where they become useless."

"It's fine, sweetie. I've changed the locks on the house twice since you disappeared, and I can't give you keys right now, either. We'll take care of it."

"The places where you choose practicality will never cease to bewilder and delight me," he said, stepping through the door into another narrow hall. I frowned as I followed.

"This doesn't look like the rest of the compound," I said. "Neither did your room. Too small, too square, too . . . not anatomically optimized for whoever used to live here. What's the deal?"

"This place was built for people whose needs were not a biped's," he said. "After discovering that it contained too few rooms optimized for human use, I set to convincing the stone to allow me to make some."

That was a daunting thought. Sorcerers, as far as I was aware, were usually proficient in a single element, with both Thomas and Annie favoring fire. "You . . . convinced the *stone*?"

"Yes. It was a profligate waste of power, but I was angry, and I was panicked, and I had no idea how much I would come to need it later."

At the end of the hall, he paused to light a lantern, revealing a room that was the mirror of his bedchamber, sans window, occupied by a large table. I pulled away from him immediately, turning toward the nearest wall. It, like all the others, was covered in a large, obviously hand-drawn map. The closest one showed what I guessed, given my limited experience so far, was probably the compound where we were standing. I glanced to Thomas, eyebrows raised, and he nodded in confirmation.

"My council meets here," he said. "We needed to be able to chart our defenses and our resources in an organized manner."

"Hence the lock."

"Yes. If the compound were ever to be taken, Sally and the others would get the noncombatants here as quickly as they could, then seal the door behind them. In less dangerous hours, the door opens for me, for her, and for selected members of the council." He gestured toward another map, this one larger and more abstract.

"This map shows you the extent of my territory. We can't get aerial views, of course, but we have no accessors here to calculate the property taxes." He managed to sound faintly amused.

I moved closer to that map, blinking at it for a moment before turning to face him. "This looks like an entire village?"

"Yes," he confirmed. "Not everyone who lives under my protection can fit inside our household. There are fields to be maintained, if nothing else, although we've had sparser crops every year. The water is drying up, and the soil is turning fallow. Aside from that, there are craftsmen who need more space than the compound allows, guards to be trained, and children to be schooled."

"How many people are we talking here? Ballpark figures are fine if you don't have exact numbers."

He sighed and pinched the bridge of his nose before saying, "Three hundred and sixty-two as of the last census. It was five hundred when the barrier closed. I can't keep them alive much longer."

"Fortunately, you won't have to."

The next map was more absence than actuality, showing the outlines of several jagged, irregular areas. The center area matched the shape of Thomas' territory. "The neighbors," he said. "I have no idea whether the exterior borders are still accurate. It's been years since we've had the resources to go out and verify them. It's been years since we've had the resources for a lot of things that should be done."

The last map was his territory, again, at roughly the same magnification as the second, but with a charcoal circle drawn to overlap it, centered on the compound. That line had clearly been rubbed out and redrawn several times, each circle smaller than the last. I blinked at it, then turned an inquiring look toward him.

"The line of our magical defenses," he said. "Within that circle, the air is purified and replenished, and the translation spells function. Outside it . . . I can't protect them. I can't protect any of us."

He sounded so utterly miserable that I wanted to kiss him until he smiled again. Instead, I damped the impulse down and asked, "How many of your people are trained for combat?"

"A little more than half. I think the most recent roster put it at two

hundred and three. Of those, a hundred and twelve serve as guards."
He moved toward the door. I followed. "The rest have families to care
for or work in the fields or the village. I don't demand service, only
that everyone do what they can to help our community survive."

"Sounds fair enough, especially for an autocratic warlord."

He offered me a faint smile before stepping out of the room.

I followed, extinguishing the lantern behind me.

The throne room was still empty. He took my hand as we walked
across it, retracing the path of my earlier flight. I glanced at him sidelong, aware that I was looking at him a lot, as much to reassure myself
that he was still here as to assess his mood. He was looking straight
ahead, profile still so achingly familiar. He might have doubted me.
I'd never done the same to him.

We walked down a curving hall I didn't recognize, bypassing the
courtyard, winding up back at the entrance to the room where I'd
been taken after I woke up. I balked, stopping dead in the middle of
the hall, and Thomas pulled me along with him toward the door.

"You can't avoid them just because you made some natural if incor-
rect assumptions," he said. "Come along. Please."

I stopped fighting and let him lead me through the door. The room
was empty, no guards or women in pajamas. I looked at Thomas, be-
mused. He smiled a little. "Wait," he said.

"If we're just going to stand here, we could pass the time by making
out," I suggested.

"We're about to have company."

I didn't have time to ask him what he meant by that before Sally
stepped through one of the arches on the opposite wall, followed by a
group of women, roughly half in the pajamas they'd been wearing the
first time I'd seen them, the others in more practical rough cloth and
leather. A few had children with them, ranging in age from toddlers
to teens. None of the kids were in pajamas. Only about half of them
had shoes.

Thomas turned to face them, his smile growing, and called, "Sally!
A word?" He didn't move away from me. That was something of a relief.

"Sure, boss," she said, and shot me a poisonous smile as she sauntered past us to the storage room where we'd met—oh, wait, where I'd
beaten the crap out of her.

"We'll only be a moment," said Thomas, and kissed my cheek before he followed her.

"I'll be fine," I said, waving him off as I focused on the new arrivals.
"Hello. And you would be?"

"We are the Autarch's senior women," said the one who appeared to be the leader. She looked perfectly human, as long as I ignored the two extra arms, one below each of the standard pair. One hand rested on the shoulder of a child with the same arrangement of limbs who stared at me with huge, liquid eyes. "We were told you wanted to meet the children. My name is Aadya."

"You were?" I glanced at the door Thomas and Sally had vanished through. "Well, that was a little presumptuous of whoever told you that, but sure, we can roll with it. Nice to meet you."

"Their fathers patrol the walls and work with us in the fields and hall," continued the woman—Aadya—calmly. "We have been told we can admit this to you, for the deep fiction does not extend to your ears."

"The deep fiction being . . . ?"

"That our beloved Autarch gathers the women who enter this land unwillingly to himself because he cannot be satisfied in the absence of his lost bride," said the woman, patiently. "It is a great and terrible love story. The children sing it every Winterbreak, to celebrate."

"Huh," I said.

"But he takes us to his home and hearth and leaves us to our own devices," she continued. "We are free in his custody, as we couldn't be outside these walls, and those of us who wish children and find mates of a compatible species are encouraged to bear them, providing we will claim him as their father, for the sake of leaving his rule unchallenged."

"That's ridiculous and patriarchal as hell, but I'm coming to expect that from this dimension," I said. "It's nice to meet you. But shouldn't we be preparing for a war?"

"Yes," said Sally, emerging from the other room with Thomas at her heels. She shot me a measuring look. "Are you ready?"

I met her assessing gaze with my own. "Born ready," I said.

Thomas came up behind me, and I stepped back so that I was half-resting against his chest. He slid an arm around my waist.

"My Autarch," said the woman who had spoken to me before, "is your mate a warrior, too?"

"You have no idea." He smiled. "The Haspers won't know what hit them."

Fifteen

"I knew what I was doing when I asked her to marry me, all three times. I'm just lucky she finally realized I was doing it."

—Thomas Price

Walking across a blasted plain to fight a hostile warlord, you know, like a really clever person who wants to live to see tomorrow

THE ARMORY AND THE women's quarters were located on opposite sides of the complex center, meaning that what followed was a lengthy walk, maybe fifteen minutes in all, through long, almost featureless halls. Thomas had gone off to convene his council of advisers and do whatever else it was he did before going into battle. Without him present, Sally and I were saying as little as possible in an effort not to antagonize one another. Well, I was making an effort, anyway; maybe she just didn't feel like talking to me. "Did you build this place?" I asked when I couldn't take the silence any longer.

"Me? No. All the land grabs were finished a long time before I was born," she said. "Benefit of having an Autarch who doesn't really age; you have time for some pretty extended projects. But he didn't build it either. Whoever lived here before things got bad built it." She shrugged. "We don't know who they were. Maybe they died out centuries ago, maybe they just couldn't stay here after the wells dried up, and some of the people in the gangs we try to hold off are their descendants. Either way, boss says this place was a ruin when he found it, and he spent a long time and a lot of resources building it back up into something that could protect his people. Even before the magic got involved, when it was all manual labor and struggle."

I nodded. "That sounds like Thomas."

"You know he's not the same guy, right?" She looked at me. "I'm not the same girl, and I've only been here for seven years. My family's probably still alive. According to you, James finally got out of that little shithole town where we both expected to live until we died. I could go home, except for the part where I couldn't possibly, because I'm not the girl they've been waiting for all this time. I'm someone new, and her skin won't fit me anymore."

"I know," I said. "You could say the same thing about me if you wanted to. Trauma changes who you are, and there's no way to say 'well, I'm finished with this, I'm going to move on now.' You have to figure out how to reconcile it with everything else you understand about yourself, and sometimes it really sucks."

Sally raised an eyebrow. "You're surprisingly calm about this."

"I've had a lot of time to come to terms with the fact that I'm essentially broken," I said. "I was worried until I got here that I'd have broken in ways that Thomas couldn't handle, and I still might be—I'm sure we both have some nasty surprises under the surface, just waiting to be discovered. That's another way trauma works. For every bruise you can see, there's another spot where it's just all about the internal bleeding." I still couldn't think too hard about what Thomas had said about Naga and his choices. Had he really been using me to harvest dimensional pneuma, treating me like a snake cult all his own, a battering ram determined enough to keep slamming through the walls of the world until I broke myself? If he'd had a less invasive way to keep me in fighting shape, it seemed really likely.

For fifty years, he'd been the ally I trusted above all others, even my own family. If I thought about it, I could remember hundreds of little course corrections, gentle suggestions I'd interpreted solely as him trying to help, and not as him trying to protect a resource. I might not have been able to get out of this place if I'd found it before finding the books, before Annie killed the crossroads . . . but I could have *been* here. I could have been here *years* ago, if not for Naga interfering with the direction of my journey. I would still have been damaged. We both would have been. But we would have been damaged together, and, suddenly, that seemed like a luxury beyond all measure.

"Hey." Sally snapped her fingers. "Come back. Wherever you're going off to, it's not your mission. You get that this is dangerous, and the boss will literally murder me if you get careless and get yourself killed, right?"

"I didn't spend fifty years finding him to go and die before he could leave the toilet seat up again," I said. "Calm down, princess. I'll be fine."

"Good," said Sally. "Because I'm still not *completely* on board with the idea that you are the person you're claiming to be. It's all a bit too convenient for me. New arrivals stop coming, and you just *happen* to finally get here, and to not have aged, and surprise, the arrivals stopped because ding-dong, the witch is dead, and it's the boss' granddaughter who did the killing? *And* you know James? It's all a little too on the nose to be realistic. You can see that, right?"

"I can," I agreed. A lifetime of walking in a haze of weird coincidence and convenience has left me well aware of how weird my life can be—and how much people tend to assume that "my life is built on a foundation of weird coincidence" will mean "my life is always perfect, and everything goes my way." The least likely result is bad just as often as it's good.

"And all that being said, whether I believe in you or not is sort of irrelevant because *he* believes in you. He really thinks you're his dead, missing, octogenarian wife," said Sally. "You convinced him, and I guess that means you've halfway convinced me, because he was always going to be the hardest sell."

I knew we were getting closer to the armory from the sound of shuffling feet and clanking metal, and I straightened my spine before we came around the bend in the hall to see about a dozen men in leather and hammered metal armor standing outside another of those rounded doors. They all stood at attention when they saw Sally, barely seeming to notice me. That was a nice change. I'm so used to being the scariest thing in the room that I'd almost forgotten things could work any other way.

Sally shot me a last, warning look and slipped through the door, leaving me to face the group of guards alone. I smiled wanly.

"You hit me," said one of them.

I blinked. It was one of the ones who'd been between me and the exit back in the women's quarters. "You had the voulge, right?" I asked.

He nodded, slow and sullen.

"It was a nice weapon. I appreciated it a lot." It was probably back in the armory by now. Maybe Sally would bring it out for one of us to use.

"I don't understand how you can go so quickly from assaulting a guard to joining an expedition into the badlands," he said, stiffly.

"Oh, that's easy. I'm the Autarch's wife."

The group exploded into mutters and whispers. I looked at them placidly. There was no way they hadn't already been informed of who

I was, but hearing something and having it confirmed were two different things entirely.

Sally emerged from the armory, pausing to toss me a heavy leather jacket. I caught it, giving her a dubious look.

"Put this on," she said. "You're basically unarmored right now, and it's cold as hell out there. If you go out there and get yourself killed, it's going to break him, and he's all that's been holding this place together. If you die in the wastes, you doom us all."

The muttering stopped as the guards stared at Sally. Hearing and confirming were different. Confirmation from someone they knew and trusted was something else altogether. I looked at the jacket in my hand, wrinkled my nose, and tossed it back.

"Won't work with my pack, and being unarmored only matters if they hit me," I said. "Don't worry about me getting cold."

"Right, because you're indestructible."

"Nope, just lucky, exceptionally hard to kill, and covered in single-use charms intended to keep me alive in any terrain."

"You better be right about all this. Or I'll kill you myself."

"I didn't realize you were a necromancer." I beamed at her. "We ready to go?"

Sally looked annoyed but let me have the point. "The others are waiting outside, and the messengers have already been dispatched. They're each carrying a portable translation and amplification charm—and those take a lot of juice to make, so you better be serious about getting us out of here." She turned to the guards, stomping one foot with a ringing sound. "Together, *move*," she snapped.

She had a cheerleader's cadence that I recognized all too well, and the tone of a warrior. Whatever she'd been back in Maine, she was powerful here, and her men fell into position without hesitation, forming a phalanx around us. Sally began to move. The rest of us moved with her, the guards in anticipation, me to avoid being left behind.

"Between the way the Autarch constructed our outer defenses and the lookouts we have patrolling, we know roughly when and where the enemy will be arriving," said Sally as we walked. The door wasn't far. One of the guards pushed it open, revealing the half-dead land I'd seen when I first arrived. One by one, we stepped out, the last guard closed the door behind us, and we were alone in a hostile landscape.

That was nothing new. I've been alone in a hostile landscape one way or another for most of my life. We started forward, into the dead land.

I paused after about twenty yards, looking back at the compound

Thomas and his people had claimed for their own. I still couldn't figure out where I'd seen it before, or why it all looked so damn familiar.

Sally wasn't wrong about the cold outside the walls. I pressed two fingers to the skin below my jaw as I started walking again, focusing on the match tattooed there, and a wave of warmth washed over me, chasing the cold away.

Every step kicked up a small cloud of dust, and while some of the bushes were very obviously dead once I got close to them, others shied away from me, reacting almost like sea anemones in the presence of a predator. A world of reactive vegetation was nothing unique, but I've always found plants that move to be more fun than the other kind. Sadly, I didn't know if they'd have defenses—toxins or stinging sap— and we were in a hurry; I couldn't allow myself the brief luxury of prodding them unless I wanted to risk losing an hour to an allergic reaction. Sometimes being responsible is the boring way to do things.

Two more detachments of guards came to join us as we walked, none of them giving me much more than a second glance. I was with Sally, they trusted Sally, I must belong here. I wondered what she'd done to earn such faith from these people, many of whom were visibly scarred, none of whom were obviously human. By the time Sally called for a halt, we were a force easily fifty strong, bristling with polearms, swords, and bows.

There was nothing in front of us. No people, no visible threats. I glanced at Sally, trying to assess the situation. She shook her head and gestured to the air, a little bit above head height. I looked again, squinting when it still looked like nothing in particular. Finally, I saw it: there was a faint soap bubble shimmer in the air, like a film of rainbows overlain across the rotting sky.

"That's the edge of the Autarch's protection spells," she said, voice tight. "Not much beyond that point. Including air. Air is important. Most people need it if we want to live."

"So this is where we fight?"

"No, this is where we take a really damn deep breath, and where you trigger those bubbles the boss said he saw on your arm."

"Shoulder, actually," I said, as coolly as I could, and pressed my hand against a line of bubbles tattooed at my shoulder. My head spun even as the dust and dryness seemed to vanish from the air. I hadn't realized how thin it was even on this side of the barrier. "A little blood sugar's a fair trade for a lack of hypoxia, I guess. How are you going to be okay?"

"Practice," she said. "We're like those Olympians from Colorado at this point. The ones who've trained for so long in crappy conditions that we're superheroes when we get down to sea level. Only what we're training for is fighting people where there isn't enough oxygen in the air."

"What fun hobbies you people have," I said.

She smirked at me, then gestured for the group to resume walking.

The barrier offered no resistance. Even with the charm, I could tell the air was thinner there, making it harder for me to draw a full breath. At least it was still breathable. The charm would last about three hours as long as I didn't run into any burning buildings; it would run out faster if I made it deal with actual smoke.

Outside the barrier, the sky was even uglier, the rotting yellow color of a bruise that had barely healed past the purple-black stage, the shade that meant something was dying. If there was a sun somewhere up there, I couldn't see it, lost as it was behind the layers of dust, ash, and cloud. The world looked sick because the world *was* sick. More, because the world was dead.

The world had been dead for a long, long time. It had just remained tethered to the crossroads somehow, tied to their poison in a terrible way I didn't quite understand, and they had been feeding it by throwing their exiles here. Every time the crossroads threw someone away, they'd been feeding magic back into the biosphere. Not enough to heal it—not enough to grow into a new membrane or to bring the dead, decaying thing it was back to life—but enough to let it limp along in a state of suspended animation, never fully collapsing.

And then they'd thrown Thomas through, clever, clever Thomas, who was so much more adaptable than most of his kind, who had already learned the techniques for tucking magic into his flesh for later use, ink and sigils and potential, who had found a way to tap into that shallow well and use that magic as if it were his own. He'd been protecting the other exiles, making this world a better place for them to live, and hastening its death at the same time.

He might have known that. He might have considered it a good thing. Better a hundred good years than five hundred years of endless suffering as the biome rotted to the point where it could no longer support anything resembling life. Or he might have been acting as a sorcerer, not a conservationist. He'd never been a part of my family's obsession, had married in as an adult and been imprisoned at the same time, making it impossible for him to do more than help with research. Field work and seeing the impact of little changes to the ecosystem had never been an option for him. He might never have realized what he was potentially doing.

Or he'd realized it and confirmed he wasn't doing it, and I was completely off-base, woolgathering as I walked. But it made sense, based on everything I'd managed to learn about the way this system worked, and the way he and Sally both agreed this reality was falling apart faster now that new arrivals from the crossroads weren't falling out of the sky. There was no new magic coming into the world. What little did arrive, Thomas took and hoarded, and however good his reasons were, however necessary his actions, the fact remained that he was like the man with the only well for miles around, taking all the water for his own lands.

It felt weird to be thinking critically about the man I'd come here to find while on my way to parlay with his enemies, but it was also necessary. A clouded head never does anyone any good, that's what my grandmother used to say, and Grandma was almost always right about almost everything. Enid Healy was the culmination of a hundred generations of careful Covenant breeding plans, and they were lucky she hadn't burned the damn place to the ground on her way out the door.

A line of dust had appeared in the distance. Sally signaled us to stop again, then gestured for the guards to fan out and form a line.

The land wasn't entirely flat; near the dusty plumes, I could see the kind of rocky outcroppings that I associated with Arizona and with certain episodes of *Star Trek*. The thought made me want to laugh. I swallowed the sound, only snorting a little in muffled mirth. Why did I keep getting into fights in places where Kirk and Spock would have fit right in, with their polyester and their bright Technicolor future? Desert landscapes are cheap to film in, sure and they seem to occur on any planet with a biome capable of supporting humanoid life, but it was still funny.

"Boss says you know what we're up against," said Sally, apparently taking my snort for dismay.

"Yup. I've been to the place where they live. Didn't like them then, don't like them now."

"They're not easy to kill."

"Nope." A thought was starting to form. A bad one, which probably meant it was the best idea I was going to have today. "Sally, you should let me go out ahead. I can shoot their front line, thin their ranks before they engage with you directly." It was the sort of technique that had been keeping me fighting for fifty years. I just needed her to go for it.

She looked at me doubtfully for a long moment, as the guards looked anxious and the plumes of dust got closer. Finally, she sighed.

"Fine, whatever," she said. "Just don't get yourself killed. I don't want to drag your corpse back to the boss. Not when we're this close to total disaster."

"You got it," I said brightly. Then I took off at a run, heading into the dusty distance.

Here we go again.

Sixteen

"I looked at that girl and I knew two things: that she was going to drive her daddy out of his mind, and that I was never going to love anything else the way I was going to love her. And God help me, both those things were true."

—Frances Brown

Running across a desolate wasteland toward a potentially unwinnable battle because that's always a great idea

SALLY PROBABLY THOUGHT I was being foolish, and she wasn't entirely wrong, but I knew these people. I knew where their weak spots were, and I knew that their idea of tactical cooperation was even lousier than mine. It made sense that if they'd been able to access the crossroads—whether ours or a local equivalent—a lot of them would have thought making bargains was a great idea, and it made even more sense that they'd have been able to thrive in the killing jar of an evil cosmic entity. Their home world was already basically a cross between *Mad Max* and *Lord of the Flies*. This just gave them a slightly shittier stage to perform on.

I stopped when the dust got close enough that I could see individual shapes moving through it, crouching down and hiding myself as well as I could behind one of the rocky outcroppings while I took stock of the situation. There were about fifty shadows all told, and while that might have made the force Sally was leading seem excessive, each of them was large enough to make two-to-one odds roughly fair for us. The shadows had a remarkably degree of morphological consistency, which made me think people from their world were extremely fond of making bargains—that, or they had aggressively dominant genes, which made no sense. There was no way these people were mammalian, much less cross-fertile with anything that wasn't essentially a reptile.

Sometimes biology gives me a headache. Everything I learned in school, that I thought was the calculus of life, was basic math at best, and it's all so much more complicated than we ever knew it was. Every new world just adds another layer of "no, seriously, what the fuck?" And a lot of the time, you can't really stop to make sense of it, because when something is trying to chew your face off, you don't generally get the opportunity to ask it how its reproduction process works.

How these people could be here didn't matter, not really. What mattered was that they were here, tall and angry and armed with cudgels and clubs. And running straight toward me. Couldn't forget about that part.

Once they were inside shooting range, I straightened up. Yes, that made me a bigger target, but as none of them had anything I recognized as a distance weapon, I wasn't terribly worried about that. I shoot better standing up. Trying to look utterly unconcerned, I sauntered forward.

"Hey, boys," I called, once I was close enough to get their attention. "Long way from Helos, don't you think?"

There had to be a larger group somewhere that wasn't part of this assault force, because they were all male as far as I could see, lacking the distinctive red-scaled mask of females of their species. For there to be this many of them, they must have had a breeding population, even if it was small; I didn't know enough about them to know whether they were egg-layers or what. And in this moment, it didn't matter, as they stopped running in order to snarl and glare at me, clearly posturing to seem bigger and more terrifying than they were.

They didn't have to try all that hard. At seven feet tall, heavily muscled and heavily scaled, they were big and terrifying enough.

"Now forgive me if I get this wrong, but I'm assuming you weren't invited to come for a visit, right?" I directed my smile at the largest of them. "I think maybe you ought to move along."

The one I was smiling at traded his snarl for a roar that would have been a lot more terrifying if he hadn't sounded like a squeaky toy being stepped on by a horse. He charged for me, mouth still open. That was his first mistake.

As established much earlier, the scales on the people from Helos made them slightly harder to shoot, but not enough so that it was any kind of real problem. Even if it had been, things with open mouths might as well be wearing a sign that says, "Hit the bullseye, win a prize."

I'm not the best sharpshooter in our family, but this guy was charging for me and closing fast, and he had a big mouth. I fed him a bullet and he fell, still running, in a heap on the cracked earth. His companions stared for a moment before they roared, almost in unison, and rushed for me.

Nothing like a good shooting gallery to make the afternoon more exciting. My first eight shots were clean, and eight bodies hit the ground. My next two missed their mark and only wounded, maybe because they were getting too close. With only two bullets remaining, I started producing knives from inside my clothing and hurling them at the soft parts of my attackers, embedding them in throats, eyes, and other vulnerabilities. Six more fell.

I was beginning to give serious thought to falling back when a volley of arrows flew over my head and cut down four more of the big lizards, followed by the sound of Sally shouting. With a roar I could feel down to the soles of my feet, the remaining Haspers charged forward, and the battle line surged forward to meet them. One of the lizards swatted me to the side as they ran, not taking the time to finish me off, which I appreciated. I don't like being finished off.

I hit the ground hard enough to bruise and rolled to the side, blinking dust out of my eyes as I turned to watch the two groups collide. The guards, moving with Sally, were far more controlled than the Haspers had been, and clearly had some sense of troop discipline and tactics. Good to know that they hadn't let being stranded in a death world make them sloppy.

The reason for such a focus on polearms was more obvious once I saw them going up against the giant lizard-people. Putting their knives on the end of long sticks, when they didn't have ready access to firearms, meant they could counter at least a little of the improved reach and height of their opponents. More of the Haspers went down. So did a few of the guards.

Sally was a spinning tornado of knives, moving fast and low, slashing at joints and exposed weak points, gutting and moving on. I admired her technique, even as I picked myself up off the ground. I shook my head, trying to clear the ringing out of my ears. Then I shot another pair of lizards and backed away, getting a decent distance between me and the fight before holstering my guns and whistling shrilly. "Hey!" I yelled. "Hey, over here!" I waved my arms over my head. "Exposed and alone and unarmored! Come and get it!"

The Haspers not currently engaged began to run in my direction, forming a nicely unified pack. I like a unified pack. I like the way it splashes when you lob a grenade into the middle of it, and I like it even better when none of its component parts knows what a grenade *is*, so they react like you've just thrown a rock or something. To be non-specific.

The sound was immense, the echoes rolling through the badlands and into the rocky *Star Trek* bluffs ahead of us. The silence that followed was even louder. A few fights were still going, but they were smaller now, multiple guards against single Haspers, and they were done in short order.

Sally strolled toward me, pausing only to kick a few of the corpses before giving me a sharp look. "Do you always showboat like that?"

"Only when it seems appropriate." I rubbed my elbow, hand coming away sticky with blood. "Ow. I thought Thomas said a show of force would be enough to make these people back down. What happened?"

"Things have gotten a lot more desperate since the last time we clashed with them quite this openly," said Sally. "We have more resources than they do. They were probably hoping they could overwhelm us fast enough to finish our entire front line."

She had taken a hit to her shoulder at some point during the fight, and it was already beginning to darken, turning lividly purple and black and spreading tendrils of angered veins down her shoulder and upper arm like some kind of odd growth. Looking at it made me feel like I could sketch a map of her capillaries.

Sally glanced at it, then shrugged. "I bruise easy," she said, like that was all the explanation I needed. "We won, they didn't knock us down, now we go home for a clambake and a beer. Or we would if we had either of those things here."

"Right." I looked at the field of fallen bodies, past the Haspers to where the guards were gathering up the remains of their own. "And we have to offer to help these people escape when we leave this place?"

"Messengers have already gone out," said Sally. "Remember? Anyone who's willing to come peacefully will already know that the offer's on the table. Anyone who isn't, we leave behind."

She grabbed the arm of the nearest Hasper, grunting a little with the effort of dragging it back toward the others. I blinked. "What are you doing?"

"We aren't the O'Vera; we don't eat the fallen. But we still have to take what we can from the bodies. It's time for looting."

"Oh, goodie," I said dryly. "My favorite."

It didn't take us as long as I would have feared to strip the bodies of everything usable, including the arrows that the guards had pincushioned them with, and my own knives, which I retrieved and wiped meticulously clean before tucking them back into their sheaths and scabbards. Sure, I was covered with blood and ichor, but I don't rust. Knives do. There was still plenty of time left on both the charm keeping me warm and the one keeping me oxygenated when Sally whistled, waving for the rest of us to follow her back toward the barrier line.

None too soon, if the increasingly labored breathing of some of the guards was anything to go by. There's only so much you can do with conditioning, and bodies need to breathe. It's a fact of biology.

Our line was more ragged and less efficient, and not only because some of the guards were carrying the bodies of their fellows. I guess when you're going up against cannibals, you don't leave the ones you lose behind. I had a lot of sympathy for that.

No one spoke as we walked, and we'd covered no more than a third of the distance when I saw movement ahead and stopped, waving for the others to do the same. Sally shot me a curious look, then swore as she followed my pointing finger toward the motion on the horizon.

"They're too small to be Haspers," she said, voice low. "But most of the other options suck just about as much."

"Yeah, but Thomas set out the welcome mat, so we may as well at least *try* to approach them like we're friendly, huh?"

Sally looked at me dubiously. "Nothing here is friendly."

"So we can be the exception, until they mess with us. And if they do that, well." I grinned at her. "I have more grenades."

We kept moving forward as a group, more on edge now, until it became clear that we were approaching a ragged group of mostly women and children, with some teen boys, humanoid in basic form, although their skins were striped like a shaved tabby's, darker bands of skin atop a pale background, and their hair continued the trend by growing in stripes of silver and deep brown. They could almost have fit right in back in Sally's hometown, blending into a human population without raising many eyebrows. Their clothes were brown to blend into the landscape, clearly made of something like a rough canvas, and loosely fitted, although that may have been a function of the fact that they didn't appear to have any actual seams, just knotted ropes.

"Murrays," said Sally, tone dark. "More of our neighbors." She waved us to a halt and whistled. The group turned to look at us, shivering. Most of them needed thicker clothing; some didn't even have shoes. This was not a well-armed and armored militia. Whether we called their leader a warlord or a children's entertainer, they were clearly starving, and clearly unarmed.

"Neighbors who aren't trying to kill us right now, so I'll take it," I said, and waved, before cupping my hands around my mouth and calling, "Hello, the Murrays! Are you here to fight us, kick off an ambush, or ask for sanctuary?"

Several of them exchanged glances before one, older than many of the others, said timidly, "The last one, I think, if 'sanctuary' means the same as 'shelter.'"

"It does," I confirmed. The translation spells were working, but that didn't make them perfect. I pressed one hand flat against my chest. "I'm Alice. This is Sally."

The woman looked at me, narrow-eyed and anxious, as the others shifted and fidgeted behind her. They were silent, even down to the youngest child. Their cheeks were hollow, their eyes sunken into their faces and too large for the rest of their features. Some carried food and water, of which there was dismayingly little; these people were here because they were out of other options. All but the youngest children stood on their own, the infants and toddlers bundled onto the hips of adults. No one was carrying much, which explained at least a little of Sally's wariness. This didn't look like was an exodus.

"Nem," said the woman, finally. "We come seeking sanctuary."

"Your messenger came, dropped the sky on our heads, and ran before the Patriarch could order him killed," said another of the women. "We talked over what he'd said and what we know from our own fields, and we decided that we'd rather take our chances than stay where we were and keep starving to death. We know the undying wizard will probably kill us, but at least it'll be faster than withering away. Not that we have a choice anymore. If we tried to go back now, the Patriarch would kill us for leaving."

"Only because you killed three of the Patriarch's men," snapped one of the teen boys.

The woman gave him a disdainful look. "They were going to sound the alarm."

I decided to like her. From the small, satisfied nod Sally gave, she had decided much the same. Raising her voice, she said, "The Autarch was sincere in his offer of shelter, food, and safety until we can exit this place. No one is going to harm you unless you present a threat."

The newcomers looked like they didn't quite believe her—I guess good things weren't very common in their lives—but they fell in willingly enough as we started moving again, our group expanding to surround theirs, with Sally moving at the front and the guards largely clustered around her. The rest filled out the sides, or walked with me at the back, pacing the slower strangers.

We walked until the shape of the compound appeared in the distance, and several of the younger women stopped dead. The guards who had been serving as unofficial escorts stopped in turn, intentionally rattling their weapons. Sally looked back at us impatiently, then at me, and gestured for us to keep moving.

"What are you doing?" I asked. "We're almost there."

"I can't," said one of the girls. "I'm sorry, I thought I could, but I can't, I can't, I can't hand myself over to a monster just because he says he means me no harm. I may not be able to go home, but I can't go inside those walls. Women who enter the undying wizard's clutches don't come out again."

"So why did you *bring* us here?" demanded the teen who'd spoken before. She shot him a sour look.

"Because you're not a woman," she said. "You can enter and live, and leave this world, and be free. Go for my sake, even if I can't come for yours."

It was as touching as it was pointless. I sighed, forcing my expression to stay as neutral as possible as I said, "Thomas—that's his name, Thomas, not 'the undying wizard'—isn't a monster," I said. "He sends his people to collect new arrivals to protect them from people like your Patriarch, who didn't think women should get a choice in who they belong to."

"I always thought that was a little bit ironic," said Nem.

I looked at her curiously. She shrugged.

"I sold my soul and family name to escape a marriage I didn't want to be entrapped by, and when the unanswered prayer took me and hurled me through creation in exchange, I landed here, and was trapped into a marriage I would never have agreed to, had I been given half a choice." She sighed. "And now I am old, and have never married, for all that I have long had a husband, and will never see my home again."

"You might," I said. She looked far enough from human that I had no idea what species she was or how long its members lived, but she wasn't ancient. "If we do this right, we all might. But we don't have a lot of time, and the charm letting me easily breathe the air outside the compound won't last forever, so if we could get moving?" I paused. "If the crossroads put you here, how have you been able to survive? The air isn't any good outside the barrier."

"Our root stock is Lilu," said Nem, almost proudly. "The air cannot poison us, for our bodies refuse to be so easily killed."

I blinked. "Huh," I said finally. "I guess that's one way to do it."

The Lilu aren't that unique, as biological organisms go; all bipeds are built on essentially the same biological plan, and if not for the protein issues, a lot more of us would probably be cross fertile. That's the real secret of the Lilu, as far as I can tell; they don't have allergies, unless you count aconite, which mostly repels them. The only thing that can poison a Lilu is, again, aconite, which isn't even found in most dimensions.

The air was better this side of the barrier, but not as good as it was inside the compound, and even Sally was starting to show some signs of strain, while these exhausted, starving people were all perfectly fresh. Maybe their lungs worked more efficiently on top of everything else?

Musing on biology was fun, but it wasn't getting us to the compound, or me back to Thomas. I focused on the woman who'd objected. "The man you call the undying wizard is my husband, and I don't share," I said. "Even if he wanted to hurt you, I wouldn't let him. I might hurt *him* for suggesting it. So can we keep moving? Please?"

One of the smaller children whimpered—the universal sound of the hungry child. That seemed to decide her. The woman looked to the kid, sighed, and nodded.

"We move," she said.

And we did.

None of the Murray women were particularly interested in making conversation as we walked, too exhausted and beaten down to really feel comfortable talking to someone they saw as allied with one of their oldest enemies. The woman and the teenage boy who seemed to enjoy squabbling with her were walking together, heads almost touching as they muttered between themselves. I dropped back to walk beside them.

"Hey," I said after a moment, when they didn't react to my presence. "You two all right?"

They looked around at me, almost guiltily. That was . . . concerning, under the circumstances. I frowned.

"You better not be planning anything. I don't usually invite people home for dinner right after I meet them, and I'm not going to appreciate it if you abuse my husband's hospitality."

"We're not planning anything," said Cer. "The Patriarch was always very clear that anyone who enters the territory of the undying wizard disappears and is never seen again. This is hard for us. I'm sorry."

"My sister was married to the Patriarch upon reaching her maturity," said the boy, trying to sound unconcerned, anxiety slipping through in his tone. "If your husband attempts to claim her, he'll be asking her to break the bonds of her fidelity, and the unanswered prayer will strike them both down where they stand."

The unanswered . . . the older Lilu woman had said the same thing. "Do you mean the crossroads?" I asked cautiously.

"Some people call the prayer that," said Cer. "They're wrong. Faithless and wrong."

Right. "And your Patriarch married you when you were, what, eighteen?"

"When I ceased to be a child." She ducked her head. "There is not much food to be had. My mother was much younger than I am when she bore the first of my siblings. It's possible that I'm flawed in the eyes of the world. The Patriarch would surely have cast me aside soon."

The more I heard about this Patriarch, the less I liked him. It seemed as if he was the reality of what Thomas had been trying to make himself look like to the world outside his walls: abusive, parasitic, and awful. "What, is this the dimension of dudes making bad decisions that the rest of us just have to live with? Are any of these stupid factions led by women? Don't answer that. If you say yes, I'll want to go talk to them, and if you say no, I'm going to turn around and march back to wherever the hell it is you came from in order to tell your Patriarch to go fuck himself."

"He wouldn't like that," said the boy.

"That's fine. I don't like *him*."

"You seem angry," said Cer, sounding confused, like she couldn't understand why I would be.

"I mean, you're the Lilu. Can't you tell?"

They both shook their heads. I didn't groan. It was a near thing.

Their unwillingness to take us at our word when we'd been telling them the truth suddenly made a lot more sense. Lilu can control the emotions of others via their pheromones, which makes them ineffective against people who lack nostrils, or personal pheromones, or have head colds or sinus infections of any kind. If they want you to feel something, you'll feel it. A surprising number of them have won Tony awards. An unsurprising number of them have failed to make the transition into screen acting. They need to be in the room with the people they're trying to influence.

Most Lilu can also read the natural emotions of the people near them, feeling what needs to be twisted and amped up, figuring out what stimuli their targets will have the best reactions to. If these people had been able to read our emotions when we approached them, they would have realized that we were sincere—not that we were telling the truth, because feeling emotion isn't the same as detecting lies, but that we meant what we were saying. It would have helped them trust us. But they couldn't, and so they didn't.

Anyone with even a drop of Lilu blood seems to get the poison resistance and the lack of allergies as part of the package—back when I spent more time with the Campbells, they had a geek whose whole act was based around drinking assorted various toxins, including mercury mixed with arsenic. He never got sick, not once, and when he did eventually die, it was of old age, not liver failure. He was one-eighth Lilu on his mother's side. He didn't have any of the empathy or pheromonal control, just the poison immunity, and he learned to work with what he had.

He was a fun guy. Knowing him is probably why I had such an easy time accepting Ted. Well, that, and Jane had long since made it very clear that I had no authority over her life, not even down to questioning the species of the man she married.

But like poor dead Oliver, or my own grandchildren, many Lilu crossbreeds seemed to lose part or all of their empathic and pheromonal abilities. Just to verify, I asked, "So you can't read people at all?"

They nodded glumly, looking like they expected to be punished for their weakness. I silently reminded myself that going off to find and murder their Patriarch would not only be antisocial but counterproductive, since we were trying to convince these people that we *weren't* all maddened killers. Instead, I sighed, and smiled.

"That's fine," I said. "My grandson reads just fine, but he has virtually no control over his pheromones. All he does is make people lust over him, sometimes so badly that they can't do anything else. We keep hoping he'll get better as he gets older, but so far, no luck in that area. We don't care what you can do, only that no one's forcing you to do anything."

"You're forcing us to march," said the boy.

"No, I'm asking you to keep moving if you don't want to die out here," I said. "It's a shitty choice, but it's still a choice, and it's yours to make. If you want to stop here, knowing you can't go back, that's up to you. We're offering you a chance. That's all we have. That's all any of us have."

He frowned, then inclined his head. "My name is Lyn."

"Well, we're glad to have you with us, and it's nice to meet you, Lyn," I said. "I hope you're both okay with surviving and being fed and maybe finding a less shitty place to live."

"It doesn't sound real," admitted Cer. "You say you speak for a monster, and that you're going to give us everything we ever wanted. Are you the avatar of the unanswered prayer?"

The idea was repulsive, but also entertaining, in a terrible way. The crossroads would *hate* to have people wandering around the cosmos who thought I somehow spoke for it. I wasn't nearly enough of an asshole for that. "Not necessarily, but I'm trying to clean up the mess they made," I said. "So if you can't read emotions, and you can't tell when we're trying to deceive you, I'm guessing you also can't tell whether or not we have bad intentions."

"You're leading us to the undying wizard," snapped the boy. "Of course you have bad intentions."

"I guess we'll know one way or the other soon." We had almost reached the compound. Both of them paled when they saw it, realizing that they were passing the point of no return. "Come on. Give us a chance."

Sally and the guards were hurrying toward the wall, sweeping their share of Murrays along with them, until only the three of us were malingering at any distance. Cer gave me a half-desperate glance, eyes searching my face for any indication of how this was going to go. Finally, she sighed, and offered her brother her hand. He took it, and together they followed me toward what I knew was safety, and they still half-expected to be certain death.

Good to see my knack for making friends was still alive and well.

Seventeen

"Sometimes the right thing and the best thing and the good thing and the thing you want are four different things, and you have to try to figure out which one of them will do the least amount of damage."

—Enid Healy

Approaching the wall of the compound belonging to the man I've been seeking for the last fifty years, pretty well ready to go the fuck home

SALLY AND THE OTHERS were waiting for us at the wall. She gave me a sardonic look.

"Can't go back in without the Bride of Frankenstein."

"He was a mad scientist, not a sorcerer," I said.

"Sure, but 'the Bride of Gandalf' doesn't have the same ring to it." She gestured to the door. "You get to do the honors."

Meaning she was concerned that if I wasn't visible when the door was answered, she'd have issues. That was something I could respect. I stepped forward and knocked, smiling to myself at the familiarity of the action. It brought back the echoes of years of trips to see Thomas when he'd been "Mr. Price" and I'd been the library lady delivering cake or cookies to his door. I don't have much to be nostalgic about from the gap between the end of my college days and the beginning of my marriage. What I do have is precious to me.

When no one answered, I knocked again before stepping back to wait. The Murrays clustered up behind me, murmuring anxiously among themselves. I cast them as close to a reassuring look as I could manage, and they kept murmuring, clearly discomforted. The guards formed a loose ring around us, keeping us all shielded, at least a little, from the rest of the outside. It wasn't much, but it was something.

And the door still wasn't opening. I turned and knocked again, more forcefully.

"Are they going to let us in?" asked Lyn.

"If they don't, they're going to be sorry," I said, voice going a little singsong at the end. These people barely knew me, and still they knew enough to take that as a bad sign and step back, eyes going just a little wider.

The guards tensed at the sound of footsteps coming from our left. I glanced to Sally. "One of yours?"

She shook her head, expression drawn. "No."

"Any chance the Haspers have more forces out here?"

"They don't do lying in wait. Too subtle for them. But they're not our only neighbors."

"Great." I was almost out of bullets, I couldn't keep chucking grenades this close to the compound, and we were running out of time. I started hammering on the door.

I was still pounding when it swung open and I all but fell into the hallway, stumbling past the woman I'd been introduced to as Aadya. She shot me a startled look, transferring it to Sally as the other woman followed me through the open door. "Did the two of you go out looking for strays?"

"We took out the jerks who were trying to huff and puff and blow your house down, and we picked up these folks along the way. They were answering the summons from *your* beloved leader." I waved for the Murrays to follow me inside. "Come on, all you, get in here. We can't keep the door open forever."

I was asking them to enter the stronghold of their oldest enemy, someone many of them had grown up fearing and hiding themselves from. But I had also taken the time to talk to them, and they were exiles now; whether they liked it or not, we were the best chance they had left. One by one, they came inside, and when the last of them was inside, Sally leaned over and pulled the door closed.

There was a finality to the sound of it latching that made me wonder about magical locks, and how secure we actually were in here. The walls seemed thick enough, but Thomas said that some of the people from the neighboring dimension were also in this one. How were our aerial defenses? How secure were the windows?

"The Autarch will not like this," said Aadya.

How much was she going to like it if I redirected all of my current frustrations onto her? I swallowed my rising temper, forced a smile, and said, "I think you're wrong, since this was his idea. Don't scare the nice people. They're already anxious, and I for one don't want to deal with a stampede of panicked Lilu."

"Lilu?" said Aadya. "These are the Murrays, if I'm not mistaken."

"Yeah, and with a name like that, at least some of their founders probably came from Earth, but we can worry about that after we've given them something to eat and a place to rest," I said.

One of the smaller children started crying softly, out of hunger if nothing else. Aadya thawed somewhat, inclining her head.

"Of course," she said. "Children never go hungry here. If you would all come with me?" She gestured broadly with all four arms before she turned to make her way down the hall. The Murrays followed, more quickly than they had followed me. I guess food is a better incentive than violence. Cer and Lyn were the last to go, stealing anxious little glances in my direction until I smiled and waved them on. I didn't need to pick up any strays this trip. Not when it looked like we were already taking Sally home.

Sally, who was looking at me with amusement in her eyes. I bristled a little. "What?"

"You know, I expected the boss to be into getting his savior complex on, the same way he always does. I didn't expect you to be into it. I also didn't expect you to be that prepared for the boundary line."

"What were you going to do if we reached it and I stopped breathing?"

"Shove you back onto the good side and send a couple guards to walk you home," she said unrepentantly. "Boss may have thought it was a good idea to send you with me, but I didn't know how well you could handle yourself, or whether you were going to freak out the second you saw things get messy. That's on me. I underestimated you, and while I'm not going to apologize for wanting to protect my people, I won't do it again."

That was understandable, even admirable, no matter how little I liked it. "Good thing I had a breathing charm on me," I said.

"Yeah. Boss warned me about that one," she said. "He's got a whole list of magical effects he thinks you can manage with what's written on your skin, and a list of what he thinks the side effects will be. Did you know that if you triggered too many of those in quick succession, you could put yourself all the way into a coma?"

"Yup," I said.

"Can I take the speed and chipperness of that answer as an indication that you've done it?"

"I don't know. Can I take the fact that you keep acting like I'm somehow infiltrating your base to make problems and not because I *belong* here as an indication that I'm allowed to push you out this door and lock it behind you? If we're asking crappy questions, I mean."

Sally laughed. "Okay, okay, fair enough. The boss will be thrilled to see us all safely back home, with no major injuries, a threat eliminated—or at least reduced—and a whole bunch of new mouths to feed."

"Assuming they don't start any trouble," said one of the guards.

Sally shot him a glance. "If they try, I'll play the xylophone on their ribs. Now come on. I understand there's snacks on offer."

As a group, we tramped down the hall, following the path charted by Aadya and the Murrays, moving deeper into the estate. When we passed a wide doorway, the guards who were still carrying their fallen companions stopped, looking to Sally. She nodded, sharply.

"Take them to the meeting hall to lie in honor until they can be given to the fields," she said. "Tell their husbands and their wives that they died fighting for the glory of the Autarch and the protection of their people, and tell them that I understand the knowledge does nothing to stop the pain."

"We shall," said one of them, quietly, and they walked through the door in a smaller, sadder group, taking the bodies with them. Sally looked at me.

"The war we're fighting here . . . it's not a game," she said.

"I never thought it was."

For a moment, she stared at me challengingly. Then she thawed, sighing. "Just as long as you know."

We continued on, fewer than we'd been before, but still standing.

Maybe that was all that mattered.

Aadya had taken the Murrays to the kitchen to raid what looked, to me, like a fairly pathetic continental breakfast—hard bread, mealy fruit, and strips of some unidentified meat that I was at least reasonably sure hadn't come from anything intelligent—but which the Murrays had already fallen upon like it was the greatest feast they had ever seen by the time we arrived. Which, to be fair, it might well have been. None of them had been eating regularly. Some of the women chewed bites of bread and meat before offering it to the children, openly weeping, and not one of them tried to refuse anything they were given. Pickiness is a product of plenty, after all.

Watching them made me miss my own children, who hadn't been children in a long, long time, who had always felt like they had the privilege of being picky. Other than Nem, who had had good reason to make a choice she clearly regretted, I didn't think any of these people had made crossroads bargains: they looked too much alike, unified by a blend of genetics enabled only by the Lilu aspects of their heritage. They had been born here. They had expected to die here. And not a single one of them deserved it.

I turned my face away, momentarily closing my eyes, and opened them when a hand touched my upper arm. Sally was standing closer than she ever had before, looking at me sympathetically.

"It's hard here," she said. "It always has been, and it's only been getting harder. But it's not going to be hard for too much longer."

Either we'd be out of here, or we'd all be dead. Strangely enough, I found that encouraging.

"I think we'd have a riot on our hands if we tried to take these nice people away from the food," I said, and looked to Aadya. "Can you keep them from eating themselves sick?"

"I've raised three of my own," she said, amused. "I can babysit."

"Good. 'cause I need to report in before I head back to the wall to join the rest of the guard," said Sally. "And if I don't get the lady here back to the boss before he loses his patience, we're going to have issues."

I couldn't feel bad about my presence hurrying us along. Sally and I left with about half the guard, leaving the others to stand watch over the Murrays as we made our way to the throne room to report to Thomas and his council.

Normally, I would have wanted to stop and clean myself up before any more potentially fraught introductions, but as the only place I knew of to change my clothes was on the other *side* of the room, that wasn't so much an option. The guards peeled off when we were about halfway there, heading for the wall Sally had mentioned, and we carried on alone to the throne room.

It was empty when we arrived, but the door to the council chamber was standing open, and soft voices drifted from inside. Sally made straight for the door. I stopped outside, standing there for a long moment before I took a breath, steeling myself, and stepped inside.

Thomas, Sally, and several men in linen robes were gathered around the table in the center of the room. I paused in the doorway, trying to identify their original dimensions. None of them looked familiar in the slightest, save for the fact that they all followed a roughly bipedal body plan, which is more common than not in the dimensions that can support human life. Finally, I walked toward them, hoping I wasn't about to get another exciting round of "who are you and why are we supposed to trust you?" It hadn't been fun coming from Sally, and at this point it was starting to get a little old. Thomas glanced up and sucked in a sharp breath at the sight of me, that familiar pained inhale that usually came right before someone said, "Oh, *Alice*..." in a pitying tone.

Not that Thomas had ever been much for pitying me. I still wasn't in the mood for being fussed at, no matter how much I might deserve it. "You should see the other guy," I said brightly. "Hi, honey, I'm home. Hello, gentlemen. You weren't here when I left."

Everyone in the room turned to stare at me, almost as one. One of them, who could have passed for human if not for the two smaller sets of eyes, one above and one below the normally-sized pair, reached over and gripped Thomas' sleeve.

"You were speaking truly," he said. "Your lover—"

"Wife," I amiably corrected.

"—has come to help you save us all."

"It'd be great if everyone in this dimension could stop questioning whether or not I'm married to you. It's enough to give a girl a complex. And if by 'help him save you all,' you mean the assholes who were getting ready to attack you are dead, you'd be right about that," I said, strolling toward them. "They were trying to kill me, and I didn't like it. I take that sort of thing personally."

Thomas' look of dismay blossomed into one of almost malicious delight. Guess he didn't like being called a liar any more than I liked being called a lover. Learn something new every day. "I appreciate you handling a few little problems for me, dear," he said. "My advisers and I were just attempting to agree on a plan."

"So I see. Where were you keeping these fine gentlemen during our tour?"

"They were attending to their duties here and in the village," he said, holding out his hand in invitation.

That's not an invitation I've ever been able to turn down. I took his hand and let him pull me against his side, only wincing a little when my bruised elbow brushed his side. He gave me a hard sidelong look, clearly picking up on even that brief discomfort. I managed a smile. Nothing was broken, and I wasn't bleeding internally. He was going to have to remember what life with me was like because there were some things that weren't going to change.

"A village which is still in dire danger," snapped one of the other men. "We brought as much with us as we could carry when you called for us to take shelter within the palace walls, but the O'Vera are coming. They'll be upon us in a matter of hours. We have to protect our fields and our homes!"

"Then we'll fight them off, the same way we always have before," Thomas replied.

"They've never been sending this kind of force before," said the man. "You have to see that this is different."

"I do, and we're taking this situation very seriously, but as I've been trying to explain, we won't be here much longer, and then the fields won't matter." He turned to Sally. "How many of your guards are ready to be sent back out?"

"About two thirds, at a guess," she said. "We lost fewer than usual, thanks to somebody," she hooked a thumb toward me, "deciding she could aggro a whole pack of Haspers by herself. But we're going to need more archers—we don't have enough to protect both the palace and the farmland at the same time."

Thomas gave me a hard look. "Did she," he said, and it wasn't a question.

There was no point in denying it. I smiled at him. "You knew I was a tailypo when you picked me up."

"True enough," he said, fond despite himself. "I did."

"We have greater issues at the moment," insisted one of the advisers. "We don't need guards. We *need* an act of great and terrible magic!"

"As I keep telling you, great and terrible magic is no longer an option," said Thomas. "The pneuma of this world is dead, and we receive no additional infusions, thanks to the cessation of new arrivals."

"You closed the barrier between this world and the cosmos," said one of the men. "Can't you open them again?"

"That's part of the problem," said Thomas. "I already did."

Everyone fell silent, visibly shocked by this announcement.

"Excuse me, you did *what*?" I asked.

"While you were sleeping, I took down the barrier that was keeping people from entering this dimension. As your arrival proves, even with the barrier in place, people could get through if they pushed hard enough. Once, the crossroads did the pushing. Not anymore. They're gone. So it seemed wise to stop powering the barrier in order to conserve what magic I have left," he said softly. "This world has been dead for a long time, and we've been prolonging the inevitable for as long as we possibly could. We can't prolong it anymore. The collapse is coming. The fields will die, the wells will fail, and all will be brutality and chaos until it finally, mercifully ends."

I raised an eyebrow. "Is this really new information, gentlemen?" I could tell there was still something he wasn't saying, which was strange. It had been a while, but I still thought I knew my husband, and he was normally tediously enthusiastic about sharing information regarding impending doom.

"No," admitted one of the advisers. "But it seems very final, and there has to be another way."

"I don't know," I said. "I've seen a lot of corpses in my day. Never yet met one where I could tell it that it was time to stop being dead and get more use out of it." That wasn't technically true. My son-in-law, Martin, is a Revenant, meaning he'd been several dead men before an enterprising mad scientist glued and stapled them all together and ran the perfect electrical current through his heart. Or hearts, I've never been clear on what he's working with, and it's never seemed polite to ask.

But Martin is a special case, assembled by an expert. We didn't have two more dead worlds to splice this one into, and even if we did, we were too small to survive an electric current of that magnitude. No. There was no option that allowed human-sized life to stay here.

The one with all the eyes frowned at me. It was pretty impressive, given all the glaring he was built to do. None of them looked overly thrilled by my presence, except for Thomas, who looked quietly content, an expression I'd spent years mistaking for neutrality while we were learning one another.

A process I was more than ready to start over from the top. I stepped up to the table, skimming the tips of my fingers over their map and staring at it until I found what I was looking for, what I had somehow already known would be there. "Don't bother defending the walls," I said. "Call everyone into the compound."

"Excuse me?" said one of the advisers.

I smiled sweetly at him. "Call them all in," I said. "All your guards, all your people, any particularly beloved house pets, any living thing you want to see survive, call them in."

"What?"

"Look at this." I pointed to the edge of the walls around the compound. They extended farther than I'd been able to see from my limited exposure, stretching out to sweep mostly around the shape of what I assumed was meant to represent the village. "There's a gap in the wall. You have enemies on their way who can fly, who eat living flesh, and who would be happy to treat this gap as the best kill chute ever constructed."

Something about the shape of the full compound still nagged at the edges of my mind. I'd seen this before. This shape, this construction style, I'd *seen* it before. I just didn't know precisely where.

"So you let the invaders come," I said. "You let them burn the fields when they can't find anyone to kill. You let them do what they've come here to do. And we fight them through a bottleneck, if we fight them at all, not in a mob."

They stared at me before looking to Thomas, like children begging their father to tell Mommy to stop being so mean. He looked at me. I looked back, defiant.

"You know I'm right," I said. "I've been out there, Thomas. Even if you save your crops this time, how long before the survivors attack again? They have even less food than you do, and the air outside the barrier is barely worthy of the name. They're desperate, and they're not going to back off, and if we don't find a way out of here soon, we're not going to."

He sighed, then looked to his advisers. "My wife is right," he said. "Our walls are strong, our weaknesses are known, and our world is dying. Tell everyone who isn't already inside the palace to get inside now, and to bring whatever they don't want to see burn."

"There isn't enough space for everyone to live here indefinitely, sir," said one of the advisers.

"It doesn't matter anymore," Thomas snapped. "No one else is coming through the barrier. Alice was the end of it. The magic this world has left, the vitality this world has left, it's all here, and we're out of time. If we're going to find a way out of this, it has to happen now. Go and bring everyone inside. Tell them that this is what must be done. Tell them that the Autarch commands it. Only tell them, while there's still time. Or am I not your unquestioned lord?"

The men looked like they weren't sure of the answer to that. Several of them glanced unhappily at me, then back to Thomas. It was clear that they weren't used to women other than maybe Sally appearing at their council table, and that fact sort of made me want to scream. Out of all the killing jars the cosmos had the potential to come up with, why did Thomas wind up in the male-dominated asshole dimension?

Answer: because this was a world populated entirely by people who'd made crossroads bargains and their descendants. Sure, there

were people like Thomas, or Nem, people who had made their bargains for selfless reasons, but if the stories Mary had to tell were anything to go by, people like them would have been in the minority even
before they were faced with the need to survive in a shithole full of
monsters. The crossroads hadn't exactly been self-selecting for nice
people who didn't want to hurt anyone else. Put enough assholes in a
box and you're going to find the biggest, strongest assholes rising to
the top, like some sort of horrific algae bloom of sphincters. I moved
to stand next to him, still smiling sweetly at the group.

"Is he not?" I asked, with acid brightness.

The one with the eyes blinked all six of them, one pair at a time,
like a rolling blackout of blinking, and said, "Of course, sir." That
seemed to be the cue the others had been waiting for. They murmured
their agreement, one after the other, and began to back away.

Thomas gave a decisive nod. "Then you may go," he said. "Tell
them to come. Tell them we're locking the doors as soon as the first
sentry sounds an alarm. They can't count on having time to dawdle."

The advisers nodded and kept backing away until they reached the
door. I turned to Thomas, opening my mouth, and he gestured for
silence. I frowned at him. That had better not be a new normal in his
mind; sure, he'd been a small-time dictator for fifty years, but I've
never taken well to being shushed.

The advisers left the room. Once we were alone, Thomas said,
sounding deeply weary, "If I don't have the last word, they won't leave.
I'm not sure whose culture carried that tedious little attribute here
with it, but when Sally and I were still adjusting to her place here, she
would speak after I did, and that would start the conversation over
again. Like a perpetual motion machine of endlessly arguing about
absolutely damn everything. I'm sorry. I just didn't want to start it up
again. Now, before you start shouting at me for shushing you, can we
please go and patch you up? Infections are nothing to sneeze at in this
place, and it's not like we have access to antibiotics."

"It's really nothing," I said, shrugging expansively. "Just a few
scrapes and bruises."

"Sweetheart . . ." He reached up, very gently, to brush his fingertips
against my cheek. "While I fully understand that sometimes you're
going to risk getting injured, I don't like you being this cavalier about
hurting yourself. Please stop doing it."

"I don't think it's that easy," I said. "I've had a long time to get used
to the idea that sometimes it's the only way."

"You're never going to that so-called uncle of yours again," he said firmly. "The damage you're dealt now is damage you'll have to learn to live with for however long we both manage to stay alive."

"I know." And I did. I didn't agree that I was never going to see Naga again, but I was done with rejuvenations. I didn't need them anymore. Not with Thomas here. Not when we were finally going home. "I've had scars before."

"Not normally because you'd been slicing pieces out of yourself."

I smiled. "Oh, there were a few times," I said. "Remember the night I tried to go to Ann Arbor?"

What little humor was left in his expression drained away. "Yes, and you are never allowed to do that again," he said. "Not when it took this long for you to come home to me. Promise, Alice. Promise me that this is not all an elaborate way of catching the bus to Ann Arbor after all."

He looked so grave that I couldn't even object to the fact that he was telling me what to do. Instead, I blinked, and swallowed, and said, "I promise. I just want to get us both home. You have people you need to meet, and I think Sally might murder me after we're all dead and gone if I don't get her back to James."

Thomas laughed, still mirthlessly, and said, "There's a fair chance, yes. She's innovative. If anyone could figure out the mechanisms of ghost murder, I think it would be Sally."

"You're going to have to tell me how she wound up your right-hand woman one of these days."

"When we have time for storytelling, we're both going to have so much we need to say," said Thomas. "I'm looking forward to it."

Eighteen

"The first time Frances Healy put her little girl in my arms, the whole world changed. I'm not exaggerating. That baby pulled me far enough away from the crossroads that I got to stay my own person when that shouldn't have been possible. I'll owe her for that forever, even if she didn't know what she was doing."

—Mary Dunlavy

In the bedroom of a man who's been missing for fifty years, trying not to smack him while he performs first aid

THIS WOULD BE EASIER if you'd stop squirming so much," said Thomas.

"This would be *easier* if you'd just let me slap some tape on it and get back to work," I shot back.

My little tumble out in the field had been worse than adrenaline, shock, and a well-trained resistance to pain had been willing to let me admit before; in addition to a badly skinned arm and elbow, I had managed to dislocate my hip and crack at least one rib, maybe more. It was nothing I hadn't done full field missions with in the past. It was also nothing Thomas was willing to let me try to just walk off.

He sighed. "Because that would absolutely be the way to discourage you from damaging yourself recreationally. Allow you to run around with a potentially life-threatening injury and pretend that everything is just fine . . . because you put *tape* on it." He managed to make that sound witheringly disapproving. It was almost impressive.

Not as impressive as the pain. As soon as we'd started to leave the council room and he'd seen the way I was walking, he'd whisked me away to his room and ordered me to sit on the bed while he got his first aid kit, supplementing it with the supplies from mine, which was much better stocked. He had local painkiller made from bromeliad sap, which was helping to numb the pain, although not enough to keep me from wanting to slap his hands away.

I settled for scowling at him, clenching my fists in the blankets until my joints ached, waiting for him to be done. He was gingerly prodding my ribs back into their proper place, rolling a sheet of sticking plaster over the damaged area. I was trying not to pull away. Setting a rib without the aid of modern medicine is a team sport, or at least it is when you're not allowed to just slap tape over it and snap it back into place.

"You really don't need to do this," I said, trying to sound more apologetic than aggravated. "I still have a couple of recovery charms on me, if you'll just let me get some electrolyte powder from my bag."

Thomas scowled and kept working. "I think using those charms frivolously counts as hurting yourself when you don't have to," he said. "Your body isn't built to move that energy around, and it costs more than I like you paying."

"I wonder if there's an actual physical difference between sorcerers and non-sorcerers," I said. "We have three of you now. If we popped you all into a CT scanner, would it show something it wouldn't show for the rest of us?"

"I have no idea what you just said, but you'll have plenty of time to experiment on me later. I hope."

"You know, that's the sweetest thing anyone's said to me in years." He sighed as he pulled his hands away and leaned back, frowning. "I hope you never have cause to say that again," he said. "This should hold, for now. I'd still like you to see our medic, but—"

"But you need me with the defenders holding the line, and we're going home," I said. "Either I'll get it set on Earth, or I'll ask Helen to help me when we get back to Ithaca. Or we'll all die here. If it's that one, it won't matter if I die with a few cracked ribs, as long as I don't get hit hard enough to puncture a lung."

Thomas' frown deepened. "I wish you hadn't come here just to die with me," he said, leaning forward until our foreheads touched. He exhaled heavily, closing his eyes. "I wish you'd found me twenty years ago, when this place still had some life left in it, and we would have had time."

"Yeah, but I don't think I *could* find you until the crossroads were gone, and it turns out that took a sorcerer," I said. "Our sorcerer, that we made together, two generations ago. I can't wait for you to meet everyone."

"I hope I have the chance." He straightened up and sighed. "Alice . . . I didn't tell the council everything."

"Yeah, I figured, since it feels sort of like the timeline sped up a lot while Sally and I were out meeting the neighbors. Can I assume you're going to tell me now?"

"Yes, but first—your Ithacan friends." He sobered. "How long were they going to give you before they followed?"

"Helen said they had to go to Empusa to get back the book Naga took, but once they finished their research, if they were going to come, they planned to do it right away," I said. "Why?"

"Because when I took down the barrier in hopes of getting even a few weeks' more magical supply, I discovered that it had been helping to maintain the structural integrity of the remaining dimensional membrane."

Shit. "That sounds bad. Is that as bad as it sounds?"

He didn't even bother to nod, just closed his eyes and wearily pinched the bridge of his nose. "It is. The membrane was always going to fail completely, with the pneuma gone. It was inevitable. What I didn't realize was that without my spell holding it together from this side . . . the process is accelerating now. Even before I took the barrier down, we didn't have much time. Taking everyone into the compound only shortens what remains. Our supplies aren't infinite, and with the pneuma gone and the membrane dissolving, we're not going to be able to rebuild them. I expect the atmosphere outside my wards to start dissipating at any moment." He grimaced. "After that happens, the air inside the wards will start to slip away. I don't have enough power left to keep it here."

"So how long do you think we have?"

"I don't know, exactly. It's not like the final extinction of a world that's been essentially kept in formaldehyde by an evil cosmic force that has now dissipated is a widely-studied phenomenon. It could be days, weeks—we might have time for the food to run out, and wouldn't that be a nice twist? Especially if we're able to convince any of the O'Vera to take refuge with us, given their customary appetites." He shook his head. "I'm a fool for thinking I owe these people anything."

I knew from his tone that he didn't mean the ones he'd already taken responsibility for. I grabbed his hand, pulling him closer to me.

"No, you're not," I said. "You're a good man. The Covenant couldn't break you. The crossroads couldn't break you. This place couldn't break you. Because you're a good man, and that's why you want to help the people who didn't deserve to be here. I know that

most folks who make bargains with the crossroads don't do it for the
altruistic reasons that you did . . ." And he broke in long enough to
laugh, a short, bitter sound. I didn't let go of his hand. "But that
doesn't mean they deserve to die whatever death comes when the
world dissolves under your feet and drops you into the void. Is there
even a void in a dead universe? Can you even die? Or do you just . . .
float in emptiness, forever?"

"I don't know. I don't think anyone does."

"So let's not find out." I squeezed his hand, hard. "Helen and
Phoebe are either on their way, or they're not. Either way, can we afford to wait for them?"

He shook his head.

"Can we afford to wait until everyone left in your territory is inside,
along with any more of the neighbors who want to join us?"

He nodded.

"All right. Can you live with yourself if not everyone comes inside?
If not everyone agrees to be saved?"

The Thomas I knew would have said yes without hesitation. As
long as the people he'd claimed personal responsibility for were safe,
he'd be able to deal with whatever result everyone else brought down
on their own heads. He protected what was his, and the rest could go
hang as far as he was concerned. This Thomas hesitated, looking con-
flicted. He was silent for a long time. Long enough that I started to
worry about what his answer was going to be. But he didn't pull his
hand out of mine, and he didn't look away from me.

"Before you got here, before Sally got here, I might have said no,"
he said finally, with grating, brutal honesty. "I'm here for the same
reason as many of these people, or if not them, their ancestors. I made
a bargain. I knew what the costs could be. I knew, from the things
Mary wouldn't say—not the things she wasn't allowed to say, the
things she *wouldn't*—that I was dealing with something unnatural.
That whatever the crossroads were, they shouldn't be. And I did it
anyway, because I was too desperate and too selfish to let you go. My
selfishness brought me here, just like theirs did. Why should I escape
if they don't?"

I raised my free hand and pressed it against the side of his face
though I didn't say anything. Every word sounded like it was hurting
him, and I needed to let him get this out.

He turned his head enough to kiss my palm, then returned to looking at me solemnly. "Before the two of you arrived, I thought I'd lost
everything, and finding a way to get myself out without giving up the

selfishness that got me here would be proof that all my punishment had been completely earned. I didn't want to be the man who deserved to feel like this. I wanted to be someone better. So I would probably have said no."

"And now?" I prompted gently.

"When we found Sally wandering the wastes, when she told me what she'd done to get taken away, when I knew for sure that Earth was still there, and how long it had been . . ." He sighed. "I knew you were gone. I knew everyone I'd known was gone. But the children might still be alive, and I owed it to them to try to make it back, and Sally was desperate to get home to James, who was her brother in every way that mattered. If I gave up, I was giving up for her, too, since any way out of here would have to come through me. And so I knew that if I had the chance to leave this place, I'd take it, whether or not everyone agreed to come with me."

"Good," I said.

He wasn't finished. "And then she brought me your guns and told me they'd been taken from a woman found unconscious outside our walls, and that she thought you might be another assassin. She didn't tell me how much you looked like your picture. I think she was trying to protect me. Sally got to watch the first time I mourned for you, you see, when she told me where she was from and what year it had been when the crossroads claimed her. Before her arrival, I'd been telling myself that time ran differently here, and it hadn't been as long for you. I think the crossroads knew, and wanted me to suffer with my hope for as long as possible, because Sally was the first person from Earth I'd seen arrive in almost fifty years." He sighed heavily. "There may be another world like this one out there somewhere, filled with its own captives."

"We'll find it," I told him. "We'll get out of here, and we'll find it if it exists, and we'll get them out."

He smiled a little. "You always were so damn convinced that you could fight the world and win," he said.

"So far I've been right."

"Except when you've been wrong."

I squeezed his fingers again. "Shush, you."

"Yes, dear." He said it with such immense fondness that my heart ached a little. "Sally brought me your guns, and I knew you were gone and that the crossroads had sent someone else to kill me. For a moment I let myself hope that it might be a grandchild come to bring me home again, but surely they would have been carrying something to distinguish them from you, not wanting to cause this exact confusion. I mourned you all over again in an instant."

"And while you were doing that, I was waking up and getting ready to murder you for replacing me with a couple dozen new wives," I said.

He smiled again, more broadly this time. "As if I could ever have replaced you."

"Hey, didn't mean you weren't willing to try," I said, as lightly as I could manage, and tugged him toward me. "Come here."

"We need to go join the effort to gather my subjects, and your ribs—"

"I know both those things, and I know we've both been alone for fifty years, no matter how many people we had near us, and I know you need to be close to me as much as I need to be close to you. Much as I don't like it, I'm okay not making out like teenagers behind the Red Angel while my ribs hurt this much, but I want to hold you for a little while, and you're going to let me. You can't go to the front line, and they're not counting on me yet." I let go of his hand and pulled my hand away, leaving him looking momentarily bereft at the loss of contact before I spread my arms and said, "Just get over here."

He sighed as he climbed onto the bed beside me, and we wrapped our arms around each other and lay down, still fully clothed, with our heads against the pillow.

"Hi," I said.

"Hello," he replied, with faint amusement. "Are we returning to introductions?"

"Not nearly enough mud for that," I said. "But I'd be happy to keep meeting you over and over again, for the rest of my life, if that was one of my options. You talked a lot, but I'm not completely sure you answered my question."

He sighed heavily. "My apologies. I . . . yes. Yes, Alice. Yes, if they won't all agree to come inside and let me try to save them, if they must persist in making war when we should be making peace with one another, then yes. I'll leave them here, and I'll come home with you."

"And Sally."

"And Sally," he agreed. "You were telling the truth when you told her that you'd spoken to James, yes? I don't know how she'll react if you were lying, and that's a fight I'd rather not have to witness."

"I can't say for sure that he's *her* James," I admitted. "Maybe there's a bunch of boys named James who fit that story. But that seems a little unlikely, and everything I said about the boy I met was true. He's from

Maine, the crossroads took his best friend, he's a sorcerer, and he's with our granddaughter. She'll keep him alive until we get home with Sally."

Thomas sighed, an almost imperceptible worry leaving his eyes. I hadn't realized it was there until it was gone.

"You care about her a lot," I said.

"She's the closest thing I've had to family in a very long time," he said. "I would have been able to understand the reasons for your falsehood, if you *had* been lying, but I would prefer not to see her hurt."

"Nope," I said. "Not lying. About anything, including being okay with the fact that you've apparently adopted a teenage girl who doesn't like me very much. We're going home, Thomas. I have faith in us."

"It's an impossible task you're asking me to achieve," he said. "You want me to work a kind of magic that's never been done before, with limited resources, without exhausting myself so severely that we simply wind up stranded in whatever dimension we're spilled out into."

"I know," I said. "But like I said, I have faith in you." I closed my eyes, exhaling, allowing myself to relax into the bed. It was a decent enough bed. Not up to the standards I was used to back on Earth, but for something scavenged in a desolate hell world, it was pretty good.

Slowly, as if he was afraid of somehow overstepping, Thomas tightened his arms around me and pulled me closer, until my forehead was pressed lightly to his chest, and I could hear the long-missed familiar rhythm of his heartbeat. Tangled up and keeping close, I sighed, and pulled myself closer still.

It had been a long, hard day for both of us—a long, hard decade, really—and it was no surprise when we fell asleep, not letting go.

"Boss?" The voice was Sally's, breaking through my fuzzy, somewhat disoriented dreams like an ice pick and shocking me back into wakefulness at the same time as I heard the door slam open. She sounded alarmed.

That wasn't a good sign. I pushed myself away from Thomas, distantly relieved that this time he'd still been there when it had been time for me to wake up, and shoved myself into a sitting position, already fully awake as I turned to face her.

"Knock," I recommended in a cold voice. Then: "What is it?"

She wasn't bleeding and had no new visible injuries. Her eyes were a little wild, and her spear was wet with what looked more like maple syrup than blood, but apart from that, she could have just been waking us up to prove that she could.

"They're in," she said, sagging and leaning against the spear for support. She was panting. The sudden urge to get her a cookie and a place to sit was almost overwhelming. "All of them. They're in."

Thomas was sitting up, blearier than I was, but still waking quickly enough that we probably wouldn't be dead if Sally had been something dangerous. "It's done?"

"All of them who were willing to come," she said. "The O'Vera and another contingent of Haspers attacked while we were still getting the last of our people inside. We lost over a dozen men. Our attackers lost a hell of a lot more. They're hungry, and dehydrated, and so tired it's almost criminal. I'm surprised they were able to march on us in the first place."

As I had almost expected, a look of brief, biting guilt flashed across Thomas' face. He wasn't responsible for the death of this world, but he had still hastened its decay on some level by siphoning away the pneuma attached to the new arrivals, keeping it from dissolving normally and entering the atmosphere. Without him, this place might have had a few more years. Of course, the people here had spent all the years up until now preying on each other, and without him, there would have been no haven for the people who weren't interested in violence and rapine, but there was no way to know.

There was no way to know any of this. I elbowed him lightly. "Hey. You offered them safety. They chose to stay outside and keep attacking each other. That's not on you."

"Listen to the lady who hauled you off for naptime when we needed you," said Sally. "This isn't your fault. Hey, lady."

"Alice," I said mildly. "The name is Alice."

"So you keep saying. These friends of yours. When are they supposed to show up?"

I wasn't really interested in having this conversation again. "Whenever they do," I said. "I can't exactly call them and ask where they are. Presumably, they're somewhere between here and Ithaca. I don't think we can wait for them."

"So we're fucked, is what you're telling me," said Sally, straightening. "You came here to get everybody's hopes up, and now we're all going to die even faster than we were before. I'm sorry, boss, it doesn't matter how much she looks or talks or acts—or fucks—like your dead wife, she's not her, and she never was. She's a trap laid by the cross-roads. And we both fell into it."

This *again*? I stared at her before turning, slowly, to look at Thomas. He was watching me, visibly worried.

"You can't think she's serious," I said. "You have to be smarter than that. Come on, honey, you know me. You know there's no chance the crossroads could mimic me well enough to fool you for more than a minute once we were both awake and actually talking to each other."

"I know Mary was there almost as soon as Alice Healy was born, arms out, ready to take her charge," he said slowly. "I know there's never been a living person the crossroads knew better than they knew my wife. I know that if they wanted to, they could make her in perfect replica, craft or steal a body, change it to suit whatever they needed it to be . . . maybe even shove poor Mary's ghost inside. Torture us both at the same time to punish her for keeping me out of their clutches as long as she did." Then he looked to Sally. "But I also know that if they were laying a trap to convince me, they wouldn't have had her come here and tell me she'd been getting *flensed alive* by someone she trusted for fifty years in order to stay in one piece long enough to get to me. They would have found something less immediately alarming to explain her presence. Something less likely to cause me to lose my temper."

I sagged in sudden relief, and only Sally's presence kept me from grabbing and kissing him like it was going to be the last time. Instead, I turned to her and said, coolly, "Believe me or not, but I am who I say I am, I'm not going anywhere, and we're all getting out of here."

"Without your friends."

Thomas slid off the bed and stood. "There may be a way," he said. "Alice has been traveling through dimensions via artificial means, causing even more disruption to the dimensional membrane, and hence the pneuma, than the norm. When she told me how she'd been rejuvenating herself for all this time, she caused me to actually assess the levels clinging to her skin. She's been having it removed regularly, but even with only this trip to fuel her, she had to cross dozens of barriers to get here. She currently has enough pneuma on her for ten people. I've long suspected that the crossroads metered out the arrivals of our newcomers to keep them from revitalizing the world sufficiently to make it a pleasant place to live. They've never allowed us this much at one time."

"So, what—you think you can scrape it off her and use it to open a door?"

"I think the word 'open' might be overly generous in that sentence, as opening something implies it can be closed again," he said. He looked at me, lips pressed into a thin line. "This will hurt. Not as much as your customary means of removal, since you'll keep your skin, but quite a bit all the same. And I've never moved this much pneuma at one time. There could be unexpected side effects."

"You have my full consent to pull my pin and chuck me like a grenade at the wall of the universe so that we can all blast our way the fuck out of here," I said cheerfully, sliding to my feet. "I can take a little pain, and it's not like I can use all this pneuma for anything." And it wasn't like he was going to let me carry it back to Naga the way I'd been doing.

And it wasn't like I particularly wanted to, either. I'd always gone running obediently back before this, but Thomas' horror over the idea of me being skinned was enough to make me wonder if the little telepathic helpers who'd always been there to ease the post-treatment pain might not have been flipping a few switches while they were inside my head, keeping me from getting as alarmed as I really should have been. It would be so easy for a Johrlac to implant a few subconscious impulses and commands. It was already clear that they'd been messing with my memory, enough to remove important pieces of information about the way the whole system worked, all without leaving holes for me to recognize and investigate.

I'd have to ask Sarah to check my head when we got home. She didn't like reading my thoughts—something about the level of single-minded obsession that had driven me through the last five decades being overwhelming, which Antimony said was a polite way of saying, "Your brain is a sack of broken glass, and she's afraid she'll cut herself"—but she'd do it if I asked her to. Better to know.

Thomas sighed. "I know you have a pain tolerance worthy of dedicated scholarship," he said. "I just wish you hadn't needed it, and I have no desire to be the one to hurt you."

Sally rolled her eyes like any teenager confronted with the thought that her father was attracted to someone, and I was reminded that while right now, she might look a few years older than me, she was actually the age she seemed: she was so terribly young, barely out of childhood when the crossroads took her. They always did appreciate an opportunity to prey on the young.

"If you two are done, I need to know the plan," she said.

Thomas took a deep breath. "We'll do this in the throne room," he said. "I'll need as much space as possible, and everyone should be as close as they can be. That's the only space we have that can hold us all. Sally, tell the guards to round everyone up, and warn anyone with children that they'll probably want to bring something to block out the screams. This is going to be brutal."

I didn't like his tone when he said that. Still, I shrugged, and said, "Works for me. Sally?"

"On it, boss," she said, and turned for the door.

"Wait," said Thomas. She glanced back. "Tell them to bring anything they're interested in keeping. I don't know how much stuff we'll be able to carry with us, but based on our individual arrivals here, and Alice's supplies, whatever we can carry will make the transit."

"All right," she said, slipping out of the room and leaving us alone.

I looked gravely at Thomas. He seemed too worried for what I understood of the situation, which admittedly wasn't as much as I would have liked. "Hey," I said softly. "Hey."

He focused on me. "Yes?"

"What are you so worried about? You've gathered everyone who's willing to be saved. You've kept these people alive as long as you possibly could, and you've done a better job than anyone could have asked of you. We have one more thing to do, and then we get to rest. We get to go home, and we get to rest."

He laughed, soft and bitter. "I'm not sure I remember how to do that anymore."

"Neither do I. So we'll learn a new way of resting, together, and that'll be nice for both of us."

"Alice . . . this isn't something I've ever done before. This isn't something I think *anyone* has ever done before. What if Naga has been torturing you because it was the only way to remove the pneuma without . . . without *killing* you in the process?"

"Then I die." I shrugged. "I've been running on borrowed time since you sold yourself to the crossroads to save me. I'd rather not die when it looks like we're finally going to be together, but it's not like I didn't know what I was doing when I threw myself into a killing jar looking for my missing husband. And I'd rather you didn't have to live believing that you're the reason I'm gone, but that's because you *wouldn't* be. If this kills me, blame the crossroads. This is all their fault. They should never have accepted the bargain you offered them in the first place. But because they did, we got Kevin, and Jane, and all the grandchildren, and a few good years together."

He smiled. "They *were* good, weren't they? I haven't just been lying to myself to make this all seem like it was worth it?"

"They were the best." I took his hand, raised it to my lips, and kissed his knuckles. "If this is how I die, it's okay. I give you permission to do whatever you have to do to save as many of these people as you possibly can, and to forgive yourself after it's over. Not that I think you will. You've never been great at forgiving yourself."

"Neither have you."

"Takes one to know one," I said. He grabbed me then, yanking me toward him, and kissed me like he was kissing me for the first time and the last time and every time in between all at once. He kissed me like he was never going to kiss me or anyone else again. When he stepped away, staring at me wonderingly, I was still holding his hand. I smiled at him, squeezed his fingers, and finally did something I'd been trying not to do for fifty years. I finally let go.

It was time to end this.

Nineteen

"Your daughter will do amazing things, but you will never
see them. I'm so sorry, Fran."

—Juniper Campbell

*Stepping into the Autarch's throne room, preparing to get the hell
out of this terrible, dying dimension*

ALL THE PEOPLE SALLY and the guard had herded into the throne
room looked bad, although the Murrays were the worst. Even
compared to the others, they were malnourished and dehydrated, visibly unwell. They held themselves in rigid groups, clearly mistrustful
of everyone around them, clearly scared out of their wits. Thomas'
people also stood apart, but they were easy to find; they were the ones
who looked like they'd been eating regularly, even if not all of them
had been eating enough, or who had clean faces, or small animals accompanying them. A little boy of what I'd guess to be around five,
with horns and bright blue skin, clutched a chicken against his chest
like it was the only good thing left in the world. The chicken, which
was also blue, didn't seem to mind.

They all murmured when the two of us emerged into the room.
Thomas kissed me on the forehead. "Go to the throne," he said. "I'll
be right back."

Then he turned and made for the door, vanishing into the hall with
Sally close behind him. I walked to the throne as instructed, shrugging
off my pack and placing it at the foot before flopping onto the cushion.
The gasp from several of his guards was remarkably satisfying. I smiled
sweetly at them and leaned back into the cushions, trying to relax.

It wasn't happening. Thomas was distressed enough to keep me on
edge, even if I hadn't been steeling myself against the promised pain.
Things always hurt more when you have time to anticipate them, and

right now, I had nothing *but* time. I closed my eyes, shutting out the rest of the room, and listened to the rustle of bodies, the shuffle of feet. There were more people here than I could count, but definitely fewer than three hundred. It was so much larger of a group than I'd been expecting, but probably less than Thomas had been hoping for, given the size of his territory's population. It was all too much.

Too bad we didn't have a Johrlac. They could probably wave their hands and work some complicated math and just pop us out of here like popping the yolk out of a boiled egg, smooth and easy. A true Johrlac, anyway. A cuckoo couldn't do it. The Johrlac we have back on Earth have been stunted somehow by their lack of exposure to the dimensional hive mind that controls all of Johrlar and guides the rest of them. I don't pretend to understand it. I'm not sure any non-telepath could.

I had time to relax completely into the throne before I heard footsteps and cracked open an eye. There was Thomas, his arms full of our old friends, the swamp bromeliad. Sally was behind him, carrying a crate of what looked like ritual tools. He began laying the flowers out around me, careful to avoid the thorns. I started to sit up. He waved me back down.

"No, no, stay as you are," he said. "This will go easier if you don't move."

Okay. That was a little ominous. I raised my eyebrows and just watched him, until he offered the last bromeliad to me.

"You want to get the sap into your system if you can," he said. "It will help."

"I love these flowers," I said, and closed my fingers around the stem, barely wincing as the thorns bit into my skin. The pain only lasted for a second before it was followed by the soothing peace of bromeliad toxins, washing all my little aches away. I felt like I could breathe more easily. It was like going from sober to pleasantly drunk without needing to do any swallowing.

"Alice." I looked to the sound of Thomas' voice. "Alice, I want you to remember that you consented to this, but you can still tell me 'no' at any point. You are allowed to ask me to stop."

"I know," I mumbled.

"Do you? Because I don't care how much you think this is the only way, I'm not going to proceed if you don't want me to."

"I want to have more time," I said. "I want to have more time with you, and with the kids, and I want to see *you* have time with the kids. I want to have more kids."

"Not while you're this inebriated, dear," said Thomas, sounding faintly amused.

Sally had been unpacking the box while we were talking, laying out an array of tools and vessels around us. Thomas turned to face the room, raising his hands.

"You have known me by many names," he said. "And those names were necessary and good, for this place, for this time. We are leaving them all behind today, along with all bargains, all crimes, all rivalries. If this succeeds, we will be free of here, and those of us who came here from other worlds can hopefully go home. Those who were born here can find places to settle where the air is still good and the ground is still fertile."

"What if we're not wanted?" demanded a voice.

"We weren't wanted here, and we did okay," said Sally. "We'll figure it out. We'll survive. That's what we do. That's what we've always done. We've survived."

"I'm going to release the spells outside this room now," continued Thomas. "It will not be safe to leave here after I've done that. If something alarms you, I'm sorry, but you'll have to stay. The translation charm will not extend beyond this room. The air will not extend beyond this room."

"We'll be fine," said a voice I recognized as Lyn.

"Not everyone will," said Thomas. "Stay inside."

A general murmur of assent met what wasn't really a request by any definition of the word; he reached down, and Sally handed him a lit candle I hadn't seen her lighting. Everything was sort of fuzzy. I wasn't tracking well. Thomas blew the candle out, and the air in the room got brighter, somehow, like we were on a plane that had just fully pressurized. The murmuring got louder.

"It is done," he said, handing the candle back to Sally. Then he turned to me. "Can you still hear me?"

I could. I smiled and nodded.

"Can I have the flower back?"

I frowned, pulling it a little closer to myself.

He sighed. "Alice, I needed you slightly anesthetized, not too drugged to understand simple requests. If you don't give me that flower back, you'll keep forcing further doses of sap into your bloodstream, and you won't be able to stay awake through the necessary procedure. Please give it back."

He sounded very serious, and like this was very important. I sighed and let go.

"Thank you," he said, whisking the crushed flower away before taking my hands in his. "I'm going to begin by peeling off a portion of the pneuma. This should allow me to strengthen the effects already in play and begin attempting to construct a door. I won't take more than I could pull from an ordinary traveler. Nod if you understand."

I nodded.

"Boss?" asked Sally, unsure.

"This is what I did to you when you first arrived," he said. "It won't hurt her too badly."

"I said he could," I said, voice gone dreamy.

"Yes, you did," Thomas said. "Sally, I know you're concerned, but I promise you, I explained as much as I could before we reached this point. I can't be sure of what will happen as we continue; I've never removed this much from one person before, and yes, it could hurt her. Magic has a cost. It could hurt me, too. I have to get us out of here, and this is the only chance we have left at this point."

"I don't like it."

"I don't either," he said, with deep regret, and still holding my hands, he *pulled*.

The human body is full of things we can't see. The air in our lungs, the sugar in our blood, the electricity in our cells. The feeling of Thomas pulling wasn't like a physical thing, but it was a physical thing at the same time; there was no other way to wrap my head around it. He was using a mechanism I didn't have and thus couldn't fully tense against, like having him try to suck the air out of me during a kiss, or somehow drain the glucose from my veins.

It ached. It ached and it burned, even through the bromeliad haze. The pain was enough to make the fog less dense, and I surfaced a bit toward unwilling sobriety, flashing him and Sally a quick smile as the pulling and pressure finally faded away.

"That's not so bad," I said.

"That was just the first layer," Thomas replied, expression going grim. "It may have been *less* of a torture to remove it all on one go."

Meaning the flensing Naga had been doing might not have been the worst possible option. I forced myself to relax again, this time keeping my eyes open and staring up at the ceiling. It was covered in a mosaic pattern of abstract shapes and chunks of colored glass, and I couldn't quite understand it, but I was still effectively high enough from the sap that I just *knew* that if I did, everything would make sense.

"Again," said Thomas, and squeezed my hands.

This time the pain was more immediate, and substantially more intense, like he was peeling the skin off of a fresh sunburn. By the time he stopped and the pressure passed, every inch of me felt like it was on fire, and the comforting haze of the bromeliads was completely gone.

I lifted my head and stared at him. "Are we done?" That still hadn't been so bad. I'd gone through a lot worse. I could—

"No," he said, sorrowfully. "I am so sorry, Alice, but I need more, or we're not going to be able to open a door out of here. Attacking this barrier is like trying to bore through solid steel with a needle."

"Always thought magic would be flashier," said Sally. "Not just you scrunching up your face like you're constipated while you break a woman's fingers."

"Can't all be glamorous, I guess," I said, trying to sound flippant, and not like I wanted to call the whole thing off. "How many more layers we got?"

"Quite a few," said Thomas. "I've peeled off as much as I could get from any five other arrivals. I could stop now; I could restore all the barriers, rebuild my shield around what's left of the membrane, and still power this world for a year off what I've gathered."

"Or you could pull the pin like we both know you need to." I smiled. "Come on, buddy. I want my little red wagon."

"I love you," he said, voice soft, and leaned in to kiss my forehead before he pulled again.

The pain was immediate, and as big as any pain I'd ever felt before in my life. It made being skinned alive seem like child's play, and in a flash of sudden, horrifying clarity, I understood that while Naga had absolutely been torturing me, it probably *had* been the most merciful way to go about things. My head snapped back, eyes open and staring at the ceiling, and the picture came into sudden, horrible focus.

Snakes. The shapes around the outside of the design were snakes. Snakes with the upper bodies of humans, because I was looking at a frieze of Naga's people.

This must have been their original world. They had started here, in this dead place, before moving to Empusa, which explained why they were so interested in dimensional travel and the way worlds could interact and intersect. Which meant Naga's real crime wasn't hurting me; it was how long he'd persisted in doing it. He'd known this place existed all along. He could have sent me here the first time I asked him for help. Or maybe he hadn't known. Maybe it was lost information, or his people thought their dimension had died so long ago that it had surely rotted into nothing by now.

But he'd been so firm on the idea that I couldn't go this way, that the worlds I'd find in this direction wouldn't support life. Had he been trying to keep me from this world in specific, or had he believed its decay would have spoiled more than just Cornale? Had he been trying to protect his investment?

Everything was starting to take on a new context, and I didn't like any of it. And then I couldn't think about any of it anymore because the pain was too intense; every nerve was on fire, and my heart was hammering harder than I had ever felt it before, pounding against the inside of my chest like it was hoping to escape. I couldn't breathe.

The pain slackened off for a moment, and I tasted peppermint. Forcing my eyes open—when had they closed? I didn't remember closing them—I blinked blearily through stress-induced black spots on my vision at Thomas, who was holding a tube of peppermint glucose gel to my lips, forcing it into my mouth.

"Just breathe and swallow, sweetheart," he said. "You're doing fantastically."

"No, she's not," protested Sally. "She looks like she's about to have a heart attack. Are you trying to become a widower? Like, you got so used to thinking of yourself that way that now you need to make it true?"

"I would prefer not to kill my wife," said Thomas, removing the empty tube and dropping it to the floor. "But she made it very clear that I was to do whatever I had to in order to get us out of here, and that at least one of us had to make it home."

No, I thought. *I changed my mind. We can stay here until the ground dissolves under our feet, we can rotate in the void together, we can be stardust, but I don't want to die.*

Sadly, humans aren't mind readers, and I couldn't speak. I closed my eyes again as Thomas stepped closer, and the pulling sensation resumed, followed, in what could have been an hour or could have been an instant, by the searing, all-consuming pain.

It wasn't burning. I've been burnt before, and this wasn't that. It wasn't freezing, either. It was like . . . rotting and being roasted by the sun in the same moment, the harsh, tingling blaze of radiation ripping through my body, and it was agony, and if trauma leaves scars no one can see, this was going to leave a scar the size of my entire body. Assuming I lived that long. Assuming this didn't kill me. Please don't let this kill me. Thomas was as traumatized as I was, just in different ways, and he didn't deserve to start his journey home by killing me, not when he'd waited this long.

Not when we'd both waited this long. The universe doesn't actually listen to prayers, and while I've been to plenty of dimensions I would call hells if pressed, I've never seen a single heaven; I don't know if there's a god, or more than one god, or anyone listening beyond forces like the crossroads, who we really wish wouldn't listen at all. I still prayed as I lay there burning but not burning, rotting on a cellular level, coming apart and collapsing in on myself like a black hole.

I prayed to no one and nothing and everything. I prayed to the gods the mice had always so fervently believed my ancestors to be. And I prayed for three things.

I prayed that we'd get out of here.

I prayed that I would survive this.

And I prayed this was the journey that finally ended with my family in one piece, after so many years of being broken. Setting a bone doesn't heal it. It gives it a chance. It creates the possibility of healing, and I wanted that possibility more than I wanted anything else in the world. I didn't want Thomas to kill me trying to save us all, as much because I didn't want to die as because I didn't want him to carry the burden of having killed me. I wanted us to go home together, and to see him see our family.

And then the pain somehow, mysteriously, impossibly, got even bigger and even brighter, burning through the entire universe, and I wasn't praying anymore. I wasn't wanting anything anymore, except for the pain to stop. Nothing else would make things okay. Only the pain stopping would fix anything.

I didn't know whether my eyes were open or closed; everything was blackness either way, so profoundly dark that the possibility of light seemed like a lie. There was a vast shattering sound, like someone had struck a mirror the size of a ballroom wall with a hammer, and like any broken mirror, it rained down around us in slicing shards, and I was ripped open, laid bare before the uncaring universe. The pain got even bigger, now searing and crushing at the same time, and then, mercifully, it stopped, and so did I.

And then, against all reason and logic and reasonable, logical outcomes of the situation, I woke up, and if that's surprising to you, imagine how it felt to *me*. I mean, at first, it felt like falling down a rabbit hole through comforting numbness, dropping like my namesake into the unending dark that lay at the center of all things. I fell, and the pain fell away, so far behind me that it couldn't possibly catch me again.

Only then the fall began to slow, and I began to remember that I had a body, or my body began to remember that it had a me. It began with a low, numbing ache that spread through all my limbs in near synchronicity, which I realized after a moment was the blood beginning to circulate again. Apparently, at some point, it had stopped, which was probably why the hurting had gone away. Human people need blood circulation to be alive, and for a little while there, I might not have been.

That was fun. Well, no, that was absolutely horrifying, and I didn't like it one little bit, but dead people don't get to have opinions about things unless they come back as ghosts, and now that I knew where Thomas was, I didn't need to start a haunting. It would still be good to know for sure whether he got out, whether he'd been able to yank enough pneuma off of me to use me like the grenade I was, but not good enough to justify coming back and hanging out the way Mary and Rose had done. If I was finished, let me be finished. Let me rest.

It had been a long, long time since I'd had anything resembling a proper nap.

But the ache continued to spread through my body, until it reached my chest and became a splintering pain that seemed to ebb and flow with my breath, which was how I realized I was breathing. And if I was breathing, I wasn't dead, and that was a little bit annoying, since I had just come to terms with the idea that I was finally done. I decided that annoyance was a good enough reason to wake up, and so I did.

Opening my eyes, I found myself looking at Sally from a much closer distance than I would have expected. Her face was right up in mine, cheeks streaked with dirt and tears, hair tangled as she took a deep breath and leaned in toward me.

The pain in my chest suddenly made a lot of sense. She'd been giving me CPR. But I was awake now, and I didn't want anyone giving me CPR, especially not someone who'd been pretty unpleasant to me during our brief acquaintance.

". . . wait," I said, or tried to, anyway. It came out as more of a croak.

Sally heard me anyway. She stopped, staring down at me.

"Are you alive?" she demanded.

I took a deep breath again—or tried to. It seemed like nothing I wanted to accomplish was really working out for me. My chest refused to fully expand.

My struggle must have shown in my face. Sally grimaced. "Sorry," she said. "This was my first time doing CPR on a person, and not a training manikin. I think I may have broken a few ribs. It was an accident."

I glared at her and didn't bother trying to sit up. Broken ribs suck, and since mine had already been cracked before she started with the compressions, at least one of them felt like it had given way. Normally, I've been lucky enough to avoid that particular scenario. But if what Thomas had been saying before was accurate, my luck, which was always unpredictable, had been temporarily stripped away when he removed the pneuma. Sitting up felt like it would be taking things a step too far, at least right now, and so I stayed where I was.

It would have been polite to thank her, but that would have taken too much air. At least I could breathe normally. At least I wasn't falling anymore.

At least we had gotten out of there.

"Alice, thank God," said Thomas, suddenly appearing next to Sally. That makes it sound like he teleported or something, when really, he had just been outside my currently limited frame of vision. "You're awake. I'm so sorry. I'm so, so sorry . . ."

"S'okay." He looked like hell, as filthy as Sally, with more streaks in the dirt on his face, some from tears and some from frustrated wiping at the same while they were falling, resulting in a muddy palimpsest of a trauma I had managed to sleep—or maybe die—through. How did they get so *dirty*? Dimensional crossing wasn't a form of mud wrestling. My lips were dry. I licked them, swallowed, and said, "Knew what I was doing."

"Well, *I* didn't, and we are never, ever doing that again."

I snorted. "No," I agreed. Then: "Happened?"

Thomas took my hand and a deep breath, in that order. "We made it," he said.

I closed my eyes, relaxing as much as I could through the pain in my chest and the ache in my limbs. We made it out of that damned killing jar. We were going to make it home from wherever we were now. Everything else was extraneous.

"You can sleep if you have to, but I'd prefer it if you didn't if you don't have to," said Thomas, squeezing my hand. "Please."

"She's exhausted," said Sally.

"She's *alive*. I thought I'd killed her."

"Phoebe said—"

I opened my eyes again. My vision was a little clearer this time, and I could see a cloth ceiling stretched above us, a blue so pale that I'd initially taken it for the sky. We were in a tent. Given the shade of blue, we were in an *Ithacan* tent, meaning Helen and Phoebe had managed to find us.

"I know what Phoebe said," snapped Thomas. "And she was right, but dammit, we need to stay with Alice now." He looked back at me. "Darling, when I was looking at your tattoos, I saw several that were associated with healing. Do you know what they do?"

I considered whether I felt well enough to nod, and finally forced myself to do so.

"This is a bad idea," said Sally.

"I'm allowed to have the occasional bad idea," snapped Thomas.

Sally sighed. "I'm going to go get Phoebe," she said, and stood, vanishing.

"Bones," I said. Then, "General."

"Anything relating to organ damage?"

That was an alarming question, especially given that the spells contained in my tattoos could only be used on myself. I wanted to ask which of my organs had been damaged—maybe my lungs, if my ribs were even more badly broken than they felt—but the question felt like too much work. Instead, I frowned and asked, "Why bad idea?"

Even that was too much work. I wanted to go back to sleep.

Thomas swallowed, looking haggard enough that what I wanted didn't matter as long as I could make him stop looking like that. "It was . . . difficult breaking the barrier from the inside. It took even more effort than I had anticipated. I had to keep ripping the pneuma off of you long past the point where I wanted to stop—your blood pressure was clearly far too high, and your temperature was spiking badly, but we'd gone so far and used up so much of what we had that stopping would have killed us all, you probably included. So I kept going."

He sounded so genuinely sorry about that that it hurt to hear. I was already in physical pain; I didn't need to be in emotional pain at the same time. I tried to lift my hand to comfort him, and it didn't want to respond. Oh, that was frustrating. I frowned. I could still do that much, at least.

"But we made it! Alice, we made it. We're out. We've been trying to resuscitate you since then. You have several broken ribs, judging by the way you're breathing, and you had at least one heart attack. Possibly more than one."

That didn't make a lot of sense. CPR alone won't bring someone out of a true cardiac arrest, just keep their blood moving long enough to prevent brain damage before their heart can be restarted. I frowned more.

"I may have exhausted us both getting us out, but it's a sorry sorcerer who can be dropped into a dimension with more ambient magic than that hellhole and not manage at least a small electrical charge," said Thomas.

So he'd been shocking me back to life? Useful man. I smiled and closed my eyes.

He shook my shoulder. "I know you're tired, love, I know you want to sleep, but I need you to stay awake. It's going to take me time to recharge, even with access to a living pneuma. I can manage small, elemental things right now because I'm an elementalist before anything else. I can't manage a healing. I've never been able to do that, and there wasn't enough ambient magic in the bottle to let me learn. If you want to repair the damage, you'll have to do it yourself."

"Not right now, she won't," snapped a beautifully familiar voice. I couldn't turn my head, but I could still smile, and so I did that.

"Helen," I rasped.

"Hello, you beautiful fool," she said, voice softening. "Even Tyche's love wasn't enough to save you this time. You ran faster than we could follow, and by the time we caught up, you had already gone into the jar."

"Aikanis?" I asked. Three syllables seemed to be about my limit right now.

"Naga wasn't pleased to return the book but recognized that an Ithacan descendant's claim superseded his own. He surrendered it rather than fight with Phoebe, and oh, you should have seen that old snake squirm. He was *not* pleased to hear that you'd gone on ahead, or that you intended to enter. It could have been a suicide mission."

"Technically, it was," said Thomas. "She did die."

"And don't think I won't be discussing that with you, at length, once she's stable." The soft clop of Helen's hooves came closer. "Which she is *not* right now. Sally tells me you were trying to coerce Alice into using some of those tattoos she's covered with, and I know you weren't doing that, because we both know that her humors are already out of balance with themselves. Unbalancing them further could only have negative effects on her health."

"Which would be less extreme if her heart weren't damaged!" Thomas protested.

Helen sighed. "Aceso, grant me strength," she said, almost under her breath. "Get out of here, now."

"But—"

"There are to be no 'buts,' human. The people you saved, at the expense of your own Odysseus, need you. They wait for your wisdom, such as it is, and they put no faith in Phoebe's word. If we're to navigate them home, we'll need you to calm their anxious nerves. Get out."

Thomas looked at her bleakly, then turned back to me and squeezed my hand. "I'll be right outside," he said. "I'll be back in an instant if you need me, I promise you I will. I'm so sorry, Alice."

Helen snorted. "As you should be. Now go."

Thomas let go of my hand. I would have grabbed for him if my arms had been working. Instead, I could only watch helplessly as he straightened and stepped out of my field of vision. A bare instant later, Helen stepped into view and crouched down, placing something cool and damp that smelled of herbs on my forehead.

"Koalemos has been with that man for a very long time," she said, settling beside me. "Only the God of Fools could have sustained him in your absence. Or perhaps he watches over you both, you lucky, lucky fool. Although your luck failed you in this instance."

I made a small sound of protest. She shook her head.

"No, I mean that sincerely. Yes, you found the papers that led you to the man, if a man who would kill you to save himself, and then try to convince you to repeat the act to salve his conscience can truly be worth finding. And yes, we followed the instructions and your trail here, to poor, once-sweet Cornale, which will grow sweet again, thanks to your actions."

She pursed her lips, wiping the cool, damp thing across my forehead. "The broken vessel was shattered by the blow from within and has crumbled away. The door is gone. Not closed or sealed: removed. It no longer poisons the pneuma of Cornale."

I smiled. Good for us.

"Had you been a little less eager, we would have told you not to go through the door to begin with," she said. "When Aikanis fell through it, he was with a full detachment of cartographers and sorcerers, all of them set to support his explorations. All of them trapped by a world that they were never meant to find."

She shook her head, lips pressed into a hard line. "Three of their sorcerers gave their lives to get the rest of them out. They drained themselves to nothing, and they did their best to break the bonds holding that lost world to this one. They failed, and so felt they had failed Cornale, and Ithaca, for the danger remained. They exiled themselves. You have brought home more than a dozen explorers, returning their legacies to their families, by telling us how their stories ended. The three sorcerers who died there will be remembered for their sacrifice. Their names will be sent into glorious retirement."

"Why . . . mad?" If Aikanis had lost three men in getting out of the dead dimension, and we'd only lost me—and not for good—it didn't make sense for her to be angry with Thomas.

"Because I know you'd do *anything* for that man, even die, and I can't believe he let you do it," she said, voice going sharp. "We would have found another way."

"No . . . time," I said. I was so very tired. My eyelids felt like they weighed ten pounds each, and I could feel them starting to drift closed. "Dying."

"I know the world was dying," she said gently. "The girl Sally, she told us everything, and we believe her, because unlike you and your Penelope, she has no cause to lie. It wouldn't have fallen so easily upon your exit if it had been able to sustain itself any longer. You've done what you set out to do, and you can rest now. We'll see about repairing the damage in the morning, when you're stable, and then we'll start for home."

That sounded pleasant enough. I let my eyes close, sighing, and relaxed into the bedding beneath me. I couldn't remember ever having been this tired in my life. Maybe a few times when I'd been injured back in Buckley, but that had been so long ago that I'd started to question my memory of how exhausted I'd been. This was impossible to question.

I didn't sleep. I just drifted, lost on a tired bed of weariness and aches. I missed my tunnel and the topple through the dark. At least that had been painless and peaceful.

Helen left, coming back a while later with a bowl of rich, salty broth that she fed to me one spoonful at a time. I would have been embarrassed by my own weakness if it had been Sally, or even Thomas, but because in Ithaca, food is love, I knew she wasn't judging me. She fed me, and I ate, and when she followed the soup with sips of some sort of sweet, sugary drink I didn't recognize, I drank, and eventually she left, and I was alone again.

This time, I did sleep, at least long enough that when I woke again, it was to darkness and silence. I was still too weak to move, but someone was nestled in beside me, warm and solid. I turned my head as far as I could, which wasn't far enough, and he stirred, making a soft mumbling noise. I smiled. Thomas. I closed my eyes again.

We both slept.

Twenty

"Someone hurts your family, you make them understand why no one hurts your family twice. You make the lesson very, very clear."

—Alexander Healy

In an Ithacan tent, barely able to move, still in a presumably hostile dimension full of man-eaters, so, you know, having a great time

THE NEXT TIME I woke up, the tent was filled with morning light and Helen was sitting next to me with another bowl of broth. I tried to sit up and scowled when I still couldn't move. Okay, this was getting ridiculous.

"What's . . . wrong?" I managed to ask. Even that took too much effort.

"We think you had what the people in your dimension refer to as 'a stroke' shortly before your heart stopped," said Helen bluntly. "The strain you put yourself through by allowing an untrained sorcerer to strip the pneuma from your body so quickly was too much. There are methods for removing it safely—surely Naga must have shown you some of those, given that you've been cleaned off regularly for as long as I've known you; that old snake has to be good for something—and you followed none of them. You're lucky your Penelope was able to bring you back at all."

I stared at her, eyes wide with horror. "Fix it," I demanded.

"Damage to the brain is trickier than damage to other systems. I don't know if we can. And that wasn't the only consequence, although I expect it to be the one you care the most about."

Well, she was right about that at least. I continued staring at her. Finally, I scowled. "Tattoos?"

"All your embedded spells are still with you, and if you want to repair your skeletal system at this point, that should be within your limits. You'll need another night for soft tissue. But before you do, a moment." Helen's expression turned grave. "Phoebe is willing to repair what damage she can. She has two requirements for you, if she does."

"What?"

"You won't return to Empusa for any longer than it takes to collect whatever you may have left there. Your association with Naga is done. This is not up for negotiation."

I nodded with difficulty. "O . . . kay. And?"

"You and your Penelope have an obligation to the people you removed from the dead world. You will see them settled in a place that will have them, and after that's done, you will go *home*, and stay there long enough to get some help laying your fears to rest. You are our friend. We love you dearly. We would rather you be healing yourself in peace and safety than running around risking your life on legs that we have granted you."

I blinked, thinking this through. It sounded like they were happy enough to let me finish fulfilling my obligations, as long as I was willing to go back to Earth when I was done, and . . . get therapy? Maybe? My kids had been trying to convince me to do that for years. I smiled at her.

"Sure," I said.

Helen smiled back, with obvious relief. "I'll get Phoebe," she said and rose, leaving the full bowl of broth behind as she walked to the door. I stayed where I was. It wasn't like I had any real choice in the matter.

Two sets of hoofbeats sounded a few minutes later, and then Phoebe was there, kneeling next to me and taking my hand. "Helen tells me you've agreed," she said. "Is this true?"

". . . yes," I managed.

"Then close your eyes and trust me."

I closed my eyes. I trusted her.

Thomas' magic was the magic of Earth, no matter what dimension he was in, and it always felt a little bit like fire, even when it was being used kindly. I didn't have any magic of my own; mine was all borrowed, and all implanted in me on Empusa, where it felt like sandpaper on my skin. Not unpleasant, but absolutely abrasive. Phoebe's magic was Ithacan. It felt like a warm wind blowing off the ocean, full of stinging salt but also gentle heat, cleansing and wiping the world away.

She rubbed some sort of oil on my wrists and temples, humming under her breath. I relaxed as the pain in my chest smoothed and faded, the bones knitting back together. The ache remained, damaged lungs not popping back until she moved on to the soft tissues of my organs, and I actually *felt* the moment when my heartbeat evened out, a hitch I had barely been aware of smoothing away to be replaced by a normal rhythm.

By the time Phoebe took her hands away, I didn't hurt at all. "You can open your eyes now," she said, and I did, blinking up at her. She smiled, offering me her hand. "Let me help you up."

I took her hand. It was easy. I just thought about it, and I did it, and the fact that it felt remarkable to me was new, and different, and I hoped it wouldn't stay remarkable for long. She pulled me to my feet as she rose, and I stood without difficulty.

My knees complained a little, which was odd, but not odd enough to make me stop or sit back down. When we were done, we were both on our feet, and when Phoebe let go of me, I didn't fall down. Instead, I looked down at myself, noting that everything seemed to be intact; I was even still wearing the clothes I'd been in when we started the ritual. I ran my hands along the length of my body, then held my arms out in front of me, testing for tremors. They didn't even shake.

"You're a miracle worker," I said.

"I am touched by Perse, as you are beloved of Tyche, and like the love of any god, my blessings have their limits," she said, in a tone which implied correction. "Miracles are for the gods. I cannot fully restore what has been taken, but I can do as much as my gifts allow."

That was ominous. I blinked but decided not to push. Thomas was going to tell me all about it, I was sure, probably while apologizing for letting me suffer the consequences of my own actions. "I still appreciate it," I said. "Helen told me your conditions, and they're fine by me. I don't think Thomas would have let me go back to Naga even if you'd been okay with the idea, and I want to spend some time with my family. I feel like I don't know them as well as I want to. And Thomas doesn't know them at all, right now."

"That sounds good," said Phoebe. "You need to rest."

"Yeah, we do."

"You may not be able to receive magical healing again."

That was new. I blinked. "Oh?" But then, before I'd started gallivanting around dimensions like it was my job, I'd never had access to magical healing. It isn't much of a thing on Earth, unless you could hook up with a Caladrius, which is a big part of the reason there aren't many of them left. After I'd been bitten by the Bidi-taurabo-haza, I'd been in physical therapy for more than a year, and I hadn't walked without a limp for almost five. Losing something I hadn't been expecting to keep wasn't much of a blow, although Phoebe looked at me like it was.

Then again, Ithaca didn't have indoor plumbing, and if someone had tried to tell me I could never have a shower again, I wouldn't have taken it very well. We get used to the things we think of as normal.

"Your system can only handle so much," she said. "I would discharge those spells without spending them, if I were you."

"Can I even *do* that?"

"Yes. It's a matter of intent," she said. "Did Naga never tell you?"

"I get the feeling Naga never told me a lot of things, or if he did, I forgot them as soon as it was convenient for him that I not know those things," I said grimly. "You'll have to tell me how to do it, but I'm willing. I'll release them as soon as we get home—just in case something goes wrong in the interim."

She nodded. "That seems fair. You should go. Your Penelope is waiting, and angry to be kept so long in abeyance."

I paused. "Why do you keep calling him that? His name is Thomas."

"Because he waited on his island for fifty years for you to come and find him, and kept his faith for all that time," she said. "And you, his Odysseus, traveled through stormy seas, disasters, and the wrath of the gods themselves to find your way back to him. He was the king of Ithaca, you know."

"What?" I blinked at her, not following.

"Odysseus, the first one. He was the king of Ithaca, and his story was so beloved that our sages carried it to all the nearby worlds, including your own. His name has been retired since his death, but we use it still, for the faithful, and the lucky, and the foolish." She smiled at me. "You've earned it. Now go."

"Okay," I said, still not quite sure what she was talking about, but not really in the mood to argue, since it sounded like she was saying the Odyssey had actually *happened* in the dimension next door to our own, and that was more than I felt equipped to deal with right now. Besides, I was standing up, and that alone felt amazing. I walked toward the mouth of the tent, pushed it open, and stepped out into the daylight.

We were still on Cornale; that was obvious from the dry, cracked land around us, which looked like a verdant paradise after the dimension with no name. This world wasn't dead yet, and maybe now it wasn't going to be, since we'd managed to excise the parasitic influence of the dead world from its pneuma. This was all very confusing and made me feel more like a cell in the body of something much, much larger than I liked. I wanted to go home where I could be to scale with the problems around me, and they might be big and terrible, but they'd be comprehensible.

The people we'd evacuated with us had set up a campsite, and they mingled with Ithacan satyrs, perfectly at ease in this new place. Children ran by, shrieking with laughter. It was almost like being back at the carnival if the carnival had been mostly made up of cryptids. Although—out here—everyone was a cryptid. Earth's science hadn't verified the existence of anyone here except for me, Thomas, and Sally, and Earth's science said Thomas and I were both much older than we actually were.

Sally was the first to spot me. She was standing near a firepit talking to several of the guards, leaning on her still-present polearm, when her eyes went wide.

"Boss! Boss!" she yelled, without taking her eyes off of me. "She's awake!"

She didn't move, just stayed where she was and pointed as Thomas emerged from another tent that had been constructed nearby. He turned to follow her finger, then broke into a run, heading directly for me. I braced for impact.

It didn't come. He slowed when he was still several feet away, stopping when he was just barely within arm's reach, and stared at me, swallowing hard enough that I automatically followed the movement of his throat. I blinked. The cameo tattoo was gone, meaning its effect had been canceled or discharged. He was aging again. We both were.

That was nice. The way he was looking at me wasn't, particularly. Maybe there was something wrong with me that I hadn't seen yet. "I got something on my face?" I asked, trying to sound light and disarming. I didn't do a very good job of it. If anything, I sounded scared out of my wits, which wasn't far from the truth. Maybe he'd been so sure that I was going to die that he was disappointed that I hadn't. Maybe—

He lurched abruptly forward and wrapped his arms around me before I could finish the thought, jerking me against him and kissing me deeply. I stiffened for a moment, startled, then relaxed and kissed him back. The embrace lasted for what felt like several minutes before Sally said, from closer than I necessarily liked, "Okay, she's moving under her own power. Do you have to try to suck her face off when the rest of us are watching? Some of us don't have any good options for a girlfriend unless we want to get with one of the goat ladies, and we'd rather you got a room."

Thomas broke off enough to turn and glare at her, not letting go of me. I started laughing. Sally smirked.

"Thought that might make you let go enough for her to tell us what's up," she said. "Helen wants us to get moving by dark. The locals are apparently getting a little grumpy about us being out here, and their leadership doesn't understand enough dimensional theory to get why this is technically a rescue mission for their whole world."

"I'm ready to go when the rest of you are," I said. "I feel fine."

Thomas glanced at me, anxiety in his eyes. "Truly?"

"Okay, that's enough of that." I planted my hands on his chest and pushed myself free of his embrace. "You don't get to keep giving me funny looks and asking if I'm okay without telling me what you think is wrong. I know I had a heart attack, I know I stopped breathing, and I know Sally broke several of my ribs during CPR. I also know that Phoebe patched all those things up *and* fixed the damage from the stroke I apparently also had. She says I shouldn't be subjected to any more magical healing for a while, which is fine, since you can't do it, I can't do it, and we're going the fuck home as soon as we finish getting all these people back where they belong. I'm not really seeing what the problem is."

Thomas looked down. I raised my eyebrows.

"Not making this any easier on yourself by making me wait for answers," I said. "Actually making it harder."

"Okay, if Mommy and Daddy are going to be fighting, I'm going to be elsewhere," said Sally. "Call me if you decide to murder each other. I want to watch."

"She's much less deferential now that she doesn't have to depend on me for her existence," said Thomas. He didn't sound sorry about that.

"Yeah, I can really see that, with how deferentially she was always speaking to you before," I said. "Now tell me what the hell is going on, and why you can kiss me but not look at me."

"Magic can be very taxing," he said, slowly. "It costs the caster in some way, generally."

"I know. It's why I was passed out from low blood sugar when Sally found me. Half my pack is effectively self-rescue medications for after I've crashed my system too far out of whack."

"And magic would do something similar if you were built to channel it." He took my hand and began leading me toward a collapsible bench someone had set up nearby. Like most Ithacan designs, it had an air of the classical Greek about it, while also being made of canvas and lightweight metal. I've never been entirely clear on their overall tech level. It seems to be rustic but post-Industrial Revolution, whatever form it took in their world. "Magic, cast too far beyond the caster's capability, or channeling too much power, can do permanent damage."

"This is a lot of talking that doesn't involve giving me a simple answer to the simple question I asked you," I said, as we sat. "What's *wrong*?"

"The spell was channeled through you, as I removed the pneuma. The price that had to be paid . . . I didn't pay it."

"So what, did my face melt off or something?"

"No. You've aged. Not too much!" he added quickly, apparently anticipating shouting or something of the like. "No more than a decade by my estimation."

"Okay." I shrugged. "Just means no one's going to look at us funny when we get home. I mean, you're clearly in your early thirties. It would have been weird."

He blinked slowly. "You're not upset?"

"Sweetheart, I'm well into my *eighties*. Physically nineteen or physically twenty-nine, I'm in incredible shape for my age, and we're both alive, which is more than we expected yesterday, or whatever day it was we went to your throne room to do something massively stupid. We get to go home. After we find safe places for all these people, we get to go home, together."

"With Sally."

"With Sally, yes. I already accepted the fact that you went and picked up a kid while I wasn't looking. Given that her best friend is apparently running around with our granddaughter and her parents probably think she's dead by now, I think we have to keep her. That's fine. Kevin's house has a lot of rooms, and so does our place back in Buckley."

Thomas laughed, and kept laughing as he leaned over, draped his arms around my shoulders, and rested his forehead against my own. I smiled and leaned into him.

"You were quite mad when the crossroads took me, and you're quite mad now, and I have never been more grateful to be going home with you," he said.

"I'm glad, because you're not going anywhere else," I said, and kissed him like I meant it, and everything was good between us. After fifty years, more broken bones than I could count, and hundreds of dead ends, everything was finally good.

With Helen directing everyone, we had the camp torn down and packed up well before sunset, then followed her through the wastes toward the point where we'd be making the crossing to the next world in line. I had to admit that the Ithacan method of travel was more pleasant than my own. Instead of crashing through dimensions with the equivalent of a sledgehammer, Helen and Phoebe had a whole group of what they called cartographers, each of whom carried a set of tools that allowed them to calibrate the thickness of the dimensional walls. They knew precisely where we had to go to meet the least resistance, then painted temporary runes on rocks gathered from the surrounding area and used them to build a rough circle we could all pass through.

The stones stayed behind where, Helen assured me, the runes would dissolve in less than a day. Someone who happened upon them before then would be able to copy whatever remained if they were quick about it, but the mere act of being activated would degrade the runes enough to render them useless.

I was pretty sure that didn't work as well as Helen thought it did, which would explain why there were echoes of Ithacan runes in so many of the dimensions I'd seen, but that was an argument for another time. For now, we just needed to get away from Cornale before the locals ate us.

Unlike the pain and screaming of escaping the bottle universe, or even the shove and effort of crossing on my own, this was painless and almost straightforward. Helen and Phoebe set the circle, two of their cartographers activated the runes, and a section of the air turned hazy and faintly reflective, like the heat haze off a summer highway. One by one, we walked through and left Cornale—and the grave of a dead dimension—behind.

Twenty-one

"I just want her to live long enough to figure out what makes her happy. I just want her to be free."

—Jonathan Healy

Ithaca, a week later

MOVING AT A PACE set by the slowest members of our company meant that it had taken us the better part of a week to make it from Cornale back to Ithaca, where the fields around Helen and Phoebe's house became a vibrant array of tents and temporary campsites as our many refugees made themselves . . . not at home, exactly, but as comfortable as they could be. Most of them had never seen this much green in their lives, and watching the children stare in awe at every flower and butterfly made me oddly glad that we had started with Cornale, where at least the landscape was a little bit comprehensible to them. We were easing them into a healthier existence.

We were easing all of us into a healthier existence. One where Sally slept with both eyes closed. One where I slept at all, curled against my husband, both of us waking up every time the other so much as sneezed. One where Thomas could feed on the pneuma of a healthy world, rebuilding depleted reserves so fundamental that he should never have been able to access, much less empty, them. We were healing.

"You're sure about this?" asked Sally, who looked much more like an Earth girl in her early twenties now that she had showered, combed her hair, and traded her battle leathers for a simple Ithacan shift. She still carried that spear like it was her favorite teddy bear. I'd even seen her sleeping with it, one leg wrapped around the pole like she thought someone was going to try to steal it in the night. She might not be wearing her trauma as obviously as some of the others, but she was still wearing it.

"We're *quite* sure," said Thomas, voice gone prim and tight, the way it always did when he couldn't even disapprove of something, because he was too busy being openly outraged by it. He took my hand and squeezed it tightly, eyes still on Sally. "This needs to be done before we can move on, and we've been imposing on our hosts for long enough."

"Hospitality has no time limit," said Helen, walking into camp with a bag of apples over one shoulder. She was promptly swarmed by the younger children, while the older ones held back and watched her with hungry eyes, wrapped in the developing shrouds of their own dignity. "But still, it's nice to know that you don't plan to stay forever. Phoebe thinks she's almost finished charting a course that will touch on all the worlds and dimensions you need to visit in order to take the refugees home. It shouldn't take you more than a year, moving at a reasonable pace, and there are a few worlds blended or empty enough to settle anyone who was born in the bottle and has nowhere else to go."

"A year, we can survive," said Thomas, not letting go of my hand.

"Especially if we're going to get my things," I agreed. "I'm going to need more ammo." With no more flensings in my future and my body still not up to the strain of channeling magic, I was going to be limited to the weapons I had on hand for the foreseeable future, maybe forever. That didn't really feel like a downgrade, since one of the weapons I had on hand now was Thomas.

"And then we go home," said Thomas. "To stay."

"If you never visit at all, we'll be very annoyed at you," said Helen, handing her bag of apples off to one of the older children to distribute. "Odysseus always comes back to Ithaca, after all."

"We only have two stops to make," I said, before Helen could keep going down the Odysseus route. It made me vaguely uncomfortable, in a "I don't want to do this for another ten years because you attracted the universe's attention" sort of way. "Empusa, then Earth, and then we'll be back for everyone, so we can start moving. You can watch them long enough for us to make the circuit, yeah?"

"Of course," said Helen. "Don't be silly. Your charges will be safe."

"I'm coming with you," said Sally.

"It's not advisable," said Thomas. "Honestly, I'd be happy to skip the stop on Earth, if not for the fact that Alice refuses to go a full year without her clergy."

"The mice won't take it well if I go silent for another year and they don't have a witness with me," I said. "I've already been gone longer than I intended to be, and I owe them the chance to get answers."

"Even so," said Thomas. "It's a risk."

"I know." The risk was mostly that we'd be seen and lose the will to come back and continue what we needed to do, but I wasn't kidding when I said I owed it to the mice. They had been with me faithfully for my entire life. Leaving them out of something this important wouldn't just be unfair, it would be cruel.

"All right," said Helen, with a heavy sigh. "Be safe, you three. Be careful and be safe."

"Never learned how to be careful," I said cheerfully. "But we'll do our best."

Thomas laughed and let go of my hand, and we walked toward the transit circle that would allow us to chart a straight line to Empusa with the least power possible.

Time to go talk to a snake.

The air in Naga's compound was warm and moist, and all too familiar. We didn't see anyone as we hurried down the hall to my room, where we set about ransacking the place, shoveling weapons, ammunition, and emergency supplies out of the primary dresser until my bag was filled to overflowing, then moving on to the duffels Sally and Thomas both carried.

"Are you sure you want protein bars more than you want another change of clothing?" asked Thomas.

"I can usually scavenge something to wear; something to eat and something to shoot can be a lot harder," I said. "Priorities are good."

"If you're not taking all these clothes, can I have some?" asked Sally. "Fluffy robes aren't exactly my style."

"It's not a robe, it's a chiton, and sure," I said, gesturing toward the appropriate dresser. "Knock yourself out."

Sally set about rummaging with the enthusiasm of someone who had spent the last of her teenage years in a post-apocalyptic hellscape, even leaning her spear against the wall as she looted my wardrobe. Even accounting for our collectively limited carrying capacity, she was able to find a few shirts and a pair of black leggings that fit her, which she changed into in the corner while Thomas politely averted his eyes. I kissed him on the cheek, picking up my pack.

It rattled. I'd need to repack everything once we were finished, since it's not actually safe to have a weapons cache that rattles. But that could happen after we finished dealing with our business here.

"I'm good to go," I said. "Sally, you want to stay here and keep going through things, or you want to come with us?"

"Will I be allowed to join in the violence?"

"No, probably not."

"I have quite a bit of pent-up aggression looking for a target, and the man who spent fifty years lying to and torturing my wife seems like an excellent outlet," said Thomas, cracking his knuckles.

Sally blanched. "I'm good, I'll stay here."

"We don't actually know that he was lying to me," I said, leading Thomas to the door. "Maybe he didn't know."

"You told me what you realized about the carvings on the ceiling," said Thomas. "He's a historian. Do you truly believe he didn't know?"

"No," I admitted.

"Even if he didn't, there's still the matter of skinning you alive and modifying your memories to keep you under his control. I won't pretend I can forgive either one of those things. The two of them together . . . I'm sorry. This has to happen."

"I know." I'd never be able to rest knowing that he was still out there, that he might decide to come for me after everything. This was the only way.

We stepped out into the hall and started toward Naga's office. If he wasn't there now, he would be eventually, and we could wait for him until he came back. We were about halfway there when the feline tattoo artist stepped out of one of the smaller rooms and stopped, blinking. He looked genuinely surprised to see me.

"We were told our services would no longer be required," he said. "My apologies. We're not ready for you."

"That's cool because they're not," I said. "We're just going to see the man in charge, and then we're out of here."

"If you're sure . . ." he said uncertainly.

Thomas looked at him, expression cold, and the artist backed away.

"My apologies," he repeated, turned around, and fled.

"You're cute when you're terrifying," I said, and resumed walking.

"Am I?" asked Thomas.

"Why do you think I'm so into you?"

"Well, I *did* marry you, and I understand many people like that sort of thing . . ."

The door to Naga's office was blessedly ajar. I pushed it open and there he was, behind his desk as he so often was, bent over a scroll. Thomas and I stepped inside, stopping just past the threshold.

"Office hours end in fifteen minutes," said Naga, not looking up. "I hope your matter is a quick one."

"Good thing we're not here for office hours," I said.

He glanced up, eyes wide and, inexplicably, terrified. That terror only grew as he looked to the man standing next to me, and I finally knew something for certain, not just through the power of conjecture:

Everything I didn't want to think about the snake man who had been my helper and guide to the universe for fifty years was true. He had been *lying* to me, intentionally steering me away from the only thing I had ever been trying to find. Whether he'd done it for the sake of the pneuma I carried back to him or out of genuine concern that I'd be trapped in the bottle and die with Thomas, I didn't know. I also didn't care, because he could have allowed me to make my own choices, and he hadn't.

He never had.

"Alice," he breathed. Then: "What's *happened* to you? You're older—"

"Wiser, too, I hope," I said. "Learned a lot of stuff out there. Did you know that I was carrying enough pneuma to blow a hole in the side of a bottle world after I finished a run? Or that it could be removed without *cutting me open* if someone actually cared about leaving my skin intact? Or that my husband was actually alive out there for me to find, and I hadn't been wasting my life for the last fifty years?"

He didn't quite recoil, but his eyes widened, very slightly, confirming my suspicions. I narrowed my own eyes, glaring at him.

"I had a family to get back to," I said, voice low. "I had a life. You took that away by withholding information. I'm still the one who chose to go after him, but you're the one who decided I didn't need to know when I was going in the wrong direction. The one who decided I didn't need to know how the universe worked."

"She trusted you," said Thomas, voice perfectly calm and cold as a frozen lake in February, after the thaw had weakened the ice without breaking it. "She came to you because she trusted you, and you led her astray over and over again to keep her . . . what? Gathering pneuma for you?"

From the way Naga glanced to the side, I knew that was the answer. "I was just *livestock* to you," I said, horrified. "You took care of me, you made sure I was fed and healthy, and you sent me out to make you richer. You did it on purpose."

"What would you have had me do?" Naga demanded, with a faint air of desperation. "No one escaped Lemure after the world soul died! I was *protecting* you from being trapped forever and allowing you to hold to some measure of hope that you might one day be reunited with your mate! I gave you a longer lifespan than your species is heir to, and I kept you safe."

"You *lied* to me. You hurt me and you used me and you *lied* to me."

"I gave you everything you asked for."

"You never gave me the one thing I *needed*!"

"I gave you *time*."

"You fucked with my memories!" Naga's expression, already panicked and desperate, turned terrified. I ignored it. Stopping to acknowledge his fear would just have taken away from the momentum I was building. It's easier to bite the hand that's been feeding you when you're too mad to see straight.

I took a step forward. Thomas' hand on my wrist kept me from taking another one. I settled for glaring.

"I never gave you permission to edit what I knew," I said. "And if I did, when I was hurt and desperate, if you asked, 'Can I take away the things that might slow you down,' and I agreed, it doesn't count because you took that memory, too." My voice dropped, going low and dangerous. "Consent has to be remembered to exist."

"You did, though," said Naga desperately. "You told me you wanted to be a better weapon. You said my surgeons could remove whatever they deemed necessary."

That didn't sound like me. Forgetting something that might make me flinch when I didn't need to was one thing; giving carte blanche to mess with my mind was another. I started to open my mouth, to argue. Thomas squeezed my wrist, and I stilled.

"That dead, rotting world was yours before I was cast there," said Thomas, tone still frozen. "Whose world was this?"

"The Empusai. We didn't steal it. The original owners are still here," said Naga. "They serve us, and we protect them."

"Seems like you've been doing that a lot," I said. "Protecting people. Did you even *ask* them?"

"We did."

"And they serve the giant snake people who came out of nowhere and took over their world anyway?" I asked. "Because that doesn't seem like it's in their best interests."

"They do it of their own free will," said Naga.

"Is it the sort of free will that comes with forgetting they agreed to it?" I snapped. "Because it sounds like that's your favorite tactic."

"We're not Johrlac!" said Naga. "You were a special case."

"Gosh, it's great to be special," I said. "Fuck you."

"Taking this world for your own was an act of violence," said Thomas. "You transgress against my wife, and against this world." He released my wrist, starting to step forward.

Naga slithered behind his desk, eyes bright with desperation. "I wasn't there when Lemure fell! It happened centuries ago, and I was born here, on this world. This is my home. I stole nothing."

"Sounds like the Empusai might disagree with that," I said.

But Naga was focusing on Thomas now, seeing him as the greater threat. "Please," he begged. "Please, understand. The loss of Lemure . . . we had no warning. The dark pneuma of another world assaulted our own, tearing it away. The invader took its place for a time, tricking our people into terrible bargains that served it and never us. Until the day came when it had exhausted our resources. It could benefit no more, and it left us, moving through the dimensions in search of a fresher host. Most of us died in the cataclysm. Those who survived fled, wandering as exiles through the universe until they found another dimension that could sustain us, another world that would serve as our home, where the native life was less advanced than we were, and willing to share in exchange for the benefit of our wisdom."

"So this whole time you knew that the crossroads had a connection to your original dimension, and that they might be using it as some sort of deep freeze for the people they took, and you didn't tell me? You didn't *help* me?"

"Until you found that book, there would have been no way to get you back once you crossed the border. I was keeping you safe."

"You didn't get to make that choice!"

Thomas interjected before Naga could answer. "Tell me about the method you used for removing the accumulated pneuma from my wife."

Naga seized onto the opportunity to explain himself like it was a lifeline, which technically, I suppose it was. "The damage to her physicality tells me that you did a more ad hoc removal of your own. Surely you can see the efficacy of stripping it all away at once, leaving the subject clean and free of outside influences. We were careful to reduce trauma to the host as much as possible, we—"

"Is there any means of removal that *wouldn't* have damaged her? Physically, mentally, or chronologically?"

"Pneuma can be unwound at a more reasonable pace, but it takes time," said Naga. "Alice has always been an impatient girl. She wouldn't have been willing to sit for the time required. We needed to get her in and out as quickly as we could. The method we used with her was the method we use with our own explorers."

I couldn't argue with that, even as I turned away from him.

"Humans aren't meant to shed their skins," said Thomas. "What have you been doing with them, all this time?"

"They sell very well," said Naga, still with an air of desperation, still clearly thinking he could talk his way out of this. "More than enough to pay for the cost of her care. If you were looking for a portion of the profits, we could—"

"Stop," I said, putting a hand on Thomas' arm. I glanced to Naga. "Both of you, stop. You're right that I was impatient, and you're right that if you had asked me, I would have taken the faster, more painful option. But that's *if you had asked me.* You never asked, not without taking the memory of it away. You never gave me the chance to remember consenting. So it doesn't matter how right you were . . . or weren't. It doesn't matter. I'm not working for you anymore. We're going home."

"No, I don't think you are," said Naga, and grabbed a glass sphere from his desk, hurling it at the floor.

I threw my arm across my eyes even as Thomas was diving for the sphere, shielding me from the bright light that erupted when the glass exploded against stone. It smelled like peppermint. That would have been funny, under other circumstances.

Thomas covered his eyes, too late to prevent the flash from dazzling them, and staggered backward even as I lowered my arm and glared at Naga. He was still behind the desk, foolish enough to open hostilities, too much the comfortable academic to have thought to move.

"I never agreed to let you go," he said. "This will be easy enough to edit away. What's one more tragedy? You might have a few nightmares— even the best psychic surgery never takes a weed all the way down to the root—but you'll be able to function, able to keep doing your *job.*"

"Like fuck I will," I said, and grabbed one of the guns from my belt, dropping into a steady shooting position.

Naga still hadn't moved. He just stayed exactly where he was, smiling at me. That made me anxious. People who don't dodge usually think they have the upper hand. If they don't, it's best to demonstrate that quickly. I pulled the trigger.

Or tried to, anyway. My finger refused to move. I tried again and failed again. Looking desperately from my gun to Naga, I tried a third time. Still nothing.

"You're a dangerous pet to keep, Alice Healy," he said, finally slithering out from behind the desk. Thomas was still staggering around, unable to see anything around him—unable to see Naga approaching me. "Did you really think I hadn't taken steps toward domestication at some point? One doesn't keep a wild animal on a chain without certain precautions. One doesn't allow a rabid creature its freedom without a muzzle."

"What did you *do*?" I demanded.

"You willingly allowed my Johrlac into your head for years," he said. "You didn't fight them. Surely you must remember *that*."

"I agreed to let them take the pain away," I said.

"And you thought you were getting that comforting release for nothing? You're more the fool than I thought you were, when you came to me with breasts still dripping foul mammalian fluids, begging for a way to do the impossible. I told you then that nothing came free. I told you it would come with costs and challenges. You still agreed. You said you'd do whatever I required. You told me that you would be my tool for as long as I wanted you to be, and you were *grateful*."

None of what he was saying sounded familiar, but then again, why should it? He'd been stealing from me for years. There was no reason to think that he hadn't stolen some agreement along the way, something to salve his conscience. If he had a conscience where foul mammals were concerned.

"What," I said again, "did you *do*?"

"You can't hurt me. You belong to me." Naga slithered closer still, reaching for the gun in my hands.

"I'm afraid she doesn't," said Thomas. He didn't sound like someone who'd just had the light of a small sun poured directly into his eyes, and when I glanced at him, he wasn't staggering anymore, just standing straight and calm, looking at Naga with unflinching eyes.

Naga turned to glare at him. "What?"

"I said, she doesn't belong to you. She belongs to me, and I belong to her, and that agreement predates any agreements she may have made with you in my absence." Thomas shook his head. "We came to verify the extent of what you'd done. You've crossed quite a few lines that can't be forgiven."

"I don't care for your forgiveness," said Naga. He hissed, fangs fully extended. Then he lunged at Thomas.

Thomas, again, didn't move, except to raise one hand and hold it, palm out, toward Naga. It wouldn't do anything to stop the charging snake man—until it did. Naga froze, fangs retracting as he swayed in place, eyes going wide with surprise.

Thomas stayed exactly where he was, hand still raised. "I wanted to take you apart piece by piece," he said. "I wanted to hear you scream, and that was before I knew the damage you had done to her mind. Be grateful that in all the time my wife's fate was in your keeping, she never forgot how to be merciful. My own time was nowhere near so kind."

I lowered my gun, still unfired, and slid it back into its holster as I walked back to join Thomas, looking unflinchingly at Naga. "Not that it's going to matter much for you, but our association is at an end, and if I guess correctly, Ithaca's going to be severing a few ties. No more deliveries for whoever comes after you. No more sheep to shear. Your university is going to curse your name for centuries—if it stands that long once word gets out about how much you knew, how many citizens of how many worlds your people left to rot in what should have been a private grave."

Naga still hadn't moved. A look of faint perplexity crossed his face, overshadowed by the blood trickling from the corners of his eyes.

"I suppose that since I was gone for so long, you forgot that I was a sorcerer," said Thomas. "I'm an elementalist, to be specific. Fire. Oxygen burns. Every cell in your body contains it. They're all remembering what it is to burn right now. Take comfort, however; you'll be dead of heat stroke before you actually catch fire."

Naga made a small sound, but still didn't move.

"Goodbye, Naga," I said, taking Thomas' free hand. "I'd say 'see you later,' but that isn't going to happen, and you won't be here to see. So this is goodbye."

Naga stayed where he was, frozen and burning alive at the same time. I can't say he watched us go. I can't say he was watching anything by that point.

His body hit the ground as we let ourselves out of the room. The sound of dry wood igniting followed a moment later as his dehydrated body finally stopped fighting the fire and burst into flame.

Office hours were technically still going on.

I shut the door behind us anyway.

Epilogue

"I think, if we just give her the space she needs, if we just stand beside her and keep her from falling down, I think . . . she's going to be okay."

—Laura Campbell

The kitchen of a large family compound in Portland, Oregon

WE STEPPED OUT OF the transit circle and were home, or close enough to home as to make no real difference, the three of us standing in the kitchen of the compound Kevin had designed and constructed after he and his sister decided to settle in Portland, Oregon, with their families. Sally looked around, gripping her spear tightly for security, before her eyes fell on the toaster. From there, she shifted her gaze to the fridge and made a sound of wordless delight, surging toward it like it was the only goal in the world worth pursuing.

I raised my eyebrows, watching as she opened the door, rooted quickly through the freezer contents, and produced a box of frozen blueberry waffles. "Sally, how the hell did you know those were in there?" I asked.

"You said James was here," said Sally. "James would never stay in a house for more than about a week before there were blueberry Eggos on hand. It just wouldn't happen."

"So you believe me now."

"I'm coming around to the idea that maybe you're not completely dishonest," said Sally, dropping two of the waffles into the toaster.

"Huh," I said. "But good on you, remembering how to use the toaster. That's the fastest non-yelling way I can think of."

"Way to do what, cook waffles?" she asked. "Do you normally cook waffles by yelling at them?"

"No," I said. "To attract company."

Three tiny heads poked out of one of the doorways cut into the wall behind the counter, whiskers bobbing as they sniffed the air. I saw their eyes widen, and I pulled my hand out of Thomas', stepping quickly forward.

"I invoke the Holy Ritual of If You Wake The House I Swear To God, Thomas, I Will Revoke Your Femurs," I said, voice firm but low. "I need my clergy. Do any of you represent me, on either side of the divide?"

The mice simply stared, struck silent by the scene in front of them.

"I need you to find my clergy—doesn't matter which mysteries—and bring them here," I said. "We can't stay long."

"Okay, boss, the lady's clearly off her gourd," said Sally. "Those are mice."

"Yes," said Thomas. Then he smiled, eyes suspiciously bright. "I've missed them so much."

One of the mice finally stepped all the way out of the hole, tail held tightly in its paws, like a child worrying a piece of rope. It looked at Thomas, eyes wide and hopeful, and squeaked, "Is it true? Are you returned unto us, with all your wisdom and your ways?"

"Not quite yet, but soon," said Thomas, as Sally stared at the mice in sudden open-mouthed silence. I smirked at her.

"Sally, meet the mice. Mice, meet Sally. Thomas picked her up in a hell dimension, and I think we're keeping her. Now will you please go get my clergy?"

With a squeak, the mouse dove into the hall, and all three heads disappeared.

"*Quietly*," I added, perhaps too late to do any good, and sighed as I turned to Thomas. "This should be fast."

"What do you mean by 'it doesn't matter which mysteries'?" asked Thomas.

"My clergy splintered after you disappeared," I said. "There are two completely different faiths now. I suppose they'll have to reunify after this. That should be fun to watch."

Sally snorted, and apparently dismissing talking mice as only the fifth most impossible thing she'd seen this week, turned to digging through the fridge. I watched, half-amused, and distracted enough by the assortment of things she was pulling out that I almost missed the sound of human-sized footsteps.

Thomas was rigid beside me. I turned to look at the doorway, where a man of about fifty stood, brown hair sleep-rumpled, glasses askew, staring at all three of us. Sally ignored him, continuing to assemble the most horrifying blueberry waffle sandwich of all time and trusting us to take care of things.

Kevin stepped into the kitchen, eyes locked on Thomas, ignoring me. Sally glanced up and, seeing that neither of us was reaching for a weapon, kept working. In a very small, somewhat strangled voice, he asked, "Dad?"

"I'm sorry, Kevin," said Thomas. "I'm so, so sorry. I would have come back sooner if I'd been able to, I wouldn't have missed so much, I—"

Kevin didn't let him finish, just strode all the way across the kitchen and wrapped his arms around his missing father, pulling him into an embrace that almost made me feel bad about the fact that we'd started our own reunion by kicking the crap out of each other. Almost.

I turned my attention back to the mousehole, now keeping one eye on the door in case we'd managed to wake anybody else. After a moment had passed, the three mice from before reappeared, accompanied by three more mice, one each in the vestments of the Noisy Priestess, the Pilgrim Priestess, and—

"Of course," I said. "I meant no disrespect by failing to call you myself. I just haven't had much to do with your faith in a very long time . . ."

"We know the memories of men, even divine men, are flawed," said the mouse in the vestment of the God of Empty Rooms and Cold Regrets, eyes never leaving Thomas, who was still wrapped in Kevin's arms. Our son was weeping into his father's shoulder like his heart was beyond broken. It hurt to see. "But we Remember. We have waited, we have kept the faith, and we Remember."

"H—" began the mice.

They didn't get any further before Kevin and I snapped, in unison, "Shush." We exchanged a look, only momentarily united before he turned back to Thomas and finally let his father go.

"You're calling for your clergy," he said. "You're not staying, are you?"

"We can't stay yet," I said. "Thomas was taking care of a whole bunch of people who'd been kidnapped by the crossroads just like he was, and we have to get them to safety."

"But we'll be back, and we'll be staying," said Thomas.

"Maybe don't tell Jane," I said.

"But feel free to tell James I ate his waffles," said Sally. She had put peanut butter, sweet pickles, and what looked like leftover chicken curry between the two blueberry waffles and was holding her concoction like it was the last treasure of El Dorado.

"You are Leaving us again?" asked the priest of Thomas' order.

"But we're taking four mice with us," I said quickly. "To document what you see and learn what happened in your absence. The mysteries will not be lost—unless you exalt and wake the house. Then we'll leave without you."

"I can't believe Mom was right," said Kevin. "I can't believe you've been out there all this time . . ."

"I can't wait to get to know you the way I should have known you all your lives," said Thomas.

"It's going to take about a year for us to finish the circuit and get everyone settled," I said. "We'll call you from Michigan when we get back. I figure Jane probably doesn't want us in her backyard."

Kevin nodded slowly, hands twitching like he wanted to reach for Thomas again, to hold on tight and never let go. I understood the feeling. Stepping over to the counter, I put my hand down flat on top of it, allowing four of the newly arrived mice—the three in marked attire and one unmarked novice—to run up my arm and cluster on my shoulder. Then I stepped back over to Thomas, taking his hand.

"If you're done raiding the fridge, Sally, we can go," I said, and looked to Kevin. "I love you, buddy. And your dad and I will be back soon. I promise."

"I believe you," he said, and watched as Sally stepped over to join us. I pulled one of the last beads off my necklace, crunching it under my heel on the kitchen floor.

All at the same time, Sally, Thomas, and I stepped through the thin spot this opened in the walls of the world, and we were safely on our way. The feeling of transition was familiar. The feeling of doing it in the company of people I trusted to keep me in one piece for more than five minutes wasn't. And the feeling of doing it with Thomas' hand in mine, well . . .

That was just about the best thing in all the worlds in all the dimensions there are.

Read on for
a brand-new InCryptid novella
by Seanan McGuire:

AND SWEEP UP
THE WOOD . . .

PART ONE:

In the Hand of the Forest
Buckley Township, Michigan, 1960

1.

Montmorency County, Michigan, is a big place with a small population, and that's the way the people who live there like it. Sprawling, untouched forests exist side by side with the spreading forms of towns grown out of villages and swelling toward cityhood with every breath and birth that passes. Lakes sleep in the shadow of the trees, dreaming their deep, slow dreams, their stony bottoms littered with the bones of careless swimmers. Infant catfish build their homes in abandoned rib cages, play games of hide-and-seek through the narrow domes of human skulls. This, too, will pass, as the cities spread; these lakes will be taught and tamed, transformed into safe swimming holes and seen through the golden lenses of nostalgia. But that is a long way into the future, and there is time enough between here and there. The future is another country.

The shape of the great Montmorency Swamp is like a handprint laid flat across the land, its hidden depths filled with dangers. Quicksand and sinkholes, venomous snakes—and other, stranger threats, the sort of threats mentioned in children's stories and whispered around campfires. They say the woods are full of monsters, and they laugh because no one believes in monsters anymore. This is the summer of 1960, and the world is too enlightened for that sort of thing. Most of the world, anyway. In some small, dark corners, people still believe the evidence of their eyes, and in those places—places like

Buckley Township, pinned like a butterfly under glass between the swamp and the dark, foreboding shadows of the Galway Woods—the population has never grown beyond a certain number. More of the young folk choose to go than choose to stay with every generation. It is a town that may die in the larval stage before it grows into a city—and some folks, those who've lived there all their lives and could no more leave than they could grow wings and fly away—some folks say that's for the best.

Some folks say it's time to leave the dead to rest.

Buckley Township: founded 1822 by Robert Buckley of Buckley Lumber. Despite the wealth of the woods surrounding the settlement, the company never flourished, and collapsed by 1878. The township was left to fend for itself. Surprisingly enough, it lived—possibly because it was too damn stubborn to die. People put down roots, becoming as much a part of the land as the trees and lakes and swamp around them, and began, in their own quiet way, to grow.

Strangers came on occasion, adding their strength and seed to the town. Alexander and Enid Healy, in '05; Frances Brown, in '28; Thomas Price, in '54. They came, they stayed, and if they were the ones who walked into the woods and didn't come back out again, well, it seemed a small price for the town's survival. More, it meant that just this once, it wasn't one of their own who paid. The blood of strangers fed the trees as well as the blood of the people who'd been born there. So the residents of Buckley told themselves, and so it was, for at least a little longer, in the hand of the forest, in the shadow of the ever-watching trees.

2.

Jonathan Healy died screaming.

The echoes hadn't even faded, and Alice already knew she'd be hearing that sound for the rest of her life. It would be waiting for her every time she closed her eyes and tried to sleep. There were things she could forget, things she could block out of her mind or move past. Hearing her father's dying screams as he was ripped apart from the inside by monstrous, impossible wasps wasn't one of those things.

The buzzing of the Apraxis filled the night as they turned their attention from the fallen to the still-standing. Alice forced her numb fingers to keep moving, fumbling bullets into the chambers of her mother's revolvers. She'd already been stung, and the blood running down her arm threatened to make her hands too slippery to hold onto the gunstocks. If she dropped her weapons, it would all be over for her, just like it was already over for her father . . .

And then the wasps were diving, and there was no more time for hesitation. Gunfire overwhelmed the sound of wings, and the distant, dying echo of her father's screams.

3.

When Buckley Township was founded, the surrounding forest was viewed as a blessing; a seemingly-infinite natural resource to be exploited for the sake of wealth and prosperity. As the logging companies tried and failed to find a foothold in the Galway Woods, that attitude changed, replaced by one of quiet suspicion. Too many men went into those trees and didn't come out again. Too many children came home wild-eyed and shaking, telling tales of monsters in the wood.

After more than a hundred years in the hand of the forest, the people of Buckley knew perfectly well that there were monsters in the Galway. They just didn't talk about it. They knew, also, that some of the newer residents of the township had an unpleasant tendency to go wandering into the Galway, looking for the monsters. They didn't talk about that, either, and when the ones who went into the wood didn't come out again, well, that was only natural.

Alice Healy, on the other hand, had been in love with the Galway Woods since she was a child, and the Woods, fickle thing that they were, had been in love with her for almost as long. How a forest could love a human woman was less than clear, but everyone who saw Alice in her element knew that it was so. She hadn't gone into the Galway that night looking for trouble. It was supposed to be a standard hunting trip, a way to blow off a little steam and make sure things were staying quiet. It should have been safe—as safe as any trip into the Galway Woods could be, since living in an area with a large cryptid population gave "safe" a looser definition than applied anywhere else. Especially when you regularly went out looking for trouble with nothing to protect you but a few battered old hand-me-down charms, a vial of aconite perfume, and a whole lot of bullets.

As far as Alice was concerned, "safe" and "careful" were the kind of words you used when you wanted to get rid of somebody. "Be careful" wasn't just an insult; it was an insult bordering on a death sentence. If you polled the town for the last words of all the people who'd walked into the woods and never walked back out again, she was firmly convinced that "I'll be careful" and "I'll be right back" would be tied for first place.

It had been a long day. Between work at the children's library and dealing with the fools and busybodies who seemed to dominate the town, Alice had been at the end of her patience and not being careful when she'd decided to go out and walk the woods. That's why her father had caught her on the way down the stairs, having swapped her work clothes for jeans, a shapeless flannel shirt, and a hunting vest. She had her blonde curls pulled back in a no-nonsense ponytail, and a rifle slung over one shoulder, as well as her mother's revolvers at her hips.

"Where do you think you're going?" he'd asked.

Alice had come to an immediate stop, cheeks burning. Even though she was a grown woman and would have been a college graduate if life and the woods hadn't interfered, her father still had a gift for making her feel like she was thirteen years old. "Out?" she'd ventured.

Jonathan had shaken his head. "Not an acceptable answer, Alice. Try again."

"I just—I was—I mean—" She'd stopped, sighing. "The woods, Daddy. I was going to the woods."

"The woods," he'd echoed. His frown said all the things he didn't say aloud.

Jonathan couldn't forbid her to go into the Galway alone, and he had long since stopped trying. She was an adult, and she could do as she pleased; more than that, she could take perfectly good care of herself. She didn't have her mother's raw talent with guns, or her grandmother's skill as a marksman, but she had a generous measure of the strange luck she'd inherited from her mother to bolster her training.

Alice had run into more than her share of trouble during a lifetime of moving through those woods, and while she'd been seriously injured a few times as a teenager, she hadn't died yet. That alone was enough to testify as to her skill, both at surviving and at finding allies . . . but that was just technicalities, and they both knew it. Jonathan didn't want her in the woods, or near the cryptids, or having anything to do with the family business. Alice didn't want to listen when he told her "no," so she never asked him, and he was never forced to directly forbid her.

Alice had hastened to fill the silence that was swelling between them. "Four kids have brought me pictures of the same thing in the last two days. Some sort of giant wasp they say they saw down by Miller's Pond."

His frown had deepened. "That's where Jenny Sampson disappeared."

Alice had nodded. "It's also less than a quarter-mile from where the Billingsly twins went missing. I looked up the description in the field guides, Daddy. There's about three things it could be, and they're all nesters. I just want to get the lay of the land and see if I can find any clear trace of what's maybe out there, feeding on the kids."

She hadn't exactly done her research, but she'd read the short descriptions of the possible cryptids, and she was confident of her ability to figure out the rest out in the field. But she wasn't going to tell *him* that. He could think she'd done all her homework before heading into the final exam.

"What are the options?" he'd asked. He'd still been frowning, but distantly now; he'd been thinking, weighing the danger to the town against his desire to keep her safely home.

"Well, it could be a nest of Melnorns. They're clumsy and slow, but they eat a lot, and they like young prey. Plus they've made incursions into this part of the country before. Might also be Laicaln bees, which would be bad, since they're pretty clever, but would probably be self-correcting. They can only sting once before they die, they don't breed quickly, and they'd never survive the winter."

"What's the third option?"

Alice had managed not to wince. She'd been hoping he wouldn't ask. "Apraxis wasps. But it's not likely, Daddy. It would have to be a very juvenile hive, and—"

Jonathan had raised his hand to cut her off, expression growing cold. "Unlikely or not, there's still a *chance*. You were just going to go charging out there alone?"

"I was only going to scout," Alice had said indignantly. "I'm not *stupid*."

"Foolhardy, impetuous, overconfident, but not stupid," Jonathan had allowed. "You're not going into the woods alone."

"But Daddy—"

"I said you weren't going *alone*. Wait here while I get my coat."

4.

They reached Miller's Pond two hours later, both of them on edge and on their guard. There had been no conversation as they walked through the wood, and Alice had been unable to relax in the disapproving presence of her father. Having him there made a late-night cryptid hunt into less of an adventure and more of a punishment.

Her resentment dropped away as the pond came into view, forgotten in the face of her curiosity. There were dozens of tiny pockmarks scored into the soft mud near the water. It looked like someone had pressed the edge of a butter knife into the ground over and over again, making a haphazard pattern of lines.

Later, Alice would ask herself if she should have realized what those pockmarks meant; if she should have somehow understood from what little had been recorded in the field guides that Melnorn get all the water they need from the bodies of their victims, and Laicaln bees prefer to drink from stagnant pools, while Miller's Pond was fresh water, clear and open. If she'd read more carefully, would she have known what was waiting for them? Could they have turned back before it was too late?

All that came later, when her father's screams rang nightly in her ears and her own wounds itched fiercely enough to make sleep a fantasy. At the time, she'd merely played the beam of her flashlight over the marks on the bank, cutting one small line of light through the darkness, and looked to him for suggestions.

"Check the trees," he said, voice pitched barely above a whisper. "Melnorn nests are papery and look a lot like paper wasps. I've never seen a Laicaln hive, but they supposedly stick to hollow trees, and they block the entrances with wax." Alice nodded once, and they separated, moving in opposite directions around the edges of the pond.

There were no visible nests in the branches surrounding Miller's Pond. All the trees appeared to be healthy, with no obvious signs of decay and no traces of beeswax. Alice approached a tall oak and tilted her flashlight up toward the branches, looking for shapes that didn't belong there. The light shone greenly through the leaves, illuminating nothing.

Shaking her head, she lowered her eyes and prepared to move on. Then she froze, the hairs on the back of her neck rising as she realized something was wrong. The woods were silent. The woods were *never* silent—not unless something was getting ready to attack. She straightened slowly, suddenly tense, and turned in a slow circle, casting the beam of her flashlight around her in a steady arc.

Two-thirds of the way around the circle, the beam hit something that threw back the light like a cut jewel. All she could think in that moment was that insects had multi-faceted eyes. Careful not to drop the flashlight, Alice drew one of her mother's revolvers with her free hand, beginning to back away as she aimed one-handed toward the glitter in the distance. It wasn't moving. She took that as a good sign; she was too large for a Melnorn to view as prey if she wasn't actively threatening the nest, and Laicaln bees were slow-moving at night. She'd be fine if she kept quiet.

The buzzing started less than half a second before something that felt like an enormous super-heated needle slammed into the back of her left arm, embedding itself all the way down against the bone. Too surprised to think, she shrieked, dropping the revolver as she reached to grope at the source of the pain. The rifle she had slung over her shoulder swung around on its strap, slamming into her hip hard enough to leave a bruise she wouldn't discover until the next day.

Her questing hand hit the side of a hard, chitinous body. She forced her fingers to close and grabbed it as firmly as she could, yanking it away and flinging it hard off to one side. *Not Laicaln,* she thought, as the stinger came free of her arm with an audible sucking sound. Her flesh felt like it was on fire.

She groped until she caught the butt of her rifle. Swinging it up, she fired twice at the buzzing coming from the direction where she'd flung the creature. She didn't take time to aim. She didn't need to; her shots were followed by a thin, echoing shriek before the silence returned, heavier now than ever.

And then her father was there in front of her, his own rifle raised and held against his chest. "How's your arm?" he demanded.

"Bleeding," she said, as she bent and retrieved her revolver from the ground. "We need to get a tourniquet on it. Daddy, was that—"

"No tourniquet," he said. "That was an Apraxis. You need to bleed the venom out."

So it was bad enough that death from blood loss was preferable to risking the poison staying in her arm? Alice nodded once, pressing her right hand over the wound, and tried not to think about it. "At least we know what we're dealing with now. Let's go home."

"That's my girl," he said.

"Is someone there?"

The voice came from the woods behind them. It was high, tremulous, and frightened—the voice of a little girl lost in the woods. Alice's head snapped up.

"That's Jenny," she said.

"Or that *was* Jenny." Jonathan's voice held a grim note of warning. "Remember what we're dealing with here."

Apraxis hives started out small and fairly easy to destroy, but they didn't stay that way for long. The entire hive absorbed the intelligence and memories of each victim, learning at a steadily increasing rate, even as they incubated additional drones in the bodies of the dead. A single Apraxis hive could easily wipe out a good-sized town if it wasn't caught early enough.

It had been over six days since Jenny Sampson disappeared. Much as she wanted to hold out hope, Alice knew better. "They're learning," she said. "Let's go."

"Please, oh please, is someone there?" The voice sharpened, taking on a more anxious pitch. *"Miss Healy, is that you? Please, I'm so scared. There are these big bee-things, and they keep buzzing all around me. Please, is someone there? Won't you help me?"*

"Don't listen," Jonathan said.

Alice nodded, lips pressed into a thin line. "I won't."

"We're going to need backup on this one. Backup, and some sort of flamethrowers." Jonathan turned to offer Alice his hand.

"I know where you live, Miss Healy," said Jenny Sampson's stolen voice. It sounded more conversational now, calmer, and Alice could finally hear the buzzing underneath it. *"I've been there before. You let me sit on the porch. You gave me lemonade. Can I come over to play?"*

Jonathan froze, stiffening. Alice glanced toward the dark wood, looking for the source of the voice. There was nothing there. "Don't listen, Daddy. You can't let them goad you."

"They know where we live," he replied. "Apraxis wasps don't have to be invited in."

"Daddy—"

"You're already hurt. Stay here and cover me. I'll be right back."

"Don't be stupid!"

"I'm not being stupid, and I'll be careful. The hive can't be very large if they're still resorting to sneak attacks and lures. This is the time to stop them unless you want a visit in your bedroom tonight."

"Daddy . . ."

"Wait here. I'm just going to get a location on the hive and see how many of them we're actually dealing with."

Alice grabbed for his hand as he turned and walked away from her. She missed by only a few inches, but it wouldn't have done any good if she'd caught him. He had fifty pounds on her, and he wasn't injured. Three steps and he was gone, fading into the woods. The voice of Jenny Sampson giggled in the distance, but otherwise, the night was silent. Even the frickens had stopped their chirping mating calls.

And then the screaming started.

Jonathan Healy screamed like a man who was having his bones ripped out of his body one by one. Alice didn't think; she just reacted, letting her rifle swing wildly on its strap as she grabbed both her mother's revolvers from their holsters. There was no pain left in her arm. Pain belonged in another world, a world where her father wasn't screaming.

His flashlight had clicked on when it hit the ground. She could see a dozen pairs of glittering eyes in the diffuse light of its beam, all moving wildly around the dark, flailing form of her father. The glitter was all she needed. Alice fired without aiming, never hesitating, and one by one, the glitters fell out of the air, until only the shadow of her father remained, no longer flailing as he started slowly slumping over.

Then he fell. It only took a few seconds, as the muscles in his legs and back realized what his brain already knew—they weren't needed anymore—and gave way. It only took a few seconds. It seemed to take a lifetime.

The sounds of the wood were returning. The pain flooded back into her injured arm, now accompanied by sharp, stabbing cramps in her fingers, marking the points where she'd clenched them too tightly around the pistols. Alice didn't care.

"Daddy?" There was no answer from the figure crumpled on the ground. "*Daddy!*"

In the distance, the frickens sang.

5.

Carrying her father's body out of the woods was one of the hardest things Alice had ever been forced to do. He outweighed her even when he wasn't wearing his hunting clothes and carrying spare ammunition in his pockets, and she would have found the process difficult without an injured arm. As it was, she could only manage to go a few yards at a time before she had to stop and rest. The blood loss wasn't helping. Black spots danced at the edges of her vision, getting larger all the time.

Something will eat us before morning, she thought, with a vague, academic sort of interest. At least her bones would be in the Galway. At least she'd still be with something that loved her, even if it hadn't been able to protect her. *Something will smell the blood or hear the rustling, and that will be that.*

But nothing came.

Alice Healy staggered out of the trees and onto Highway 18 half an hour after dawn, with the weight of her father's corpse supported mostly by her back and shoulders. Her face and hair were caked with a mixture of blood and dirt that made her look like she'd just survived some sort of war, and there was a makeshift tourniquet she didn't remember making tied around her left arm. It had probably seemed important that she not bleed to death out there, but somehow . . .

Somehow it was hard to focus on that as she shuffled down the last embankment separating the wood from the highway, lowered her father's body gently to the blacktop, and collapsed on top of him, closing her eyes.

As she fell into blessed stillness, Alice thought of her mother's face; the face she hadn't seen since she was seven, when Frances Healy took her own walk into the woods. After that, there was only darkness, and the quiet resignation that came with realizing that her father had been right all along.

She should have stayed out of the Galway.

PART TWO:

The Shade of the Tree

1.

Franklin Rogers was hauling a truckload of potatoes up to Ann Arbor, getting an early start so he could make it back by dinnertime, when he saw what looked like two bodies lying in the road. Bodies near the edge of the wood weren't uncommon, especially not bodies in hunter's orange, but it was the off-season, and he hadn't been expecting them. Swearing under his breath, he hit the brakes.

Then he saw the face of the larger of the two bodies and started swearing out loud, opening his door and jumping out before the truck entirely stopped moving. "Jonathan? Jonathan Healy, are you alive down there? Dammit, Johnny, you answer me!"

The Healys were come-latelies to the town, and sure, there were some that blamed Alexander and Enid's settling there for that Price fellow moving in over on Old Logger's Road, like letting one foreigner in just encouraged more, but that didn't mean they didn't have their friends and supporters. Franklin had known Johnny Healy since they were teenagers playing down by the old quarry, making grand plans to run off to the big city and live lives of dashing adventure. He'd danced with Frances at the wedding and told her what a gorgeous bride she was. Seeing him here, like this . . .

It was no wonder some of the folks in town were starting to say the Healys were cursed, what with the way they kept going into the woods but not coming back out again. First Fran, then Enid, and finally Alex, barely two years before. As Franklin turned the top body over to see its face and caught his first glimpse of sunny blonde hair through the caked-on blood, he found himself wondering if maybe there wasn't some truth to the idea of the family curse.

"Alice. Alice, wake up now, that's a good girl. Come on, Alice. Your Poppa's going to kill me if you don't wake up." He felt her wrist—cold—before fumbling with the collar of her shirt, just enough to get his fingers pressed against her neck. He couldn't find a pulse.

"Oh, *Alice*," Franklin sighed, and turned away from her, focusing on her father.

If Alice looked dead, Jonathan looked like he'd been mauled. There were holes punched in his clothing, some the size of canning jars, others going all the way through to come out the other side. More holes marked his throat and hands, filled with black pools of newly-jellied blood. Only his face was untouched. A small mercy if there was no living family to attend the funeral viewing.

Franklin had lived his whole life on the edge of the Galway Woods, and he knew what he was seeing, even as his mind started to fabricate careful excuses for what was right in front of him. It was plain they'd been hunting together; a father-daughter excursion. Everyone in town knew they'd been arguing lately. A little hunting trip could have seemed like just the thing to ease the tensions, and it being off-season wouldn't matter, because nobody was going to accuse *Jonathan Healy* of poaching.

So they'd gone out together to start smoothing things out between them, and Johnny had walked into the crossfire of some other hunting party. Maybe one that really *was* poaching and didn't want reports getting back to town. He'd gone down, but Alice was only hit once— hit bad, if the looks of her arm were any indication—and she'd been a good girl. She brought her father's body home.

Even though it killed her to do it.

Franklin had almost managed to convince himself this was the truth when Alice groaned. "Alice?" He turned back to her. "Alice, honey, you all right?"

" . . . Daddy?" she whispered.

"He's just fine, sugar, don't you worry," Franklin said hurriedly, moving to scoop her into his arms, leaving Jonathan staring blankly at the paling sky. "Come on, now. He's asked me to give you a ride into town."

" . . . wasps," she whispered.

"There aren't any wasps in my truck," he assured her, not stopping to let himself think about how those "bullet holes" could easily have been left by stingers bigger than stingers had any business being. "Come on, now, Alice. Let's go visit the nice hospital."

She didn't fight as he loaded her into the cab of the truck or seem to notice when he put her father's body just as gently into the back, cushioning him on the potatoes that wouldn't make it to market today after all.

She never even opened her eyes.

2.

Jonathan Healy was pronounced dead on arrival at the hospital, scarcely an hour after dawn. Alice was taken straight to the emergency room, where she was given antibiotics, three blood transfusions, and seventeen stitches in the back of her left arm. Another three inches to the right and whatever hit her would have severed a major vein. She would have bled out before her father could get to her. He might have made it out of the woods alive after that if he hadn't felt the need to go after the thing that killed his only daughter. Things only played out the way that they did because of pure luck.

Healy family luck. Sometimes it's good. Sometimes it's bad. And it's always hard to tell the two of them apart.

3.

They made her stay at the hospital under observation for twenty-four hours. Alice slept for twelve of them, out so hard and so deeply that the attending nurses checked her pulse several times, just to reassure themselves she still had one.

"Let her sleep," advised the doctor. "She's had one heck of a night, and she's going to have a great deal to worry about when she finally wakes up." Medical bills, funeral arrangements, the death of her last known relative; those were certainly things she'd have reason to be concerned with.

No one really considered that she might have cause to worry about the wound in her arm, or the wounds that killed her father. No one stopped to wonder whether those wounds might have been made by the stingers of giant, intelligent wasps, rather than by ordinary bullets. Everyone knew the woods on some level, but no one thought about it in that much detail.

It was simply better not to.

Like a woman who knew she wouldn't have another chance to rest for quite some time, Alice Healy slept on.

4.

Checking herself out of the hospital was easy. All she had to do was tell the doctor, very politely, that she felt perfectly well, if a little woozy, and wanted to begin the hard, unavoidable task of arranging her father's funeral. There was nothing more that could be done for her, physically; she'd only suffered a little blood loss and a reasonably minor flesh wound. One of the nurses loaned her some clean clothes, and an orderly drove her back to the suddenly too-empty house on the edge of the wood.

Alice had spent the majority of her life learning how to handle herself around people who weren't part of the family. She was pleasant, facile, and polite for the duration of the ride—and a little distance was only natural, after all, in a young woman who'd just lost her father. She thanked the orderly for getting her home and promised to have the funeral home contact the hospital about arrangements for her father's body before the end of the day.

Her hand only shook slightly as she dug the keys out of her bag of personal effects and unlocked the front door, letting herself into the house. She even managed to return the keys to the bag, close the door, and turn the deadbolt before she sat down on the stairs and cried.

The Aeslin mice in the attic had been with them for generations; had come over with the family from England when they first split with the Covenant. They knew what it meant when two fully-armed members of the family went into the woods and only one of them returned, more than a day later and still smelling faintly of blood. They didn't intrude on her grief or bother asking her what had happened.

By the time Alice finished crying—and she thought she was probably finished crying forever; there were no more tears left in her body, she'd used them all up—the sounds of their private mourning rituals were already drifting down the stairs.

Let them mourn. She had a funeral to attend to. After that was done, she could sit down with them and tell them what had happened, so they could add the story of her father's death to their history of the family line. So it could be preserved. But all that could wait; all that was for after he was buried and gone.

"Oh, Daddy," she whispered. "I didn't even have time to pick up the bodies." There would be no final record of Jonathan Healy to add to the family's memorial collection. Just like her mother, who'd been killed by something they had never been able to identify or track. There was a hole in the history, and it was getting bigger with every loss.

The spot on her arm where she'd been stung by the Apraxis was throbbing like a rotten tooth under the stitches, despite the antibiotics the doctors had pumped into her. She rubbed it distractedly with one hand as she started for the kitchen. Coffee. She needed hot coffee brewed strong and maybe with a shot of brandy added to make her focus while she did what needed to be done. There was no one else to do it.

Fortunately, she'd been through the process of arranging a funeral before. She'd been there when her grandfather arranged the burial of her grandmother, and she'd handled her grandfather's funeral mostly on her own; her father had been too stunned by the suddenness of his own father's death to really be of any real use. It was just a matter of making a few phone calls, accepting the condolences gracefully, and saying "the usual" would be fine. A plain box, yes, of course, and the date of his death carved into the blank half of the tombstone he would share with his wife, her mother. The family plots had been paid for years ago. They'd never said so in quite that many words, but Alice was fairly sure her grandparents always knew the family wasn't going to leave Michigan alive.

Three generations wasn't that bad for a family of cryptozoologists living in exile and trying to defend humans from cryptids—and vice versa—without any resources or support. It was pure luck that had kept them fighting for as long as they had. And now it was just her—Alice, youngest and most unskilled of them all—with no one left to arrange her funeral when the time came.

"Don't dwell," she muttered through gritted teeth, and called the library—her father's library, which he'd run calmly and without dispute for as long as she could remember—to accept their tears, regrets, and solemn promises that she'd still have a job when she felt well enough to return. The children's library would be waiting for her.

"Thank you," she said, over and over, so many times that the words lost all meaning. She too numb to move by the time she got off the phone, and she let that tell her what to do, for a little while; she sat down at the table, put her head against her arms, and simply breathed, trying to remember what was supposed to happen next.

It was easier if she didn't try to think. That was a problem because she had to think; she had to go into her grandfather's library, look up everything they had written down about the Apraxis, and make sure things were really finished. It had been too easy. In the end, it had all been too easy, and she couldn't allow herself to trust it.

And yes, maybe she was looking for revenge—for some chance there was a second hive, something she could destroy without the need for mercy or conservation—but what was wrong with that? They'd killed her father. They'd earned it. For once in her life, Alice was ready to stand with the Covenant's ideals. If any of those demon bugs were still alive, they damn well deserved to die.

Time kept flickering around her like a badly-cut film as she moved through the afternoon and early evening. One moment she was in the kitchen, pouring another cup of hot black coffee and doctoring it with brandy; the next, she was in the family library, cheeks wet with her constant tears, pulling a volume from the high shelves of cryptid lore and extra-dimensional zoology.

"You have to understand something before you hunt it, Alice," her grandfather used to say. "If you don't, you're no better than a small child kicking over an anthill just for the sake of being mean."

She didn't see anything particularly wrong with being mean at that specific moment. She *wanted* to be mean. She didn't want to understand the ecological niche filled by the things that killed her father. Maybe she hadn't liked him much, but she'd loved him, and now she was alone. She wanted the Apraxis to die. She wanted them to suffer while they did it.

Her arm still throbbed. She rubbed it again, wincing as her fingers encountered the bruised place just below her stitches, and opened *Gray's Guide to Insects, Arachnids, and Exoskeletal Beings of the Cryptid World.* It was an essentially flawed manuscript filled with juvenile mistakes, but it also held a great deal of useful observation. What it got wrong, it got very, very wrong, but what it got right . . . might prove useful.

The entry on the Apraxis was in the third chapter, "Hive Intelligences." Someone—presumably her grandfather; it looked like his handwriting—had added a new title in pencil underneath the official one: "Things Not to Ask To Dinner." Smiling slightly, she checked the page numbers against the index, flipped to the right section, and began to read.

The Apraxis wasp, or "mind eater," is one of the most dangerous hive intelligences. It is highly mobile, sturdy enough to survive in most climates, and possesses not only the capacity to learn, but the ability to acquire knowledge at an accelerated rate by incubating its young in the flesh of its victims. The soldier Apraxis possesses a hollow stinger which delivers both a painful venom and small, nearly-invisible eggs with a single sting. The eggs hatch rapidly once implanted in the flesh of their victims. They mature most rapidly in a living host. Once they finish growing to adult size and absorbing the knowledge of their host, they will chew their way out. This process is most often fatal to the host, who will have been distracted and unfocused during the maturing process, due to the telepathic influence of the larvae, and may not have thought to seek assistance. Indeed—

Alice stopped rubbing her arm, feeling the animation draining out of her face. Then, taking a deep breath, she looked back to the book.

—many hosts will not even be aware they have been infested.

"That sort of thing could be pretty easy to overlook," she said faintly.

The average gestation period of larval Apraxis is three days in living flesh, or three weeks in the bodies of the dead. Burning the body will not kill the eggs but will cause them to disperse into the local soil, where they will await ingestion by a suitable host in order to finish the maturation process. Many areas have suffered repeat infestations due to improper handling of the bodies of the infected.

Her father had been stung more than a dozen times. Alice remembered that much, even though most of the details were mercifully blurred by the memory of darkness and the shock of the event itself. She'd only been stung once, in the arm, in a spot that was sore and bruised, and throbbed more beneath the stitches than the injury could really justify.

Well. It had only been a day and a half since the attack. She had time to finish reading before she went to take care of . . . whatever needed to be taken care of.

Apraxis are relatively fragile and can be killed by direct hits to the body, head, or thorax. The bladed edges of their wings can be dangerous in close quarters, but their effectiveness as weapons is reduced when the adult wasp is in flight. Nymphs can be killed through blunt trauma, or by drowning. Gasoline and the blood of Johrlac have both proven excellent for preserving the young—

"Because a cuckoo is *just* what this little slice of hell needs," Alice muttered, shuddering at the very notion.

—and some specimens have now been under study for more than thirty years. Eggs preserved in this fashion will gestate and hatch if removed from suspension and brought into contact with mammalian tissue, either living or dead. Individual Apraxis have little to no sense of self-preservation—

"Well, that's something we have in common." Alice barely noticed that she'd started rubbing her arm again, testing the dimensions of the sore place with her fingers.

—as they are bent, instead, toward the survival of the species as a whole. Entire hives have been known to sacrifice themselves in order to claim a more suitable host.

Alice simply sat there for a long moment, looking at the words and considering their implications. "Entire hives will sacrifice themselves in order to claim a more suitable host." That's what it said, right there in black and white.

There wasn't a child in town who didn't believe—really and truly *believe*—that she had magical powers, that she could make the monsters go away. There wasn't an intelligent cryptid in those woods who didn't know about Jonathan Healy and his position on things that hurt his town. The first humans to vanish were all children. Who knew how many cryptids had died before the Apraxis moved on to more protected prey?

The Apraxis said they knew where she lived when they spoke to her in Jenny Sampson's voice. The hive must have increased in number every time it took a child, and every time it took a child it heard, again, that the Healys hunted monsters in the woods. Three days to gestate in living flesh. The damned things had taken Jenny alive, and her death had been . . .

Her death had been something that didn't bear thinking about.

"It was a trap," said Alice, and rubbed her arm again. Was the bruise beneath her stitches starting to swell? She rather thought that it was.

There was nothing more of use in that book, or in any of the others, although she found several small warnings tucked in amongst the dryer passages, all cautioning the reader not to go alone into areas where Apraxis had been sighted, and especially not to go at night, as the hives tended to hunt most actively in the dark. Too little, too late. The damage was already done.

Alice replaced the books on the shelves, making sure they were in the correct order—the librarian in her coming out again, almost automatically, underscored with the macabre awareness that this could very well be the last time she used the library. If she died without an heir, her grandfather's safety deposit box would be opened, and the last letter to the Covenant of St. George would be sent. The letter that restored the family's property to them and asked them to come clean certain materials out of the house.

Three generations wasn't such a bad run. She knew that. She did, really, down to the bones of her, and yet she was crying again when she turned down the lights, and she kept crying as she closed and locked the library door. She hadn't been out of tears after all.

5.

It took the better part of an hour to get everything together. Finding a clean scalpel wasn't hard; neither was finding an oilcloth to spread over the kitchen table. But her chain mail gloves were in the barn, and after she spent twenty minutes finding them, she wound up needing to go right back out again in order to find a pair of forceps small enough to slide into an incision without tearing her bicep open. She was already missing half of her left calf. She didn't need to spoil her arm as well.

The gas cans were in the shed on the other side of the house. At least the canning jars were easy to find, tucked safely into boxes in the basement.

Alice surveyed the items arrayed on the table. Home surgery, she thought grimly, is never as simple as you think it's going to be. Not that she really expected this to be simple once it was underway. The egg or eggs had been inserted near a major vein, and from the feel of her arm, the larvae had managed to burrow down to nestle against the bone. She'd need to cut deep and fast, without incapacitating herself, and extract the nymph one-handed before it could burrow deeper into her flesh. Worst case, she'd bleed out before she got it out of her body, and the gestation period would take a little longer as it finished inside a corpse.

"Well," she said, as philosophically as she could manage, "I suppose I've finally found something I like less than library board meetings." She sat, moving the forceps and the jar of gasoline into easy reach before pulling a chain mail glove onto her right hand.

The stitches on her arm were slightly above the tender spot. That made sense; the eggs were extruded through the base of the ovipositor, which had been roughly four inches in length. Alice traced the bruise with her fingers, noting the points where the pain was most severe. Then she picked up the scalpel and calmly drove it into the meat of her arm.

The blade was sharp, and it didn't hurt nearly as much as she'd been afraid it would. She'd only cut a few inches when she heard a thin keening noise, like a kitten crying through a window. The sound was grating—fingers scraping along the inside of her skull—and worse, it was coming from inside her arm.

Moving quickly now, Alice dropped the scalpel, grabbed the forceps, and shoved them into the wound. They hit something that resisted like bone when they were barely half an inch past the skin. She clamped them shut, pulling as hard as she could.

The keening grew in intensity to match the pain, which was now shooting along her arm in vast, pulsing blasts. Alice ground her teeth together, biting the inside of her cheek to keep herself from screaming, and kept pulling until the forceps came free with an audible popping sound, pulling a squirming horror nearly the length of her index finger into the light. It was milk-white underneath a thin film of viscous, watery-looking blood. The buds of its wings were furled tightly against its back, and its mouth was working constantly, mandibles opening and closing as it shrieked at her, voice whistle-sharp and piercing. It stabbed the air with its half-formed stinger, trying to strike at anything in reach.

"Bastard," she hissed, and plunged the forceps into the jar of gasoline, holding them under until the nymph stopped squirming.

After the movement died, she dunked the forceps into her waiting mug of hot water before picking up a towel and wiping the worst of the blood from her arm. She felt the area around her incision as she did. The pain wasn't lessening, and there was a second sore spot, smaller but definitely swollen, about an inch below the first one.

Alice closed her eyes for a moment, sighing, and reached for the forceps again.

The second nymph was less developed and hence easier to extract. It helped that the trauma to her arm was becoming severe enough for shock to set in, numbing the pain. As it was, she had to pause several times, biting her cheek while she waited for the room to stop spinning.

The third nymph was the smallest but had been warned by the sudden disappearance of its siblings; it fought her every inch of the way, biting down and clinging with tiny claws as she pulled. It kept squirming even after she had it free, nearly knocking over the jar of gasoline before she could get it immersed and slam the lid into place.

She sat there for several moments, hand clamped tightly against her arm, feeling for sore spots as she watched the nymph slowly stop moving. She didn't feel any more of them, and that was good because she didn't have the strength for another extraction. "If I'm not done, I'm done," she said, and was dismayed by how far away her own voice sounded. "Oh, that's no good. Get up, Alice. You still have work to do."

Her legs didn't listen. Not moving was better, they argued. Shock would keep the pain from coming back. She could watch the infant Apraxis float in their sea of amber, and maybe that would teach her . . . something . . . about where they'd come from, and why. Even if they didn't, she'd be motionless. Wasn't that better than trying to move around?

"I have to get up now," she said, closing her eyes. "Come on, Alice. Don't be a silly. Get up." No, argued her legs. Her arms were joining the mutiny. Sitting was better. She should sit.

If she sat, she was going to die.

Was that such a bad thing? If she died, the Covenant would come to town. They would dismantle the house, taking everything the Healys had learned during their short-lived rebellion, and take it back to Europe, where they could use it to teach other people not to make the same mistakes. It wouldn't be lost. Just . . . reclaimed, in a way, by the people they'd tried to leave behind. They wouldn't be forgotten. There were worse fates.

But she didn't want to die.

So what? Three generations wasn't such a bad run—hadn't she had that thought herself, more than once? The Healy luck couldn't last forever. Maybe it was better to stop fighting than to be the only one left clinging to something that was better off gone.

No one would think to tell Thomas if she died. He'd find out when the Covenant arrived.

That was enough to make the mutineers pause in their argument. Alice pursued that line of thought, telling herself fiercely, *If you give up here, he'll never know. Or maybe he will because the Covenant will tell him. Do you want him to find out that way? Do you want them to tell him about your diaries, or about the picture under your pillow? Get up. Don't do this.* "Just get moving," she snarled, and then—to her great surprise—she was.

She cleared away the jar of gasoline, the scalpel, and the forceps like she was sleepwalking, tucking them into a cupboard before getting out a loaf of bread and a plain kitchen knife. She rubbed the blade thoroughly in her blood; there was plenty of blood to go around.

It took forever to walk to the phone, take it off the cradle, and dial for directory assistance. "Operator," said the distant, tinny voice of Maisie Baker.

"This is Alice Healy," Alice said, her own voice sounding nearly as far away as Maisie's. "I was making dinner, and I heard a sound, and I jumped with the knife in my hand, and I'm afraid I've hurt myself. Can you please ring the ambulance for me? Thank you, so much." She hung up without waiting for a reply.

She made it to the front lawn, pausing only to lock the door carefully behind herself before shock and blood loss overtook pure stubbornness and she collapsed. The ambulance arrived ten minutes later and found her lying there, covered in blood, barely breathing.

For the second time in under a week, Alice Healy went to the hospital.

6.

They couldn't call it a suicide attempt, not exactly; not even a foolish girl would try to kill herself by opening a vein in her upper arm, and Alice Healy was far from foolish. It didn't matter that the edges of the wound were unusually clean. She'd been clutching a bloody bread knife in one hand when she was found, and there were bread crumbs inside the wound. No one was going to argue with evidence like that.

"Grief confuses a person. It can make them clumsy," said the attending doctor. For the most part, people were willing to accept that. It was easier than the alternatives.

Alice herself was serene when she woke up, all apologies and bashful embarrassment over her own clumsiness. The loss of her father had overcome her while she was cooking, she said; she'd been slicing bread and heard a noise that sounded like a footstep, and she'd stabbed herself in the arm in the process of turning toward it. "I don't believe in ghosts or anything," she said, with a small, nervous laugh, "but I'm not in the habit of being alone out there. It's an old house. It makes noises, sometimes."

"If this is going to be an ongoing problem, Alice, maybe you should consider moving closer to town." The doctor gave her a serious look. They'd known each other for years; they'd gone to school together, and while they'd never been friends, he had a certain measure of respect for her, odd as she could sometimes be. "There are quite a few rooms for rent for a respectable young lady like yourself. You could move away from the memories. Start over again. Or move back once you'd found yourself a fellow, start a new family."

It was good advice if you were talking to a woman who planned to eventually get married and settle down with her new husband. For Alice, it was something like suggesting she pack her things and relocate to Jupiter. Still smiling, she nodded, replying, "I'll think about it. I was born in that house, though; I'm not sure I'm ready to let go quite that much."

"Just keep it in mind, and try not to hurt yourself again," he said. "Your system can only take so many blood transfusions before it stops recovering."

"I'll do my very best," she said.

"Good." He rose from the chair beside her bed. "I'll get you your clothes and release papers."

"Thank you," said Alice.

Her smile lasted until he was out of the room. She sagged against her pillows, closing her eyes. She'd successfully removed all the nymphs. There were no more odd bruises or unusually sore spots on her arm, and given the size of the ones she'd found, they couldn't move through the body without leaving some signs behind. Now what?

Now she needed to get out of the hospital, go home, and start putting things into a more lasting order. Now she needed to bury her father, who had been dead for two and a half days. That was less than half of the first week the nymphs would need to spend gestating in his body before they reached full maturity and broke free. They needed three weeks in total. She had time.

Thinking logically, she knew she'd have an easier time of things if she could do it now and get to the nymphs before they reached adulthood. There was just one problem with trying to extract them now: the books agreed they grew more slowly in the dead, and while she might kill any nymphs by burning the body, she wouldn't destroy any un-hatched eggs. Anything small enough to be overlooked by the doctors who'd stitched her up would be nearly impossible to find in a corpse. And getting her father's body away from the morgue without releasing it to the funeral home would be even harder. Maybe if she hadn't wound up in the hospital . . .

But then, if she hadn't wound up in the hospital, she'd be dead, too. They'd both be incubating their deadly new family members some-where deep in the woods, out of sight until they hatched and could lay siege to an unsuspecting, undefended town. No, it would have to be a burial and a grave robbery. Not particularly ladylike, but it wasn't like she had a choice.

She managed to keep herself from either laughing or crying as they brought the papers in, and she checked herself out.

7.

Buckley Township was too small to have anything as metropolitan as a cab, but the receptionist had a brother who was willing to give Alice a ride home. He dropped her at the foot of the driveway, asking sev-eral times if she was sure she could make the walk on her own, if she was sure she should be alone. She smiled and smiled and ground her teeth and felt like screaming the whole time she was convincing him to leave her, and she walked up to the house alone, pausing on the porch until his headlights faded and then using her toe to trace a circle on the boards.

"Mary, if you can hear me, I could really use you about now," she said, voice low. "I know we haven't been talking much, but Daddy's dead and I'm afraid."

There was no reply. She waited several minutes, hopeful to the end, before she sighed, and turned, and let herself inside.

The mice were waiting for her on the stairs. It looked like the entire population of the attic had come down. They formed a sea of black, brown, white, and patchwork fur, spreading out to completely cover the bottom six steps. Tiny oil-drop eyes watched her step inside, but none of them said a word until the door was closed and locked behind her. The mice knew the rules as well as any Healy.

"Hello," said Alice wearily, dropping the keys into her coat pocket as she turned to face the colony. "Did you need me for something?"

The current high priest of her congregation stepped forward. His ceremonial headdress of beads, bones, and crow feathers was attached to an ivory thimble that rode low over his muzzle in what was doubtless an impressive display, if you happened to be another mouse. "There was blood in many places in the Room of Eating," he declared, thumping the step with his kitten-bone staff for emphasis. "One who had been in the walls when you departed came to us saying that you spilled your own blood in mourning for the God who was your father. We called for the Phantom Priestess, to ask if you yet lived, but she did not come. Are you well, Priestess?"

Lovely; now even the damn Aeslin mice thought she was suicidal. "I had to remove three Apraxis nymphs from my arm before they burrowed their way out of my flesh and devoured me alive, actually," she said, rubbing the side of her face with one hand. "It was an act of self-preservation, not mourning, I promise. I'm sorry Mary's being cagey."

The mouse tilted his head to the side, regarding her. "Then you do not seek to join your forbearers in the Land Where All Is Well, Turn Out the Damn Lights and Go to Bed?"

"What? I . . . oh. I see." Alice sighed as comprehension dawned. Sometimes she still had trouble understanding the mice, even though she'd grown up with them. "That's one of your terms for Heaven, isn't it?" The entire sea of tiny bodies rippled with an almost tidal motion as the mice nodded. "I don't want to go to Heaven, no. Or Hell, or anyplace else that involves being dead. But thank you for your concern."

"The God is gone," said the priest, continuing to watch her. "Will a new God be coming before us, to aid you in preservation of the way?"

Alice paused. The Aeslin had been living with the Healy family for a very long time. They knew just about everything there was to know about their history—more than anyone had ever written down. "Has there ever been a time without a God before?" she asked as lightly as she could manage.

"No," said the priest, as the mice behind and around him murmured negation. "There have always been two to guide and protect us, a God and His Priestess. Sometimes more are granted unto us, and we rejoice, but always, there have been two. When does the new God arrive? Will you go to the God of Inconvenient Timing?"

The question was so innocent. She knew they didn't mean anything by it. It still burned. "He . . . a new God isn't going to be arriving, and Thomas isn't going to come," Alice said slowly. "This is a new time, a time when it's just . . . when it's just us. All of you, and me."

The mice exchanged shocked whispers before the priest looked up to her again, asking hesitantly, "This is a time for learning and purification? To prove we remain worthy?"

"Yes, that's exactly what this is," said Alice, trying to mask her relief. There was an art to talking to the mice, assuming you wanted them to actually pay attention. How was she supposed to say, "When the cryptid wasps swarm out of Daddy's corpse and eat me, you're going to have to go stay with Mr. Price until Naga can get to this dimension to pick you up." It wasn't the sort of thing she'd ever needed to say before. Finally, she settled for the reasonably neutral, formal-sounding, "There may be some other changes ahead of us. Things aren't going to be the way that they were. But you have to prove yourselves worthy before you can learn what's next."

"Worthy of what, Priestess?"

"I don't know," Alice replied. Then she smiled, sadly. "I guess we'll find out together, won't we?"

8.

The funeral was held on Sunday.

Alice hadn't been able to come up with an excuse to make it a private ceremony. "Friends and family" wouldn't be exactly private, given how much of the town had known her father, and "just family" looked too much like her sitting alone with a corpse. There wasn't even religion to fall back on—the Healys were well-established as Easter Sunday Presbyterians, showing up for church only when social custom absolutely demanded it and mostly steering well clear. In the end, she simply had to agree to go along with the burial and start making plans for digging her father up again after it was over.

She greeted the mourners with a small, distant smile, shook hands and accepted hugs from people who'd known her all her life. The whole time, she was wondering whether her arm was recovered enough to let her handle the shovel properly. She barely saw the faces of the people offering their condolences. They would all go home at the end of the service talking about how sad it was, how tragic. Poor Alice, so clearly crushed by the loss of her father, left all alone in the world.

In actuality, Alice was just distracted, and starting to think—not for the first time—about how much easier things would have been if she'd been born a boy. Not only would her father have been a lot less likely to try to keep her out of the woods the way he did, she'd have been able to make big, strapping farm boy friends who'd probably see "Hey, come out and help me dig Daddy out of his grave so we can get the demon wasps out of his corpse" as an invitation to good, clean fun. Girls weren't supposed to rob graves. Girls were supposed to darn socks and do needlework.

While Alice could certainly see where a steady hand and a lot of needles would help when it came to getting rid of the nymphs, that didn't help her with actually getting her hands on the body.

The first few greetings were hard. "I'm sorry" and "if there's anything we can do" and "he was a good man" all seemed fresh and new, like they'd never been said before. She smiled fixedly, took the offerings as they were intended, and didn't answer the nebulous offers of aid by asking people how good they were with a shovel. She did all right throughout the viewing, and through the brief sermon that started the actual ceremony. She was beginning, stupidly, to believe she might make it through the afternoon without breaking down completely.

Then the eulogies began.

Jonathan Healy had been a good man; he'd worked long and hard for the community, for the library, and for the improvement of the library; he'd always had a kind word and a helping hand for those less fortunate than he was; the list of his virtues went on and on, expanded on by every person that stood to speak. Jonathan Healy loved his wife, honored his father and mother, and loved his daughter, who had done him the honor of seeing him as close to home as she could.

Alice had never in her life been so glad to be left sitting at the sidelines. She cried from the first word through to the last. By the time everyone had finished volunteering to speak, there'd been no time left for her to give her own eulogy, and that was just fine, because what could she have said? "I'm sorry I got you killed" didn't seem appropriate, and neither did "be seeing you soon." So she just wept.

It might have been easier if Thomas had been there, or Mary, or even Cynthia who owned the Red Angel. But Thomas couldn't attend, and Mary wasn't answering when she called, and Cynthia wouldn't have been comfortable at a human funeral. Alice had to muddle through on her own.

They buried Jonathan Healy next to his wife. Alice threw the first handful of dirt onto the grave, along with a small bouquet of yellow flowers that only a few puzzled members of the crowd recognized as aconite. Then she turned and walked away, heading for that battered old white truck of hers, the one she'd insisted on driving, even though a dozen people offered to give her a ride to the funeral home. She politely declined the offers of a room for the night, a hot dinner, or just company until she felt better. She was fine, she said; she only wanted to go home and sleep.

Once the last of the well-wishers had been waved off and she was allowed to get into the truck, she turned on the engine and drove out to Old Logger's Road, where she parked just out of view of Thomas' house—close enough to see the light from the windows reflecting off the trees, but not close enough for the man inside to see her—and put her head down against the wheel and cried herself to sleep.

She stayed there until morning.

9.

How does one relatively petite woman with an injured arm excavate six solid feet of earth, break through a cement grave liner, haul the corpse of a two-hundred-pound man out of the grave, replace the soil, move the body to a well-lit place, and still have the strength to deal with what could potentially be hundreds of demonic wasps in an unknown state of maturity? Almost as importantly, how does she do all of that and still retain the capability to dispose of the body afterward?

Answer: she doesn't.

After a week of studying the problem from every angle she could think of and a few she probably shouldn't have, Alice was forced to admit that she couldn't see an answer. She'd called for Mary every night, seeking backup, and her phantom babysitter had never appeared, leaving her to puzzle things out on her own.

The cemetery was too publicly situated to allow her to perform a simple grave robbery; she'd have to get in and out with impossible speed, even if she did it in the middle of the night. Heavy rains would have helped by softening up the ground, but the summer remained stubbornly dry. The wounds in her arm were healing, and no new nymphs appeared; that didn't alter the fact that she'd sliced fairly deeply into the muscle, and her lifting power—which was never anything to brag about—was seriously impaired.

Attempts to summon Naga had met with silence. The cryptid professor was probably off on another school trip, putting him out of range of her little pre-mixed hex bags. She had to face the facts: she was never going to get her father out of the ground. Even if some miraculously lucky series of events allowed her to manage it, she'd never be able to get the body back to the house or stay on her feet long enough to dig out all the nymphs. There was just no way.

"I have to wait for them to hatch," she said, leaning her elbows on her grandfather's battered old writing desk and dropping her face into her hands, eyes closed. "I have to wait for them to hatch, and hope the ground slows them down enough to let me shoot them one at a time."

Once upon a time, she would have considered that an exciting challenge, something fun to do with her evening before she had to come home and put the dishes away. That was before she saw her father die. Things had changed.

Maybe she would've been able to find something, *anything* that would work if there'd been anyone in a position to help her . . . but there wasn't anyone, and there weren't any other ways. It was going to come down to her, the new-hatched Apraxis wasps, and as many guns as she could carry to the cemetery. Who walked—or flew—away would be determined then and there.

Two weeks to the hatching. That's what the calendar said, and all the books seemed to agree. The Apraxis would gestate for twenty-one days before chewing their way free, with all her father's memories and intelligence intact in the form of a newly-dispersed hive mind. "Because that's not creepy or anything," she muttered, rising to put the books away.

The time for studying was done. Now was the time to put her affairs in order.

10.

It took two weeks for Alice Healy to get ready to die.

She began by formally requesting a leave of absence from her job. The library board was painfully willing to grant it, agreeing without hesitation to her carefully-worded offer to come back to work at the beginning of September. The children's library was sparsely used during the summer, they said; most of the kids were at camp, or swimming in the lake, not spending their days indoors with the books. One of the interns would mind her desk while she was away.

Alice smiled, thanked them for understanding, and took the files holding all the retired Monster Wall drawings out of her filing cabinet when she left.

The library did hold one surprise: she'd expected the sketches on the Wall to be at least a week old, since she'd been gone that long. Instead, she found that the children had continued posting their monsters and had started posting hand-drawn "get well soon" cards right along with them. One particularly well-done sketch showed a sad-looking boogeyman trying to feed her chicken soup, with "fel better miss Heely" woefully misspelled underneath the picture. She looked at it until she felt herself getting ready to cry again and took it with her when she went.

It took the better part of a week to clean out the barn. She baled hides, filled jars with scales, teeth, and claws, and labeled the various canning jars of organs and fluids that had been accumulating around the place for the past several decades. When the representatives of the Covenant arrived to clean up the family affairs, she didn't want them to think the Healys had turned into barbarians. She polished the tools and sharpened the knives, and she planned.

The books all agreed that burning wouldn't destroy the eggs, but none of them claimed that the adult wasps were fireproof. She could probably rig some sort of flamethrower, assuming she didn't mind setting her own hair on fire. Start with bullets to pick off as much of the early waves as she could manage, move on to flame when they started to outnumber her, and then, if that worked, she could go back to bullets for the stragglers. All she had to do was keep them from escaping, and from stinging her again.

Maybe there was a chance that she'd be able to . . .

"Don't be a fool, Alice," she said aloud. "Kill them all, but don't start planning on staying alive." It seemed better not to start down that path. Hope makes you worry about how much you're bleeding. Fatalism makes you do more damage before you die. Given the options, and what the Apraxis could do to the town if they managed to get loose, she knew which she was going to choose.

It took another two days to clean the downstairs, with the mice watching raptly all the while. The old priest came down to observe her as she cleaned out her father's study. After an hour, he sat down on the blotter, regarding her steadily.

"You are preparing for a journey," he accused.

"I suppose that's true," she said, wiping the dust off a mounted cockatrice.

"Will we be accompanying you?"

"Not this time."

"We accompanied those who came before you across the Great

Water," the priest said solemnly. "We will gladly go with you on this journey."

The image of arriving at the Pearly Gates with an honor guard of cryptid mice who worshipped her as a demi-goddess arose before Alice could smother it, and she smiled, putting a hand over her mouth to muffle the expression. "I'm sorry, but you really can't come with me this time."

"I see." The priest continued studying her. "You go to follow those who came, and went, before you."

Alice hesitated before nodding, very slowly. "I suppose I do, yes."

"And there is need for this thing?"

"There's great need. I wouldn't . . . I wouldn't go if there wasn't great need. I'm sorry."

"You do not need to offer apologies, Priestess. What you will do is what must be done. So it has always been." The priest shook his head, reaching up to remove the ceremonial headdress. "My time as priest grows short. Soon, I too will take that journey."

The admission sent a pang through Alice's heart as she realized what the tiny priest meant. "I'm so sorry to hear that." It had always been hard for her to tell the ages of individual mice. She knew from the bestiaries that Aeslin could live fifty years or more, but in the end, age came for them just like it came for everything else. "Maybe we'll see each other at our destination."

"The Gods have always been kind," the priest replied. "We will all be joined, and gladly, in that place."

Alice shook her head. She couldn't help envying his certainty. Maybe she wasn't a cryptid mouse worshipping a family of slightly off-kilter cryptozoologists, but she'd never really believed in an afterlife beyond Mary's twilight, either. "I won't leave you alone here. I . . . I'm leaving a message for Naga. He'll come and get you and take you wherever you want to go."

The priest held up a paw in negation. "If you go and do not return for seven days, or if others come in your stead, we will make our own way. There are places which will welcome us."

"I see." Alice leaned down to put her hand in front of him. The old priest rose slowly, stepping onto her palm, and leaned on his staff as she lifted the hand to eye level. "This is one of those times when I shouldn't ask, isn't it?"

"It is so, Priestess."

"All right, then; I won't." She moved the hand to her shoulder, holding it there as he stepped off and settled in her hair. "I need to clean the pantry. Come with me?"

"I would be honored, Priestess."

"I'm glad." She turned off the light and closed the door, asking as she did, "Will you tell me one of the stories about my mother?"

"Of course, Priestess." The old mouse cleared his throat, and began to solemnly recite: "It was in the year of the great dryness, when the Patient Priestess did shout No, No, That Is Not the Way to Dig a Well . . ."

Sometimes the only thing to do is prepare.

11.

The world ends every time a person dies, because for them—unless they manage to come back as some sort of unquiet ghost, which had always struck Alice as being something uncomfortably like cheating—everything is over. Die, and even though the world may keep on turning, it no longer turns in a way that you're ever going to see.

Keeping that in mind, it struck her as vaguely improper for the world to be ending on a Wednesday. It should have been a Monday, at the very least; some sort of day that was suited to a suicide. Ah, well. The dying don't get to be picky.

She spent the morning loading the back of the truck, pausing between loads to write the letters she'd been putting off since the day she realized what she'd need to do. One was for Naga, explaining exactly what she wanted done with the few things in the house that she considered truly hers. One was for Clark, her only college boyfriend, who would have been her college fiancé, if things had gone just a little differently. One for the men from the Covenant, telling them where the traps were. One for Mary, asking where she'd been when Alice needed her, why she hadn't been there in the end.

Maybe that letter was a little bit cruel. But sometimes the truth was a cruel thing.

And one for Thomas Price, explaining absolutely everything else that needed to be explained. "We only get to do this once, Alice," her grandfather used to say. "Oh, sure, there're souls, and maybe they come back around again, but they don't come back as us, now, do they? And ghosts aren't the same as living people. Ghosting's not a way to settle your affairs from the grave. You make sure you tie all your knots just as tight as you can, because no one's going to batten down the hatches for you when you go."

She was tying knots. She was taking down the sails and battening the hatches because that was what a person did when they knew they were going to die; they made sure the dishes were clean and dry, that the towels were folded neatly in their chests, and that the library was properly indexed.

They also filled the truck with cans of jellied gasoline, accelerants, butane torches, ammunition, and any convenient sniper rifles that happened to be lying around the house. As a last resort, she threw a belt of concussion grenades that had been in the attic since the family moved over from England into the passenger seat and closed the truck's back gate. If everything else failed, she could blow herself to Kingdom Come, and take as many of the bastards as possible along with her for the ride.

It was almost funny, Alice thought grimly. She was getting ready to go and commit suicide—there was no other term for facing a swarm of cryptid wasps on your own in a graveyard without backup on the way—but she'd be damned before she'd be quiet about it.

There was only one thing left for her to do by three o'clock on the afternoon of the last day of her life, and it wasn't something she could handle at the house. She walked through the halls one last time, looking at the carefully dusted shelves and the carefully straightened pictures. It looked almost like a museum; a memorial to something that was long since dead and gone. Maybe, in a way, that's what it was.

The high priest and a small band of acolytes waited for her on the kitchen counter, their tails coiled tight and anxious around their legs. "Have you come for the taking of leave?" he asked, leaning heavily on his kitten-bone staff.

"I have," she said, walking over to the counter and kneeling to put the mice at the level of her eyes. "I'm sorry. I wish . . ."

"Wishes Are For Fools and Madmen; Actions Are For the Brave," intoned the priest, with that particular stress on the first letters of each word that told her he was reciting. The mice were the only creatures Alice had ever met who could actually *pronounce* capital letters.

"Who said that?" she asked.

"The Patient Priestess, Enid Healy, who begat—"

"I know who Grandma Enid begat. But thank you for making sure." Alice smiled, offering her hand toward the mice, palm upward. "Thank you for everything."

"We will see you again, Noisy Priestess," said the priest, putting his free paw lightly on the tip of her index finger. "We have always had one blessing that was denied to you and yours, for you are of the divine, and have needed it not."

Alice blinked. "What blessing is that?"

The mice weren't built to smile, but they could still show amusement. The mouse priest did so, flattening his whiskers and twitching his tail at her as he replied, solemnly, "We have faith."

PART THREE:

Trade Today For Tomorrow

1.

The last thing Alice did before leaving the house for what she assumed would be the final time was go into the room that had belonged to her parents and open her mother's jewelry box. It was sitting on the dresser, where it had been untouched for over seventeen years. The last time it had been opened was the day after Frances Healy walked into the woods and didn't come back out, when her grieving husband put her jewelry away for the last time.

Alice picked through the jumble of bracelets and earrings without partners, finally extracting the prize she had come to find: her mother's engagement ring. The silver had tarnished, but the diamond still glittered as brightly as she remembered. Most engagement rings are made of gold. Frances Healy's was made by melting down a silver bullet dredged from the corpse of the first werewolf she ever shot. And that, in a way, says everything anyone will ever need to know about the Healys.

Carefully, Alice strung the ring on a plain gold chain from her own jewelry box, fastening the clasp at the nape of her neck. She sat there for a few minutes, resting on the edge of her parents' bed, fighting back the urge to cry. Finally, quietly, she said, "Meet me at the door, Mama. I'm scared."

Then she stood, turning off the lights as she walked first out of the room, and then out of the house itself. Seven hours to moonrise, when the nymphs would begin emerging from her father's body.

Time to go.

2.

If Thomas Price was surprised to find Alice on his doorstep wearing jeans, a blood-stained white tank top, hiking boots, and an olive-green vest that started life as military surplus, he didn't show it. If the gun belt strapped low around her hips was unexpected, he didn't show that, either. He just held the door a little further open, saying, "Miss Healy. I wasn't expecting you this evening. Would you care to come inside, or is this intended as strictly a brief visit?"

"It's actually more of a social call," replied Alice, offering a strained smile as she stepped past him into the house. "I hope I'm not interrupting anything?"

"Nothing of any real importance," he said as he closed the door behind her.

She flashed him a briefly amused look, taking in his damp, uncombed hair, and the somewhat undone state of his shirt. "You missed a button," she said. Then the reality of the statement sunk in, and her cheeks flushed.

"That's been known to happen from time to time," said Thomas slowly. "Usually when I'm not expecting company. How have you been, Miss Healy? I've been worried since I heard . . ." He stopped, not quite certain how to proceed.

"Better than I expected, not as good as I might have hoped," Alice said, blush fading as she ducked her head. "I'm sorry I didn't tell you myself."

"You've been busy." She'd been busy, and there hadn't been a damn thing he could do to help her. Maybe if he'd been able to leave the house . . . but that door was closed, had been closed for years, and he had no one but himself to blame for it.

Himself, and the woman standing in front of him, alive and breathing. Maybe it hadn't been a fair exchange, his freedom for her life—an exchange she still might not know the terms of—but it was done, and even now, he couldn't find it in himself to regret it.

Alice squared her shoulders, seeming to make a decision as she straightened up and met his eyes full-on, with no polite attempts at glancing away. "I know I didn't call ahead, but it seemed important that I come tonight. You see, Father's death, it . . . put some things into perspective for me, some things I'd been thinking about for an awfully long time. And I felt that, since we've known each other for so long, I owed it to you to come over here and . . . and let you know."

Thomas frowned, looking from the guns belted at her hips back to her face. She looked tired. More accurately, she looked like she hadn't slept for over a week. There were dark circles beneath her eyes, not even cursorily covered with foundation powder, and her normally bright hair was dull from insufficient care. It fell in soft, uneven waves, rather than holding together in her customary, overly-careful curls. He thought it looked better this way, but much as he wanted to be distracted by her hair—by the idea of burying his fingers in it and finally saying the things he'd been trying not to say for years—something about her words was making him uneasy.

"Let me know what?" he asked.

"I'm . . ." *I'm stupidly in love with you, Thomas, I have been since I was a teenager, and we have six hours before I go to the graveyard and don't come back because nobody's luck can last forever. So I came here because I didn't want to die without saying it to your face, and there just isn't time to play around anymore. We used all the time up on . . . on gingham dresses and upside-down cakes and being polite with one another. I'm here to ask you not to be polite to me, just for tonight. Because I won't be here tomorrow.*

"Miss Healy? Alice?"

Alice shook her head, smiling slightly as she came out of her fugue. "I'm sorry. I'm still a little distracted, I suppose. Forgive me?"

"Always," said Thomas, with complete sincerity. "You were saying?"

"I was saying . . ." *I love you.* "I'm leaving Buckley forever, Mr. Price. I'm being picked up tonight by an old friend of my mother's on his way through town, and he's going to give me a ride to Ann Arbor." She hadn't intended to lie, but it rolled easily off her tongue. "I'm just here to say goodbye."

Something in her words didn't ring right. Thomas indicated the gun belt. "Do you customarily go fully armed when you're getting rides from friends of the family? I wasn't aware that was an American custom."

"Didn't Grandma ever tell you that Momma was carnie folk? I know you remember me going off to spend summers with the carnival."

"She did, yes, and I remember. I've met your aunt Juniper. Still, it seems a little odd."

"Believe me, the guns won't be a problem. I think they're pretty much expected with this crowd. Like wearing calico to the first spring picnic."

"I'll bow to your expertise in this matter. Will you be . . . returning any time soon, Miss Healy?"

"No. No, I really don't think so." Alice smiled again, glancing down to keep him from seeing the way the expression didn't reach her eyes. "I'm leaving for good this time."

"I see," he said neutrally. *What are you going out there to kill, Alice? Why are you so sure that it's going to kill you? You were supposed to be retired. Your father told me that you were. Why are you finally looking at me like you're a real person again, and lying when you tell me where you're going?* "I'm very sorry to hear that."

"I'm afraid it can't be helped. This is something I need to do."

"There's nothing I can say to change your mind?"

"No, there isn't," she said. She didn't have to feign the regret in her voice. That, at least, was entirely honest. "I have a few hours before my ride gets here, and then I guess it's time to get on the road."

"Will you write this time?"

Alice hesitated. The resignation in his voice hadn't sounded forced; it sounded as real and as complete as her own regret. "If I can," she said.

"I'll miss you." The admission was softly made. It had the weight of years behind it.

"I'll . . . I'm going to miss you, too."

He watched her for a few moments, waiting for her to say something—anything—more. She looked away without speaking. With a sigh, he did the same.

"Well. I suppose you have things to do before you go. Other calls to make, other recluses to see," he said, beginning to carefully redo the buttons on his shirt. He didn't have to look at her if he kept his eyes on his hands. "Please do take care out there. I understand that it's quite a large world, and it would be easy to get lost."

"Mr. Price . . ."

"Yes?" He looked up, fingers going still.

Alice's first shooting lessons were with her grandmother, of all people: the single member of the family who spent the least amount of time on the firing range because she had the least need for the practice. "If you need to aim, you've already missed the shot," she used to say. "Just fire. Your hand knows the way better than your eye does."

She stepped forward before she could second-guess herself again. Slinging her arms around Thomas' neck, she pressed her body hard against his until she could feel the sheath of the knife she'd always pretended not to know he wore beneath his shirt digging into the skin of her belly and kissed him.

She didn't need to aim.

3.

There was a moment of startled hesitation during which neither of them really breathed. After that, Thomas didn't need to aim, either. He kissed her back, immediately and without any reservations. She started to pull away, surprised by his participation—she'd been expecting to kiss him and run before he could react, not find herself getting thoroughly kissed in return.

He slid his arms around her as soon as he felt her starting to retreat, flattening his hands against the smooth outlines of her shoulder blades and spreading his fingers wide to cup her back. He kept kissing her as he pulled her harder against him. Alice's confusion managed to last a few seconds longer before the rest of her informed it that she had better things to be doing than worrying about whether or not Thomas had lost his mind. Freeing one hand from around his neck, she slid her fingers up and into his hair, and hung on.

Thomas eventually broke away, pulling back just far enough to look at her without actually letting go. Alice met his eyes, her fingers remaining caught in his hair as she fought not to run.

Well, she thought, *I guess this answers the question of how I convince myself to leave. I've never actually gotten him to throw me out before . . .*

"Miss Healy?"

Alice swallowed. "Yes, Mr. Price?"

"I'm afraid you may have mumbled a bit at the end there." His expression was entirely serious, but she thought she heard amusement in his otherwise dry tone.

In for a penny, in for a pound. "I'm so sorry about that," she said. "Here, let me try again." She leaned up onto her toes, tightening her fingers in his hair, and resumed kissing him.

This time he was expecting her, and more, this time she was expecting him to kiss her back, leaving them both with the attention to focus on other things. Alice ran her left hand down the back of his neck, making the small hairs there stand on end before dragging her nails lightly back up to the base of his skull, where she twined the fingers of both hands together and held on like her life depended on it. Thomas left one hand where it was, but dipped the other down lower, resting it against her hip, fingers still splayed.

Alice broke the kiss this time, tilting her head back to offer him a small, only slightly worried smile. "Did you hear me that time?"

"I think so," he said, with a solemn nod. "You said something like this." He kissed her for a third time, holding it for only a moment before he pulled back and looked at her. "Am I close?"

"Very," she said, and smiled.

That expression was nearly enough to make Thomas pick her up, carry her into the kitchen, and lock her in the pantry until she told him what was going on. *You really are intending to die tonight, aren't you?* he thought. *That's the only reason you're letting me see you the way you really are.* "I thought I might be," he said aloud. "Were you telling me this for any particular reason?" He brought his right hand around as he spoke, sliding it up her back and moving to cup her cheek. His thumb stroked the side of her face, almost idly.

"I didn't want to go without saying it at least once," she replied, smile fading as her expression grew grave. "Mr. Price . . ."

"I think that, given what we've been saying to one another, we can consider ourselves to be on a first-name basis," he said. There was a measure of amusement in his tone, despite the growing conviction that anything she said—in words, anyway—would be either a lie or something he really didn't want to hear. "It's Thomas, in case you've forgotten."

"Thomas," she repeated, voice going soft. She took a moment to study his face, considering what she was going to say next.

The years inside had changed him, although not in the usual ways. He was paler than he'd been before, which was to be expected—no sunlight, after all—but he didn't have the soft, sheltered look most invalids and recluses tended to acquire. If anything, he looked like a man who did hard physical labor all day, worn down to whipcord leanness and sharp angles. She sometimes fancied she could cut herself on his cheekbones. Even the pallor suited him, in its way, making his eyes seem all the bluer. He didn't look any older than he should have, save for his hair, where gray was marching through the brown at a truly impressive speed.

He had the look of a man who didn't sleep much. She'd learned to recognize that in her own mirror a very long time ago.

Thomas spoke before she could finish collecting her thoughts, asking mildly, "You're not going to Ann Arbor, are you?"

"No, I'm not," she admitted. "I'm sorry I lied to you. It just seemed . . ."

"Easier?"

"Kinder," she said, with a small shake of her head. "But I guess easier, too. I just wanted to say goodbye."

"It took you this long to work up to saying 'hello,' and you want to say goodbye already?" He stroked the side of her face with his thumb again. "I suppose I shouldn't complain. You could have left without saying it at all."

She dropped the hand that had been twined in his hair and wrapped her fingers lightly around his wrist. "No, I really couldn't have. Not this time."

"That's something, anyway." He leaned in to kiss her again, breaking her hold and sliding his hand down to join the other one, so that he was cupping her hips a few inches above her gun belt. Ending the kiss, he said, "Your father told me you'd retired from the family business, as it were. Is this a relapse, or have I been laboring under a misconception?"

"Retired?" Alice blinked at him, startled into brief laughter. "He told you I was *retired*? Is that why you've been so willing to—Thomas, I assure you, I am *not* retired. I'm the . . . what's the opposite of 're-tired'?"

"A Healy?"

"Exactly." She paused. "About tonight . . ."

"Given that you're not retired, and you're apparently not going to Ann Arbor, I think I have a reasonably decent idea of what you're planning to do tonight, even if I haven't got all the details." Thomas frowned. "I do have to ask you one thing, and I have to ask that you please not lie to me when you answer."

"All right," she said softly, trying to hide the tension he could feel tightening her body. "I'll do my best to answer whatever it is."

"Thank you." This time, he kissed her slowly, carefully, like he expected her to pull away. He released her when the stiffness finally left her back and shoulders, and asked, "Is there anything I can do to help?"

"I don't think so," she said. "I should go."

"I was afraid you'd say that," he said, not letting go of her hips. "I've missed you."

"What?" Alice paused, looking at him quizzically. "I've been back in town for years now. I've come to visit every week. How have you missed me?"

"You never came back to town, Alice, not that you were willing to admit to me." He raised one hand to her cheek, stroking her hair back from her face and letting himself take a moment to watch the way it tangled around his fingers. "You went to college, and you didn't come back. You sent someone who'd been a long-term victim of a cuckoo attack back in your place."

"I was *never* that bad!" she protested.

"No?" he asked. "You left with violent tendencies, unladylike language, and a strong but not unwelcome tendency to wear inappropriate shorts while sitting on my porch eating frozen juice pops in a vaguely obscene manner. You came back in a nice gingham dress, gave me some home-baked muffins, and complimented me on the curtains. Which are, by the way, entirely hideous."

Alice stared at him for a moment before finally admitting, in a faint voice, "All right, maybe I was that bad."

"I was actually looking into spells for undoing mental possession, until your father offered to, ahem, 'break my arrogant face' if I so much as looked in your direction," said Thomas, pulling his hand away from her cheek and adjusting his glasses. "He said you were getting away from everything that wasn't normal, and I just assumed that after everything that happened that it was, well, what you wanted."

"Thomas . . ." She reached for his hand, pressing it back against her cheek. "That was never what I wanted."

"Really?" he asked. "What was?"

She leaned in and kissed him again rather than answering, this time freeing both her hands to begin undoing the buttons of his shirt. The fabric was damp from where it had stuck against his post-shower skin and grabbed at her fingers as she slid them inside and spread them flat against his chest. Thomas made a small sound of surprise. She hesitated, but only for as long as it took for him to get his hands back around her hips and yank her closer.

Taking that as approval, Alice worked her hands further inside his shirt, nails scratching lightly as she ran them down his chest and stopped, just below his navel, fingertips pointed downward. They were both breathing a little raggedly as she broke away, tilting her head down, eyes half-closed.

"This," she said, between breaths. "This is what I wanted. Just this."

"Alice . . ."

"Don't." She looked up. "I have six hours. That's all. And then I have to go."

He regarded her solemnly. "But not to Ann Arbor."

"No, not to Ann Arbor. To Detroit, I suppose, or Grand Rapids, or . . . or anywhere you want to think of me as going. But there's only one train out, Thomas, and it leaves in six hours, and I have to be on it. I haven't got a choice."

Moonrise. You're leaving at moonrise. Did you really think I wouldn't notice that little part of your itinerary? "Six hours it is, then," he said. "What were you proposing we do with that time?"

Alice slid her hands farther down the flat incline of his stomach, until her fingers grazed the waistband of his pants, and then dipped slightly beneath. "I thought maybe we could keep talking."

"Gladly," he said, and kissed her again.

4.

There are a great many kinds of kisses in the world. The kisses they passed back and forth between them were a conversation, in their own way; "Are you sure you have to go?" was answered with, "If I didn't have to go, I would never have been able to come," and there was no answer for that, save for regret over all the time that had been casually, unintentionally wasted. By both of them.

Thomas pulled his hand away from her face, dropping it to her hip before sliding both hands around to the front, where he unfastened her gun belt with two simple flicks of his thumbs. Alice broke away to give him a quizzical look, and he flashed her a quick, half-amused grin.

"Where did you think your grandmother always took these to be repaired?" he asked. "To the tooth fairy?"

"Oh, the tooth fairy doesn't come to our place anymore," she said, sliding her own hand around to his side and unfastening the straps holding his knife-holster in place. "She got tired of being shot at."

"Holding a grudge?"

"No, just target practice."

Thomas shook his head, laughing for what felt like the first time in years, and bent to kiss her again as he pulled her with him toward the couch. The floor was a dangerous labyrinth of stacked books and half-repaired weapons, but he navigated it with grace, never missing a step.

"Showoff," murmured Alice, pulling his holster away and dropping it to the floor.

"Says the woman who shot the tooth fairy," he replied, and dropped backward onto the couch, pulling her down with him.

"I don't like things that buzz," she said as she straddled his lap, bracing her knees on either side of his thighs as she began undoing his belt. "I've never liked things that buzz. Nothing that buzzes should come sneaking into my room and putting things under my pillow in the middle of the night."

"I'll try to make it a point not to," his breath caught as the fingers of one hand slid below the top of his pants, "buzz."

Alice's expression sobered, even as she splayed her left hand flat against his chest and pinned him back against the couch. "I'll hold you to that," she said, voice gone suddenly quiet.

"I'm sorry?" What she was doing with her right hand was making it difficult to focus on what she was actually saying.

"It doesn't matter," she said, kissing him again.

There was a moment where he could have argued with her. The moment passed. He tangled the fingers of his left hand through her hair as he used his right to unzip her vest and peel it away. Several throwing knives and a box of shotgun shells thudded to the floor, disregarded by both of them as the tempo of Alice's fingers increased. She bent forward to rest her forehead against his shoulder, and he bit down on the curve of her neck, sliding his right hand up and under the back of her tank top. Alice made a small, surprised noise, but didn't pull away. Her left hand slid down his chest to join the right. The rhythm faltered for a moment as she adjusted her fingers, and then resumed itself, her hands moving in long, slow strokes.

Thomas continued working his hand up under the curve of her back until he reached the strap of her brassiere, tangled as it was with the shoulder holster she was wearing on her right arm. The same quick motion of his thumbs that had removed the gun belt unfastened the clasp, and he began working at the straps on her holster, undoing buckles during the lulls in her rhythmic stroking.

There were no sounds but their rapidly-quickening breath for several minutes after that. Alice focused on the motion of her hands while Thomas worked to remove her shoulder holster, finally managing to peel it out through the armhole of her shirt without breaking her concentration and begin trailing kisses down the side of her neck, bracing his hands at the small of her back to keep her balanced. Alice responded by biting his collarbone, hands increasing tempo once again.

He rocked his hips up to meet hers. She answered the motion in kind, her hands continuing to work as he dug his nails into the small of her back, mapping the thin lines of scar tissue that crisscrossed her spine. For a moment, they simply rocked together, until he sagged backward with an incoherent noise, and she pulled her hands free, twining her arms back around his neck.

"Mmmm?" she inquired, kissing his ear.

After a moment of looking for the appropriate words, he finally settled for, "Do I even want to know where you learned that sort of language?"

"I went to college, and I read a lot," she said, cheeks still flushed. Running her fingers along the back of his collar, she frowned. "Is this a garrote?"

"That depends." He slid his hand down to the waistband of her jeans. "Is this a small-caliber pistol?"

Alice smiled blithely. "Maybe."

"In that case, maybe it's a garrote." Thomas turned to kiss her shoulder again. "Why do you ask?"

"Didn't I just get you out of the shower?" Alice asked, rolling her shoulder back to allow him easier access.

Kissing the hollow of her collarbone, he said, "Yes. That's why I'm so woefully underdressed."

"Three ways to kill a man is underdressed?" she said dubiously.

Thomas pulled back, eyeing her. "*Three* ways to kill a man?"

"The knife I took off your belt, the garrote, and the folding sword at the back of your trousers," she said, with a blink.

"You think I only have *three* ways to kill a man?" He shook his head. "Frankly, Alice, I think I'm rather offended."

"Oh." Expression grave, Alice leaned back, away from him, and removed first her shirt, then her already-unfastened bra. "Does this help?"

Thomas considered her, studying her breasts, stomach, and shoulders before turning his attention toward the bandages still taped around her left bicep. Then he nodded and tugged her close again. "Yes, it does. I'm substantially less offended now, if slightly overdressed."

"You were underdressed a moment ago," she said, before she kissed him, twining the fingers of her left hand into his hair again. "We're making progress."

"Progress is good," he agreed, taking the pistol from the back of her jeans and setting it carefully on the table next to the couch before sliding his hands down below the level of her waistband, cupping her rear in his palms. "Mankind has always favored progress over stagnation."

"So let's progress."

There was no need for further conversation for some time after that. Alice removed his shirt, discovering two more weapons in the process—the knife in his left shirt sleeve wasn't surprising, but the derringer in his right sleeve was, at least slightly; she'd never considered him that much of a gun man—and began performing the long-delayed task of mapping the tattoos covering his arms and torso with her tongue. He leaned back long enough to catch his breath, then began stripping her in return, removing the knives from her belt one by one before undoing the belt itself, working it carefully out of the loops of her jeans.

The scarring on her stomach distracted him briefly. He splayed his hand against it, looking up, and waited for her to stop kissing the side of his neck before he said, "You didn't have this when you went away."

"Mmmm?" Alice lifted her head, brushing her hair away from her eyes as she looked at him with bafflement. "Went away where?"

"To school. You didn't have this when you went away to school." Her sweater had been pulled up almost to the base of her ribs that day in the forest when he traded his freedom for her life. Looking at her now, there was no question that it had been a fair exchange. He kept his hand splayed against her stomach, feeling her breath through the heat of her skin. "What happened?"

Alice gave him a look that was half-amused, half-exasperated. "I'm nearly naked and sitting in your lap. Even if you want to tell me you're not interested, your body isn't voting with your brain on this one." She placed a hand on the front of his open trousers, kneading gently. "Do you really think now is the time to quiz me about my scars?"

"I think you're leaving for Ann Arbor in a little over five hours," he said, calmly. "Am I going to get another opportunity?"

She hesitated for a moment before putting her hand over his, holding him to her. "It was my freshman year. Cheerleaders kept disappearing, so I went hunting. It turned out one of the biology majors had managed to get himself infected with some sort of parasitic slimemonster that kept taking over his body and, well, having a cheerleader buffet. Not alkabyiftiris slime, but close enough to make me uncomfortable. He didn't want to give up his new bodily roommate. So I shot him. Seventeen times. And he handed me a bunch of my own skin. But it grew back. His skull didn't."

"Ah." Thomas shook his head, expression wry. "How very retired you were."

"At least it was educational. There are a lot of colors inside a possessed biology major." She lifted her hand to tap one of the tattoos on his chest. "Now it's your turn. What does this one represent?"

Glancing down, he said, "Protection against hostile spirits, succubae, and banshees of all varieties."

"Yours are more useful than mine," she said, before kissing the spot she'd tapped. "All mine do is raise nasty questions every time I see a new doctor."

"Indeed." He kissed the side of her neck again, before asking, almost offhandedly, "What happened to your arm, Alice?" *How did your father really die? Where are you going tonight when the moon comes up?*

"I cut myself making dinner," she said smoothly. "Sometimes I'm so clumsy it hurts. Literally, when it puts me in the hospital."

"Ah." *You still won't tell me, then.* "I'll have to remember that."

No, I won't. "I'm not feeling clumsy right now," she said, and twisted herself to straddle his lap more solidly. "Are you?"

"Clumsy, no. However . . ." Thomas extricated both hands from the tangle of their bodies and gathered Alice into his arms as he stood. After a single startled squeak, she wrapped her arms around his neck, letting him support her back and knees. "I think this is a conversation better continued elsewhere."

"Elsewhere being . . . ?"

"I was considering the bedroom. Unless you had a better alternative?" He paused. "Or I've managed to misinterpret our discussion . . ."

"Thomas, for me to be making more blatant advances, I'd have to be moving an entire army into position around your capital city." Alice shook her head. "I didn't think to bring any archers."

"And there's definitely no room in your pants for the cavalry," he said gravely. She hit him in the shoulder with the heel of her left hand. He smiled. "The bedroom it is, then, before you break out the catapults."

"Siege weaponry as a seduction tool isn't very useful with most gentlemen." Alice leaned in to kiss him languidly. It seemed to work well, and so she kept kissing him as he walked them across the room, breaking away only when they reached the stairs.

"I don't know," Thomas said, beginning to climb up toward the second floor. "Most men are fond of large weapons. I think it's more that most women never consider bringing ballistae into the courting process."

"Thank God." Alice put her head against his shoulder, letting herself relax. "We might not be having this conversation if someone else had been willing to threaten you with a frontal attack."

Thomas paused to look down at her. She tilted her head slightly back to get a better view and then smiled at him.

"Actually," he said, "I think we would be."

5.

For the first time in well over a week, tangled in unfamiliar sheets and pressed against Thomas' side like she was afraid he might vanish at any moment, Alice slept.

Thomas didn't.

They had so little time left, and he wasn't going to miss a second of it. He already regretted all the questions he'd never get to ask, all the things he'd never get to tell her.

He lay awake, tracing the scars on her right shoulder with the fingertips of his left hand and trying to keep himself from watching the clock as it ticked slowly down toward time for her to leave for . . . wherever it was that she was actually going. Moonrise. She was leaving at moonrise, and she was wearing a silver ring around her neck, and that was a line of thought he didn't particularly care to follow any further.

He knew the Healy attitude toward infection. It never ended well. At least, not if you were even remotely fond of the infected being amongst the living, rather than part of the somewhat larger family memorial wall.

According to the clock, the moon would rise in an hour and a half, and Alice would be leaving for . . . not Ann Arbor, exactly, but Detroit, or Grand Rapids, or whatever other name he felt like putting on "not here." The only place he really wanted her to be was "here, with me," and he knew—from what she'd said, from what she hadn't said, from what they'd said to each other with hands and lips and years of apparently mutual frustration—that it wouldn't be fair to even think the words too loudly. For whatever reason, she truly didn't believe staying was an option. If he pushed her, he might lose even the little time they had.

She didn't believe telling you how she felt was an option, either, and look how that turned out, a corner of his mind offered, with traitorous mildness. *She knows what she wants, but she doesn't know how to go about getting it. You could just let her sleep. Let her figure things out in the morning.*

And if she's a lycanthrope? he asked himself.

If she's a werewolf, the gun in the nightstand is loaded with silver. You can handle it yourself. She shouldn't have to do it alone.

Thomas let himself consider that as he continued to map her scars. He'd done worse things than killing a lycanthrope who didn't want to live with her condition—and besides that, death wasn't the only option. Perhaps it was the most appealing, if you happened to be a Healy, but death closed off all the others. The chance of a cure . . .

The chance of a cure had been pursued for centuries, and no one had ever managed to find it. No. "Wake me when it's time?" she'd asked when they both saw that she was drifting. "I don't want to go yet." And because he didn't want her to go, either, he'd promised to wake her up.

Thomas Price was a man of his word. If he broke it now, she'd never trust him again. That wasn't how he wanted to end things, not when they'd taken so very long to begin.

Fingers restlessly tracing the topography of Alice Healy, he settled back against the headboard, and watched the minutes counting down to goodbye.

6.

Later, the whole night would seem almost like a dream, from unexpected beginning to inevitable end. The knocking at the door—Healy women had always knocked at that door, starting with Enid and running all the way down to her granddaughter, even when no one else bothered—the conversation that didn't use words, but instead relied upon the ghosts of words that died unspoken; the time on the couch. The journey up the stairs that took a matter of minutes and seemed to take a thousand years. It was all jumbled up, frustrations and longing and fear spilled out too fast upon the floor, so nothing was entirely clear.

He knew she'd squirmed out of his arms when they reached the bedroom, dropping her feet down to the floor before offering her hands, like she was giving him some sort of present neither one of them fully understood. He knew he'd taken them, and they'd simply stood there for a few minutes, looking at each other.

Neither of them was wearing anything from the waist up unless you wanted to count Alice's necklace. Somehow, he was fairly sure her father wouldn't have approved.

"Alice . . ."

"Five hours to go," she said and smiled. The acceptance in that smile—the acceptance, the resignation, and yes, the love—was impossible to deny, much as he might have liked to. "Don't you think we've talked enough?"

"Five hours," he said reluctantly. "It isn't enough time."

"I'm sorry. It's all I've got."

"Next time, let's not wait so long?"

"Next time, I promise to talk to you while there's a little more day-light left."

And then she was kissing him again, and somewhere between the door and the bed, they both lost what clothing they had left, and fell naked into the sheets, and time . . .

Time ceased to matter for a little while, until it was three hours to go, and Alice smiled at him again, sleepy under the tangled hayride sheaves of her hair, and said, "Wake me when it's time? I don't want to go yet."

And because he was an honest man, and a fool, and yes, in love with this stupid, suicidal woman who was plainly expecting to die before morning, he nodded, and kissed her on the forehead, and said, "Rest."

And she had.

7.

"Alice."

She stirred in her sleep as he shook her, making a small, protesting noise, but didn't open her eyes.

"Alice."

She still didn't fully react. He shook her again, slightly harder.

"Alice. Don't make me ask you again." Three times was a fair effort. If she didn't open her eyes after this, he . . .

"I'm awake," she said blearily as she sat up, raking her hair away from her face with one hand. "Where's my gun?"

She woke up and looked for the weapons. Reluctantly fond, Thomas wondered again how the hell he could have believed for a minute that she was actually retired. He should have known better all along. "Depending on which one you consider 'yours,' it's either on the floor, downstairs, or on the nightstand."

"Right, I . . . what?" Opening her eyes, she twisted around, and blinked at him. "I'm here."

"Yes."

"*You're* here."

"Seeing as how I can't leave this house without unleashing an apoc-alypse of biblical proportions—or at least exploding or something of the sort—I don't think that's much of a surprise to anyone but you."

His confinement wouldn't last much longer. As soon as she died, the bargain would be fulfilled, and he'd be free to go. Free . . .

It still wasn't a fair exchange.

Alice—who'd never known the exact terms of his confinement, and, God willing, never would—continued blinking. "*We're* here."

Thomas smiled despite himself. "Yes."

"We're . . ." Alice paused, looking for a decorous term. There wasn't one. " . . . really kind of naked right now."

Thomas was growing decidedly amused. "You don't wake up quickly, do you? Yes, we're naked. This is my house, this is my room, and this is my bed. The gun on the nightstand is your gun, as evidenced by the slightly broken trigger. Which I can fix for you if you can postpone your departure for a while longer."

"Departure," Alice echoed, and looked toward the clock on the wall. "Half an hour."

"I thought you might appreciate a little time to get ready before you had to go," he said carefully.

"Thank you," she said, turned around, and kissed him again.

There had been a certain amount of leisure when he carried her up the stairs, when she removed his trousers—time was short, but moonrise was still far enough away that it could be treated like another country. Now, it was just around the corner, and time was more than short. Time was past.

His hands found her waist and jerked her across the bed to him, one sliding down to brace against her buttocks, the other up to the middle of her back. Alice responded by hooking one arm around his neck and dropping the other to his groin, breaking off the kiss long enough to whisper harshly, "Ten minutes."

"Fifteen," he countered.

"Help me get dressed. Buckles are hard."

"Deal," he said, and kissed her again.

8.

Fifteen minutes passed too fast for words to measure.

The bruises on his back would last far longer than that. So would the ones on her unbandaged arm and right hip, where his fingers had gripped her as if holding on tightly enough could make it so he would never be forced to let go. Pressed up against the borders of a deadline, facing the cold and looming country of the future, neither of them felt the need to be gentle. That time had passed.

If anything, they were writing their farewell notes to one another, with sweat and bruises to serve for ink, with skin and muscle as the paper to place the words upon. Every scratch spelled out "I'm sorry." Every "I love you" was a purple-black bruise that would shift slowly to yellow around the spreading edges, like a flower opening its petals. In the absence of more permanent memoirs, this goodbye would, at least, be something to remember for a day or two.

For those who had a day or two left to remember things in.

The clock counted down the minutes to farewell, and they burned every second like it was a candle, lighting it at both ends, fanning the flames with lips and fingers on skin, bodies pressed against each other so hard that their muscles were stretched and singing from the strain.

Thomas wound his fingers into her hair and slammed her into the mattress, leaving her gasping for air as she locked her legs around his hips. "Stay," he said, voice pitched low.

"I can't," she said, between breaths, and raised herself to meet him. "Come with me."

"I can't," he said, and entered her.

There were no words spoken aloud after that; only words written on the canvases of their bodies, his hand on her breast and between her legs, her hand at the small of his back, their lips chafed and very nearly burning where they touched.

And then there was no more time.

No more time at all.

9.

Neither of them spoke much as Alice dressed, beyond her periodic requests for him to pass her one weapon or another, and the occasional request for help with a particularly troublesome buckle. Words would have done no good at all; not until they were armored from one another by clothing and convention. All he had to say to her was "stay." All she had to say to him was "no."

She looked up as she fastened Fran's gun belt around her own waist, leaving her fingers on the buckle. "Thank you," she said.

Thomas raised an eyebrow, pulling his trousers up around his waist and tying the cord. "For what?"

Alice shrugged, very slightly. "Letting me stay?"

"If you must thank me for something, thank me for letting you leave," he replied flatly. He picked up a knife from the bedside table, sliding it into his waistband. "I'd really prefer you didn't."

"Ann Arbor calls," Alice said, as lightly as she could manage. She studied him for a moment before reaching around to the back of her neck and undoing the clasp on her chain. Her mother's ring dropped into her waiting palm, draped with the loops and snarls of the necklace it had dangled from. "Here."

Eyebrows raised, Thomas looked from the ring to her face. "You're offering me your mother's engagement ring?"

"Until I can come back for it, yes," Alice said.

He snorted. "There's no need to lie on my account. I'm a grown man. I know a woman who's walking off to die when I see one. Even if she calls it 'Ann Arbor.'"

"Or Grand Rapids," Alice said, still holding out the ring. "I'm not lying on anyone's account, Thomas. If I can come back—if there's any possible way to get a return ticket on this trip—I will. I'll come back here, to you, and get my mother's ring. But if I don't make it back, the Covenant gets the house, and everything in it that Naga doesn't remove before they get here. I somehow doubt they'd give you anything to remember me by."

"And here I thought I was only getting bruises out of this arrangement," he said, taking the ring from her hand. He studied it for a moment before saying, almost distantly, "Your grandmother would have approved of this, I think."

"You mean she'd have threatened to shoot you for deflowering me, and then demanded to know when we were getting married?"

"Just so." He fastened the chain behind his neck, taking some comfort in the feel of the warm silver hitting at the hollow of his throat. *I wish you'd tell me where you were really going, Alice. I wish I could go with you.*

But then, isn't it the nature of men to wish for what they'll never have?

Alice leaned over and pressed a soft kiss against his cheek. "I love you, Thomas Price. Just so it's been said once, out loud. I don't want any confusion on that point."

"So noted," he said. "I love you, Alice Healy. Again, simply to prevent confusion in the future."

"Of course." Smiling wanly, she stepped to the front door and put her hand on the knob. Pausing, she looked back at him. "Are you going to be all right?"

"I think I can survive reasonably well without your company," he said dryly. "If you mean, 'Will you be all right with the fact that I'm clearly marching off to die,' well, that's a little much to ask of me." He paused in turn, and then sighed, adding, "But I'm glad that you came."

"So am I," she said, and stepped out the door, into the darkness.

Thomas followed to the threshold—as far as the spell that bound him would allow him to go—and watched as she walked down to the driveway, climbed into the driver's seat of her truck, and drove away. Then he stood there a while longer, just in case she changed her mind and came back. Just in case this hadn't been a dream.

When the white face of the moon rose pale and gleaming above the trees, he turned away, stepped back from the threshold, and closed the door. In the distance, gunshots sounded, coming fast and frantic . . . then stopping entirely.

Alice had gone to Ann Arbor.

10.

No one who felt like living a long and productive life went into a grave-yard in Montmorency County after the sun went down. Even the teen-agers, half-feral with hormones and testing the boundaries of authority, learned that lesson quickly; failure to catch on resulted in removal from the gene pool, and kept the things that prowled the graveyards relatively well-fed.

Sometimes there is nothing at all romantic about "the circle of life."

Alice pulled up outside the cemetery gates with ten minutes to spare; not much time, when one considered the magnitude of what needed to be done, but it would hopefully be enough, and she had no regrets. Some things needed to be said before you took a seat on the last train out of town. Otherwise, they'd join the ranks of all the things you never said at all.

She'd called for Mary several times during the drive, and Mary hadn't come. She was doing this alone. Touching the spot where her mother's necklace had been, she opened the driver's side door, climbed out into the night, and got to work.

The frickens sang in the distance, trading their cheerful back-and-forth chorus of chirps and trills. Alice found the sound deeply reas-suring. She was sure they'd stop when the Apraxis nymphs started emerging from the ground; being tiny cryptid frog-chickens living in a place where everything occasionally wanted to eat you resulted in a highly-tuned sense of self-preservation. As long as they sang, she was as safe as any lone woman who didn't have a tank had ever been in a Buckley graveyard at night.

The first thing to do was get inside. The gates were, of course, chained at sundown; they were also left unguarded, since no one really considered grave robbery much of a threat in the modern world. One good blow with a crowbar, and the gates were spread to welcome her in.

"I do so love modern technology," she said, tossing the crowbar aside.

Hauling her things from the truck to her father's grave took longer than she liked, but at least the reasons were good. The Healy family plot was tucked into a far corner of the graveyard, well away from any convenient gratings, plots of unusual flora, or escape routes. Alice couldn't help smiling as she doused her father's grave with kerosene. She hadn't been alive when the plot was chosen, but she'd seen the mice reenact the process of selection often enough in the sacred ritual of If We Get Buried There, Jonathan, Something Will Steal the Bodies and Reanimate Them, and How Do We Explain That To the Neighbors? Really, Try To Think For Once.

"Only you, Mom," she said, and patted her mother's headstone lovingly before beginning the process of embedding road flares all around the still relatively-fresh outline of her father's grave. The frickens were still singing. There was still time.

She was carrying the last of the butane torches to the makeshift storage area she'd established behind her grandparents' headstone when the frickens finally stopped. The animation went out of her expression in an instant as she dropped the torches, grabbed the first sniper rifle that came to hand, and crouched down to wait.

The ground heaved, once, then twice, like the belly of a pregnant woman getting ready for birth. Then it went entirely still, an island of motionlessness in the silence of the night. Alice braced the rifle's muzzle against the back of the tombstone, eyes narrowed, and waited.

The first of the newborn Apraxis burrowed out of the ground at the base of the headstone, where the passage had been easiest. There were fragments of silk coffin lining clinging to its razor-edged wings, lending the thing a macabre carnival air. It twitched them once, twice, and then rose unsteadily into the air, testing its freedom.

Alice blew its head off with a single muffled shot, and it fell back to earth without a sound.

The next three went the same way; they emerged alone, rose from the ground, and died before they had time to make it more than a few feet from their point of hatching. Alice was starting to think this might be easier than she'd dared to hope when the fifth emerged.

This one came up right next to one of the fallen. It paused, prodding the shattered carapace with a foreleg, before glancing around the area with what she could only refer to as wariness. She froze. Most insects could only really see motion. Alice wasn't sure that applied to Apraxis—so few people had survived an attack that there had never been any good notes taken on their visual perceptions—but she was certain she couldn't outrun them.

Still soundless, the wasp turned and burrowed back under the ground. The rules had just changed. She'd known they would, but still, she'd hoped for just a little bit more *time* . . .

Alice set the sniper rifle aside, still moving with patient, expressionless calm, and picked up her shotgun. It had a fairly wide radius when loaded with buckshot. The radius got better if you happened to mix the buckshot with magnesium, which had an unfriendly tendency to ignite from the force of being shot out of the barrel. There was a chance the gun would blow up in her hands, but at that particular moment, it was a risk she was willing to take.

The ground heaved again. Alice crouched lower and pulled back the hammer on the shotgun, waiting.

And then the surface of the grave split like a piece of rotten fruit, and the true battle finally began. The wasps swarmed up into the sky in a gleaming cloud, their wings humming in a tune that part of her wanted to drop everything and listen to. Only part, however; the part that had already gone to Ann Arbor. Part of her was still tangled in the sheets of a bed she'd never seen before, and that part, the greater part, was damned if it was going to die before it got the chance to go back and reclaim her mother's ring. Eyes narrowed still further, Alice lined up her shot on the center of the swarm.

"Oh, Alice," buzzed the wasps, in her father's voice. "You could never be a good girl, could you, my Alice? You could never be obedient, but you're trying now, my dear, you're trying. You thought I wanted this, didn't you? The gunfire and the good death. No, Alice, no. Some things are better than ending. You be good now. You mind your father now."

Alice fired. Wasps showered down on the grave like rain, broken by buckshot, burning from the magnesium. The swarm scattered in all directions, and she grabbed her pistols, firing at every glint of motion that came close enough to threaten her. She never stopped to aim. If she had to aim, she was already dead.

Something struck her in the shoulder, leaving behind a burning wound that felt all too familiar. She dropped the gun in her left hand and whipped around with a speed born entirely of desperation, grabbing the wasp before it could disengage from the bone and squeezing its center carapace until it shattered beneath her fingers.

It died screaming in her father's voice.

"Alice, Alice, Alice," scolded the swarm. *"That's no way to treat your father. Be good, now. Come with me. It only has to hurt if you let it. It can be pleasant. I can make it painless for you, and we can be together forever."*

Alice might have laughed if she hadn't been bleeding. "My father spent his whole life sending me away," she said, trying to keep the swarm distracted as she fumbled for one of the sniper rifles. More wasps were emerging from the grave with every passing second. She had to stop them, or the town would be lost, whatever happened to her.

"I was wrong. Let me make it up to you. Let us be together now, Alice. Let me give you the sky, and the night, and the freedom to fly."

"Golly. Do I get a little red wagon to go with that?" She found the rifle and double-checked the chamber before leaning around the edge of the headstone, pointing the barrel toward her father's grave.

Jonathan Healy had been thorough, dogged, and detail-oriented. He had possessed the Healy tendency to assume he could survive practically anything. But he'd never had the luck or level of creativity that his daughter inherited from his wife, and so the wasps that stole his memories didn't realize what Alice was doing until the third shot was fired, and the first road flare burst into flame, and the grave began to burn. The emerging wasps caught fire as they spread their wings, and they screamed as they burned. Fire wouldn't destroy any unhatched eggs. It would absolutely eliminate the newborn wasps.

"Oh, Alice," sighed the swarm, stolen voice tinged with anger for the first time. *"I'm afraid you'll have to be punished for that."* It rose into the air, wings glinting with light from the fire below.

"I guess that means no on the little red wagon, huh?" said Alice, grabbing for her pistols once again.

What came next was chaos. The wasps descended and scattered around her, forcing her to stay with single shots instead of the shotgun's dispersion pattern. They made no effort to preserve individual lives, but instead took darting runs toward both sides at once, forcing her to choose which angles to defend. She was doing some of the best shooting of her life, albeit aided by the sheer number of opponents, and she was losing.

Ann Arbor, here I come, she thought, after the second sting slammed into her left thigh, after she had crushed the offending wasp beneath her hand.

"This shall not stand!" cried a small, indignant voice. Unable to believe what she was hearing, Alice turned to see the mouse priest standing on her father's headstone, backlit by the dying flames. He was surrounded by a small circle made up entirely of the elder members of his congregation, mice long past their prime and moving toward the grave. "Blasphemy!"

"Get out of here! It's not safe!" she shouted.

In the firelight, she almost thought the mouse priest smiled. "We have faith, Priestess."

"Little mice, little Aeslin, do not be here," buzzed the swarm, sounding almost amused. *"This is none of your concern."*

"You are the Eaters of Souls and Knowing," replied the priest. "Take us. All that has been the family you choose is in us. We know all things that should be known. Let our Priestess go, for if the line ends, we shall have no gods. But with you, we might be gods. That would be enough."

He was lying.

Alice realized that even as the swarm began to turn, coming together, circling the grave. The mice were lying. They didn't believe being eaten by giant evil wasps would make them gods; it made no sense. Their idea of Heaven included cheese and cake and all the Healys that had come before, not frozen preservation in the minds of the Apraxis. This was a lie. They had come to save her. They were old, and they would be honored forever for what they did tonight, if she had the strength to survive it.

You zealous little fools, she thought, and reached for the grenades.

"All things," buzzed the swarm greedily, in her father's voice. The promise of knowledge was something the Apraxis couldn't resist. *"All things."* And it descended, coming together in a great clump of wings and stinging barbs, obscuring the mice from view.

There was no other way. Alice threw the grenades, two at a time, and watched the grave go up in flames. The screaming of the Apraxis was so loud she never heard the screams of the mice at all.

She braced herself against the tombstone after the explosions stopped, listening for the sound of wings. There was none. Still, she took her shotgun, using it to lever herself to her feet, and walked to the smoking remains of her father's grave, looking gravely at the pieces of carapace that littered the ground in all directions.

"I'm not that easy to take advantage of, Daddy," she said, only half-aware that she was crying, and turned away, beginning to gather as many of the intact bodies as she could find.

The old priest's kitten-bone staff was lying beside one of the nearby headstones, propped up so that she wouldn't miss it. She cried harder when she realized what it was, dusting it off with the utmost care before she tucked it into her pocket.

In the end, she didn't get out of the graveyard until nearly midnight. That was all right; the police wouldn't show up for hours.

11.

Loading the truck took longer than it should have. She could barely use her left arm; there were three stings in the area of her shoulder, one of them cutting all the way to the bone, and another two in the forearm. She hadn't bothered to count the punctures in her legs, back, and buttocks—it seemed like a losing proposition. She was going to live.

For three days, anyway, at which point she would die horribly, unless she could find someone who felt like digging Apraxis nymphs out of her flesh. Somehow, she didn't think that would be all that difficult.

Alice climbed into the driver's seat once the last of the guns were slung behind the seat, and the bodies of the intact Apraxis had been carefully wound in tarpaulins and tucked into the back of the truck bed. Putting her hands against the wheel, she stared dully through the windscreen and gave serious thought to passing out. The police had to have heard the explosion, but she knew they would be "mysteriously" detained from reaching the graveyard until well after the sun came up. The human instinct for survival at its finest.

Really, she could close her eyes, go to sleep, and wait for the sun to come up.

At which point you'll be dead of blood loss, you dizzy cow, and what good is that going to do anyone? she thought fiercely.

It would do all the good in the world, her body argued, on account of her not needing to move around once she was dead.

"This is a stupid argument, and I want my little red wagon," she muttered, put the truck into gear, and drove away from . . .

. . . well, away from everything.

12.

The drive from the cemetery to Thomas' house would have taken approximately ten minutes, under normal circumstances. "Normal circumstances" assumed the driver would be using both arms, capable of focusing on the road, and not blacking out every mile or so. Alice was lucky; not only did she not drive entirely off the road, but she didn't meet any other cars in her long, unsteady trip across town.

Healy luck. Sometimes it's good, sometimes it's bad, and sometimes it can be hard to tell the difference.

Thomas was sitting at his kitchen table, staring at the back door and wondering when he'd have the nerve to test the barrier. If she was dead—if she was truly dead—he'd be able to go outside. He could find her body and give her a decent burial. He owed her that much, didn't he? But still, he couldn't move, not until he heard the sound of a truck pulling into the driveway. The motor ran for a moment, then cut off. He glanced to the clock.

It was almost five in the morning; the moon was still up. Just some tourist, then, or some drunken hunter who'd pulled up to the wrong house. A door slammed outside. Footsteps on the walkway.

He was in the front room before Alice knocked—or, more precisely, before Alice thudded her forehead several times against the door, since her left arm was dangling uselessly, and her right was being used to keep her upright. His first impression upon opening the door was that there was more blood there than woman. What little of her wasn't covered with dried or drying blood was still bleeding actively, and the whole of her stank of gunpowder and ichor.

She'd never been lovelier.

"Hi," she managed, after a moment of mutual staring. "Forgot my coat."

"I was wondering if you'd come back for that," he said as he offered her his arm. "So you're not a lycanthrope, then."

"No—why did you think—? No, don't tell me. I'm not a lycanthrope, but I'm going to bleed on your floor."

"I think I'll risk it. Didn't you like Ann Arbor?"

"It was boring there. Nobody had any little red wagons. I have lots of Apraxis eggs in my back. And in my arm, and leg, and other places. Can you get them out for me?" Alice leaned heavily against him as he guided her inside. "I've lost a lot of blood—and mice. Lots and lots of mice. I can make more blood, but only if you get the eggs out. I won't be able to help. I think I need to pass out now."

Somewhat alarmed, Thomas wrapped his other arm around her to hold her up. "There will be no Apraxis eggs when you wake up."

"Oh. Good." Alice smiled and fainted.

Three generations isn't a bad run for a family of slightly feral cryptid hunters living in hiding and working without any real backup. Four generations, on the other hand . . .

Well, that's even better.

Price Family Field Guide
to the Cryptids of North America
Updated and Expanded Edition

Aeslin mice (Apodemus sapiens). Sapient, rodentlike cryptids which present as near-identical to non-cryptid field mice. Aeslin mice crave religion, and will attach themselves to "divine figures" selected virtually at random when a new colony is created. They possess perfect recall; each colony maintains a detailed oral history going back to its inception. Origins unknown.

Basilisk (Procompsognathus basilisk). Venomous, feathered saurians approximately the size of a large chicken. This would be bad enough, but thanks to a quirk of evolution, the gaze of a basilisk causes petrification, turning living flesh to stone. Basilisks are not native to North America, but were imported as game animals. By idiots.

Bogeyman (Vestiarium sapiens). The thing in your closet is probably a very pleasant individual who simply has issues with direct sunlight. Probably. Bogeymen are close relatives of the human race; they just happen to be almost purely nocturnal, with excellent night vision, and a fondness for enclosed spaces. They rarely grab the ankles of small children, unless it's funny.

Chupacabra (Chupacabra sapiens). True to folklore, chupacabra are blood-suckers, with stomachs that do not handle solids well. They are also therianthrope shapeshifters, capable of transforming themselves into human form, which explains why they have never been captured. When cornered, most chupacabra will assume their bipedal shape in self-defense. A surprising number of chupacabra are involved in ballroom dance.

Dragon (Draconem sapiens). Dragons are essentially winged, fire-breathing dinosaurs the size of Greyhound buses. At least, the males are. The females are attractive humanoids who can blend seamlessly in a crowd of supermodels, and outnumber the males twenty to one. Females are capable of parthenogenic reproduction and can sustain their population for centuries without outside help. All dragons, male and female, require gold to live, and collect it constantly.

Ghoul (Herophilus sapiens). The ghoul is an obligate carnivore, incapable of digesting any but the simplest vegetable solids, and prefers humans because of their wide selection of dietary nutrients. Most ghouls are carrion eaters. Ghouls can be easily identified by their teeth, which will be shed and replaced repeatedly over the course of a lifetime.

Hidebehind (Aphanes apokryphos). We don't really know much about the hidebehinds: no one's ever seen them. They're excellent illusionists, and we think they're bipeds, which means they're probably mammals. Probably.

Huldra (Hulder sapiens). While the Huldrafolk are technically divided into three distinct subspecies, the most is known about *Hulder sapiens skogsfrun*, the Huldra of the trees. These hollow-backed hematophages can pass for human when they have to, but prefer to avoid humanity, living in secluded villages throughout Scandinavia. Individual Huldra can live for hundreds of years when left to their own devices. They aren't innately friendly, but aren't hostile unless threatened.

Jackalope (Parcervus antelope). Essentially large jackrabbits with antelope antlers, the jackalope is a staple of the American West, and stuffed examples can be found in junk shops and kitschy restaurants all across the country. Most of the taxidermy is fake. Some, however, is not. The jackalope was once extremely common, and has been shot, stuffed, and harried to near-extinction. They're relatively harmless, and they taste great.

Johrlac (Johrlac psychidolos). Colloquially known as "cuckoos," the Johrlac are telepathic ambush predators. They appear human, but are internally very different, being cold-blooded and possessing a decentralized circulatory system. This quirk of biology means they can be

shot repeatedly in the chest without being killed. Extremely dangerous. All Johrlac are interested in mathematics, sometimes to the point
of obsession. Origins unknown; possibly insect in nature.

Laidly worm (Draconem laidly). Very little is known about these
close relatives of the dragons. They present similar but presumably
not identical sexual dimorphism; no currently living males have been
located.

Lamia (Python lamia). Semi-hominid cryptids with the upper bodies
of humans and the lower bodies of snakes. Lamia are members of
order synapsedia, the mammal-like reptiles, and are considered responsible for many of the "great snake" sightings of legend. The sightings not attributed to actual great snakes, that is.

Lesser gorgon (Gorgos euryale). One of three known subspecies of
gorgon, the lesser gorgon's gaze causes short-term paralysis followed
by death in anything under five pounds. The bite of the snakes atop
their heads will cause paralysis followed by death in anything smaller
than an elephant if not treated with the appropriate antivenin. Lesser
gorgons tend to be very polite, especially to people who like snakes.

Lilu (Lilu sapiens). Due to the striking dissimilarity of their abilities,
male and female Lilu are often treated as two individual species: incubi and succubi. Incubi are empathic; succubi are persuasive tele-
paths. Both exude strong pheromones inspiring feelings of attraction
and lust in the opposite sex. This can be a problem for incubi like our
cousin Artie, who mostly wants to be left alone, or succubi like our
cousin Elsie, who gets very tired of men hitting on her while she's trying to flirt with their girlfriends.

Madhura (Homo madhurata). Humanoid cryptids with an affinity for
sugar in all forms. Vegetarian. Their presence slows the decay of or-
ganic matter, and is usually viewed as lucky by everyone except the
local dentist. Madhura are very family-oriented, and are rarely found
living on their own. Originally from the Indian subcontinent.

Manananggal (Tanggal geminus). If the manananggal is proof of anything, it is that Nature abhors a logical classification system. We're
reasonably sure the manananggal are mammals; everything else is
anyone's guess. They're hermaphroditic and capable of splitting their

upper and lower bodies, although they are a single entity, and killing the lower half kills the upper half as well. They prefer fetal tissue, or the flesh of newborn infants. They are also venomous, as we have recently discovered. Do not engage if you can help it.

Oread (Nymphae silica). Humanoid cryptids with the approximate skin density of granite. Their actual biological composition is unknown, as no one has ever been able to successfully dissect one. Oreads are extremely strong, and can be dangerous when angered. They seem to have evolved independently across the globe; their common name is from the Greek.

Sasquatch (Gigantopithecus sesquac). These massive native denizens of North America have learned to embrace depilatories and mail-order shoe catalogs. A surprising number make their living as Bigfoot hunters (Bigfeet and Sasquatches are close relatives, and enjoy tormenting each other). They are predominantly vegetarian, and enjoy Canadian television.

Tanuki (Nyctereutes sapiens). Therianthrope shapeshifters from Japan, the Tanuki are critically endangered due to the efforts of the Covenant. Despite this, they remain friendly, helpful people, with a naturally gregarious nature which makes it virtually impossible for them to avoid human settlements. Tanuki possess three primary forms—human, raccoon dog, and big-ass scary monster. Pray you never see the third form of the Tanuki.

Ukupani (Ukupani sapiens). Aquatic therianthropes native to the warm waters of the Pacific Islands, the Ukupani were believed for centuries to be an all-male species, until Thomas Price sat down with several local fishermen and determined that the abnormally large Great White sharks that were often found near Ukupani males were, in actuality, Ukupani females. Female Ukupani can't shapeshift, but can eat people. Happily. They are as intelligent as their shapeshifting mates, because smart sharks are exactly what the ocean needed.

Wadjet (Naja wadjet). Once worshipped as gods, the male wadjet resembles an enormous cobra, capable of reaching seventeen feet in length when fully mature, while the female wadjet resembles an attractive human female. Wadjet pair-bond young, and must spend extended amounts of time together before puberty in order to become immune to one another's venom and be able to successfully mate as adults.

Waheela (Waheela sapiens). Therianthrope shapeshifters from the upper portion of North America, the waheela are a solitary race, usually claiming large swaths of territory and defending it to the death from others of their species. Waheela mating season is best described with the term "bloodbath." Waheela transform into something that looks like a dire bear on steroids. They're usually not hostile, but it's best not to push it.

PLAYLIST:

"We Both Go Down Together" . . . . The Decemberists
"Lovin' Baby Girl" . . . . Melanie
"Kate and the Ghost of Lost Love" . . . . Dave & Tracy
"Old Soul" . . . . Thea Gilmore
"The Horror and the Wild" . . . . The Amazing Devil
"Won't Want For Love" . . . . The Decemberists
"All the Time" . . . . We're About 9
"Alice" . . . . Tom Waits
"No Body No Crime" . . . . Taylor Swift
"Almost Home" . . . . Hem
"People Like Us" . . . . Matt Bomer
"Come Up With Me" . . . . Thea Gilmore
"Half Acre" . . . . Hem
"Bury Me Standing" . . . . Oysterband
"Better Dig Two" . . . . The Band Perry
"Glitter & Gold" . . . . Barns Courtney
"Hell is For Children" . . . . Halestorm

ACKNOWLEDGMENTS:

Here we go again, and finally. You see, *Spelunking Through Hell* was literally the book I used to pitch this series in the first place, and everything since then has been one long con to convince you all to care about this vaguely disturbed, definitely damaged woman and her wild, possibly futile search for the man she lost fifty years before. Alice came before everything else. Given how hard she seems to be to kill, I fully expect her to be coming after everything else at this rate, and she's going to keep stabbing, shooting, and swinging all the way down. And quite honestly, I can't say I'm not excited to go along with her every step of the way. She's my imaginary friend, and I love her dearly, and I hope by this point you all love her too.

I have no intention of moving any time soon, not least because as I write this, we're still in the middle of a global pandemic, no matter how hard we may all want to pretend that it's over. Here's a hint: as long as we're still fighting new variants and wearing masks whenever we enter a public place, it's not over, and taking off your mask because you're tired of it doesn't end it, either. It's the necessity, not the activity, that's the defining factor. So I am still in Seattle, and thankfully, I still like it here, so that's a good thing, given, again, vaguely trapped in place for the time being. I hope you're all holding it together as well as can reasonably be expected under the circumstances.

Travel in 2021 . . . let's see. Well, I went to Spain, for a large, mostly outdoor book festival, and now can check "travel internationally during a global pandemic" off my list of things I never really expected to

Acknowledgments

be doing. I had an awesome time, and ate a lot of very interesting cheese, which did a lot to balance out the sheer stress of traveling under such non-ideal circumstances.

Thanks to Chris Mangum, who maintains the code for my website, while Tara O'Shea, who manages the graphics. The words are all on me, which is why the site is so often out of date. Something's gotta give, and it's usually going to be me! Thanks to everyone at DAW, the best home my heart could have, and to the wonderful folks in marketing and publicity at Penguin Random House.

Due to unexpected circumstances, my agent, Diana Fox, stepped up and did way more heavy lifting on this story than is her norm—or is technically a part of her job description. I'd still be a lot deeper in the weeds without her. So thanks to Diana, for making sure we got here.

I am so intensely pleased to have finished off this piece of Alice's story, and moved the whole family one step closer to dealing with some of their more pressing problems. I'm hoping that Alice can get some rest now that this is out of the way. I doubt it, but a girl can dream.

Cat update (I know you all live for these): Thomas is a fine senior gentleman now, and while he has a touch of arthritis, his sweaters help to keep him warm, and I've set up cat stairs all over the house so he can still come and go as he pleases. Megara remains roughly as intelligent as bread mold, and is very happy as she is—this is not a cat burdened by the weight of a prodigious intellect! Elsie is healthy, fine, and very opinionated, and would like me to stop writing this and pet her. Tinkerbell is a snotty little diva who knows exactly how pretty she is, and Verity would like to speak to the manager. Of life.

And now, gratitude in earnest. Thank you to the people who kept showing up when the conventions and book events went virtual; to Kate, for being one of the rocks that keeps me solidly anchored; to Phil, for continuing to put up with me; to Michelle Dockrey, for existence and random online commentary; to Chris Mangum, for being here even when it's inconvenient; to Whitney Johnson, for Thursday night salad runs and general sanity; and to my dearest Amy McNally, for everything. Thanks to the members of all four of my current ongoing D&D games. And to you: thank you, so much, for reading.

Any errors in this book are my own. The errors that aren't here are the ones that all these people helped me fix. I appreciate it so much.

Let's go home.